ONLY IN MY DREAMS

As time slipped away Greyson held her around the middle, his face nuzzled in her neck, snoring lightly. To have someone love you an entire lifetime carried a heavy burden. With all the life mistakes she had made, Sutton questioned what she had done to deserve his undying commitment to a relationship that might never be. She placed her fingers against the squared sideburn intersecting his cheekbone. His intensity left her dazed. Truly, she loved him, but with all that had occurred lately, it would be easy to misinterpret the love of their long-standing friendship with the special type of love Greyson confessed to last night. Sutton kissed the top of his head.

How did I let this get out of control? Sutton asked herself, wallowing in turmoil. She would never do anything to hurt Greyson, but she needed time away from him to think. His life had been put on hold while she lived in a nightmare world filled with deceit and broken dreams. While he waited to love her, she was beginning to doubt that a good marriage could even be possible.

ONLY IN MY DREAMS

Kimberley White

ARABESQUE

★ BET BOOKS™

BET Publications, LLC
http://www.bet.com
http://www.arabesquebooks.com

ARABESQUE BOOKS are published by

BET Publications, LLC
c/o BET BOOKS
One BET Plaza
1900 W Place NE
Washington, DC 20018-1211

All Kensington Titles, Imprints and Distributed Lines are available at special quantity discounts for bulk purchases for sales promotion, premiums, fund-raising, and educational or institutional use. Special book excerpts or customized printings can also be created to fit specific needs. For details, write or phone the office of the Kensington special sales manager: Kensington Publishing Corp., 850 Third Avenue, New York, NY 10022, attn: Special Sales Department, Phone: 1-800-221-2647.

First Printing: May 2003
10 9 8 7 6 5 4 3 2 1

Printed in the United States of America

ACKNOWLEDGMENTS

Greyson and Sutton can't wait to share their story with you. . . . Imagine it. The perfect man sacrifices his hard-earned career to find you. His motivation is his love for you. His goal is to marry you, and keep you happy for the rest of your life. *Only In My Dreams* is a little different than my previous novels, but don't worry there's plenty of steamy romance.

A special thank you to the readers who supported me at book signings. Especially those who went the extra mile and posted a review on Amazon. With your support, many more romances will come.

Go Pilots! Class of '85.

Writing is a solo journey with many twists, turns, ups, and downs. There is a network of writers out there who offer support and keep me sane. Thank you all.

To the keeper of my dreams, Glenn "Montell" Townes: Good luck on the quest.

Prologue

Greyson Ballantyne ducked under the archway as he exited the room where the groomsmen were dressing for the wedding. Its festive atmosphere conflicted with the heaviness of his heart. The roar of the groomsmen joking and celebrating behind the door followed him into the hallway. He moved away from the sounds to gather his thoughts.

"Listen, baby, do you think this wedding is going to change the way things are between us?"

Greyson recognized the male voice immediately. He sidestepped down the hallway, keeping his back against the wall, until he could hear the conversation clearly.

"Why are you marrying her?" The woman sniffled.

"This is business. I've told you that since day one. I have plans for a big future and I need her beside me. She has a way of charming potential clients."

"I still don't understand. I could learn—"

The man's voice became rough, unyielding. "I don't have time for you to learn. I have two more years to reach the goals of my five-year plan. Nothing is going to interfere with that." His voice softened. "Now as soon as I get established, she's history and I'm coming back for you."

Greyson could not make out the muffled, whimpering response.

"We don't have much time left to be together. Come here."

Greyson's heart beat rapidly, contracting into a tight-fisted

ball. His temples pulsated. What should he do about the information he had overheard? He pressed into the wall as if he
could mold himself into it, removing himself from the situation. Nervously, he tugged at the jacket of the new tuxedo he
wore for Alex's wedding. Alex—the man whose voice filled
the shadows. The voice of his lifelong nemesis rang loud and
clear. Since they were kids, the two had a friendship forced
by proximity and maintained by Greyson's brothers' relationship with Alex. Alex had forced Greyson into competing over
everything—women, grades, lifestyle. Alex's life mission
seemed to be rubbing Greyson's nose in his successes.

"Hey, Greyson," Chevy, his little brother, approached
from behind, "have you seen Alex?"

Before Greyson could answer, Alex stepped out of the
shadows alone. "What's up?"

"The preacher wants to see you." Chevy directed him to
the room where the groomsmen were gathered. "Are you
coming, Grey?"

Greyson cleared the contempt from his throat. "I'm
going to check on things out front."

He climbed the stairs as quickly as his long, lean legs
would allow. Topside, guests were being seated in the
church pews unlike downstairs where the caterers scurried
about the hall where dinner would be served. The DJ bus-
ied himself setting up his stereo equipment in the corner
away from the wedding party table. The hustle and bustle,
along with the sting of what Greyson had overheard, made
him weary. He roamed the church he had attended since
birth until he found a secluded area where he could sit and
compose his scattered thoughts.

"Sutton?" he asked, surprised to see her sitting alone in
one of the church offices.

She looked up at him. Today—dressed in a cream wedding gown of lace and pearl, her rusty red hair elegantly
styled beneath a pillbox hat with a short veil—Sutton
looked more beautiful than he had ever seen her in the
twenty-plus years he'd known her.

"Hi, Greyson." She moved over to make room for him on the chair. She gave him the you're-a-good-friend smile she reserved for him when he entered her space.

"Hi, you." He fit his towering body next to hers, making her appear more fragile than usual. He lowered his voice to the level befitting a church. "Why are you in here?"

She held her hands out in front of her. "Look at me. I'm shaking. I've never been this nervous in all my life."

"You're supposed to be nervous. In less than thirty minutes, you'll be a married woman." Saying the words with a false smile, Greyson's chest tightened. Inhaling became difficult.

"This is supposed to be the happiest day of my life. I don't feel that way. I feel scared."

"What?" he asked, taken aback by her confession.

Sutton turned her head away.

"Are you having second thoughts?"

"Second. Third." She studied her fair skin through gloved fingers.

Greyson sat stunned. Neither spoke. The organist began to play a smooth ballad.

Greyson replayed the conversation the groom had in the shadows with the unidentified woman. Untapped love gave him the notion; desperation made him speak without thinking. "Sutton, you don't have to do this. Say the word and I'll whip you out the back. We'll disappear for a few days. I'll take you to my town house in Chicago. You can clear your head and then handle Alex."

Sutton smiled. She placed her hand next to his cheek. The lace felt rough against his skin. The aroma of her perfume heightened his awareness of her beauty. "You have been saving me since we were kids. What would I do without you?"

What will I do if you walk down the aisle and marry Alex? My life will never be the same. "You don't have to find out."

Sutton's red head angled in question. She took in a deep

breath that heaved her cleavage above the scalloped edge of her dress. Greyson longed to stroke her there.

"I'm being silly." She smiled. It wasn't a true smile. "Do you have a handkerchief?"

Greyson dug into the breast pocket of his tux and handed her his silk handkerchief.

"How's my makeup?" she asked after dabbing at her face.

The soft lines of her face captivated him. The intense eyes that forbade you to look away held him prisoner. Silky, flaxen skin glowed against her wedding gown. Wisps of soft rusty red hair remained her trademark. "I have never seen you look more beautiful than you do at this moment. Alex doesn't deserve you."

"You're sweet." She patted his knee.

Greyson caught her hand under his. His hand moved past her gloved fingers, up her arm to rest on her shoulder. Sutton fell over into the massive girth of his chest. Having her need his strength made him pull her deeper into his protective fold. His hand stroked her chin. Her bewildered eyes smoldered with desire. Without thinking, Greyson let his emotions lead him to her freshly painted lips. She leaned into the kiss. He wrapped her in his arms.

"Greyson," she whispered when she pulled away. She stood and backed away from him, her lace-covered fingertips pressed to the place his lips had vacated.

"Sutton, wait." He rose and moved toward her but she took two steps back.

"No." She held up her hand, stopping his progress. "We need to take our places."

"Sutton, how can you go through with marrying Alex after what just happened?" he asked, desolation dripping from his lips.

"Nothing—nothing happened here. I was scared. You were confused."

"I'm not confused. I know what I've been wanting for over twenty years—"

"Don't. This is not the time or the place." Sutton backed

to the door, shaking her head. "Don't do this to me. Not now."

"If not now, when?"

"Greyson, I'm marrying Alex."

In a cloud of cream taffeta and lace, Sutton turned and fled the room.

Greyson watched the train of her dress disappear down the corridor. He wanted to tell her that Alex was already cheating on her. That he didn't really love her. That she was slated to be his trophy wife. He wanted to demand that she abide by the fear that had her trembling in his arms with uncertainty only minutes ago. He wanted to confess the true feelings he had been harboring for her over the years. But as he had done all his life, he remained silent while Sutton looked to another man for love.

One

Five years later

Being tall, dark, and handsome paid Greyson Ballantyne's tuition through Harvard Law School. Being intelligent, ambitious, and hardworking made him the first black senior partner at Hunter, Roe & Volney.

Greyson placed the last of his plaques inside the white packing box. He taped the top to secure the contents. Hearing the light banter of his associates outside his office, he pushed his door closed before anyone could enter with questions about his future. He stepped over to the black vertical blinds and used the cord to close the slats on the busy streets of downtown Chicago. Tourists strolled down Michigan Avenue with bags bundled underneath their arms. He wanted to escape this place, which choked the life from him.

He had risen to the top of corporate law at a firm where any tactic was allowed to win a case. When Hunter, Roe & Volney recruited him directly from school, he thought the offer was the opportunity of a lifetime. And it had been. This small-town, southern boy had learned about a way of life completely foreign to him. The lawyers who were his mentors taught him more than any law professor had ever done. He rolled his hefty salary, intense knowledge, and life passion together to put him on a course where money would never be a problem. Since starting at the law firm, he lived below his means, stashing away every penny he could get while formulating his business plan. Now came the time to leave. Today he would walk away a winner from big-city, corporate-law life.

"Are you sure you want to do this?"

Greyson spun around to see Belinda, a recently hired research assistant, had joined him. He instantly felt the need to justify his actions. "I was going to call you before I left town."

"No." She sauntered up to him, resting her hands on his lapel. "No, you weren't."

He did not bother to dispute the truth of her statement.

"Leaving—when you're on top—makes an impression. Are you sure it's the one you want to make?"

"I'm sure."

"Are you sure you want to leave me?"

"Belinda." Greyson backed out of her grasp. One lonely night his pent-up passion erupted, causing him to make a mistake that he had regretted many times since.

"It sounds as if you're dismissing me."

"I've apologized many times." He truly regretted succumbing to his lust with a woman with whom he had no emotional attachment. It was never his intention to hurt or use her. The adrenaline of winning a major case, loneliness, and need directed his behavior that evening. "If I could do it all over, I would have never taken advantage of the situation—"

Belinda's hands found their way to his lapel again. "It's not taking advantage if it's what I wanted to happen. What's not right is that you're walking away from all that you've accomplished. That you're walking away from me."

"I've told you that I'm not happy here." His long arms spread wide. "This is not me. I'm from a small town in the mountains—"

"I know. I know. A small town where black men don't date white women. Is that it?"

"It's never been about that."

"Oh, no?" Belinda flipped her brunette hair over her

shoulder and crossed her arms over her petite chest. "What we feel for each other should not be bound by color."

Greyson shook his head. In all their previous discussions he had never been able to make her understand.

"Then tell me that your parents wouldn't have a problem with you bringing me home."

"My parents support their children in whatever makes them happy. I can't lie and say that they pictured interracial relationships for their children, but if it were what I wanted, they'd want it too. This is about much more than you and me. What you and I had was a one-time, lust-based affair. Nothing more."

"I don't agree. I can tell it was more. I can feel it."

"It could never be more than that because I'm in love with another woman."

Belinda looked as if she had been struck.

Greyson tried to soften the harsh realism of his words. He had never before admitted that to anyone aloud. He did not want to shame Belinda, but he needed her to have a firm understanding of the situation. "Like I said, this is not the lifestyle for me. I'm not happy here. I want to return to my hometown and live a quiet life. I want to help build up the town that has begun to crumble since the paper mill closed down. I have the means. I have to do it. I *want* to do it. I want to shed my designer suits and don overalls and a straw hat. Now that I've saved enough money, I can."

Belinda snickered. "You want to chop wood and milk cows? Greyson, please. I've seen you in action. You love sitting at the bargaining table and walking away a victor. I've witnessed your tenacity when interviewing a potential witness. I've seen the way you smile when a client signs over a big, fat check paying your fees."

"That's the entire problem. I don't want those things to be the only sources of happiness in my life anymore. I want to smile when I come home to the woman I love. I want to feel happy when I tuck my kids in at night."

"And where is this woman who's going to make you ec-statically happy? Why isn't she by your side now?"

Greyson's jaw tightened. *She married a man I despise. A man who was never good enough for her. A man who died while with another woman.* To Belinda, he answered, "She's waiting for me. She just doesn't know it."

Greyson packed the white box containing his awards in the back of his gray Volvo wagon. Matching luggage filled the rest of the spacious trunk. He removed the designer jacket to reveal broad squared shoulders covered by a powder blue dress shirt. In his breast pocket was his final check from Hunter, Roe & Volney. A check for close to a million dollars. In a silver embossed envelope on the front seat sat a portfolio containing his investment profile, stock certificates, and insurance policy. He gazed up at the skyscraper that had secured his future.

"No regrets." Greyson smiled. He hopped in the front seat and pulled away toward his future.

After a twelve-hour drive, Greyson turned up the winding red-dirt drive of his parents' home. Fatigue never bothered him on the drive; his excitement supplied an extra boost of energy. He had never considered flying into Charleston, West Virginia, renting a car, and then driving home to the sleepy town nestled in the foothills of the mountains. He savored every laborious step to return where he belonged.

The head of the Ballantyne family, Jack, climbed down from his tractor. "Mar-beth. Mar-beth. The eldest is here."

Greyson's mother rushed out onto the porch, wiping her hands on the green apron that encircled her waist. He had been craving her cakes and pies the last four hours of the drive. Marybeth Ballantyne would have a spread large enough to feed twelve linebackers waiting for her eldest son when he returned. Of that, Greyson was sure. Her hand covered her mouth. Tears sprang forth when Greyson exited the car. He took the porch in two steps and swept his mother up in his arms, twirling her around.

"Put your Mama down and turn 'round so I can see ya." His father's voice rang with familiar authority.

Greyson did as he was told. "Hi, Pop."

His father tried to contain his pride but a smile spread across his lips. "You look good, son. Been away from home too long."

"I know, sir." Greyson shook his father's hand and then pulled him in for a hug. "Where are my brothers?"

His mother answered. "Chevy came by here and picked Kirkland up about two hours ago. Chevy said he had an errand to run for you. He was real secretive about it, too. They promised to be back by the time you got here."

"Don't worry about those boys. They'll be home by the time we sit down to supper. Grab your gear and get cleaned up."

"Yes, sir."

This is what he had been missing.

The tiny upper loft that served as the bedroom for Greyson and his two younger brothers during their childhood hardly accommodated his size now. He could barely move around the tiny matchbook-sized bathroom. Water pressure in the shower was almost nonexistent. The house remained as neat and clean as he remembered, but it seemed to have shrunk since his last visit five years ago. He rummaged through his bags for a comfortable old sweatshirt and jeans. He came down the stairs as his brothers entered the front door.

"Look who made it." Kirkland noticed him first.

"Came crawling back, huh?" Chevy kidded him.

The massive stature of the three men easily filled the parlor. They joined in a group hug as Pop Ballantyne watched from the archway, his chest swelling with pride over what he had produced.

"Did you take care of it?" Greyson asked after they finished the getting-reacquainted banter that brothers are prone to.

"I had to take charge of the situation," Kirkland bragged. "Chevy ain't right in the head sometimes."

"Listen—" Chevy started, but their mother interrupted with a call to dinner.

The boys answered their mother's summons without delay. In the moderate kitchen, she had set the table for the four most important men in her life. She sat at the end opposite her husband, who graced the table with prayer before they began eating. Greyson sat to the left of his father, Chevy next to him. Kirkland sat across from Chevy, doting on their mother during the entire dinner. As the youngest, Kirkland had felt obligated to remain close to home and after college began working in the state capital of Charleston as a contractor. He spent more time with their parents than the other brothers and adored his mother. He fawned over her endlessly, always reminding Pop when an anniversary, birthday, or romantic holiday was near. Tonight, he prepared her plate and jumped out of his seat to fulfill any whim she might imagine. Their mother protested with a smile and a pat on his head.

They sat around the table, a large bounty of home-cooked food separating them. Fresh golden-brown biscuits slathered with butter sat next to a platter of fried chicken. Greens seasoned with ham, corn pudding, and macaroni and cheese rounded out the side dishes. Along with the fried chicken, their mother had prepared barbecued ribs and a baked ham. Halfway through the meal, she informed them that a stuffed turkey was baking in the oven.

Chevy kicked Greyson under the table several times, drawing attention to their little brother's fawning behavior. Living near each other, they were more prone to bickering than Greyson was with either of them.

Chevy looked like a carbon copy of their father. A hardworking man who enjoyed working with his hands, he focused on forestry during college. Chevy made a modest living in the small town with the forgotten art. He lived ten minutes from his childhood home, alone in a modern house resembling a log cabin. He ignored the children who teased him with a song about a hermit living in the woods. His hazel eyes dropped to his scuffed boots when he passed a pretty woman in town. Only in the company of his family did he open up and display his shining personality.

Greyson had always been the jewel that lit his mother's eye and puffed out his father's chest. His father worked double shifts seven days a week to pay Greyson's way through four years of college. His striking, chiseled face and tall, commanding body caught the interest of a talent scout, who offered him modeling jobs in men's fashion magazines. The money, along with an affirmative action–based scholarship, paid his tuition through Harvard Law School. Tonight he would begin to repay his parents and the small mountain town for the blessings he had received during his life.

His father spoke; everyone quieted down. "Tomorrow I'll take you around town. I want to show off my Harvard graduate son to the snobs who said my kids wouldn't amounta nothin'."

"Yes, sir."

"Every one of my sons has made me proud." His voice cracked. He hid his face behind a mug of cold beer.

Mama diverted attention away from her husband's open display of emotion. An old-fashioned man with old-fashioned values, Pop believed to reveal his feelings left him open to be perceived as weak, especially in front of his wife and children.

"This town ain't what it usta be," Pop said. "A lot of the same families still live here but it don't sparkle like it usta."

"That's why Grey came back," Chevy started.

"Mom, Pop." Greyson took a break from his second helping of apple pie and vanilla ice cream.

"What is it, son?" his father asked.

"Pop, you and Mama have sacrificed so much for me—for all of us—we wanted to pay you back."

Kirkland placed his hand on top of his mother's while he clarified. "It was Greyson who came up with the idea and most of the capital. Chevy and I are following his lead."

"What's going on?" His mother smoothed back her graying hair.

"I quit my job at the law firm and I'm moving back home."

"Greyson." Mama grasped her chest.

"Are you sure about this?" Pop asked. "Not much for a lawyer to do 'round here."

Greyson nodded. "Positive. I made a good living with Hunter, Roe & Volney, but this is where I belong."

Chevy took over. "We've been making plans that we wanted to keep to ourselves until Grey came home." He pushed his empty plate away. "The three of us have decided to go into business together. We bought the old paper mill and have been renovating it. We're going to reopen it and bring this town back to life."

"The old paper mill?" Pop questioned. "In these modern times, no one makes paper that way anymore, do they?"

"Exactly, Pop." Chevy went on. "We want to make quality paper and accessories. With a computer and fax machine in every home, we can make a fortune."

Kirkland's soft voice of reason piped in. "We know it's going to be hard, but we're committed. We have a good business plan and marketing strategy. After we get up and running, we plan to expand the business."

Chevy looked between his parents and brothers. "We can't sit by and watch this town die."

Pop turned away to shield the pride that sparkled in his eyes.

Their mother openly cried with joy. "I'm so proud of you boys."

"Greyson has more." Kirkland smiled at his mother, handing her a napkin.

"What?" Mama asked with an inquisitive smile.

Chevy laid the bait. "You know that big blue house down the hill with the white shutters?"

"That cute cottage they've been building for almost a year?" Mama clarified.

"That's the one."

Greyson pulled a set of keys from the pocket of his jeans. "It's yours."

Mama jumped up, knocking over her chair. "Ours? How is it ours? Jack, do you hear this foolishness Greyson is talking?"

"I heard, Mar-beth. Don't tease your mother like that, son."

Greyson smiled, his throat constricting with joy. "Chevy and Kirkland have been overseeing the builders. Everything you've ever dreamed of is in that house. It sits on enough acres so that you can move all your animals there, Pop. It's my gift to you for everything you've ever given me."

"Honey." Mama looked to her husband. Kirkland hurried to right her chair.

Pop stood from his place at the table. "I can't let my child buy me a house. Put your money away 'til you can buy a house for your own wife and kids. We've been living here since before you were born. We can live here the rest of our days."

Marybeth's face drooped. She returned to her seat; her husband had made his decision.

"Pop, I understand how you feel. I'm building myself a home here. We're working on rebuilding the town. What kind of son would I be if I didn't do for my own parents? Believe me, I can afford it. I worked my fingers to the bone for the past ten years so that I could give this to you. Don't insult me by not accepting it."

Chevy and Kirkland's heads went up. They had never heard their father's decisions challenged.

Greyson, seeing his father was on the fence, pushed harder. "Look at Mama's face. She wants this. She's worked for it. You've both earned it."

Chevy found the courage to agree with Greyson. "You really do deserve it, Pop."

Greyson went on. "Mama scrubbed floors in Charleston to buy us clothes. You worked at the paper mill to pay for this house. At the same time, you farmed animals so that we could eat. Well, it all paid off. The three of us have college educations and we're all doing well for ourselves." He paused to read his father's face. "We've gone through a lot to make this nice for you. Kirkland designed the house. Chevy had it furnished. Take the house, Pop."

Pop turned his eyes to his wife's face. She pulled her eyes from her lap to meet his. Her wishes were unmistakable.

"Mar-beth?"

"I want it only if you do, Jack."

Pop looked at each of his sons. His stern, tired gaze lingered on Greyson's stone-chiseled face. "This won't hurt your pockets?"

"Grey is doing really well," Chevy offered. "You should see the big house he's building. As a matter of fact, you can. It's the big one up the mountain behind the row of houses across the way."

"The one looking down on us?"

Greyson nodded. He held the keys out for his father. Pop nodded toward his wife. Marybeth took the keys and danced around the house.

After all the excitement, Kirkland headed home, Mama and Pop retired to bed, and Chevy and Greyson took a walk around the property. They stopped at the fenced-in area that held the hogs.

"It's going to be a mess moving all these pigs." Greyson remarked over the loud snorting.

"I hired someone to do it."

Silence bonded them to old memories.

"This is a good thing you're doing for the town." Chevy slapped his brother on the back.

"We're in this together."

They shared a hug.

"Your timing couldn't be better." Chevy turned to face Greyson, resting his back against the wooden fence.

"I've been keeping my eye on the town. If we don't save it now, it won't last much longer."

"True, but that's not what I meant."

"What are you talking about?"

Chevy turned in the same direction as his brother, watching the pigs settle down for the night. "Sutton's back in town. The Galloways are having a memorial for Alex at the church."

Greyson's heart leapt at the mention of her name. The last memory he had of her, standing at the front of the town church in a cream wedding gown, assaulted him. The feel of her lips was as vivid as if the kiss had happened hours before instead of five years ago.

Alex was killed in an auto accident a month ago. The funeral had been private, family only. Greyson sent flowers to the Galloways and to Sutton when his mother called him with the news. He couldn't bring himself to call Sutton with his condolences. If he were honest, he'd admit that Alex's death had increased his urgency in returning to Hannaford.

"Is she all right?" Greyson asked, after a long break in the conversation.

"I haven't seen her. I went by the Galloway place but they're keeping her under lock and key. No one in Hannaford even knew about the accident. Rumor is, she and Alex weren't getting along. The Galloways are trying to keep her away from the town so that no one will know what a jerk he was to her."

"What did he do?" If Alex weren't dead, Greyson would wring his neck for hurting Sutton. He pictured Pop in the barn carrying a squawking chicken in one hand and an ax in the other as he approached a tree stump.

Chevy shrugged his shoulders. "Women, I heard."

Greyson remembered the shadow conversation.

"This might seem like bad timing, but this could be your big chance. I know how bad you had it for Sutton. If I were you, I wouldn't let her get away again."

Chevy would never know how perfectly this fit into Greyson's plans. He had figured on having a monumental battle with Alex over Sutton one day. He would never rejoice in Alex's tragic death, but Chevy was right. Sutton was free; he was moving back to Hannaford Valley. His plan might come together better than he had imagined. After settling in town, he had planned to pay Sutton a visit in Ohio and make his move. Now that she was in Hannaford, he wouldn't have to. Fate was helping to pull them together.

Chevy's soft-spoken voice continued. "Do you know about Sierra?"

"Who's Sierra?"

"Sutton and Alex's little girl."

Greyson was stunned by the announcement. A ready-made family? His dreams had always been about him and Sutton getting married and one day starting a family of their own. He never planned to raise Alex's child.

"I guess you didn't know."

"No, I didn't," Greyson mumbled.

"They were married. Did you think they wouldn't have the house, the kids, the whole thing?"

"Mama never mentioned it." But she wouldn't have a reason to. Sutton and Alex lived in Ohio and didn't stay in touch with anyone except their parents. "I never thought about it. Alex didn't want any kids. Remember? He used to tell us that all the time."

"He must have changed his mind. Have you changed yours?"

Greyson played out the implications. He hadn't planned on Sutton having any kids but he was fond of children. He knew that when he married Sutton they'd have two or three of their own. He had given up his life in Chicago with the hope of winning Sutton. He couldn't turn back now.

"Grey, I feel sorta responsible for Sutton marrying Alex. I gave you bad advice five years ago. Now's my chance to make it right. If you still love Sutton as much as you used to, you shouldn't let anything keep you from her."

Greyson tried to picture what the little girl looked like— a combination of Sutton and Alex. He imagined she'd have

Sutton's sassy attitude and Alex's high-spirited ways. More importantly, he tried to place himself in the little girl's shoes. Her father had just died. How would she feel about another man moving in on her mother?

"What are you gonna do?" Chevy asked as they turned to walk back to the house.

"I'm not going to let Sutton get away this time."

TWO

Sutton's brownish red hair took on a fiery appearance under the black veil of mourning her mother-in-law insisted she wear. Sutton would be happy when she returned to Ohio. With all of the emphasis on appearances, she wondered how much the Galloways loved their only child, Alex. Mother Galloway sat next to her in the pew, crying enough to confirm her grief but not enough to make a spectacle of herself.

The second service would not have been necessary if the funeral had been open to all of Alex's acquaintances. Instead, a private service had been held on the Galloway land in Hannaford Valley. His family kept possession of the house even though Alex had moved his mother to Ohio.

Several more people came up to Sutton and offered their condolences. Her parents, along with Sierra, had gone home hours ago. Sutton longed to join them. She had fulfilled her obligation to her husband when she refused to consider divorce—even after the third affair.

Mother Galloway leaned over. "I think the entire town has come out. We're going to leave now. You should stay a little while longer in case stragglers come."

Not wanting to argue, Sutton nodded in agreement. Mother Galloway led her group of followers out of the church. The bunch consisted of the women she called her friends: socialites from Ohio. Sutton thanked them all for coming, kissed Mother Galloway properly on the cheek, and settled into her seat. The cushioned benches were a contribution from Alex shortly before his death.

All the major events in Sutton's life had occurred in the town's church. She remembered the details of every event chronologically: baptism, high-school graduation, marriage, and now her husband's memorial.

The small town had been built around the church. The point of the steeple marked the town's existence to those passing through the mountains. Age had humbled the majestic structure, but it remained the focal point of Hannaford Valley. Stained glass windows covered each wall. The janitor could be seen shining the windows weekly, no matter what the season. Being a refuge, the church never closed. The pastor could always be found bustling down the aisles, practicing his sermon in his office, or helping with a church function. All the important town meetings were held there, instead of the city hall building.

Sutton remembered how the wives of Alex's business partners had snickered when she described the way she had grown up. She and Alex had fought terribly when they returned home that evening. Under no circumstances was she to talk about the simple, loving small town where they were born and raised when they were socializing with his clients. Whereas she cherished her upbringing, Alex was ashamed of it. He said it weakened him in the eyes of his superiors.

A calming breeze moved through the church, gently removing her from the dwelling place of bad memories. An extreme silence hushed every noise in the building, so she could hear the nighttime insects coming alive outside. A need, deeply ingrained in her being, enveloped her and filled her with complete satisfaction. Yes, Sutton remembered feeling this way before. Safe, loved, happy. The aroma of freshly ground woodsy spices wafted to her on the next breeze. This feeling, as if a presence was near that had been assigned to watch over her in adverse times, had visited her before, the last time being before she marched down the aisle. She dismissed the invisible embrace as redirected nervous tension caused by her husband's memorial.

The sound of the church door opening behind Sutton made her swing around. The church was empty. She gathered her purse and prepared to walk to her parents' house. She stopped halfway up the carpeted aisle. At the end of the red carpet, near the exit, stood a man as tall and lean as the trees engulfing the small town.

"Sutton?" He had not lost his southern twang, unlike Alex, who had practiced daily until his disappeared.

She had not seen him in five years. Not since he tattooed her with a kiss her husband's lips could never erase. "Greyson Ballantyne, is that you?"

He came closer. His manly body wore a black suit, white dress shirt, and black silk tie. Even though the southern accent remained, his appearance was big city. He looked much more adult than she remembered.

"Still sporting that red hair." Greyson's closed-lip smile lit his eyes.

Sutton's hand went to smooth her hair. She bumped her black veil and quickly remembered her purpose for being at the church. She was publicly mourning her husband's death. It must be blasphemy to have butterflies in her stomach when Greyson watched her.

"I haven't seen you in five years." Sutton tried to make light conversation.

"Yeah. The last time was in this church." He hiked his thumb in the direction of the office where they shared their forbidden kiss.

Sutton's eyes went to the carpet.

Greyson cleared his throat. "My condolences."

"Thank you." Sutton gathered the courage to lift her head. Over the years, his skin had retained its dark, sharp handsomeness. His angular jaw ran parallel to his high cheekbones. His full lips framed a set of perfect white teeth.

"Are you leaving?" Concern marked his words.

Sutton nodded. "It's getting late."

"Do you need a ride up to the Galloway place?"

"No. The Galloways are heading back to Ohio tonight. I'm staying with my parents for awhile."

Greyson nodded his understanding.

"I'll walk home. I need the air."

"I'll see you home," Greyson readily volunteered. He placed a firm hand on her back and escorted her out of the church.

"What are you doing here?" Sutton asked as they strolled down the deserted street toward her parents' home.

"I'm moving back."

"Really?"

"Yeah, I realized that this is home."

"What are you going to do? There aren't any places to practice law here."

"I'm going to take some time off. Help my parents get settled. Once they're okay, I'll go back to work. How about you? Have you had a chance to think about the future now that . . ."

"It's all right. You can say it. Now that Alex is dead."

They walked several feet before Sutton spoke again. "I really don't know in what direction life will take me. I suppose I'll stay with my parents until I have to go back and settle Alex's will. After that, I don't know."

"Well, we're here." Greyson announced as they reached the white picket fence surrounding her parents' front yard.

"Thank you for walking me. Would you like to come in? I know my parents would love to see you."

"No, it's getting late."

"Where are you staying?" Sutton felt desperation in knowing that he would be leaving her.

He nodded up the road in the direction of his childhood home. "I'm staying with my folks. They'll be moving into that new blue and white house down the hill soon. I'll stay on at their old place until I find something."

"Maybe we'll have time to talk before I leave." The image of how handsome Greyson looked in his tux at her wedding flashed before her.

"I'd like that."

The porch light clicked on.

"You better go inside."

Sutton nodded and ran up the porch stairs to greet her father. She forbade herself to look back.

"Is Sierra asleep?"

"Yeah, your mother put her to bed about an hour ago. Was that the Ballantyne boy?" Mr. Hill asked, peeking through the drapes of the front room. Other than walking a little slower, her father had not changed with the passing of years.

"Greyson walked me home from the church." Sutton peeled away the veil and opened the first two buttons of the shirt constricting her neck.

"Don't tell me he's going to start sniffing around here again. Never could get rid of that kid."

"Daddy, don't be hateful." Sutton wrapped her arms around her father. She gave him a quick kiss on the cheek, which melted away the brashness of his attitude.

He sat down and patted the sofa next to him. Sutton joined him. The house was dark and quiet and moving shadows jumped off the walls near his bedroom.

"Is Mom asleep?"

"She turned in right after she put Sierra down." He smiled wide, exposing his new dentures. "That's one precious girl you got there."

Sutton matched his smile. "That she is."

"As sweet as candy. She knows how to wrap Grandpa around her little finger already." He became lost in thought as he stared toward the staircase. "She's dealing pretty well with her daddy's death."

"She'll be okay. Sierra didn't know her father very well."

"How could she not know him well?"

"Alex hardly ever came home. When he did, he didn't have time for Sierra—or me."

Her father's eyes blazed with anger. Sutton patted his work-worn hand. "But that's in the past." She changed her attitude as quickly as she changed the subject. "I wanted to ask you if Sierra and I could stay with you and Mom for a little while. Just until Alex's will is read and everything back in Ohio is settled."

"Of course. You don't need to ask. I don't think you could get Sierra away from your mom right now if you tried. She's never really had the chance to get to know her." He laughed. "She's planned this shopping trip in town for them tomorrow. Why don't you go along? Get your mind off your troubles."

"No, thanks. I think I'll sleep in tomorrow." She stood and placed another kiss on his cheek. "Good night, Daddy."

After a quick shower, Sutton climbed into bed next to Sierra. Alex had insisted that they never let Sierra join them in bed, but tonight he was not here. She moved her daughter next to the wall and lay facing her. Sierra's honey-colored skin belonged to Alex, along with her stubborn attitude. The long, bright red hair she inherited from her mother. Her tomboyish ways came directly from day care, but Alex was determined to remove them when he selected the upscale preschool she was to attend next fall.

Sierra helped Sutton to fight off the lonely nights more times than she could count. Sierra had been Alex's gift to Sutton after her second threat of divorce. He promised her they could have a baby with every major argument. It soon became a dysfunctional power game between them.

Sutton desperately wanted a baby and Alex used that desire to get him out of tight spots in their marriage. He often told her he felt it was too soon. At first it was his five-year plan that took precedence, and then his ten. When Sutton threatened to leave him after a crazy woman showed up at their condo breaking the windows with rocks, he impregnated her to encourage her to stay.

That night, like so many before and after, was typical of the drama surrounding the five years of their marriage. Every time Sutton gained the courage to leave, Alex squashed it. There would be a work crisis. Or Mother Galloway would appear on her doorstep to explain the uncontrollable libido of the Galloway men. It was their wives' curse to bear. Sutton wished someone had warned her before she signed up for a lifetime of Galloway sex antics.

There were naked women in his office. Crank phone calls at all hours of the night. Unsigned letters. Pictures of Alex's bare rear between another woman's thighs. Visitors. Scenes at restaurants. Angry husbands. Crashing shopping baskets at the supermarket. Private detectives. Snickering, pointing, and rolling of eyes.

A twinge of guilt moved through Sutton. She would always care for Alex—they were friends since childhood—but she had stopped loving him long ago. She could pinpoint the exact moment her feelings changed. It happened when Greyson pressed his lips to hers while she wore her wedding dress.

That one kiss opened the door on feelings she had always ignored. When they played together—Sutton, Alex, and the Ballantyne brothers—it was always Alex who flirted with her. Greyson was reserved and friendly, almost distant. Sutton had always had a crush on him but he never noticed her. During adolescence, Alex became her boyfriend and the rest progressed naturally.

Sierra turned to face her. Sutton pulled the blanket to her shoulders. She was officially a widow, a single mother. Alex's estate would have to support them until she could figure out her next step. He had never allowed her to finish college. When Sierra was born he insisted Sutton become a full-time mother and housewife. Prior to that she played the perfect wife of his five-year plan. Her head began to spin. Why hadn't she educated herself after the first affair? What if he had left them? She would have been destitute. It was just as bad that she let him confine her to the house while he bettered himself and she doted on him.

At twenty-eight, it was not too late to correct her mistakes and start over. She would make a happy, loving home for Sierra. She'd visit her parents more often like she wanted to. She'd check into finishing college and build a career of her own. She'd paid with broken dreams for supporting Alex; his money would now be put to good use.

Three

Three Months Later

Sutton sat next to Mother Galloway in Alex's lawyer's office. Dressed impeccably, Mother Galloway crossed her leg over her thigh and folded her hands in her lap. Her fondness for hats materialized today with a small round object that Sutton thought resembled an inverted saucer. She always felt like a child next to Mother Galloway, who had a way of looking down on you, with the arching of her brow, making you feel privileged to be near her. Sutton compared her conservative houndstooth pantsuit and pearl stud earrings to the elaborate suit and diamond necklace Mother Galloway wore.

All of the formalities of the will had been handled and now the lawyer was beginning to read Sutton's destiny. The dollar amounts were huge. Alex bequeathed to this person and that. Property was left to people with female names whom Sutton had never met. She glanced sideways at Mother Galloway, who remained stiff and unreadable. Sutton's time of embarrassment was over. She wanted a bottom-line figure so that she could go about planning her future.

Mother Galloway shifted slightly toward the lawyer when he recited what Alex left her. Alex had purchased the home Mother Galloway was living in and signed ownership over to her. The Mercedes she drove was paid in full before his death, and that too had been signed over to her. Various insurance policies naming Mother Galloway as beneficiary would pay her way to fancy fundraisers for the rest of her life.

The lawyer continued, "The assets I have mentioned thus far have been distributed prior to this reading—as Alex wanted it. The boat, land, and rental properties were purchased by Alex and signed over to the receiving party before his death."

"What are you saying?" Sutton asked, confused by the legal process.

The balding lawyer cleared his throat. "Alex realized he was in financial trouble and had begun to hide his assets by signing them over to various individuals."

"Various individuals being his mistresses."

"Now, dear." Mother Galloway patted her hand in a patronizing way that made Sutton want to move to the other side of the room. "Please finish reading the will."

The lawyer scratched the bare spot of his head. "There would really be no use in continuing. You see, the IRS has seized all the remaining assets."

"What do you mean?" Mother Galloway asked.

"Your son was being audited by the IRS because of his failure to claim income. The IRS placed a lien on all his assets two months before Alex died. You were aware that he didn't file a tax claim in 1996, 1998 or 1999?"

"No," Sutton whispered. "Alex handled all our finances." She didn't fully understand what the man was trying to say, but a mild panic bristled beneath her skin.

"He didn't file a return during those years, and as you know, he made a substantial amount of money. The IRS has frozen all the bank accounts and put a lien on the condo and the cars."

Mother Galloway patted away the dribble from the corner of her mouth. "He couldn't possibly owe the government that much money. My son came to Ohio and worked his way to the top of his field. Why, last year, his department was named marketing team of the year. He increased his employer's profits by sixty percent during the time he was there. He had quite a bit of money; he could easily pay any debts he accumulated."

"Alex was a friend as well as a client," the lawyer reminded her.

"Check the figures."

"I have."

"Check them again!" Mrs. Galloway momentarily lost her composure.

"I've gone over the numbers, Mrs. Galloway. More importantly, the IRS has gone over the figures. If there is anything left, they will release it to Mrs. Galloway." He nodded toward Sutton. "But I have to be honest, I wouldn't count on that happening."

"Surely there is some mistake." Indignation seeped between Mother Galloway's words. "My son would not leave his wife and child in this position."

"I doubt that he meant to. As I said, he realized his problem and had started signing over his assets. His untimely death must have interrupted what he was trying to do."

"What are you saying?" Sutton asked, her mouth as dry as dirt. Listening to them talk, she had not been able to contemplate the consequences of the lawyer's words and speak at the same time.

"I'm sorry, Mrs. Galloway." The lawyer found it hard to look Sutton in the eyes.

"You're sorry," she said sarcastically. "Now I understand why Alex demanded we wait three months after his death to read the will. He knew I would try to get the boat, cars, and homes back from his mistresses. I should have known this had something to do with the other women he was seeing."

"Sutton." Mother Galloway touched Sutton's arm to quiet her.

She pulled away, refusing to humor her mother-in-law. "No, Mother Galloway. How could Alex do this to me? To Sierra? Even after he's dead, he's disrespecting his family."

Mother Galloway glanced at the lawyer, embarrassed.

"What exactly does all this mean? After the mistresses have been paid and the IRS bill is settled, what's left for me and Sierra?"

The lawyer scratched the bald spot of his head. "Mrs. Galloway, Alex has no holdings."

"No holdings? Are you saying that I'm penniless?"

Four

"Daughter?" A soft knock followed.

Sutton turned in her bed to face the door. "Come in, Daddy."

Mr. Hill came into the room, closing the door behind him, and claimed a place next to Sutton on the bed. "Your mother took Sierra to church. The women are having a fundraising meeting. Someone donated a huge amount of money to the church and they're going to decide how to spend it."

"That's nice, Daddy." Sutton's voice had lost all its zest. She sounded pitiful even to herself. She tried to shield her feelings by offering a slight smile.

After a brief pause her father asked, "What are you going to do?"

Sutton sat up against the headboard drawing her knees into her chest. "I don't know. Most of what I own is in this room." She motioned to the suitcases neatly stacked in the corner waiting to be unpacked. "Mother Galloway called in a few favors and the IRS is going to allow me to retrieve some of our things before they sell the condo. At least Sierra and I will have clothes to put on our backs. I might be able to get her toys. The IRS made it clear that I wouldn't be able to take anything of real value." She ran her hand through her hair. "I have a thousand dollars in cash but that won't get me very far."

"Your mother and I have told you we love having you and Sierra. Why don't you consider settling back here? You can stay with us until you get back on your feet. The way I see it, you have two choices. Stay here with us or go back to Ohio and move in with Mrs. Galloway."

"I'd like to stay here a bit longer. Besides, I could never live with Mother Galloway. Alex would control me from the grave."

"Of course." He patted the top of her head. "Why don't you get out of bed? Your mother is worried about you sleeping all day."

"Daddy, I don't have the energy. I'm confused about what to do next. I need time to think."

"Honey, you'll feel better if you get up and about. It's pretty out. Why don't you walk into town and meet your mother at church?"

Sutton, seeing the desperation and concern in her father's eyes, agreed with a nod.

"That's my girl. I have to drive to the capital today. Want me to wait for you?"

"No. I think I'll walk to town like you suggested."

Mr. Hill stepped to the door. "You have a good day. See you at dinner."

Sutton labored over dressing. After a long bath and light breakfast, she searched her suitcases for something to wear that would lift her spirits. She settled on a light-weight, tea-length yellow dress covered with a flower pattern. Knowing she would be walking, she stepped into her favorite tan mules and tied a sweater over her shoulders. She hadn't visited the salon since staying with her parents, and her hair had grown down to her shoulders. She brushed her reddish-brown tresses back and creased a tight flip at the ends with her mother's electric curling iron. A stroke of blush to her cheeks and a dab of pink to her lips were added to make her appear more carefree than she felt inside.

Sutton stepped out onto the front porch into unseasonably mild April weather. The bright sun made the sixty-degree temperature feel warm and summery. Once she stepped out on the porch, she decided to venture down the road in the opposite direction of the church.

She strolled past the old Galloway house, where she played as a child. The tree house in the front yard had grown tattered. The Galloways had abandoned the house when Alex's father made enough money to move up the hill, looking down on them all. A bit further down the road, on the opposite side of the street, still stood the Ballantyne house. Backing it were acres of land used to raise farm animals. The large vegetable garden had been a showpiece of Mr. Ballantyne's for years. The flower garden out front was Mrs. Ballantyne's pride.

Sutton's tour of her old neighborhood covered a long stretch of land. The houses did not sit on top of each other like in the city. Here in the small mountain area, her house was closest to town and she had to walk south to reach the Galloway and Ballantyne places. Each house was separated by trees and farmland.

Sutton considered stopping in on Greyson as she continued past his house. Everyone in town knew he was staying there alone while his parents had relocated only a week ago into their new home. She had not seen Greyson since the night of Alex's memorial and supposed he had become a hermit, much like Chevy. Although, some would say it was she who had become the recluse. Shame kept her indoors away from the gossips who wanted to say, "I told you so."

Before Sutton had realized it, she was at the new Galloway place. She glanced at her watch and calculated that she had been walking for about forty-five minutes. As long as she had come that distance, she decided to visit the cross Mother Galloway had erected as a tribute to her only son.

Sutton stood silently at the memorial site. She wanted to say comforting words to Alex telling him how much she missed him; she couldn't. The words would not come. She still harbored anger over the deceit of his multiple affairs. He had taken care of his mistresses in his final hour, but had deprived their child of her legacy.

She did regret that her daughter would grow up without a father and she shared that with Alex's memory. She softened her stance when his gift of Sierra warmed her heart. Alex did love her, he just didn't understand how to treat the ones he loved. She said private words of forgiveness with which her heart couldn't concur. As she turned and walked back toward town she heeded her father's advice. It was time to get out of bed and start a new life.

The cirrus clouds parted and the sun became brighter, hotter. The familiar calming breeze that moved through the church enveloped her as she walked. A hush settled the farm animals nearby. Suddenly, Sutton felt optimistic about her future, about her daughter's future. The aroma of freshly ground woodsy spices wafted to her.

"Sutton?" Greyson drew out her name with country flavor.

Sutton turned to see Greyson behind her wearing a gray jogging suit with "Orlando Magic" embroidered in blue and silver letters across his wide chest. A matching baseball cap shielded his eyes from the sun. His freshly shaved face smiled brightly. Even casually dressed it was obvious why he had been chosen to model professionally.

"Hi." Sutton waited for him to fall into step beside her. "What are you doing out here?"

"I saw you when you passed the house. You looked troubled so I thought I'd make sure you were doing okay. So," Greyson locked his fingers behind his back, "how are you doing? This is a lot to deal with."

Sutton kicked the red dirt. "Do you know?"

"Know what?" Greyson glanced down at her. "I know that you're trying to deal with your husband's death."

"Don't try to shield me now. You've always been honest with me. Do you—and the whole town—know that my husband left all his money and belongings to various girlfriends? Do you—and the whole town—know that I'm penniless?"

A gust of wind passed over them. "Yes, I know. And from what my mom says, the town is talking."

Sutton pounded her fist into her thigh. "Even from the grave . . ."

They walked in silence down a stretch of dirt-covered road.

"Let's walk this way. I want to show you something." Greyson guided Sutton through a patch of trees she remembered as a favorite childhood play place. His firm grip on her arm gave her momentary security. "What are you planning to do?"

Sutton swatted a fly from her path. "I have to find a job right away."

"How long will you stay with your parents?"

Sutton shrugged. "Ohio wasn't really for me. I didn't have any true friends there. The slow pace of Hannaford Valley is more my style. If I can find work, maybe I'll stay here."

In the distance Sutton could hear bulldozers and men shouting. "My mother says they're building a house over that ridge." She pointed in the direction of the noise. "You can see it much better from the windows at the back of my parents' house. That's going to be some place. More like a mansion. I wonder who in this town can afford something like that."

Greyson nodded, his eyes heavily cloaked in thought. "Hey, let me show you something." His large, soft hand swallowed hers as he led her at a run across the open field that ended at the back of his family's property.

Sutton stopped a few feet from the structure. She rested her hands on her knees while catching her breath. The task of breathing became more daunting because she could not stop laughing from happy memories. "I can't believe it's still standing."

"I was walking out here last night, taking a look at the land when I found it. I had forgotten all about this."

Sutton stood at a distance as she watched Greyson approach the structure. The wooden shack stood underneath a crab apple tree. The falling apples were one reason they chose the spot for their clubhouse. Sutton, the Ballantyne brothers, and Alex spent an entire week one summer hammering old boards together to make this special place. The boards were cut unevenly, and the spaces between allowed the rain inside, but they cherished the privacy. Greyson tested the stability of the warped wood. It creaked but did not shift under the weight of his pushing and pounding. The clubhouse that seemed larger than life when Sutton was eight barely came midway to Greyson's thigh today. He tugged at the door until it popped open on its makeshift hinges. He smiled back at her before he dropped to his knees and crawled inside.

Minutes later his hand came through the opening. "Come inside the castle, my princess."

"I'm not crawling inside that musty, old, bug-infested, condemned playhouse."

Greyson stuck his head out, his face radiant with mischief. "See, that's why Peter Pan wanted to stay a kid. Now that you're all grown up, this place isn't good enough for you."

Sutton parked her hands on her hips. "Now that I'm grown up, I know how nasty bugs are."

"Girls." Greyson crawled out of the clubhouse and held his ground squarely in front of her. "I have a confession. When I found this place last night I cleaned it out. I knew I wouldn't get you inside otherwise."

Sutton twisted her mouth to one side in disbelief.

"Really, I did. There's even a clean blanket inside. I was going to come to your house this afternoon and bring you over."

Sutton's eyes went to the old structure.

"Please, come inside and sit with me for awhile." Greyson held out his hand. Sutton studied it, and wanting to experience the silky softness again, placed her hand in his.

Sutton hiked her sundress above her knees and followed Greyson inside. Back into their carefree past. Not only had he spread a red, black, and green checkered blanket over the dirt floor, he had placed a lantern in the corner of the room. Greyson's large body filled the small house. Sutton lay on her side facing him. She relived many good memories as her eyes roamed every corner of the shack.

Greyson fixed himself on his side, facing her, and crossed his ankles. "Tell me what it was like to be married to Alex."

Sutton tossed her head back. Greyson always provided the ear for her therapy sessions during their teen years. "It wasn't at all what I expected. I can't speak ill of the dead, so I'll only say that I pictured marriage as a partnership where you worked to provide for your children and make happy memories that lasted a lifetime."

"And it wasn't that way?" Greyson removed his baseball cap and placed it on the blanket in front of him.

She momentarily lost her thoughts in his striking eyes and thick eyebrows. "No, it wasn't. Most of the time I was alone—until Sierra came along."

"Sierra, your little girl. You didn't mention her at the church."

"Seeing you again took me by surprise."

Greyson's lashes flipped up, his gaze held an intensity that made Sutton's body heat at its core. "I'd like to meet her."

A wide smile split her face. "Sierra and Alex have always been separate in my mind. I had my marriage to Alex, and I had my life with Sierra. Alex wanted it that way. I guess I wanted it that way, too. I didn't want to taint my baby."

"Why did you stay with Alex once things got bad?"

"I don't know. I justified it to myself in several ways. It was expected. Alex would never agree to divorce. Mother Galloway told me the shame would ruin everyone involved. I wanted my daughter to have two parents. I really don't know now that I look back on it all."

Greyson nodded his understanding. He placed his palm down on the blanket in front of him. The lantern made a gold bracelet sparkle against his dark skin. She felt the urge to reach out and turn it round and round on his wrist.

"How about you? Did you ever get married?"

"Couldn't find anyone who would put up with me."
Greyson laughed at his own attempt at humor. Sutton could
not join him. Imagining him focusing all of his attention on
some other woman made her insides recoil. She knew it was
wrong, but she was happy he had not made a commitment to
another woman.

A long moment passed where they watched each other,
then they bashfully looked away, and time traveled to a
simpler era.

"Are you over him?"

The blunt question surprised Sutton. "Alex? He'll always
have a special place in my heart. We were all friends. We all
grew up together. And he was my husband."

"Do you still love him?"

"Greyson." Sutton's eyes darted around the shanty. "Why
are you asking me about my feelings for Alex?" She dis-
guised the warm sensation in the pit of her stomach with a
nervous giggle.

"I'm asking because I want to know if it would be inappropriate to kiss you right now."

Before Sutton could choke out another reply, Greyson's lips
were pressed against hers, rekindling dangerous memories of
the last time they kissed. Her eyes fluttered before closing. In
the sudden darkness that followed were sounds of cheers and
clinking glasses, visions of an expensive wedding gown with
a man's hands caressing the fabric—a man's hands other than
her husband's. When Greyson's tongue wet her lips, Sutton
felt as if she were still sitting in the church office sharing passion with a man who was her husband's groomsman. Not
only did the world's time clock stop, it rewound, pulling them
back into the past, to the day they should have stopped the
madness and did what their hearts bid.

Greyson pulled away, keeping his lips dangerously close
to hers. His hand cupped her cheek. "Sutton."

The way he whispered her name screamed pent-up passion and the escape of forbidden lust. Sutton's eyes opened
to study his chiseled chin and high cheekbones.

"Why did you kiss me that day?" Sutton had wondered about this many times in the years that followed. "Why did you kiss me on my wedding day?"

"I wanted to kiss you every day of my life. I wanted you to be mine every day for years but you only had eyes for Alex."

Sutton shook her head vehemently. "It wasn't Alex I wanted. Alex wanted me and he told me that every day until we were married. You didn't. Why did you wait all those years, never giving me a clue, and then kiss me on my wedding day?"

"I knew it was my last chance. In a matter of minutes you would marry a man who not only didn't deserve you, he didn't love you."

"Alex may not have been perfect but he loved me."

"No, he didn't. You were part of his plan to become a success. I heard him with another woman that day. He confessed it all to her."

Sutton felt as if the small shanty had fallen on her head. "What?" she whispered. "What did you say? You heard Alex with another woman the day of our wedding?"

Greyson rambled the details of the shadow meeting. "I tried to put it out of my mind. Until now I didn't know I remembered it so vividly."

"Why didn't you tell me?" Sutton sat upright, her words vibrating off the close proximity of the walls. "You let me make a lifelong commitment to a man who you believed didn't love me? You were my friend. Why would you want me to suffer like that?"

"I didn't know what to do, Sutton. I thought he'd come to his senses once you were married. When I came across you in the office I was trying to figure out what to do. Then we kissed. I asked you to leave the church with me, remember?"

"You kissed me. You knew about Alex and took a shot at me for yourself. Is that what you're doing right now? Trying to get back at Alex by kissing his widow?" Sutton scrambled out of the small wooden structure.

Greyson followed, calling her name. "Sutton, wait up. Let's talk about this. You don't understand."

Sutton marched off across the field. "You and Alex always had that sick rivalry type of friendship. It was like you hated each other but couldn't stay away from each other."

Greyson followed her. "I never liked Alex. Alex's friendship was with my brothers more than me. The only reason he asked me to be a groomsman was because Kirkland told him it was the right thing to do. I hung around Alex to be near you."

Sutton let the words ricochet off her back. She refused to fall for the sweet talk, tender touches, and soft kisses. "But you let me marry a man you believed didn't love me."

Sutton needed to be far away from Greyson. She ran across the open field in the direction that would take her back to the main road. Back to the security of her father's house. Greyson continued to call out, begging her to give him a chance to explain his reasoning. Sutton's foot kicked a rock. She slipped off the platform of her mules while the hem of her dress snagged the toe of her shoe and she went down in a fresh black mud puddle. She caught herself with the palms of her hands. Her left wrist burned upon impact. Mud splashed up, covering every inch of her dress.

"Sutton." Greyson's worried face appeared inches from hers. He bent down next to her in the mud. "Are you all right? Are you hurt?"

"I'm fine."

He helped her to her feet. Sutton tried to pull out of his grip. Black mud stained her from head to toe.

Greyson examined her by walking in a complete circle around her body. Sure that she was okay, he pulled his sweatshirt over his head and slipped it around her shoulders. Sutton started to protest but the sight of his broad bare chest muted her.

"Let's head back to my place. I'll drive you home."

"No. I can get home by myself."

"Don't be stubborn. It's not ladylike." Greyson swept her off her feet into his arms.

"Put me down, Greyson Ballantyne." She crossed her hands in front of her as he pressed her against the warmth of his chest.

"No. I'm carrying you back to my place and then I'm driving you home. If you have a problem with that, try to get away from me."

Knowing that she could never match his strength, Sutton relented and let him carry her to his Volvo. She rested against the ripples of his chest. Her face bumped the crook of his neck as he crossed the uneven field. The masculine scent of woodsy herbs comforted her. She fought his alluring qualities. Letting her marry Alex was wrong. She held onto that truth when his grip tightened around her back and beneath her thighs.

Greyson gently placed her on the front seat of his Volvo wagon. He bent down, placing his face next to hers. "Are you sure you don't want to get cleaned up here before I take you home?"

"I'm sure." Sutton pouted.

Greyson secured her door before sliding into the driver's seat.

Just before he turned into her driveway, he broke the silence. "I've asked myself a thousand times why I didn't stop the wedding and tell you about Alex. I think it was because I wanted you to be happy and it seemed Alex did that for you."

He pulled up next to her house and put the car in park. "I held out hope that there was a spark between us—that's why I kissed you. I wanted to see if I had a chance. You made it clear that Alex was your future. Not me."

Sutton's lips parted. Maybe in some way, Greyson not telling her was partly her own fault. If he would have barged into the church office with the story he told her earlier, would she have believed him? Probably not. She would have chalked it up to jealousy and the rivalry Alex and

Greyson carried over the years. If that was true, then why did she kiss him back? If she was so tuned in to Alex and being his wife, why did she kiss Greyson minutes before walking down the aisle?

"Grey—"

Mr. Hill stepped out onto the front porch. "Sutton? You in that car?" He made a windmill gesture with his hand. "Come on inside now."

Sutton obediently opened the door and climbed the front porch stairs.

"What happened to you?" He father took her by both arms and checked for injuries.

"I fell while running, Daddy. I'm fine." She turned over her shoulder to see Greyson driving down the road back the way they had come.

"Was that the Ballantyne boy who dropped you off? What's he have to do with my daughter coming home covered in black mud?" He ushered her inside. "I'm telling you that boy has always been sniffing around you and I don't like it. Can't he see you're still grieving for Alex?"

Five

The library would have a copy of the capital's newspaper. Sutton left Sierra making cookies with her mother and walked to town to search the employment section. Before she could get her own place and a car, she needed to find work. The ailing town didn't offer many options. It didn't help that she only possessed two years of post-high-school education. Alex had wanted a stay-at-home wife and mother. Finishing college without any funds now seemed like a dream that would never come to fruition.

Sutton sat at a table in back of the one-story library scanning the newspaper. A shadow moved over her shoulder, covering the paper.

"Maddie!" She jumped out of her chair and shared a long, rocking hug with her old high school friend.

"I heard you were back in town for awhile. I've been meaning to come by but didn't know . . ."

"It's hard when someone dies."

Maddie took a seat in the shiny wood-grain chair next to Sutton. "You're too young to be a widow. All things considered you look fabulous."

"So do you. You still look eighteen. Catch me up."

Maddie gave an abbreviated, hushed version of her life. Never married, she took care of her parents until her mother died last year. Her father suffered a massive stroke a year ago and remained in poor health. "I thought about you all the time. The way you and Alex made it out of this town. I envy you."

"Are you thinking about leaving?"

"I was at one time. Before my parents became ill. I like it here, but I want to get married and have a family of my own. There aren't many prospects in this tiny town, but I have to take care of my father."

Sutton nodded. After her life with Alex, marriage was in the far recesses of her mind, but she could understand her friend's desire.

"What are you doing?" Maddie pointed to the newspaper scattered about the table.

"Job hunting. I need something right away."

"What do you have in mind?"

"Any work will do."

"The library needs someone. I'm here alone most of the time. The mayor approved financing for an assistant months ago but there hasn't been any interest. I went to college to be a librarian. It would be nice to settle into the job and not have to carry the load alone. We're not like the big-city libraries, but we're all Hannaford Valley has. Interested?"

An hour later, Sutton had completed a job application, tax forms, insurance, and benefit information. She left the library with a spring in her step and her mind racing to the future. The library job was a small victory but it was one in the direction of independence. The hours were consistent and would leave time for her to pursue schooling. The steady paycheck would help her get a place for herself and Sierra. All things considered, life was looking up.

The ache in her wrist, a reminder of her fall, began to throb. Despite the ice pack applied during the night, it still hurt. The swelling had gone down but a bruise remained. While in town she decided to stop by the doctor's office on the other side of the Piggly Wiggly grocery store.

The doctor told stories of every childhood injury she had suffered before he wrapped her left wrist in an Ace bandage and advised that she keep it immobilized for two weeks. He promised that the injury was not serious enough to interfere with her new job at the library.

"Uncle," said the low commanding voice of Todd Carter, "don't you think getting an X-ray would be a good idea?"

Doc Carter scratched his white beard and peered through thick glasses. "It might not be a bad idea at that. Take care of her, Todd." He shuffled out of the room.

Sutton and Todd shared a smile.

"He's getting on, but he's still good at what he does." Todd's bright skin contrasted with the deep sable of his beard and mustache. "How have you been doing?"

"With everything that's been going on in my life lately, other than this small setback, just fine."

He nodded as he jotted something on her medical record.

"Are you a doctor now? I hadn't heard that."

Todd glanced up from the chart. "I'm a nurse."

Rumors of his too-feminine ways resurfaced.

"Let me walk you next door for your X-rays. With this new setup Unc put in, you don't have to go outside. We knocked out the back wall and put the addition here." He opened a door that led into another reception area. He ushered her past other waiting patients. "It made no sense to send our patients all the way to the capital for simple X-rays that could be taken and read here in a matter of minutes."

"Looks like you're helping your uncle keep up with the times."

"I'm trying. Auntie passed on a while ago and he's slowed down a great deal since then. I've been trying to talk him into getting a partner. Someone recently out of medical school with fresh ideas and knowledge of modern medical advances."

"That would be good."

"Have a seat here, and I'll find a technician to take your pictures."

Sutton watched him walk out of the room on the tips of his toes. During high school Todd had been ostracized for his less-than-manly ways but no one ever substantiated the rumors. And no one could ever convince her that being homosexual—if he was—was a danger to the people around him. She shook her head. Some of the beliefs about small-town living were true. The residents stood on ceremony, honored traditions long forgotten by others, and a rumor beat the truth nine out of ten times.

The X-rays were negative, which kept Sutton from having her left arm placed in a cast. Her father would have had a nervous breakdown if he believed Greyson had broken her wrist. She noted the time and hurried home. Not paying attention while she sprinted down the sidewalk, she bounced off a solid mass.

"Sutton Hill." Chevy grasped her shoulders to keep her upright. Whenever she encountered a Ballantyne her balance went off-kilter. "I wondered when I'd run into you. Did I hurt you?"

"No, I'm sorry. I bumped into you."

Chevy offered his condolences and made the usual catch-up small talk. "My truck is parked across the street. Would you like a ride home?"

"No. I'll walk."

"If you're sure." Chevy hesitated. "Grey mentioned what happened out at our place yesterday. He didn't say it was that serious." He nodded toward her newly bandaged wrist.

Sutton gave him the short version of the story, taking the blame for her own clumsiness.

"Still, Grey will feel bad. He's already moping around about the fight you two had. He wouldn't tell me what it was about."

"Better to keep it between us. It wasn't all that important." Sutton tried to downplay the whole incident. Chevy had always protected her as if she were his little sister. If it meant taking her side against Greyson, he would. No use in placing a wedge between two brothers. This was between her and Greyson. She was starting to realize it always had been.

Sutton smiled and started down the walk with a quick wave.

"Hey, Sutton." Chevy held the brim of his hat as he jogged to catch up to her. "My parents have been wanting to see you. They keep asking us if we've been by your place. My mother is planning to invite you to dinner Saturday. You know they moved into a new house. She wants to have a dinner to celebrate."

"That's sweet of her, but I don't think I can make it." Sitting at the table with Greyson, watching him eat with the same mouth that had lured her into inappropriate kissing sessions, was a temptation she could avoid.

Chevy laughed and removed his wide-brimmed straw hat. "Are you really going to turn my mother down?"

Sutton thought it out. No, Mrs. Ballantyne rarely took no for an answer.

"That's what I thought. Bring your little girl, too. I'll come for you about six o'clock?"

"Six is good."

Chevy replaced his hat, tipped his brim and headed in the opposite direction. Chevy Ballantyne was the last living buffalo cowboy. Rumor spread across the valley that he lived alone in a cabin in the woods because he had strange tendencies that ladies should not know about. Sutton knew better. Of the Ballantyne brothers, Chevy was the quiet, introverted one. Sutton would never place him in the middle of a big city and expect him to make it without severely injuring someone he felt offended his honor code, but otherwise he was a gentle giant. His brawn and rugged good looks, paired with his sensitivity and good-natured heart, made him the catch of the century. Unfortunately, no woman had discovered this pot of gold.

Sierra bounced down the stairs and ran across the yard to greet her mother.

"You have a boo-boo."

"Yeah, I do, so now I have to pick you up in my right arm."

Sierra giggled while she scrambled up into her mother's arm.

"Why are you outside by yourself?"

"I'm playing with my dolls."

Sutton viewed the evidence once she stepped up on the porch. "Why don't you pick up your toys and come inside? It's almost dinnertime."

Sierra hopped down and began to pick up her things. Her hair had been restyled since the morning. A part separated her scalp into two equal sides and long red braids cascaded down her back. Sutton remembered the style from her own school days.

Sutton stepped inside and heard her mother speaking in a hushed voice. "It's not right not to tell her."

"I don't care," her father answered. "I don't want you saying anything to her. It's been my responsibility to raise Sutton and I make the decisions when it comes to her."

"You're not raising her anymore. Sutton is a grown woman with a child."

Sutton followed the voices to the kitchen.

"I say I'll handle this. Are you going to challenge me?"

Silence was the answer.

"That boy has been sniffing around my girl for years. Do you see the way he looks at her? All like he'd eat her up if given half the chance. Well, he won't get the chance if it's up to me. Alex has done that girl enough harm. I never approved of her hanging around with that bunch of boys anyway. It wasn't right for a young girl not to have no other young girls as friends."

"She had—"

Sutton stepped into the middle of the battleground. "I had girls for friends, too, Daddy. I just wasn't as close to them as I was to Alex and the Ballantynes."

She kissed her mother and then her father.

"What happened?" Her mother left the stove to tend to her daughter.

"Doc Carter says I sprained it when I fell yesterday."

Her father grunted. "Sit down at the table." He pulled out a chair for her.

"It's not bad. Doc says to limit using it but I'm right-handed, so that won't be hard to do. He says it's okay for me to start work as planned."

"Work?" Her mother's face beamed with excitement.

"I ran into Maddie at the library and she hired me on the spot. It's nothing fancy, but it'll pay the bills and provide medical benefits for Sierra and me."

"I knew you wouldn't stay down long." Her mother went to check something bubbling on the stovetop.

Mr. Hill joined his daughter at the table. "Don't you be in an all-fire hurry to get out of this house. Mom and I love having you and Sierra. I don't want you to leave here until you're steady on your feet."

"We won't." Sutton patted her father's hand. Her mother smiled over her shoulder. Having Sierra in the house gave her another daughter to dress and spoil. After Sutton, she'd been unable to have more children, although they had desperately wanted a houseful.

"Now what were you arguing about when I walked in?" Sutton knew by what she'd heard it had something to do with Greyson.

"We're just looking out for you, sugar, that's all." Mr. Hill returned the gesture of patting her hand. Mrs. Hill averted her eyes.

Sierra skipped into the kitchen and stood next to her grandmother at the stove. "Can I help?"

Sutton watched as her mother patiently handed Sierra the utensils and demonstrated how she should place each setting.

"She seems to be doing all right with all of the excitement," Mr. Hill whispered in Sutton's direction. "Excitement" was how her parents referred to Alex's death when Sierra was around.

Sutton nodded. "Sometimes I think it wasn't such a bad thing that they weren't close."

* * *

Sutton went to the Ballantyne dinner alone. Her parents insisted on taking Sierra to the capital, where they had a day of movies and McDonald's planned. Giving Sierra the choice was needless. What kid wouldn't choose McDonald's over a night of old people sitting around a table eating?

Sutton sat wedged between Chevy and Kirkland. The two big men dwarfed her at the table. She remembered the very summer when they received their growth spurts and grew taller than the trees in the everglade. Their skinny bodies filled out with muscles and their waists shrank inward, giving their physiques a perfect inverted triangle appearance.

"Here's Greyson now," Mrs. Ballantyne said, as the wind chimes hanging above the front door rattled.

Greyson came into the room apologizing. "Sorry I'm late. The flights leaving Chicago were delayed because of the weather and—"

All eyes turned to Greyson when he abruptly stopped speaking. His eyes were locked on Sutton. He hadn't seen her since the mishap with the mud puddle. Tonight her cherry-colored hair was wound in soft curls that framed her face. The emerald dress she wore plunged deeply in front, exposing a blush to her fair skin that matched his surprised expression. Her pouty lips were tinted pink, and green eye shadow accentuated her sexy brown eyes.

"Sutton, I apologize. I didn't know there'd be company."

Sutton nodded, making a point of keeping her eyes from his.

Greyson knew she must still be angry with him. If not for what his father would do if Grey interrupted his mother's dinner party, he'd pull her to the back of the house and try to explain.

"Is that all you're going to eat, Greyson?" his mother asked. His normally voracious appetite left him and was replaced by frustrated sexual hunger as he watched the graceful way Sutton slipped the fork into her mouth.

"It must have been the flight. I'm a little jet lagged," Greyson explained.

Kirkland reassured their mother, "Greyson can take care of himself. Don't worry, Mama."

His mother watched him until she was convinced he was not seriously ill. "Who's ready for dessert?" she asked a short time later.

Sutton stood with his mother. "Let me help you with that, Mama."

Greyson's eyes narrowed. She still called his mother Mama. How could she be so closely knit with his family and not sense his intentions to make her a permanent, legal member of their clan?

"Nonsense. You sit down and rest that arm. Didn't Doc Carter tell you to take it easy?"

During the dinner Sutton had kept her left hand in her lap and Greyson had not noticed the bandage until that moment. A twinge of guilt moved through him. He would do anything to have the injury himself. He wondered if Sutton was in pain. Did she blame him for her fall? How badly was she hurt?

"It's not as bad as it looks." Sutton's protest fell on deaf ears. Mrs. Ballantyne was already in the kitchen.

Chevy stood and helped her back into her seat. Greyson observed the tenderness he used to do so. He slammed his water glass on the tabletop as a first warning to Chevy.

Pop Ballantyne glanced Greyson's way. Then, he directed his youngest, "Go help your mother."

Kirkland quickly did as he was told.

"Sutton," Pop said, "Chevy said he ran into you coming out of Doc Carter's office. Everything okay with your arm?"

"Yes, sir. Just banged it up a little."

Chevy rested his elbow on the table and used it as a prop for his stubbly chin. "Tell Pop your good news."

Greyson's chiseled chin twitched again. He wanted to pick the water glass up and hurl it across the table at his brother. This newly rediscovered closeness to Sutton was going to stop.

Sutton looked at Chevy with smiling eyes. "I'm taking a job at the library and moving back to Hannaford Valley."

"Good, child." Mrs. Ballantyne reappeared with a chocolate cake. Kirkland followed with vanilla ice cream, bowls, and spoons.

"That's what I told her when I heard." Chevy delighted in the information. "Hannaford Valley really is your home. This is where you should be. All your family is here—"

"Including us," Mrs. Ballantyne added.

Chevy nodded and continued, "This is where you should be, surrounded by friends to help you through this difficult time." His hand rested on Sutton's back.

"Chevy—" Greyson warned through clenched teeth.

Chevy removed his hand. Everyone else looked bewildered by the outburst.

Mrs. Ballantyne served Sutton after her husband. "I met your darling little girl at the church. Any time your folks can't keep her, you bring her around here."

"Yes, ma'am."

"You should see Sierra around her Uncle Chevy. We hit it off right away," Chevy bragged.

"That's right, you did." Sutton cut into her cake. "That surprised me, too. She usually doesn't take to strangers."

"Chevy," Greyson's tone commanded everyone's chatter to stop. "What are you doing spending so much time around Sutton and her family?"

"I-I—"

"You what?"

Pop Ballantyne turned a harsh gaze on his eldest. "Watch your tone at my table."

"Sorry, sir." Greyson's eyes studied Chevy with a silent warning. His gaze questioned Sutton's actions toward his brother. He apologized to his mother and dropped his eyes to his dessert.

Six

After dinner, Greyson slipped the dark jacket of his suit back on and waited. He sat tight-lipped in the great room while his family gathered around the new television and watched an action movie whose sound blasted from the stereo speakers. And he waited. His mouth puckered in a frown when his mother sat with Sutton, showing her pictures of their past. And waited. Waited while watching Chevy's every move. Waited and learned how Sutton had come to be at his parents' house for dinner. Waited, waited, and waited. Until finally Kirkland kissed their mother goodnight, saying he had a long drive back to the capital. Mama was tired and decided to turn in. Pop wasn't far behind.

"Last one out, lock up," Pop instructed. All of the boys had keys to their new home. He refused to lock his children out of his life.

"Chevy, I think I should be leaving," Sutton said after the light down the long hallway dimmed.

Chevy grinned at Greyson. "Lock up, big brother."

Greyson slowly, deliberately unfolded his tall body with a menacing easiness that meant trouble was on the horizon. "I'll lock up after you leave. Alone."

Chevy's chuckle halted when Greyson's eyes flashed in his direction. "What are you doing, Grey?"

"Sutton is going to stay behind. We need to talk about a few things."

Sutton shrank back under his intimidating gaze. "It's late."

Greyson shook his head. "Don't care how late it is." Each word became a chore to turn out. He turned to Chevy. "I'll be by your place tomorrow."

Chevy's mouth dropped but he remained silent. Greyson hoped he correctly heard the words as a warning.

Chevy got a head start on explaining himself. "Look, Grey, I—"

"Good night. I'll see you tomorrow."

Chevy looked to Sutton. With unconvincing bravado he said, "I brought you. It's my responsibility to get you home."

Greyson loosened the cuffs of his white dress shirt and began to roll them up to his elbows. He stood with his feet apart, a silent challenge. Because Greyson was usually the cerebral, yielding brother, Chevy didn't know how to interpret his big brother's unfamiliar, bold actions.

Sutton touched Chevy's arm. "I'm sure Greyson will see me home."

Chevy watched her, turned to Greyson and thought it wise to leave without further debate.

The paneling covering the walls made the great room dark and warm. The oversized furniture masked the room's true size. Sophisticated electronic equipment made the room a showplace. Mrs. Ballantyne's touches were evident in the color coordination of the furniture, drapes, and knick-knacks.

"What just happened here?" Greyson folded his thick arms across his chest. "Are you dating my little brother now?"

"Greyson, don't yell at me like that. What business is it of yours whom I date?"

He kicked the ottoman out of his path and reached Sutton in two long strides. "It's my business because you and I were kissing a few days ago. Then you sank into the grieving widow mode and now you show up as my brother's date."

"First of all, me not wanting to see you had nothing to do with playing the grieving widow, as you put it."

"That's what your father told me when I called."

Sutton faltered with his disclosure of this information but recovered quickly. "I can't help what my father led you to believe. Maybe he didn't want to tell you the truth because he was afraid you wouldn't understand."

"Is that a crack about me not telling you about Alex?"

Sutton stomped her foot on the hardwood flooring. "How could you keep his secret?"

"I told you—"

"I think about all the years of misery and I can't help but blame you for part of it."

"Me? If you were so damn miserable, why didn't you leave? This isn't nineteen twenty-seven, where your husband could command you to stay."

"That's not fair. You don't know—"

"Don't know what? What, maybe you liked being Alex's wife a little more than you're admitting now."

"You have no idea what it was like."

"You stayed."

"I wasn't happy."

"You married him. You married him right after kissing me at the church; nobody made you walk down that aisle. And you had his child."

"Keep Sierra out of this. This is between you and me. I will not have you dragging her into the middle of this mess we've made."

Greyson's eyes glanced away quickly. "I shouldn't have said that." His cheekbone flexed. "Are you dragging Chevy into this? You know how this town talks. Everyone will think you're a couple."

"Chevy knows we're friends. He understands that. You're the only one who seems to be confusing my relationship with him."

"What about us? Am I confused about your relationship with me?"

"You should have told me what you knew about Alex. You were supposed to be my friend. You don't understand how I feel."

Greyson snatched her up by the shoulders, lifting her to the tips of her feet. He pressed his lips against hers until she stopped pushing against his chest. He flicked his tongue against the corner of her mouth until the last of her resistance melted away. His eyes watched her expression soften as he transferred his passion across the full pout of her lips.

He pulled away. "Tell me I don't understand that."

"Greyson?" Pop appeared in the doorway.

Greyson released Sutton. She turned her back to them.

"Yes, Pop?"

"Your Mama and I can hear you all the way down the hall." He looked past Greyson's broad shoulders. "Everything all right in here?"

"We're fine, Pop." He stepped to the door, blocking his father's field of vision.

Pop Ballantyne lowered his voice. "I don't want no foolishness up in this here house."

"We're working some things out. That's all." Greyson pushed the door closed. "Sutton and I have a lot to talk about. We'll keep it down. Didn't mean to disturb you."

Pop looked skeptically between the crack of the door in Sutton's direction. "Good night." He showed Greyson the face of his wristwatch. Nine-thirty.

"Good night, Pop."

Greyson composed himself by rubbing a hand down the bridge of his nose and across his jaw line. He touched Sutton's shoulder and directed her to sit on the sofa. He shielded their words from his parents' ears by turning on the stereo.

Greyson kneeled before Sutton, resting his hands on her knees. "You can use all the words in your repertoire to try and convince me otherwise, but your kisses tell me all I need to know. I should have stood up and told you how I felt a long time ago—I didn't. Any part I had in your unhappiness, I accept responsibility for. The question is, what do we do now?"

"We don't let this happen again. No more kissing. We continue the friendship we've had all these years and that's it."

"I don't understand. Why are you rejecting me?"

Sutton paused in thought. "I'm a penniless widow with a child. I'm not exactly thinking about becoming involved with another man at this time. I want to be free to have what I want. To pursue what I need. I want to make a home for Sierra. I don't want to go from one man to another."

Greyson felt her slipping away. "When you turned twelve, I was seventeen. Did your father ever tell you I asked his permission to date you?" The shock on Sutton's face served as his answer. "He said what any sane father would have. Not as long as he was alive. Twelve and seventeen." Greyson shook his head. "When you think of it in terms of numbers, it seems absurd. When you think about it in terms of you being a mature twelve-year-old who was developing into a woman who I didn't want to see get away, it makes perfect sense."

"Greyson, I didn't know—"

"I asked again when you were thirteen: still too young. When you turned fourteen, Alex asked. Alex asked and your father said yes. I don't hold any ill feelings toward your father. If you had been my daughter I would have wanted you to date the wealthiest man in the valley, too."

Greyson's fingers caressed the bandage on her wrist. "What no one knew was that right before you turned thirteen we kissed. Remember that?"

"My first kiss," Sutton whispered, her eyes flashing seductively.

"Although we only kissed that one time, I was crazy over you after that. I could tell you didn't think of it like I did. I was much older and knew it meant more. For you it was about learning how to kiss. I was going to teach you how to kiss so when you found your first boyfriend you'd be ready.

Remember? Who better to teach you than your best platonic friend? What you don't realize is that it's never been platonic for me. And it never will be."

Sutton's eyes rose to meet his. "This is overwhelming, Greyson."

"Isn't love supposed to be?"

Before Sutton could answer, he pulled her by the waist as he stretched his long body across the carpet. He placed her next to him while his hands examined every inch of her face. Her breathing sped up as his finger explored the plunged neckline of her dress. He straddled her middle and leaned down to kiss her. There was no resistance this time.

Seven

"Mommy." Sierra stood even with the kitchen tabletop, tugging at Sutton's sleeve.

She'd done it again. Zoned out while thinking of the kisses she shared with Greyson.

"Yes?"

Sierra's eyes were as round and as shiny as marbles. "Mother Galloway is here."

Sutton made out Sierra's attempt to announce her grandmother's arrival. The distress on her daughter's face was completely opposite the joy she saw when Sierra spent time with Sutton's parents. Sutton stood and brushed off her jeans and sweater. She wished for enough time to change into something more suitable, but her mother was calling from the living room. She used her fingers to comb her crimson strands of hair into place. She did the same for her daughter. Noticing the wild frivolity of her daughter's French braids, she suggested Sierra go up to their room to play.

Sierra zoomed out of the kitchen and Sutton answered her mother's second announcement of her mother-in-law's arrival.

Mother Galloway looked picture perfect, as usual. She wore a burgundy pantsuit tastefully adorned with a pearl necklace and earrings. She clutched a matching purse to her side as if someone in the house would actually attempt to wrestle it away from her.

"Mother Galloway, how are you?" Sutton kissed her

cheek and they sat together on the sofa. Her mother was gone by the time she looked around.

Mother Galloway's disapproving glare set the tone for their meeting. "I'm doing fine, Sutton, but you don't seem to be. I saw Sierra out front, all dirty and tattered. Is this what you've been reduced to?"

Sutton dulled the tip of her sharpened tongue. "Alex did leave us penniless."

Mother Galloway shrank back momentarily.

"But you're looking good," Sutton added.

Mother Galloway situated her purse on her lap. "My son's lawyer contacted me this week. The IRS is ready to liquidate the condo. It has been sold by auction and the new owners take possession in seven days. The government will allow you two days to gather essentials for you and Sierra. I assume you can make that."

"I don't know if I can. I'm working now." In truth, she didn't want to relive the memories of her empty marriage or be haunted by her dead husband's belongings.

"Working?" Her nose scrunched up, as if Sutton had just confessed to being a porn star.

"I found a job at the library. It should tide me over until I get back on my feet."

"Well, you'll have to forget working for a couple of days. You have to sign papers and remove your belongings before the new owners take possession of the condo."

"I can't afford a trip to Ohio right now. Can't you sign the papers?"

"The lawyer says no."

More likely, she didn't want her name on any papers that the IRS would have access to. It had not escaped Sutton that Mrs. Galloway continued to live in the manner to which she was accustomed, even after Alex's death. She never doubted that Mother Galloway had been a part of Alex's deception and had gotten her fair share of loot.

Mother Galloway continued, "I'll pay your airfare and put you up in a hotel until your business is finished."

Bingo. Alex had made sure Mother Galloway would be taken care of after his death.

Mrs. Galloway stood, ending the conversation. "There will be an e-ticket waiting at the airport."

Sutton walked her mother-in-law out to her Mercedes and waved good-bye as she drove away. Her connection with the Galloway family would never be terminated. If nothing else, they would be tied through Sierra. Mother Galloway had never been mean to Sutton, but she had never been warm, either. And Sutton was positive that Mother Galloway was privy to her son's wrongdoings. Hence the numerous expensive gifts Alex bestowed on his mother. As long as the goodies kept coming, Mother Galloway looked the other way when her son was absent at family gatherings, or when she herself was used as an alibi for his late nights.

"Hey, Pop. I didn't hear you come in." Greyson scratched his bare stomach while making his way to his kitchen. "What do you need?"

Pop Ballantyne adjusted the strap of his overalls. "I wanted to talk to you about the other night." He sat at the kitchen table where he had fought hard to provide food for his family. He loved his new home and furnishings, but his heart belonged to this house.

"What about it?" Greyson straddled a chair and prepared a bowl of corn flakes.

"For some reason Chevy thinks that you're looking to talk to him."

Remembering the way Chevy touched Sutton during dinner made his anger rise anew. He answered, tight-lipped, "I am."

"Well you make sure that's all you do." He dropped his voice as if there were others in the house to overhear the conversation. "I saw the way you were carrying on with Sutton and I'm not sure I like it. She's still grieving over

Alex and you have her pinned up in my great room making the moves on her. It ain't right."

"You don't understand, Pop. I wasn't 'making the moves' on her. We were kissing."

Pop seemed surprised he would openly admit what he was sure his father knew. The boys had always kept a close relationship with their father, openly discussing anything from sports to sex without ceremony. The surprise on Pop's face was due to having an open discussion about Sutton, a young lady he thought of as the daughter with which he never was blessed.

Greyson dismissed his father's expression and continued. "Why is everybody in this town incessant on keeping Sutton in a state of grieving over Alex? Sutton and I have unfinished business that has nothing to do with her and Alex. There's a lot you don't know about those two."

Pop slapped his hand down on the table, causing the bowl of cereal to vibrate. "I know a coupla things, and I know that people in this town talk. The Ballantynes have had a hard time making a name here. Your mother and me moved here right after we were married and no one accepted us as part of the town family."

"You've told me that."

"Did I ever tell you why?"

Greyson shook his head while adding sugar to his cereal.

"Your Mama was pregnant with you when we moved into this house." He dropped his voice. "Pregnant and showing."

That meant his mother had gotten pregnant before they were married. Greyson listened more intently, not certain how he felt about hearing this intimate information.

"I could care less what these people say or think as long as my wife is happy and I raise good boys. But your mother ain't like that. For some reason she wants the townspeople to like her. She's always busy volunteering for this or that. She genuinely likes helping others, but I know she also feels like she has to work that much harder to fit in. I don't want no rumors about you and Sutton destroying what she's done here. It would kill her."

The naïveté of the people of Hannaford Valley made Greyson want to deliver a lecture on modern times. But this was their way of life. This is the way of life he had given up everything to return to. In a small town such as Hannaford, reputation was everything, and he had not considered that in his boldness to win Sutton.

"I'm sorry, Pop. No disrespect intended."

His father nodded. That easily, all was forgiven.

Greyson continued. "Let me explain my side before you leave. I love Sutton Hill. I always have loved her but I was too stupid to stand up and fight for her. I let her be swept away by Alex. I knew he was no good for her. All these years I've been miserable without her in my life. There has not been a day that I haven't pictured her face. Now that I have a shot at being with her, I can't just stand back and let her get away again."

Pop regarded him with a strange expression.

"Do you know what I mean?"

Pop nodded. "This sounds similar to the conversation I had with your grandfather when I asked permission to court your mother."

"And he said?"

"No. Run me off with a shotgun."

"And what did you do?"

"Sneaked her out the window of the room she shared with her sisters." A slick smile covered his face. "Sneaked her out and away from that old fool."

"Then you understand. I have given up everything to move back here and convince Sutton to marry me. That's what this is all about. It's true I want to help the town flourish again. I wanted to repay some of what you and Mama have done for us. My commitment to you, Mama, and the town stands, but I'd be lying if I didn't tell you that Sutton is my main motivation for leaving Chicago and coming back here."

"Yeah, I understand loud and clear." Distress made Pop lean forward and press his finger against Greyson's bare chest. "I want *you* to understand loud and clear." He sat back and placed his hands flat against the tabletop. "You decided you're going after Sutton, okay. You made a commitment to this town, me, and your mama, okay." His eyes found Greyson's. "Once you make those kinds of choices, you gotta be in it for the long haul."

Pop studied his hands for a long moment before going on. "Do you think sneaking your mama out that window didn't come with consequences? I thought I was being a cool cat—bragged about it all over town. I liked your mama, wanted to spend time with her, knew she was fallin' fast for me. I just didn't expect to fall so hard for her. When she turned up pregnant, all hell broke loose. This cool cat was gonna be somebody's father. Shoot, I was driving moonshine to get the money to take her out."

"Pop—" There's only so much Greyson wanted to know about his parents and their personal life.

Pop's eyes cut into him, keeping him quiet. "When she came to me crying, asking about what we were gonna do . . ." Emotion made him look away until he could speak without his voice breaking. "I looked at that beautiful, warm woman and asked myself, what is this flower doing with this weed? That was the first time I realized I loved your mama. That was the first time I realized what it was to be a man."

Another pause. "I decided right then and there that I would do right by Mar-beth and my kid. I took her away, married her, and started my family. Times have been hard here and there, but I never turned my back on her and I never did anything to hurt her. I love your mother."

"Pop, you don't have to tell me that," Greyson said softly, feeling the thickness of the emotional confession coat his skin.

"I'm telling you all this to make a point. Once you take on Sutton, you have to be prepared to stand by her—no matter what problems come. That girl just lost her husband.

She has a baby. I heard all the talk about what Alex did to her—that leaves a lot of pain. The town's gonna add its two cents. You ready to take on all those troubles? Or are you trying to pin her up in my house stealing kisses like y'all are still kids?"

Greyson took a firm stand. "I said I love her. I love her. Always have. I'm not running away—no matter what happens. This time I'm going to fight for her."

His father studied him with the same intensity he used on his boys back when he was trying to discover who threw a baseball that broke the back window. "Mean that, son?"

"Yes, sir."

"I was beginning to wonder if I'd ever have a grandchild. And it'd be nice to have more women around. You boys are all wrapped up in work. I thought your mother and I would have to do without those things."

"Not if I can help it."

Later that day, Greyson, dressed in worn jeans and a flannel shirt, stood on the front porch of Chevy's log cabin.

"What?" Chevy pulled the door open after Greyson's third round of pounding. He stepped back. "Pop said he talked to you."

Greyson stood in the doorway wearing a menacing snarl. "Now *I'm* here to talk to you."

"Listen, Grey . . ."

Greyson backed him into the house. When he couldn't contain his laughter any longer, he burst into a loud rumble. "I'm not going to do anything to you, Chevy."

Chevy exhaled a sigh of relief. "I'm not worried about you. I just didn't want to have to explain to Pop why I had to put you in the hospital. Mama would be all upset."

Greyson jumped at him. Chevy stumbled backward, falling back into an easy chair. Greyson doubled over in laugher, and after a moment, Chevy joined him.

"I wasn't hitting on Sutton," Chevy apologized after their laughter faded.

"Yes, you were."

"Flirting a little, but I know how you feel about her."

Greyson walked around the large room of the cabin, surveying the animal trophies Chevy had collected from hunting. He ran his large hand across the glass tabletop of a dining-room table made mostly from a huge tree trunk. He marveled at the intricate detail of the pattern of stones around the fireplace. "Did you do all this work yourself?"

"Most of it. Kirkland helped a lot. Some of the men at one of his construction sites pitched in with the heavy work."

"How many bedrooms?" Greyson stopped near a long hallway.

"Let me show you." Chevy bolted up from his seat and gave his big brother a pride-filled tour of the cabin, pointing out every detail in workmanship and design.

The master bedroom was situated in the rear of the cabin. The room was at least fifty percent of the size of the entire cabin. A fireplace much more intricately designed than the one gracing the living room adorned this room. A large triple-pane glass window looked down on a grove of trees. On the opposite side of the room was a sliding glass-door that led to a back porch surrounded by so many flowers that the aroma wafted inside immediately upon opening the door. The master bath was amazing. Built-in shelves held plants that grew down to the floor. Plush salmon carpet cushioned Greyson's step. Through a connecting walk-in closet was a vanity station. Greyson saw the vanity had a mirror to the ceiling and fluorescent lighting.

Greyson followed Chevy through the house for the tour of the kitchen, a second bath, and another bedroom he was currently using as a planning station for his work.

"About Sutton," Greyson started once they were settled in the living room again.

"I invited her to dinner because I knew you would like to

see her. I should have figured you'd get jealous. Grey, you know I've always had a soft spot for her. She's like a little sister to me."

"I know. It's all right. As long as you know when to back off."

Chevy nodded. "How did things go after I left?"

Greyson gave him an abbreviated version of their time together.

"You're on the right track." Chevy offered his support.

"Listen," Greyson cleared his throat before starting such a sensitive conversation, "I noticed the vanity. Have anyone in mind when you built it?"

Chevy shifted uneasily in his seat. "I have the ideal woman in mind. I just haven't met her." He tsked. "The women in this town think I'm some sort of freak. Maybe I am. I love living out here in the woods isolated from everyone else. I went to college to study a dying profession like forestry. Every time I get around women, I clam up."

Greyson didn't know what to say that would heal his brother's pride without sounding insincere or wimpy.

Chevy continued. "I'm thirty years old. I want a wife and kids like everyone else."

"One thing I know is that you'll never find a wife if you don't leave this cabin. I also see the way women look at you when we go into town together. The rugged, angry black cowboy is back in style."

They laughed.

"Don't make fun of me, Grey. I'm serious."

"I know. Since I'm back we'll work on it."

"Keep this between us? The last thing I need is Mama parading a bunch of women in front of me."

Greyson rose up to slap his brother's palm. Chevy had kept his secret about Sutton all these years, so how could he not do the same?

"As long as we have an understanding about Sutton."

* * *

Opening himself up to emotional scrutiny made Greyson seek refuge with his mother. Mama greeted him in the front hall with a warm hug that enveloped him in her softness. He sat on a plastic covering in the garden next to his mother while she weeded the area around her rose bushes.

"Are you staying for dinner? We're having banana pudding for dessert."

Greyson patted his stomach. "Mama, are you trying to make me fat?"

"I'd like to see a little more meat on your bones." She grinned, her eyes flashing pride. "You put on about five pounds and you'll have all these girls running afta you."

"Listen to you."

She raised an eyebrow. "I know your dad had to go talk to you. He wouldn't tell me what was going on, but I have my own ideas."

Greyson was not going to share his romantic conquests with his mother. His father had done enough sharing already that morning.

"I saw Sutton earlier."

"Really?" Greyson sat forward wrapping his arms around his legs.

"She was at the church helping her mother. Looked like she wanted to be anywhere but there. Reminded me of how you kids used to get all antsy in church every Sunday."

Greyson tuned out his mother's reminiscing as he pictured a tired Sutton at the church looking for a way to escape.

Greyson stood and dusted his pants. "Mama, I have to go."

"I thought you would."

Less than an hour later, Greyson descended the stairs of the church basement looking for Sutton.

"Whew," Mrs. Hill said as she wiped imaginary sweat from her forehead. "Sutton's upstairs hiding from me, I'm sure. After a few hours of work, she started getting anxious to leave. I guess I did work her pretty hard. We're about done here." She looked around at the mounds of boxes packed and ready to go into storage. "I was about to call her father to pick us up."

"I could see you home," Greyson offered.

Mrs. Hill craned her neck to see what he was carrying. Piecing things together, she said, "No, Mr. Hill is waiting. You see that Sutton gets home safely."

"Yes, ma'am."

Greyson climbed the stairs two at time. He checked the sanctuary first. The reverend was pushing a cart of Bibles down the side aisle. He said, "I think I saw her in the back."

"Thank you." Greyson hurried off, his excitement building with each step.

"See you in church Sunday," the reverend called after him, making it sound like a warning.

After checking one empty room, Greyson knew exactly where he'd find Sutton. Positive karma flowed as he took measured steps. The door was closed. He paused with his hand over the doorknob. Where else would she seek asylum? Greyson opened the door of Sutton's safe haven. He remembered his last visit to the church office.

The desk lamp framed Sutton's cherry hair and fair skin. Greyson stepped into the room and waited for her to notice him. With mixed emotions of regret, fear, and longing percolating in his chest, he braced himself for Sutton's reaction.

"Greyson, what are you doing here?" She beamed intoxicating excitement.

Her smile made Greyson know everything would work out for them. No matter what obstacles came their way, they would live happily ever after.

"Greyson?" Sutton rounded the desk. "What are you doing here?"

"My mother said she saw you here earlier and you looked like you could use a break."

Sutton nodded, folding her arms over her chest. "My mother has worked my fingers to the bone."

Greyson was lost in her beauty.

"What's that?" She pointed to the bulging overnight bag he carried.

"This?" He smiled, remembering his mission. "This is dinner." He closed the door and turned the lock.

"What are you up to?"

Greyson opened the bag and smoothed a blanket over the floor. He followed with the dinner his mother had packed for them.

Sutton lifted the lid on the plastic container filled with banana pudding. "This smells too good."

"Hungry?" Greyson asked as he finished arranging the food and plates.

"Starving."

"Well, sit down." He helped her down beside him. "I told your mother I'd get you home. I told the reverend I'd be in church Sunday."

"You took care of everything, huh?"

"Yep." He put yellow squash onto a paper plate for her.

"I don't like squash."

"Me, either. My mother said to eat every bite." He lifted his shoulders in defeat and moved on to the green beans. He finished with the fried chicken.

Sutton placed a golden-brown biscuit on each of their plates and handed him a soda. Greyson took her hand and said a quiet prayer to bless the food. He pulled her plate over and speared a piece of squash, "After you."

Sutton closed her eyes and opened her mouth.

Greyson hesitated, contemplating replacing the fork with his lips.

"That's pretty good."

Greyson tasted his own squash. "Gross."

Greyson had finished his chicken before Sutton broke the silence. "I really needed this. How did you know?"

"I needed this—really bad."

Sutton's eyes fluttered downward. "You're so sure about everything and I'm wallowing in confusion."

"That's because you're trying to analyze everything instead of going with your gut."

"What do you mean?" She lifted her eyes to him.

"We're sitting in the same office we kissed in five years ago, alone. Don't you feel the vibe we left behind?"

"I always feel a vibe when you come around. It has nothing to do with this office."

Her confession left him speechless.

Sutton lifted a biscuit to her lips. Greyson pushed it away and replaced it with his lips.

"Ready for the banana pudding?" Sutton asked, attempting to look cool and composed. But her breaths came too short, heaving her breasts.

"You do that and I'll"—he searched through his overnight bag—"pour us a glass of wine."

"Greyson!" Sutton feigned offense. "In church?"

"You know the story of turning water to wine better than I do." He found two clear plastic cups, poured their wine, and handed her a cup. He set his wine down long enough to spoon the first helping of pudding into Sutton's mouth.

"Ummm. Your mother reinvented the banana for this one."

Greyson scooped up a spoonful of wafers and fed them to her.

"You're something else. I wish we could do this every day."

He twisted a strand of ruby-kissed hair around his finger. "We will. I promise. Our time is coming."

Eight

After signing the closing papers and endorsing the profit check to the IRS, Sutton, under watchful eyes, gathered her and Sierra's clothes, shoes, and toys. After all was done, she had spent four days away from her pride and joy, had missed work, and had been badgered daily by Mother Galloway.

Sutton moved quickly around the bedroom she'd shared with Alex. The memories of the day they moved into the condo swirled around her head when she entered his closet. All of his suits hung undisturbed. His shoes shone from their place on the shoe rack. She pushed the button of his electric tie rack and tried to place the occasions he had worn each one. When she felt herself becoming misty, she ended her journey through her past, left the closet, and pulled the door of the bedroom closed.

She remembered the police had come around ten the night Alex died.

Sutton had long ago abandoned waiting up for Alex. Dinner was ruined as usual, so she pitched it into the garbage disposal. She wandered into his home office and took the seat directly across from his desk. She remembered sitting there, staring at the vacant ergonomic chair while trying to figure out what held him at work for so many hours of the day. The sign that there was a new woman in Alex's life came whenever he increased his hours at work. Shame would keep him from spending time with Sutton and

Sierra; he found it difficult to look them in the eyes after giving his family time to another woman.

Sutton sat studying the neatly stacked work papers and the mini humidor that held contraband Cuban cigars offered as a gift by a past client. She had decided months ago that she would not question his late nights anymore. What good did it do? Alex would lie. Sutton would become upset. Knowing this, she couldn't figure out why she was drawn to his home office that night. When he came home she wanted to be in bed lounging, reading a book as if she had not noticed his absence.

The doorbell chimed, bringing Sutton out of her trance. She tightened her robe around her waist, checked the time, and went to the door. Even as she crossed the expanse of the condo, she questioned opening the door at night while home alone with Sierra. No one ever came to the condo at night.

Sutton checked the peephole. A policewoman stared directly into the small hole. The male officer had his back turned, making gestures with his arms. Riotous noises exploded in Sutton's head. She knew the officers were coming with bad news. Her first thought was to pretend not to be home; that way they couldn't deliver the news. Her body felt as hectic as the noises directing her movements. She struggled internally with every gesture needed to turn the lock and then the knob, letting the police in along with their news.

"Yes?" her voice never sounded mousier.

"Mrs. Alex Galloway?" the female officer asked.

When the male officer swung around, Sutton read his expression and her legs buckled beneath her. She hit the cold marble foyer with a thud as her head hit the welcome mat.

The female officer patted her hand. "Mrs. Galloway, are you with me?"

"Is it my husband?"

"Yes, Mrs. Galloway."

"Is he dead?" The words left the putrid taste of bile on Sutton's tongue.

The officer nodded. "A car accident on the interstate."

The male officer's hands came beneath Sutton's armpits and lifted her to her feet with little effort. "I'm sorry for your loss. Is there someone we can call?"

Mother Galloway intercepted all information the coroner and police gathered. She filtered the facts and slowly fed them to Sutton over a seven-day period. Alex was driving too fast. The roads were still slick from afternoon rain. He was traveling in the direction of home, but not from the direction of the office.

"Any messages?"

The desk clerk handed Sutton a stack of white slips. Mother Galloway wanted a report before Sutton left for the airport in the morning. Sierra had called as she did every day. Old acquaintances had learned Sutton was in town and wanted to get together for dinner. She balled the slips up as she stepped onto the elevator. They wanted the scoop on what Alex had done. One of the messages was from a woman Sutton suspected possessed inside knowledge because, although she couldn't prove it, she knew the woman was having an affair with Alex.

Once inside her room, Sutton came across a message that surprised her. Greyson Ballantyne had called and left a return number. The number contained only four digits. After the grueling week she'd spent packing away sad memories, his comforting voice would be welcomed.

"Front desk."

"This is Mrs. Galloway in 422." A shiver ran through Sutton; she hadn't referred to herself as Mrs. Galloway since the funeral. "There's a message here from Mr. Ballantyne, but there are only four digits given in his phone number."

"One moment, please." The desk clerk quickly returned to the phone. "I was checking our carbon of the message, Mrs. Galloway. There are only four numbers because that is an in-house line—his room number. Simply dial those four numbers and you'll be instantly connected. I can do that for you if you wish."

"No." Sutton snapped. She settled down. "No, thank you. I'll call directly."

Sutton cradled the phone in her lap, contemplating her next move. Why was Greyson in Ohio? What business did he have here? How did he know what hotel she was staying at? A crazy stirring of excitement made her smile. The mystery of him near her—from the room number, in a suite above her—made her mind picture heady scenarios inappropriate for a widow. Her hands shook as she punched in the numbers. On the third ring she decided to hang up and compose herself.

"Hello, Sutton," Greyson answered as her finger went to disconnect the call.

"How did you know it would be me?"

"You're the only one who knows where I am." His deep voice toyed with her.

"Why are you here? How'd you know I was here?"

"I found out where you disappeared to from your mother. I ran into her when I helped Mama haul some things to the church. I'm here because I want to spend time with you. Discreetly. Without the entire valley watching us. When can you be ready for dinner?"

Sutton suppressed her smile. "I never said I'd do dinner with you."

"Don't be stubborn. It's not ladylike. Can you be ready in thirty minutes?"

"I didn't come to Cleveland to entertain."

"Fine. We'll stay in. I'll be down for you in ten minutes."

"But—"

"See you in ten minutes." Greyson softly replaced the receiver.

"This is dangerous and you should call back and cancel." Sutton's rational mind argued with her mirrored reflection.

Her body throbbed with anticipation. She thought of Greyson Ballantyne. Brown as sand burned by the Bahamian sun, a chiseled face carved from granite, skyscraper tall, and with a southern twang that flowed rhythmically off his tongue through full brown lips. He modeled professionally, for goodness' sake. Her rational mind lost the debate.

"What's the worst that could happen?" she asked aloud as she applied the curling iron to a small patch of hair at the nape of her neck. "Ouch!" she shouted when the iron scorched her. "Yep," she conceded, "that's a possibility."

Sutton slipped a creamy turquoise sweater around her shoulders. "I know the possibilities and I have to be mature enough to handle them." She tucked her shirt inside her black khaki pants. She checked herself in the mirror on the back of the closet door, wishing she had packed a pretty dress. A soft tapping sounded at the door. She slipped on her shoes and hurried to open the door.

"Hi." Greyson stood leaning against the frame with a single rose resting between the ripples of his chest. Sutton wanted to vie for position with the flower against the wool blend, tight-fitting black sweater that outlined every wave of his muscles. Naturally—as any woman would do if a gorgeous man showed up at her door with a rose—her eyes moved south. Past the black belt that flowed through the loops of his black dress pants. Down the fabric that covered his thick legs. Back up to the tell-tale spot that every woman wanted to know she commanded.

Greyson cleared his throat. Embarrassed, Sutton turned for her purse. He followed her inside the room and she immediately realized her mistake. Being alone with Greyson could be dangerous. As his cologne filled the room, her mind's calculator clicked on. How long had it been since she'd made love? To answer that question, she had to add days from well before Alex's death.

Sutton picked up her purse from the bed and righted herself, to find her back pressed against Greyson's front.

"This is for you," he whispered near her ear as his arm came around and handed her the perfect rose.

"Thank you." Sutton lost the "I'll play it cool" battle when her voice came out strained and weak.

"You are welcome." He blew a puff of air in her ear after the completion of the sentence.

Sutton's rational mind said, "You see where his head—heads—are. Don't leave this hotel room!" The needs of her body commandeered her mouth, "Are you ready?"

Once downstairs at the restaurant off the main lobby of the hotel, Greyson told the hostess, "Thank you, but we can seat ourselves." Before Sutton could question him, he took her hand and guided her through the maze of tables scattered randomly about the dining room. They passed couples nuzzling in dark corners, families with unruly children, and a man and woman eating dinner while ignoring each other. Sutton knew those dinners well. The guilty Friday night hurry-up-and-eat-because-someone-is-waiting-for-me dinners. A tug from Greyson pulled her out of the past.

They stopped in the middle of the restaurant. Sutton had expected Greyson to choose a booth in the back in the corner in the dark.

Across one of the gold-trimmed china plates lay a single red rose. Sutton looked up at Greyson.

"Have a seat." He pulled out her chair. He sat next to her and rearranged his place setting to accommodate the change. A waiter appeared with a chilled bottle of wine. "Please leave it." Greyson interrupted the man's grand presentation of opening the bottle and righting their wineglasses. The man dipped slightly at the waist, placed the bottle near Greyson's elbow and left them alone.

"I want tonight to be our first date—a real date." Greyson filled Sutton's glass and then his own. "I've lived this night over and over again in my mind. I want us to start on new, neutral ground."

"Agreed." Sutton clinked her glass to his.

"Great." He placed his glass on the table and planted his

elbows on each side of his china place setting. "Tell me about yourself, Sutton."

She took in a deep breath that made her chest rise. She noticed his eyes follow the swell. "I'm a thirty-year-old widow with one beautiful daughter."

"I've heard about that charmer of a daughter you have. Any chance I might meet her when we get back home?"

Sutton shifted uneasily. Introducing Sierra to a man at this stage might be premature for their relationship. Also, she had to consider how Sierra would take to having a strange man move into her life.

"Is there a problem?" Greyson's all-knowing eyes pierced hers.

"Meeting Sierra will be rough."

"Why?"

"With Alex's death—"

"I understand. We have plenty of time to discuss me meeting Sierra. We have a lot to do between us before we bring her into this."

Sutton's tension eased when she realized Greyson was on the same page about her daughter.

Greyson finished his glass of wine. The waiter returned and they placed their orders.

"You know, Sutton, you're more than a widow and a mother. Tell me about you."

"Me?" Sutton asked after a long pause. "Now that you've asked, I see that I've lost myself. I have been so focused on being a good wife, helping my husband advance his career, and saving my marriage that since those things have dropped off my priority list, I don't know what to do with myself."

"I understand." Greyson's hand rested on hers. His large, smooth hand cloaked all her fears. "Maybe you can start by asking what you want to do with your life."

"Hmm. Still hard."

"Let's go about this another way. What have you enjoyed most about your life to this point?"

"That's easy. Sierra is my pride and joy."

"Would you consider having more kids?"

"Definitely. With the right man."

Greyson nodded, as if saying he had no worries. "What else?"

"I liked the two years I spent in college. I liked the whole learning process. The lectures, studying, books."

"Now we're getting somewhere. Have you considered going back and finishing your degree?"

Sutton nodded. "That was my plan until I found out that I needed to work two full-time jobs just to make ends meet for Sierra and me."

"I can help you with that. I can give you the money—"

"No."

"I'll make you a personal loan until you get back on your feet."

"No," Sutton said. "There's no way I'd take a dime from you."

"Why not? We're friends, aren't we? I'd be honored to help you."

"I know, but I don't want to be beholden to anyone again. This whole experience taught me that. I thank you, but no."

Greyson nodded his understanding. Disappointment glinted behind his eyes. "Do you think you'd ever get married again?"

"I would." Sutton did not hesitate with her answer. "I'd do it differently this time. The man I'd marry would love living in the hills of West Virginia. Corporate holdings and advancing his career wouldn't be important. There would be no Armani suits in his closet or designer cologne on his dresser top. He'd hate meetings with clients, entertaining, and social events. He'd be a hardworking man without the bulging bank account."

Sutton knew that Greyson was all of these things. He would be an attentive husband and father, loyal to his family. Working with his hands wasn't considered an insult or beneath him. Although well educated, he wasn't trapped in the rapid-rise-to-the-top, acquire-all-the-money-you-can-make lifestyle.

The burnt expression on Greyson's face confused Sutton.

"You're very specific in what you want. Any room for flexibility?" Greyson asked.

The waiter began placing their food in front of them.

"I've been the wife of one of those men. It left me hurt, angry, and unable to properly grieve the death of my life partner."

"You made a terrible mistake marrying Alex." Greyson pushed his plate aside and pulled Sutton's in front of him. He used the tools supplied by the waiter to peel open the lobster and remove its meat. "Don't you see that you didn't marry your life partner when you married Alex?"

Sutton watched the aggressive movements of his pampered fingers as he prepared her surf and turf. He glanced up at her and, seeing that she was watching him intently, lifted one corner of his mouth in an unreadable smile. "You can ask me."

Sutton warmed with his ability to read her. "I have nothing to ask."

Greyson slid her plate back to its proper place. He pierced a fat piece of lobster on her fork, dipped it in butter sauce, and held it to her mouth. He fed her with the caution of a new father feeding his infant child. Watching her chew, he turned his attention to preparing his own food in the same fashion he had done hers.

"You are such a coward, Sutton. Ask me what's on your mind." His lip lifted again.

"Okay," she dabbed at the corner of her mouth with the white linen napkin, "how do you know Alex wasn't my life partner?"

"Because I'm your life partner." He used his fingers to pop a piece of white lobster meat into his mouth. Smiling, he plucked a chunk of lobster off her plate, dipped it in the butter and lifted it to her lips. Sutton's lips parted slowly. Greyson placed the meat on her tongue, his fingers lingering in her mouth until she closed her lips around them. Seductively, he eased his fingers past her lips.

"What does that mean?" Sutton asked as he started in on his steak.

"Umm. This is great. Here, try some." Again his fingers were inside her mouth. He made a straight line from her mouth to his. The thing he did with his tongue and finger was enough to have them removed from the establishment. Sutton searched the room to see if anyone was watching. A middle-aged woman at the next table grinned in her direction before whispering in her date's ear. They rose and left, her date tossing a few bills on the table before their hasty departure.

"It means, my dear, that you were meant to be with me. I was meant to be with you. Somewhere along the way, we got lost and missed each other. And when we found each other again, we didn't believe it so we let a terrible wrong occur without stopping it."

"I don't appreciate you referring to my wedding as a terrible wrong. You make it seem like it was the greatest tragedy since the Titanic."

"One day I'll show you it was." He dipped more of the lobster meat in butter. This time he used a fork.

Nine

Sutton's statement cut Greyson to the core. Tonight he was going to share his plans with her. His plans for re-building the town. His wishes for his parents. He was going to tell her about his dream for them to get married. The top-per of the evening was going to be the house.

After hearing Sutton say that she would never be with a man of means, a corporate player, he felt disconcerted. Would his wealth turn her off? Could she see that he was some of those things she wanted to avoid but none of the bad things Alex was? Did she understand that he had given up the corporate life too, unable to play its games anymore? After being hurt so badly by Alex, would her mind allow her to see the love he had for her?

As Sutton finished the last of her meal and their evening drew to a close, Greyson told himself to take advantage of the time they had together. Once they returned home to work, family, friends, and town gossips, this freedom would be lost. Before they returned to Hannaford Valley, Greyson wanted to know where he stood with Sutton.

He signaled for the waiter. The restaurant had grown crowded during the hour they spent eating and talking. The noise level rose and the volume of the music grew louder to surpass it.

"Man, Sutton, I had no idea you could put food away like that." He winked at her as he reviewed the bill. He sifted through his wallet for his platinum card. He hesitated, not liking the message it would send to Sutton, and opted to pay the bill in cash. "Keep the change," he told the waiter.

"This was fun," Sutton said as they stepped on the elevator. Greyson followed her at a distance, checking out the waves her behind made with every step. She'd come into the thick thighs and round rump somewhere around fourteen. He imagined pressing his growing hardness into the healthy flesh of her behind, lying between her thighs with the mounds pressed into his lower abdomen.

"I can't believe you came all this way to take me to dinner." Sutton took her top lip between her teeth and when she released it, pink lipstick smeared her teeth.

She was nervous. Greyson liked having this powerful effect on her. He stepped up to her, close enough to feel her breasts graze his sweater.

"You have lipstick on your teeth."

"Oh." Sutton went for her purse.

"Use your tongue." Greyson suggested, taking her chin in his palm and lifting her head to him. She obliged. He felt his own mouth water with jealousy. Why didn't he suggest he use his tongue?

He did not release her. "To answer your question, I didn't come all this way for dinner. I came all this way to make love to you."

Sutton's eyes fluttered with surprise. Her chest began to rise and fall with quick, choppy breaths. This new boldness caught her off guard. He'd spent night after night rehearsing the things he would say to her if given the chance. He'd tucked his entire life away for this woman. His quiet, studious manner was not going to cut it. He wanted Sutton and she would know it every day of their lives.

"Greyson, I don't know what's going on—"

"I'm trying my best to show you."

He stepped up to her.

She stepped back, trapping herself in a corner.

Sutton said, "It was the wine at dinner."

Greyson locked his eyes with Sutton's and descended to

meet her lips. All of the babbling stopped when his tongue chased hers. He pressed her into the wall of the elevator and started a deep grind he hadn't used since the girl's locker room in high school. Raw, carnal urges drove him deeper into the heated area of her body. Her moans of joy controlled his hips.

The elevator stopped on Sutton's floor. Greyson moved to hold the door open for her. "Before you step off this elevator Sutton, think of me. I want you. You want me. I can feel it in your kiss." The boldness left his voice and the natural desires of a man replaced it. "We've made this mistake once before. Let's not make it again."

Sutton brought her eyes up from the multicolored carpet of the elevator floor. The door chimed, signaling it had been held open too long. "What are you asking me to do?"

"I want you to search your feelings and determine if I'm the man you want to be with."

"I promise I'll think it over tonight."

Greyson shook his head. The door chimed again. "I need an answer right now. This is our time. Now. If you feel what I feel, go up to my room with me."

"I can't make a decision this important in an instant."

"If what my instincts say are true, you made this decision a long time ago. You just need to share it with me tonight."

"You don't know what you're asking."

The door chimed.

"I don't? Look at me. Here." Greyson pointed to his eyes. "You look in my eyes and tell me I don't know what I'm asking. Tell me that I'm confused about my feelings for you. Tell me that I'm wrong about what you feel for me."

Greyson knew she could not lie to him. Even if she could say false words he would see the truth written across her face. Her shoulders loosened. Her eyes softened.

After a long moment where Greyson didn't breathe, Sutton said, without explanation, "Good night, Greyson."

"Wait, I'll walk you to your door."

"No, please. Good night." Sutton hurried away from him. Again.

Mother Galloway's eyes narrowed with embarrassment. Her insides burned with betrayal. She crumpled the linen napkin in her lap and tossed it into her plate of unfinished dinner.

Her dinner companion did not attempt to be discreet. "Isn't that your daughter-in-law?" She tsked. "With that man?"

Mother Galloway cut her eyes away from the archway of the restaurant across the table to her companion, slicing a line in the conversation that should not be crossed. In Hannaford Valley, no one would have dared called attention to Sutton's indiscretion, at least not in Mother Galloway's presence. But here in Ohio, she was still trying to establish her place of belonging with the black elite.

The haughty woman lifted the eyeglasses dangling on a chain around her neck. She glared at Sutton leaving with Greyson's arm draped over her shoulder.

Mother Galloway smoldered.

The dinner companion turned to Mother Galloway, studying her reaction over the rim of her glasses. "How long has Alex been gone?"

Ten

Greyson watched helplessly as Sutton disappeared down the hallway. Dumbfounded, he wondered how to proceed from this point. He had laid all his feelings out to her. He questioned if it was too soon after Alex's death. Could she smell the redolence of vicious corporate law on his clothes? Did he read her all wrong; did she have any feelings for him at all? Defeated and perplexed, he hung his head after using his keycard to access his suite.

He replayed the events of the night, lingering on their kiss in the elevator while showering for bed. Memories plunged deep into his heart and pulled out the event that had started his torture. He sat in front of the television and re-lived the night that had threatened to dismember his soul.

January 1, 1995

They clinked their glasses together for one last New Year's toast. When the hoopla had died down to a continuous murmur, Alex demanded everyone's attention. He considered himself the leader of their pack, and Greyson both envied and despised him for having the gall to make such an assumption.

"Fellas, fellas . . ." His eyes followed two skimpily dressed women as they flitted around the table. One of the women returned the stare and gave a quick wink with her

large hazel eyes before turning away. "Wow." Alex said in his southern accent as he shook away the lustful thoughts. "Attention please, fellas."

The Ballantyne brothers listened intently.

"I asked y'all to celebrate New Year's Day with me because . . ." He looked at each of them, building the suspense. "Because this will be the last year I can do this with y'all. I asked Sutton to marry me last night."

"Did she say yes?" Kirkland barked with a hearty laugh.

"Of course."

Sudden, all-engulfing darkness. The only ones in the bar were Greyson and Alex, surrounded by stark blackness. Alex's lips were moving, his eyebrows shot upward in an animated fashion as he spoke, but Greyson could not hear what he was saying. Now that he noticed, he could not hear any sounds. He checked for signs that he was dreaming—that he wasn't actually under water. His head felt submerged. His eyes burned. He couldn't breathe. A strong hand clasped his shoulder.

When he regained his faculties, Alex continued to brag. "She knows a good thing when she sees it. Always has. Fellas, this train is moving out. Sutton and I are getting married and moving to Ohio."

"Ohio?" Chevy glanced at Greyson, waiting. He kept a restraining hand on his older brother's shoulder. "What's in Ohio?"

"A big corporation who wants old Alex Galloway as part of its team. I'm tired of living in my old man's shadow. I need to get out of this town and make my own money."

"Listen, that's great." Kirkland stood and embraced Alex over the table. "I was beginning to wonder how long it would take for you and Sutton to finally tie the knot."

"It's time. We've been dating since she turned fourteen." Alex barked out a laugh.

Chevy released Greyson's shoulder and shook Alex's hand. "Yeah, Alex, congrats." His eyes bore into Alex's as his tone turned serious. *"You know how I feel about Sutton. Don't hurt her."*

Alex laughed it off and turned to Greyson, waiting.

"I hope you're happy," Greyson said in a manner that bordered close enough to sarcasm that Alex hesitated before leading the conversation again.

"I want all you knuckleheads to stand up with me. Make sure I go through with this here thing," he joked, his mouth heavy with drawn-out southern grammar. Greyson thought marrying Sutton would be an honor, not a joking matter. *"Kirkland, you've got to be my best man."*

They embraced again. Greyson could never understand his youngest brother's alliance with Alex. Kirkland admired Alex more than he admired his own big brothers.

"When's the day?" Chevy asked cautiously.

Greyson's chest tightened with anticipation. How long did he have to live?

"Last Saturday in May."

"May?" Greyson's alarm stopped Alex's rambling. *"Why so soon?"*

Alex's eyes narrowed in his direction. *"You have a problem with that date? Somewhere you need to be?"*

Greyson checked his inappropriateness. *"No. I thought these things took a long time to plan."*

"They don't." Alex lost his upbeat attitude when addressing Greyson. It quickly returned when the woman who winked at him moments ago approached the table to ask for a dance. Alex took her hand; Kirkland accompanied her friend to the dance floor.

"I'm leaving." Greyson grabbed his winter coat off the back of his chair. *"Can you pay for my drinks?"*

"No problem." Chevy stood with him. *"Where are you going?"*

"I have to see Sutton."

"Wait." Chevy grabbed Greyson's arm before he could shove it through the sleeve of his coat. *"You can't come to*

town for the holiday and stick your nose in her business. Sutton is grown now."

"Are you saying that you agree with this? Look at Alex out there."

They both turned to the dance floor where Alex was engaged in a steady bump-and-grind session with the winking woman.

"This is between Sutton and Alex. Do you think she has no idea what he's like? We all grew up together, remember?"

"Maybe she doesn't know. You see the way he transforms into Mr. Perfect whenever she's near. He's always been that way with her. I need to be sure she knows what she's getting into."

"Why? Are you doing this for her? Are you sure you don't want her to know about how you feel for her?"

"What would be wrong with that?" Greyson spat out at his meddling brother.

"Everything. It's selfish. You've been living in Chicago for the past five years; before that you were off at school. Alex may have a lot of faults, but despite how ambitious he's always been, he stayed here in Hannaford Valley with Sutton. We don't know what goes on between those two when we're not around. Maybe he really does love her. Maybe this is all a show for our benefit—bragging rights."

Greyson took the sting of Chevy's statements.

"It's not fair to walk into Sutton's world and shatter it all because you want her with you instead of Alex. It's too late."

Frustrated and defeated, Greyson put on his coat and buttoned it to the collar. "I'll see you at home." He walked away sluggishly.

"Are you all right?" Chevy called. "Do you want me to go with you?"

Greyson waved his hand through the air and stepped out of the bar.

Chevy was definitely right. He had left home and begun a new life. He couldn't expect Sutton to turn away from Alex and wait for him. She had no idea how he felt about her.

Chevy was right.

But Greyson's entire life was spent loving Sutton and not being able to tell her. Alex had always been in the way. His family's struggling farm had made him unworthy next to the prominent, lone Galloway son. He was making something of himself now; he possessed a law degree from Harvard and held a prestigious job with a high-ranking Chicago law firm. He was almost worthy. He was coming to the point in his life where he could knock on Sutton's father's door and ask to see her without shame. Tonight, Alex's announcement made it necessary to jump in before he was completely ready. He made his way to Sutton's house quickly. He rang the bell and Mr. Hill answered.

"It's kinda late, son," Mr. Hill scowled.

"I'm sorry, sir, but it's important I see Sutton."

Dressed in his nightclothes, a checkered robe covering him, Mr. Hill stood guard over his daughter.

"Who is it, Daddy?" Sutton bounced up behind him. "Greyson, come on in."

Sutton led him past her father into the living room. The television was playing a repeat of the previous night's Dick Clark's New Year's Special.

"I didn't mean to come this late," Greyson apologized.

"It's okay. My parents just went to bed. I was watching television. Sit down."

Greyson wanted to bolt to the door. Why had he come?

Sutton's blinding smile and fiery red hair made her appear more beautiful than usual. He wondered if her beauty had anything to do with her engagement and her sudden unavailability.

Sutton sat across from Greyson on the sofa, waiting. He had not been able to form an intelligent sentence when he needed one. Every word he spoke was an effort in phrasing so not to expose his breaking heart.

"Why'd you stop by? Alex said you all were going out to celebrate."

"We did." *He opened the top button of his coat.*

"*Do you want me to hang your coat?*"

"*No. I'm not staying long.*"

He hesitated.

She waited.

"*Alex said he proposed.*" *Greyson couldn't acknowledge they were getting married yet. Not without breaking down.*

Sutton bounced on the sofa. She pushed her left hand in his face. "*I'm so glad he told you. He asked me not to say anything until he could talk to all of you together. Isn't it great?*"

If the huge marquise-diamond ring sitting on her finger was an indication of Alex's true love, Greyson had no chance in the world with Sutton Hill. "*It's big.*" *He tried to laugh while pretending to examine the ring. Never. Never again would he look at that ring. It symbolized the end of his life.*

"*You're happy?*" *Greyson asked lightly, but he pushed his feet firmly against the floor to prepare for the answer. He had a fake smile waiting for her reply.*

"*I am.*" *She admired the ring.* "*I truly am.*"

When their eyes met, Greyson saw something there he had never seen before. She always gave him pretend-sister smiles and polite hugs. As she thought of her wedding, her eyes danced with something foreign to him. She was happy. She was happy in a way he had never made her.

Greyson conceded. "*I wish you the best.*"

He opened his arms. Sutton fell into his embrace.

He held her a long time.

Long enough for the wave of tears to pass.

"*What're you doing here?*" *The tip of Alex's lit cigarette led his way out of the darkness. Alex was a few inches shy of Greyson's height. He carried pretty-boy features that the girls in high school always whispered made nice-looking babies. His father's money had always allowed him to dress well and drive a new car. The looks and the money*

spurred a catch-me-if-you-can arrogance in Alex that al-
ways enticed the women.

Greyson waited until he met Alex at the driveway before answering. "I came to see Sutton."

"What do you have to see my fiancée about at this time of night?" He consulted his gold watch before scowling at Greyson.

"Actually, we talked about you two getting married."

"Remember, I'm the one marrying Sutton." Alex's fingertip probed Greyson's chest. "Stay away from her. I see the way you still look at her. You lost, fella." He took a long drag from his cigarette before tossing it away. He blew the smoke into Greyson's face. "All these years and you're still carrying a torch for Sutton. You're pitiful."

"And you're pathetic. You don't love her. Why are you marrying her?" Greyson felt his fists clench. He stuffed them into the pockets of his winter coat in order to avoid a riot on the Hills' front lawn.

"Why I'm marrying Sutton is absolutely none of your business. Listen, I'm going to tolerate you because Kirkland is my best friend. And Chevy is all right. But I've never been able to stomach you for long periods of time. I asked you to be a groomsman out of respect for Sutton and Kirkland. Don't make me ban you from the festivities."

"So why are you marrying Sutton?" Greyson exaggerated the still unanswered question.

"Have I made myself clear? Sutton is mine. Stay away from her and we'll have no beef." He pulled a cheap motel room key from his pocket. "Now I have to go. I have other business to attend to. Do I need to escort you outta here?"

Eleven

The aroma of flowers consumed the room. Sutton flipped the light switch. Red roses were everywhere. In a vase next to her bed, in the bathroom, and on the table in the sitting area. Red and white rose petals were scattered across the sheets of her turned-down bed and over the carpet.

She pressed her back to the door. What had stopped her from accepting Greyson's proposal? Actually, it had little to do with her feelings for him and more to do with the fears left behind by Alex. Entering into another relationship this soon could be dangerous. She hadn't learned what her first mistakes were. How could she attempt to correct them with Greyson?

She assessed her surroundings, lifting a perfectly designed rose to her nose. When would they have this chance again? What did her rational mind think? What did her body scream?

Greyson made her feel like watermelon Jolly Rancher candies. As a child, after two weeks of being good and doing all her chores without being reminded, Sutton received her fifty-cent allowance. Red pigtails flying in the wind, she would skip, humming all the way, into town to the Five and Dime for penny candy. She'd only spend five cents a day, choosing to make the warm sensation last nearly two weeks until allowance time rolled around again.

Too anxious to wait until she got home, Sutton would sit outside the Five and Dime with her legs crossed and open the first candy. She'd hold it up to her eyes examining it thoroughly before slipping it past her lips.

She used her tongue to swish the hard candy right and left inside her mouth. Fresh watermelon coated her taste buds. Sunny days warmed; wet, rainy days became dry. Sutton lifted her hands to her cheeks and pressed, hoping to contain the sweet, juicy flavor and make it last longer. She'd inhale the fruity scent swirling around her head. The flavor and aroma mixed, sending her mind miles away.

Tonight, Greyson, standing tall and dark, rekindled the feel of watermelon Jolly Ranchers candy. The sweet masculine aroma of his cologne made her mouth water.

When had he made arrangements for her room to be decorated with roses?

Sutton inhaled deeply, allowing her chest to swell with giddy thoughts of passionate kisses late into the night. Greyson wouldn't let her squirm away from him easily. He'd shower her with romantic remembrances of their past until she melted into his waiting arms.

Greyson answered the phone in his suite after the first ring. "Yes, Sutton?"

"Can I come up?"

"I left the key in the red envelope next to your bed."

Twelve

"Greyson?" Sutton called out when she entered the expansive suite.

"I'm in here. Follow my voice."

She did.

She froze in the doorjamb of the suite's elaborate bedroom. Before she could take in the Jacuzzi, wet bar, and big-screen television, her eyes fell on Greyson. Standing in the shadows, with the black sweater straining to cover his biceps and the black dress slacks molded to his thighs, she remembered a Calvin Klein underwear ad he had posed for years ago. He stood modeling the underwear with his arms crossed over his chest; his lips were curled into an expression that could be conceived as a scowl or a come-to-me-because-I-need-to-make-love-to-you plea. Tonight he wore that same game face and she knew exactly what he meant.

Sutton's eyes dropped to her feet. "The roses were nice. I thought they were a fluke at first. They weren't. You remember."

"I'd never forget."

Sutton shifted her weight from one foot to the other, still avoiding Greyson's piercing eyes. Now that they stood alone in his hotel room, the intimacy made her begin to doubt her decision. She was not behaving like a recent widow with a little girl.

"You look nervous."

"I am. A little." Sutton's eyes shot upward in a quick flash.

"I've been waiting for this moment for so long." Greyson's voice broke.

Sutton's eyes came up slowly, afraid of the intensity Greyson's eyes would reflect. When she found the courage to meet his gaze what she saw made her squint to read it clearly. Wild passion fighting for release only scratched the surface. Behind his eyes was a tenderness that made her want to take him in her arms and rock him against the security of her chest. His tenderness shielded a longing that had long ago turned into hurt.

Greyson lowered his head and gathered his thoughts. As his head rose, his chest heaved with a full intake of breath. His voice, with the elongation of vowels dipped in melted chocolate, returned. "I've been waiting for us to be together all my life. Now that it might actually happen I'm not sure what to do."

Sutton tried to smile to show that she understood.

"I won't be with you if you can't give yourself to me without question."

"I have questions about how logical we're being," Sutton admitted. "I don't have questions about how badly I want to be intimate with you."

Sutton stood captivated as Greyson crossed the room. He peered down at her, lost in thought. His hand cupped her cheek. She leaned into his touch. His fingers massaged her scalp. Having bright red hair as a child had been a focal point of teasing. As an adult, her hair had browned but stray, bright-red strands intermingled throughout her scalp, giving her hair a reddish appearance when the sun hit it. As Greyson massaged her scalp and pulled her head into his chest, her hair felt like a crown of glory.

"Why did you come to my room?" Greyson's question materialized through short puffs of air.

His fingers found a place in her scalp that triggered her intimacy button. Her body softened and a warm flush tinted her skin. At that moment, she could not even remember her name. She wanted to touch him. Memories of running her finger across the magazine ads that showcased his visual charms passed through her in a hot wave of desire.

Greyson's arms locked around her waist. He waited for an answer.

"I came because—" Stark insight halted her words. She hadn't come to his room because he was the sexiest man she knew. She hadn't come because she was overcome with grief. She hadn't come because she was lonely or confused.

Greyson's serious attitude and unbridled intelligence made him appear larger, stronger than any other man she'd ever met. Maturing into a man honored him with broad shoulders, a tapered waist, and sharp facial features. The combination of good looks and a shining personality resulted in a man who possessed it all by Sutton's estimation. Over the years, she'd thought of him. Wondered "what if." And she'd never been able to shake the hold he had on her. That was why she stood before him in his hotel room this night. Because she wanted him as much as he wanted her— she always had.

"Sutton, I'm waiting for an answer." Greyson pulled her closer. His fingers squeezed her hips.

"I'm here because this is where I need to be."

Greyson's head lowered. His lashes hooded his eyes. His lips seized hers while scooping her up in his arms. Sutton fell down on the bed with the ease of a feather floating to earth. Greyson clasped her fingers between his and fanned her arms out across the mattress, leaving her wide open. His mouth covered hers while unbuttoning her blouse. Every one of his movements was slow, tantalizing, and very deliberate. Sutton felt crazed while waiting for him to undo each of the buttons of her blouse. When she tried to help, he pushed her back into the mattress and spread her arms at her sides.

"Pretty," Greyson commented when her intricately woven, sky-blue lacy bra was exposed. "Sexy." He hummed his delight while suckling her breasts through the fabric. A sharp twinge electrified the buds straining against the cups, demanding freedom to experience his lips uninhibited.

Greyson slipped his fingers beneath the elastic straps of her bra and slipped them over her shoulders. "Beautiful." His head disappeared into the space between her full bosom. He kissed her there. Again. His tongue traced a small circle. His fingers kneaded her right breast; his mouth enveloped her left nipple.

Sutton stroked the top of his head as he searched for a rhythm that pleased them both. Finding it, he settled into his task. His slow, light suckling increased in speed. The suction pulled her deeper into his mouth. His fingers pinched her other breast. She moaned against the vacuum that pulled at her core. When the pain became too bittersweet to tolerate, he moved to the other breast, massaging the pain that his lips left behind.

"Sutton." Greyson lifted his head and studied her expression. Finding what he needed, he returned to his task.

Sutton squeezed her eyes closed, wishing she could blame her wild abandon on having too many drinks at dinner. The high she was feeling could only be attributed to the deft movement of Greyson's tongue flickering across her nipple.

Greyson's finger slipped past the waistband of her pants. The button popped, and he lowered the zipper in one swift move. He leaned over her, kissing her neck while moving her pants down over her hips. His kisses trailed across her belly. His tongue teased the edges of her panties. Sutton thrashed on the bed, hoping for more but not daring to ask. Greyson used both hands to gather the underwear at her hips. He grabbed the top of the waistband between his teeth and pulled them down inch by agonizing inch over her thighs. The intermittent grazing of his mouth over the sensitive areas of her inner thighs drained all her composure.

Sutton moved up in the bed, never taking her eyes from Greyson. He stood at the foot of the bed and pulled his sweater over his head. A fine mist of hair covered the muscles of his dark chest. One side of his mouth lifted seductively. He bent and kissed the top of her foot while opening his belt. He whipped the belt from his pants and tossed it across the room.

"Sutton," he feigned shock and turned his back to her as he opened his pants and let them fall to the floor. The same mist of hair covered his thighs. Sutton imagined her fingers gliding up and down his legs, sampling the silky fine hairs. He returned to the bed and suspended himself above her while taking ownership of her mouth. During the next kiss—the one that ignited fireworks in Sutton's head—Greyson removed his briefs.

His hand entered the steamy area separating their bodies. "You're hungry for me."

She answered by lifting her hips from the bed.

Greyson's tip pulsated against her thigh. He pulled a package from underneath the pillow where she rested her head. Paper ripped. His hands moved fiercely. With an arch of his back, he guided himself between her thighs, giving her a sample of what was to come.

"Are you—" he used his free hand to hold her chin. "Are you all right?"

"Yes," Sutton breathed her answer, unsure of why he asked.

Sutton lay completely frozen as Greyson eased another inch into her.

"You're tensing up on me." Greyson stated between puffs of air that warmed her cheek. Bewildered, he asked, "What are you doing?"

"Nothing." Sutton answered, equally bewildered.

"That's the problem, Sutton."

"This is the way I always—" she thought better of finishing her reflective statement. Alex had been her first and only lover; she married still a virgin. He liked her compliant and docile. She was doing as he had instructed. As she had been taught.

"I don't want you this way." Greyson remained suspended above her body, some inches in but demanding more entry. "You show me how you feel," he demanded. "You show me everything you're feeling. Tell me everything you want. Give me all you have." He pressed his forehead to hers. "Got it?"

Sutton nodded. She lifted her head to taste his lips. Greyson yielded his tongue to her. With one pumping motion, he entered her. Sutton took in a breath that lifted her chest from the bed. His final thrust filled her, breaking the barrier usually reserved for virginal experiences. Greyson felt the depth of his penetration too and pulled back. Sutton wrapped her arms around him and grabbed his round backside, pushing him in further. The pain made way for an abandoned display of emotional lust. She caught his waist in the vise of her thighs.

Greyson's kisses remained the constant in their lovemaking. They softened the force of his uncontrolled thrusts. The kisses replenished Sutton's mouth, made dry by her panting. They pushed her to the edge as her hips rocked up, encouraging him to plunge deeper.

Greyson penned Sutton's hands to the bed and made her wide open to surrendering to her emotions. "Sutton, you feel so good." His hips flexed in unison with hers. "Tell me how you feel." Every word she uttered prolonged his thrusts and made him search deeper inside himself. He released the virile dragon that had been dormant for far too long. He told her this as they clung to each other, fighting to save themselves. Together they shivered and shook, soaking the bed with their hot juices.

Greyson collapsed on top of her. "Sutton, I love you."

Involuntarily, Sutton's body became rigid.

"What?" Greyson wiped the perspiration threatening to sting her eyes with the back of his hand. "You had to know that. Didn't you?"

Sutton shook her head. If being in love with Greyson would lead to the same dysfunctional relationship she had with Alex, love was not what she wanted or needed.

"All these years. You had to know. What did you think this was all about?"

"I—"

"I've been waiting all this time." He took a deep breath. "I want to marry you, Sutton. I want you, Sierra, and me to be a family."

"Don't joke like that, Greyson."

He pulled his exhausted manhood from Sutton and sat up next to her. "What did you think this was about?" he asked again.

"I believed we were going to start a relationship. You're thinking marriage already."

"Damn right," he clipped. "Do you think I would make love to you if I didn't want something permanent with you? Do you think I would belittle either of us that way?"

"No. I—" Heightened emotions threatened to bring tears.

"What?"

"I don't know."

"That's weak. After all the secrets we've shared over the years, the friendship we have, how could you think—You know I feel more for you than a one-night stand can begin to cover. You feel for me, too. Don't pretend that we had sex. We made love."

"I've only been widowed for four months."

Greyson waved away the statement. "That marriage was dead longer than four months." He turned and faced her squarely.

Sutton sat up against the headboard, covering her chest with the sheet. "You want me to forget all my years with Alex, all of my past, and pretend like we can be an ordinary couple? I can't do that."

"Why not?"

"Think about all of the women you've encountered. You can't act as if they never existed. Each one of those relationships helped to bring you to this point in your life."

"No, they did not. Loving you my entire life brought me to this point. Every move I've made, everything I've attempted, it's all been with the knowledge that it would be for us. Even when you married Alex, I knew. I knew that we'd be together."

"Greyson—"

"Let me finish. When I came back to Hannaford, I had no way of knowing you would eventually move back. It didn't matter to me. When it came to you, I had one thing on my mind. To make you mine. Put you where you should have been all along."

"I didn't know."

"It doesn't matter that you didn't know then. It matters that you know now. Are you telling me that this is never going to happen? Because I won't accept that."

"This is all too much." Sutton rose from the bed only to have Greyson catch her arm and pull her back.

"What's too much?"

"You. You're too much. Do you think my head is clear enough to deal with all this now? My husband just died. I've lost everything I had. My life is upside down and you want me to handle this?"

"Handle what? Why did you come here tonight? You knew coming here would mean you were consenting to sleeping with me, but you had to know it was about more than that. I can't believe you'd come to my suite, sleep with me, and then walk away—waving at me from across the street when we return to Hannaford.

"I love you. I want you forever. If you let me into your life, the other issues won't be problems. I'll love you so strongly that you won't remember Alex's name. I can support you and Sierra."

"That's another thing, Greyson. You're making all these plans and you've never even met my daughter."

"I want to meet her. I didn't know you had a child but I love you and I'll love your child."

"It's not that simple."

"I admit it took me by surprise when I found out you had a little girl. Raising Alex's child was not in my plans. I took my time and I thought about how I feel for you and what I want out of life. I will meet Sierra and I will love her and I will make us a family. You don't realize how deeply, completely I love you."

Sutton could read the sincerity behind Greyson's pleading eyes. He would be a wonderful father to Sierra. His nature made him gentle and patient. When he got to know Sierra, he would love her as his own. Sutton felt that at her core.

"Sutton," Greyson pulled her into the moist heat of his body, "tell me that I haven't waited all this time for nothing."

The steam radiating from their naked bodies mixed into a heady cloud that hovered over the bed. Being this close to Greyson's nakedness opened the door of intimacy for Sutton.

"Sutton." Greyson's voice never wavered. "I love you so much. Tell me you'll give this a chance to work."

Sutton pressed her cheek against the smooth, dark skin of his chest.

He tipped her chin up. "I will do anything—everything—to make this happen. I know the timing could be better and the circumstances could be different, but this is what we have to deal with. I'm ready to handle anything that is thrown in our way."

"I want to make this work," Sutton admitted.

Greyson exhaled loudly. His rumbling laughter vibrated against her cheek. His joy became infectious. She caressed his cheek. He snatched up her hand. His eyes focused on her marquis engagement ring and gold wedding band combination. He worked the rings off her finger and placed them next to the bed. Never losing eye contact, he pushed her back on the bed and covered her body with his.

Thirteen

The last thing Sutton remembered was Greyson covering her nude body with the sheets and quilt decorating the bed. She slept deeply. Later, she wondered if Greyson had loved her thoroughly enough to make her lose consciousness. She awoke abruptly, feeling as if she'd slept ten hours. She checked the clock next to the bed. She'd only slept an hour. Greyson's breath heated her neck with every exhalation. Seeing her ring abandoned next to the clock startled her into reality.

Sutton and Alex had hardly ever argued. When she asked for a divorce to free him to date openly he apologized, but was explicit in his refusal to ever grant her one. Arguing proved useless because Alex never wavered and she usually ended up working herself into a fit while he stormed out of the house to find comfort with one of his women. But one time she'd pushed him into a confrontation that he could not avoid.

"Hey, baby." Alex entered their bedroom and immediately began peeling away his designer suit. As was his routine, he filled her in on the details of his day while he showered and climbed into bed. Sutton had remained quiet, pretending to read her magazine. Once he found his way under the covers, she spoke.

"I went to the supermarket today."

"Hmm." Alex wiggled down in the bed and closed his eyes.

"The weirdest thing happened."

"Really?" He yawned.

"Out of nowhere, a basket came rolling down the aisle and hit me. My hip is bruised from the impact."

Alex opened his eyes. "Really?" His eyebrow rose slowly with question.

"Yeah. Hurts like hell."

"Don't curse."

"The woman driving the cart came rushing up to me. I thought she wanted to apologize and make sure I was all right. Instead she told me that you don't really love me because you love her. She said you only married me because you wanted to parade me in front of your clients and that once you were set financially, you'd have no use for me. She said it's time for me to realize that and get out of the way."

Sutton could see the wheels turning in Alex's head. He sat up in the bed next to her. "Are you hurt?" He peeled back the covers to see the horrific bruise to her hip. "Did you go to see your doctor?"

"And tell him what? That a strange woman hit me with a shopping cart and told me to stay away from my own husband?"

"I'll take you in the morning. Meanwhile, I'll rub some cream on it." He started to leave the bed, but Sutton's raised voice stopped him.

"You don't know who it was, do you?"

"Of course not. This crazy woman must have thought you were someone else."

"No. You don't know who it was because it could have been so many people."

"I don't know who it was because I'm not seeing anyone," Alex stated firmly.

"I've seen her before. I spent every minute in the bathtub while I soaked my hip trying to place her. It wasn't until a minute ago that I did."

"What are you talking about?" Alex's normally composed face began to sag with worry.

"I remember seeing her at our wedding."

"That's ridiculous. What would someone from Hannaford Valley be doing in Ohio? That's too much of a coincidence."

"I agree. The memory is vague, but I believe I remember you dancing with her at our reception. We argued about it in the limo."

"Sutton, see the doctor in the morning about your hip. Get some rest now. You're so stressed about this whole incident that you're imagining things in order to find an answer. There isn't one. None other than a crazy woman in the supermarket attacked you because she mistook you for someone else."

"I think you're right. I'll just put my mind at ease by looking through our wedding album. If I'm wrong, she won't be in any of the pictures."

"Wait." Alex grabbed Sutton's arm, stopping her from leaving the bed.

"She described every inch of your mother's house. She described every inch of your body. She mimicked every sound you make when you—" Sutton leapt from the bed. "Don't try to make me think I'm losing my mind. She knew who I was. She knew you. Who is this woman, Alex?"

Alex followed her across the bedroom. He jumped in her path before she made it to the door.

"She was a white woman. Does that narrow the field of choices any?"

Alex still appeared baffled about the woman's identity.

"I want a divorce. I've forgiven you too many times. I can't do it anymore, Alex." The tears had started rolling at this point.

"I've told you a hundred times, no divorce. NO divorce!" The tip of his finger grazed her nose.

She turned away.

"I'll take care of her. She won't come around you again."

"I don't want *you* around me again. I want out. I'm going home."

"You're going nowhere." He pushed up closer. "No divorce. No separation."

"You can't make me stay with you."

"You're not listening. This marriage is not over. We are together forever."

"Why? Why do you want me if you have other women?"

"You are my wife. That woman means nothing to me. My marriage and what I do outside this house are separate issues."

Sutton stared at him incredulously.

"Everyone has a place. I'll make sure she knows hers. You make sure you know yours. Your place is here, by my side, acting as my wife."

"I'm not doing this anymore. I mean it."

"I love you. I married you. That's what's important. Don't get this twisted in your head."

"Me, twisted? I'm here every day and night being your wife. Where are you? I don't have a husband."

Alex ran his hand over his chin. "You want me here every night. I'll be here."

"You've promised that before."

"You've never seriously threatened to leave me before. I'll straighten up this time. I promise. No more women. I'll stop working late and work more in my office here. We'll take a vacation." He pulled her resisting body against his. "I love you."

Sutton fought not to believe him.

"We'll take a vacation and get started on the family you want."

"A baby?" She had fallen into the trap easily. "Really?"

"For you: anything. I'm serious about making it right between us."

Almost a year later, after several more broken promises, Sierra was born and Alex started "working" the late nights again.

Greyson's hand cascaded down Sutton's outstretched arm, across her fingers, and ended at the rings she spun

around on the table while she relived her time with Alex.
"Sutton?"

"Yeah?" her voice sounded sleepier than she felt.

"Keep your mind on us."

He could read her in his sleep.

"Sutton?"

"Yeah?"

"I never, ever want to see those rings on your finger again."

"Is that an order?"

Greyson climbed on her back and shielded her body with his. "That is a request from the deepest part of my soul." He opened the drawer and brushed the rings inside, closing it tight.

The next time Sutton woke, the sun framed the edges of the heavy drapes covering the window. She checked the clock. She would return to Hannaford Valley this evening after having dinner with Mother Galloway. Dinner was a formality designed for Sutton to exploit her grieving-widow status with Mother Galloway's shallow society acquaintances. Mother Galloway had taken the liberty of purchasing a conservative black dress and pumps for Sutton to wear to the dinner party.

As time slipped away Greyson held her around the middle, his face nuzzled in her neck, snoring lightly. To have someone love you an entire lifetime carried a heavy burden. With all the life mistakes she had made, Sutton questioned what she had done to deserve his undying commitment to a relationship that might never be. She placed her fingers against the squared sideburn intersecting his cheekbone. His intensity left her dazed. Truly, she loved him, but with all that had occurred lately, it would be easy to misinterpret the love of their long-standing friendship with the special type of love Greyson confessed to last night. Sutton kissed the top of his head.

How did I let this get out of control? Sutton asked herself, wallowing in turmoil. She would never do anything to hurt Greyson, but she needed time away from him to think. His life had been put on hold while she lived in a nightmare world filled with deceit and broken dreams. While he waited to love her, she was beginning to doubt that a good marriage could even be possible. There were too many temptations for both men and women to do wrong. Her vision was tainted; Greyson's was rose-colored.

Sutton turned her head toward the bedside table. She'd need to retrieve her wedding ring without upsetting Greyson. Mother Galloway would blow a gasket if she showed up with her naked finger flapping in the breeze.

Another source of pain for Greyson.

Sutton sighed aloud. She felt trapped between what was morally right and what her heart desired.

"Good morning," Greyson smiled up at her and planted a kiss on each of her breasts before leaving the bed.

Sutton watched the way he walked, with a small bounce off his left foot. He possessed the perfect body. The deep dimples at the top of his haunches tantalized her. His dark skin rippled as the muscles in his thighs flexed with every bouncing step. He left the bathroom door open, humming while he washed up.

"I'm hungry," Sutton called to him.

"Order room service." Greyson stepped into the bedroom, toothbrush in hand. "I don't want to leave the room yet."

Sutton turned to the phone, avoiding the wanton expression on his face. He returned to the bathroom where she heard him start to gargle. His brazen attitude about making love still needed some getting used to. She couldn't remember the last time a man had displayed unbridled passion for her. As she dialed room service she couldn't believe the words she used and the way she gyrated her hips while they made love.

Sutton opened the drapes, letting the sun brighten and warm the room. "This room must have cost a fortune."

"I'm sure it does, but I didn't pay a dime. I won a large settlement for this hotel chain years ago and every since I've had the privilege of staying at any of their hotels or resorts for free."

She found Greyson's discarded shirt on the back of a chair and slipped into it. "Do you have an extra toothbrush?"

Greyson moved to his leather bag sitting on the counter and hunted through its contents until he found a new toothbrush. He sat on the rim of the tub watching her splash water on her face. He remained silent as she brushed her teeth.

"Are you trying to pretend that last night didn't happen?" Greyson's voice edged with intolerance.

"No," Sutton wiped her mouth on a towel and grabbed his comb and brush.

"It wasn't a sleepover. We're not kids anymore."

"I know." She vigorously brushed her hair back.

"I told you I love you."

Although the bathroom was larger than her old bedroom at her parents' house, the room seemed too small for them both to breathe. Sutton made a hasty retreat.

"I proposed to you." Greyson's voice thundered from his spot in the doorway separating the bedroom and bathroom.

Sutton froze. He had. He was speaking in future terms, but essentially he had proposed.

Greyson pressed his nude body against her as he massaged her shoulders. His manhood grew against her backside. His arms came around her hips. "There's a wall between us. One that doesn't need to be there. One that you've constructed." He shimmied his hips against her, clouding her senses. "This is simple, Sutton." His lips were next to her ear. "Listen to me. I love you. We want each other. We'll be married and live happily ever after."

"Greyson, can't you see that you're pushing me?"

"Pushing? I may be moving faster than you expected, but not faster than you need. Don't you want this?"

"I do." She paused. "It's just that I'm not ready for another marriage."

"But you will be. And when you are, I want it to be me that you're marrying. Until then, I plan to spend every minute helping you get to that point." His lips began to cascade down her neck. "Knowing you," he said between kisses and flicks of his tongue, "you're worrying yourself about what happened in your marriage with Alex. You're scared that our marriage might be the same. But how could that be? I love you. Alex never did."

"Stop saying that. You don't know what went on between us when no one was around."

Greyson straightened, but did not release the hold he had on Sutton. "Are you defending him to me?"

"I'm saying—"

"I won't take that from you. Don't stand here after we've made love and try to tell me he was a good husband and father."

Sutton couldn't tell if he was hurt or angry. She smoothed her words. "I don't want to feel that this is a continuation of your rivalry with Alex. He might not have been the best husband or father, but there was a time when he loved me. He's dead now. I don't want to speak badly of him to you. It isn't right."

From behind, Greyson molded his body into hers. "You're right. That was inconsiderate of me to say." His lips traced the notches of her spine.

"You're right about something else," Greyson continued. "I don't know what went on between you and Alex during your marriage, nothing other than the rumors flying around Hannaford. So why don't you tell me?"

Sutton wanted to preserve the carefree time they were having. If she relived all the good and bad moments of her marriage with Alex, she'd surely sink into a pit of despair. And then the guilt would come. Guilty feelings about how she could be nude in a man's hotel room four months after her husband's death.

Sutton turned to face him. "Can we talk about that another time? The purpose of you following me to Ohio was for us to have this time together without outsiders intruding."

Greyson nodded. "We'll talk later."

Sutton turned but Greyson caught her in the circle of his arms. He rested his head on her shoulder and nuzzled her hair. "What did you order for breakfast?"

Sutton worked to answer while being distracted by his roaming hands. "Pancakes, eggs, ham, coffee, juice, and fruit."

"Girl, you sure can put the food away." He laughed. "Where does it go?" He pretended to search for body fat by patting her flat stomach, firm hips, and ample breasts. "With the cook having all that food to prepare, we probably have time to get into a little something before room service arrives."

"You are insatiable," Sutton giggled.

Greyson coaxed her to the bed with his body. "I keep telling you I've been waiting to get you in this position—"

Sutton fell face down on the bed. Greyson pulled her ankles until her feet found the carpet. He quickly kneeled behind her on the floor. In a frenzied motion, he guided his hips between her thighs and entered her in one quick motion that made her cry out. He grasped her hips and pulled her off the bed to sit on his lap. Sutton's forehead rested against the corner of the bed, the quilt between her teeth to stifle her cries. He guided her hips from behind as she bounced wildly. He tried to calm her enough to direct her movements and slow down her achievement of pleasure, but Sutton did not want that. As the pain caused by the girth of his manhood made her clamp down on the quilt, something made her want more. She wanted Greyson to penetrate her soul deep enough so that she would never remember the feel of anyone else inside her. She wanted him to erase all of the times she had acted out of obligation and replace those times with the wanton need she felt when he stroked her.

"Sutton, slow down." Greyson spoke in a low, comforting

tone, enunciating every word to focus her attention. "We have time. Slow down before you hurt yourself."

On the upstroke, Sutton pulled herself away from Greyson. She swung her body around to face him. Her breathing became ragged. Strands of red hair stuck to her forehead, and her body glistened with moisture.

Greyson smiled at her. He watched her from where he sat on the carpet without touching her. He waited.

"You are a beautiful man, Greyson Ballantyne."

His shoulders vibrated with the rumble of his laughter.

"Make love to me."

His expression became serious. "What do you want from me?"

"Make love to me."

"Are you sure?"

Sutton rose and crawled over to him on her hands and knees. She held her lips an inch from his. "You wanted me to show you what I wanted. You wanted me to tell you how I feel. . . . Make me yours, Greyson. Make love to me."

"Sutton—" He turned away, momentarily hiding the sheen moistening his eyes. "Sutton, don't ever leave me." He held her face in his hands. "I will love you forever. I will take care of you and Sierra until the day I die. You will have everything you ever want or need—both of you. Just don't ever leave me. Please."

Greyson's all-encompassing, genuine love blocked any words Sutton might say.

"I'm not a weak man," Greyson explained, the emotion cloaking his voice.

"I know. I don't think you are."

"It's just that I love you so much."

Sutton cupped his face as he was doing to hers. "Make love to me now."

Greyson moved to retrieve the package underneath the pillow where she had slept. They kissed. His lips barely brushed hers, as if he thought she might shatter. He gently eased her to the carpet, moved her legs apart with the use of his knees and settled between her legs. His head fell back upon impact. He growled through a prolonged exhalation when he entered her heat. He steadied her hips until his every inch was cradled inside her walls. He rocked back and forth placing a kiss to a new body part with every stroke. Sutton's breath escaped in quick spurts as pleasure spasms weaved through her core. Greyson built her pleasure to a peak with the deep thrusts of his hips. The carpet scraped her back, leaving a burn that would remind her of this morning a week later. She called out, digging her nails into his shoulders as her body spilled over with passion. Before her own sensations subsided, Greyson's started. His manhood jerked inside of her as he tried to steady his breathing.

Fourteen

Greyson walked Sutton back to her hotel room. "How long is this dinner supposed to last?"

"I'm not sure." Sutton strung her hands around his narrow waist.

"You know I don't want you to go."

"I know, but I have to. After this dinner all of my business with Mother Galloway will be done. I can return home to Hannaford Valley and be with the people I love."

Greyson met her for a kiss. "I like the sound of that."

"The rings?" Sutton held out her hand.

Greyson begrudgingly took the rings out of his shirt pocket and dropped them into her palm.

"I owe this to Mother Galloway," Sutton said by way of explanation. She'd don the rings after he left her hotel room. "I'd better get dressed. I can't be late."

"Okay. You remember the plan? After the dinner you fly home. I'll be in California for three days for my law-school buddy's wedding. I'll come home directly after that and we'll pick up where we're leaving off. I want to take you white-water rafting."

Sutton looked skeptical.

"I'm telling you, you'll love it. Don't tell me you don't like adventure after that little thing you just did to me."

Sutton blushed. "Greyson."

"No. Look, I'm teasing. It was great. I'll get these wounds taken care of before tetanus sets in and everything'll be fine."

"Get out of here." Sutton swatted at him, chasing him to the door.

"Enjoy dinner, but don't become too at ease with playing Alex's grieving wife." Greyson turned to her in the doorway. "I love you." He kissed her quickly and disappeared down the hallway.

Mother Galloway seemed distant the entire evening. She greeted Sutton with stiff pleasantries that held no sincerity. She left Sutton with a group of old, pretentious women. Normally Mother Galloway would attach Sutton to her hip. She'd fawn over Sutton, demonstrating to her friends that she was the perfect mother-in-law. Toward the end of the evening, two hours before Sutton's flight home, Mother Galloway requested her presence in the study.

"Yes, Mother Galloway?"

"Close the door." Mother Galloway sat draped over the arm of the sofa, a glass of sherry in her hand. "Have a seat."

Sutton did as instructed. She stiffened under Mother Galloway's scrutiny. "I'd better get to the airport soon."

Mother Galloway tossed back her drink. She placed the glass on a brown suede coaster near the corner of the wrought-iron-and-glass coffee table. "You put on a good show in there."

"Ma'am?"

Being outright rude was not Mother Galloway's style.

"You are my son's widow. For God's sake, it's only been four months! Four months and you're already carrying on like a slut."

"Mother—"

She waved away Sutton's denial, bouncing up from the sofa. "Imagine my embarrassment yesterday when I saw you hanging all over that Ballantyne boy in the middle of the hotel restaurant. I couldn't explain it to my dinner companion, the biggest motormouth in the Cleveland social circle. And when I went to your room and you weren't there, I was fit to be tied."

"I can explain—"

"Please do." Mother Galloway moved with sleek gestures as she smoothed the skirt of her azure suit.

"Well," Sutton wrung her hands. "See, Greyson and I—"

"Were you seeing him behind Alex's back?" Mother Galloway paced the length of the room.

"Of course not. Everything happened so fast that I—"

"After waiting two hours for you to return to your room, I asked myself what Alex would do if he were alive to see this." Mother Galloway's voice cracked with grief. She rounded her desk and removed a picture from the wall, revealing a safe. She turned the dial swiftly—left, right, left—and yanked the door open. She removed an envelope. "He wouldn't believe me without proof." She waved an unlabeled videotape in the air. "Money will get you anything, anytime, anywhere."

Mother Galloway stalked up to Sutton and threw the envelope in her lap. "Take a look."

Sutton opened the envelope and spilled its contents into her lap. Large color glossies of her and Greyson entwined on the carpet of his suite fell into view. All angles, close up and far away. "How did you get these?"

"Keep the drapes closed next time. Do you need to see the tape?" Mother Galloway sneered.

Sutton stuffed the pictures back into the envelope, unable to speak.

"I asked myself all evening what I should do with these. It wasn't until you walked through the door that I found the answer to my problem."

"What are you going to do? This would kill my parents. Greyson and I didn't mean to hurt you or anyone else. I remained faithful to Alex every day of our marriage, even while he played around. I was a good wife to him. Now I deserve to be happy."

Mother Galloway cringed at the reference to her son's

wrongdoings. "My son gave his life to making sure you and Sierra had everything you needed. He worked his fingers to the bone to keep you in designer clothing, fancy cars, and expensive furnishings. And look how you repay him. You don't even wait until his grave is cold before you take up with the man he hated more than anyone else in the world."

Mother Galloway calmed herself. She swayed across the room and took a seat in a large Victorian chair. "He had doubts about you. He came to me on several occasions wondering if Greyson had gotten to you. When you denied him, he wondered if you had taken up with that Ballantyne boy."

"I denied Alex because he was finding what he needed outside of our bed." Sutton regretted the bold words she used with her mother-in-law the moment they left her mouth. But she had to make her understand; what she and Greyson had done was not dirty and deceitful.

"Mother Galloway, Alex and my marriage was far from perfect, but that's in the past now. Alex is gone. I'm free to live my life however I see fit." She paused and softened her voice. "What are you going to do with the video? These pictures?"

Mother Galloway returned the evidence to her safe and replaced the picture covering it. "Nothing. I'm going to do absolutely nothing with them."

"Thank you." Sutton's body relaxed.

"I'll do nothing with them as long as you do as I say. If you don't, the pictures will become evidence in my custody suit to have my grandbaby here with me."

"What!"

"Here's where you have to make a hard choice. You have to choose between Greyson Ballantyne and your daughter because if you ever see him again, I'll pursue custody of Sierra and all the world will see these pictures."

Sutton rose to her feet in protest. Her head swirled, causing her to fall back into the chair. "Why are you doing this? I did nothing but honor Alex when he was alive. How can you be this vengeful?"

"I will honor my son's memory and so will you," Mother Galloway snapped.

"He left us with nothing," Sutton rationalized.

"Your plane ticket has been exchanged for a round trip one. You'll also find a seat has been reserved for Sierra on your return flight."

"I don't understand." Sutton stood slowly, bracing herself for another bout of dizziness.

"How can I keep an eye on you and Greyson in Hannaford while I'm in Ohio? I can't. You'll return to Hannaford Valley and bring Sierra here to live. That way I can assure she's being properly educated and that you're living up to our agreement."

"I never said I would let you control me this way."

"You don't have a choice, Sutton."

Sutton racked her brain, searching for leverage against this surprise attack.

"I assume you'll be wearing my son's wedding ring for some time to come." Mother Galloway sauntered victoriously to the door. "My chauffer will accompany you. And Sutton, let's keep this arrangement confidential between us."

Fifteen

"Greyson, you look like you just won the case of the century. I know that can't be true because I heard you walked away from practicing law."

"Ryan, you look good, man." They embraced in the middle of the crowded airport. "This weather agrees with you," Greyson added, noticing his friend's tan.

"It's a whole new way of living out here. Had to let those cold Michigan winters go, man."

Ryan expertly navigated the airport, proving that he had made several trips in the last two days to pick up wedding guests. Waiting in the car at the curbside was Brice, the final member of the law-school trio. Even in the stifling heat, Brice looked like a man who had just stepped off the pages of *GQ* magazine. His wrist sparkled with diamonds, and around his neck hung a thick gold chain. Greyson tossed his luggage in the trunk of Ryan's car and they headed to his home, where Greyson would be a guest for the next three days.

"So you left Hunter, Roe & Volney?" Brice asked from the front passenger seat.

Greyson nodded. "Had to. I was suffocating there."

"I swear I don't understand you or Ryan. Both of you dropped everything and walked away without looking back. I can understand Ryan's decision a little better, but you? I thought we were on the same page."

"Had to do it."

"No regrets?" Brice asked.

"None." Greyson thought of his early-morning activities with Sutton. "None at all."

Greyson leaned forward and shook Ryan's shoulder. "Tell me about Anita. I didn't think anyone would ever replace Sherry in your eyes."

Brice groaned and flipped the visor down, shielding the bright California sun from his eyes. He pulled a pair of designer sunglasses from his breast pocket and covered his eyes.

"Sherry is not even in the same class as Anita. Anita is smart, loving—"

"And she takes no stuff. Just what Ryan needs to keep him in line," Brice added.

The men shared a laugh before Greyson inquired about Ryan's new legal practice. Ryan had been forced to reevaluate his life and career goals. His sister assisted him in learning everything he needed to know about life in LA, and Ryan set up a legal practice targeted to up-and-coming entertainers. Brice remained in Michigan, practicing trial law as a partner at a prestigious firm. After Brice finished disclosing the details of his latest criminal case, all attention turned to Greyson and his life to date.

"A paper mill?" Brice questioned wearily. "You gave up your partnership position at Hunter to move home and open a paper mill? You disappoint me."

"No way, Brice," Ryan added, not taking his eyes off the road. "I knew when you called me with this that there was more to it. There's a woman in this picture."

Greyson laughed at his friend's astute assessment. "Sutton Hill."

"Sutton Hill? Where do we know that name from?" Brice asked Ryan as if Greyson were not in the backseat readily available to explain.

"I don't know, but we know Sutton Hill," Ryan said, making a left into a residential neighborhood bordered by mountainous greenery.

Brice turned to face Greyson. "She's not the woman you used to talk about in law school, is she?" He turned to Ryan. "You remember. He used to talk about this lady—day and night. He'd never been on a date with her but was completely in love with her."

"Yeah, I remember." Ryan laughed. "That's her, isn't it, Greyson?"

"That's my Sutton."

"Oh, she's your Sutton, huh? Didn't she go off and marry another man?"

"That doesn't matter. She's mine now. Pretty soon I'll be asking you guys to fly into West Virginia for my wedding."

"Does she know about this?" Brice joked.

Ryan laughed with him. "I can tell you right now that Anita will not bail me out of jail for kidnapping a woman and forcing her to marry you."

"When I marry Sutton she's going to be a willing participant. Don't worry about that. The only reason I flew out here was to get pointers for my own wedding."

"Why didn't you bring her?" Ryan asked.

Greyson's mood dipped when he thought of her playing the desperate widow of Alex Galloway instead of being with him on the beaches of California. "There's been a recent tragedy in her life and she had to deal with that. Besides, she has a little girl who she doesn't like to leave for long periods of time. We're planning uninterrupted time together when I get back from your wedding."

Ryan pulled in front of a moderate-size Spanish Tudor. The driveway was being utilized to capacity. Two men with long hair and California tans sat on the porch stairs talking. The front door was open and the sound of laughter floated out to the curb.

Greyson asked, "This your place?"

"No." Ryan stopped the engine. "This is my sister's house. She's kindly agreed to put us up for the wedding."

"You'll love her." Brice exited the car. "Don't get caught up in the name-dropping and stargazing. Famous faces pop in and out of here like she's situated in the middle of a movie lot."

"Are you sure she won't mind?" Greyson asked. "I can get a hotel room."

"No. This has been planned since before I even asked Anita to marry me. Gale loves to entertain. I'd have you stay at my place, but Anita and I closed a couple of days ago and haven't moved in yet. Anita and her family are staying with my grandmother. I'm staying here with you and Brice." They exited the car and walked to the trunk where Brice was waiting.

"Was Kirkland helpful?"

"Oh, man. He helped tremendously. I had no idea what I was getting into. I didn't understand what those decorators were talking about. We're remodeling the master bedroom, the kitchen, and the living room. I want everything perfect when Anita and I return from our honeymoon."

"Ryan."

The three men turned to the porch where a beautiful woman with ample curves and a broad smile stood.

"Come here, baby." Ryan held out his hand to her. He looked at Greyson over his shoulder. "She's beautiful, isn't she?"

The woman bolted across the yard and into Ryan's arms. Greyson's stomach flip-flopped as he watched them embrace. Brice began unloading the luggage at the curb. Ryan whispered something to Anita that made her smile. She burrowed her face in his chest.

"Greyson, Anita. Anita, Greyson. They're always like this." Brice offered as he held out Greyson's bag. "Just ignore them." He started across the lawn to the house.

A strange feeling of desperation came over Greyson as he watched Ryan and Anita kiss. For some unknown reason, he felt Sutton slipping away, his dream of being a family fading. He couldn't understand the dread. Being with her that morning and the night before was better than any of his fantasies. This feeling was familiar, but he couldn't remember where he had encountered it—

His luggage fell to the asphalt.

Ryan and Anita separated.

"Greyson, you all right, man?" Ryan asked.

"Honey, he doesn't look well. Maybe it's the heat. This California sun takes time to get used to."

"Greyson?"

Greyson remembered this feeling. It was how his insides twisted and his heart lurched the day he watched the woman he loved walk down the aisle and marry the man he despised. He needed to speak to Sutton. He couldn't; he didn't know Mrs. Galloway's phone number. Three days would pass before he could see her and be assured that his worrying was without merit. His chest heaved with deep, panicked breaths.

"Are you okay?" Anita's inquiry came with a tender touch to his back.

"I'm fine. I'm sorry. You're right. The heat must be bothering me." Greyson scolded himself for being foolish. Alex could not steal Sutton away from him again. In three days he'd return to Hannaford and they'd be together again. Then they'd go to the lodge to white-water raft and he would get to know Sierra.

"Ryan, get his bags. I'll send my brother out to help you." Anita grasped Greyson's arm. "Let's go inside and I'll get you something to drink while you lie down."

Anita brought Greyson a glass of ice water and showed him to the room where he would sleep. She sat with him, talking and getting to know one of her future husband's best friends. They closed the door to keep the noise out while they talked. The group in the living room shared star stories, ate, and played cards.

Anita's mothering qualities comforted Greyson. He shared his history about Sutton. A few times, Anita dabbed at the corners of her eyes, stating she wanted to meet Sutton. She told him of the turmoil she and Ryan had suffered until they found their way to each other. Openly discussing his emotions for Sutton with a nonjudgmental woman eased Greyson's mind and solidified his belief that he was doing the right thing. Any doubts he harbored about giving up his position at the law firm and moving back to his small hometown dissipated.

"Anita, can I ask you to do something for me?"

"Sure." Anita sat forward in her chair, anxious to hear what was on his mind.

"I want to buy Sutton a ring. Can you take me to a jewelry store?"

Anita's broad smile returned. "When?"

"Now. Right now. I know you're busy with the wedding—"

"Nothing left to do for the wedding except show up. If I don't keep myself busy tonight, I'll be a nervous wreck by the morning." She hopped up from her chair. "Let's go."

Greyson lifted himself from the bed and slipped his feet back into his shoes. "Can we keep this from the guys? After you, I want Sutton to be the first to know."

"Afraid they'll tease you, huh?"

Greyson laughed. "They always tease me about my feelings for Sutton."

The first jewelry store Anita drove to did the trick. Greyson wanted something unique, special for Sutton. With Anita's help, he sat with the shop owner and designed an oval ring made of tanzanite surrounded by diamond chips. He guessitmated the band size based on his remembrance of the set of rings he removed from Sutton's finger the night before. With prompting and a promise of a bonus upon delivery, the shopkeeper assured Greyson the ring would be ready for pickup before he boarded his flight home.

The next afternoon, Greyson sat next to Brice in the pew, watching Ryan nervously exchange wedding vows. Anita's voice trembled, and Ryan had to steady her hand when she attempted to slide the wedding ring on his finger. Ryan stood tall and proud as his grandmother beamed from the front pew.

Love and friendship overflowed inside the chapel. Greyson hoped his own ceremony would be as moving. Twenty close friends and family members watched Anita and Ryan declare their undying love for each other. "Small and elegant," Anita had said, beaming, as they drove from the jewelry store the day before. "Ryan is not a man who has to do things on a grand scale. We're going to have a small ceremony with the ones we love and then throw a huge bash to celebrate. Did I tell you Ryan planned everything before he even asked me to marry him?"

After the wedding, the celebration went late into the night. Greyson was fortunate enough to dance with the bride before she left with her husband to start their new life together.

Anita looked up at him at the completion of their dance. "I wish you all of the magic that keeps Ryan and me together."

"Thank you. And congratulations." Greyson kissed her cheek.

Ryan stood behind Anita, waiting for Greyson to return his bride. "Hey, what's this?" His arm snaked around her waist.

Greyson extended his hand to Ryan. "She's pretty special."

"I know." Ryan shook his hand and then kissed the top of Anita's head. "Ready to go?"

Anita nodded. She shared a knowing look with Greyson before Ryan swept her away.

As Greyson drove alone in his Volvo wagon from the state capital to Hannaford Valley, he revisited his time in California. Ryan, Brice, and he were the best of friends while in college. Ryan and Brice had gone on to law school in Michigan, while he had been awarded the Harvard scholarship. The distance did not separate them. All three were awarded summer internships in New York where they roomed together to cut expenses. Greyson had flown to Michigan for their graduation. Ryan and Brice sat in the fourth row at his Harvard graduation.

Ryan had strayed from their friendship when a woman entered his life that almost destroyed him emotionally. Brice and Greyson stayed focused, helping each other make the necessary contacts to advance up the corporate ladder. Greyson won a position as the first black partner at the prestigious Hunter, Roe & Volney Chicago law firm. Brice was a dynamic criminal trial attorney and junior partner at his law firm. Greyson smiled as he assessed their lives at this point. All were successful in their own right. And as soon as Sutton accepted his proposal, he'd be happier still.

Sixteen

Greyson hopped up the steps of Mr. Hill's front porch with a bouquet of red roses in one hand and the custom-made engagement ring in the other. He rang the bell and was still chuckling at his giddiness when Mr. Hill's stoic face appeared.

"Good morning, Mr. Hill. Can I see Sutton, please?"

Mr. Hill stepped out on the porch, bringing the door closed behind him. "Sutton ain't here."

"What?" Surely Mr. Hill wouldn't try to keep them apart now that they were responsible adults.

"You heard me. Sutton came back from Ohio, grabbed Sierra, and left within the hour. Said she's moving there with Galloway. I couldn't get her to tell me what was going on, but she said it had something to do with what happened on her trip to close up the house." Mr. Hill took a menacing step toward Greyson. "You wouldn't know anything about this, would you?"

"No, sir," Greyson choked on his words. "I really don't."

Mr. Hill stared at the roses and red velvet box he carried.

Greyson slipped the ring into his pocket. "Is that all she said? When is she coming back?"

"Didn't sound like she plans to come back at all. Nearly ripped the grandbaby from her grandmother's arms. Tore my wife to pieces. And Sutton wasn't in much better shape. Whatever happened shook her up pretty bad."

"Do you have any idea where she's staying since the house has been liquidated?"

"She's staying with Mrs. Galloway."

"Can I have the number?" Greyson pleaded. He needed to get to the bottom of what was going on. He realized that he had surprised Sutton by coming on strongly with his emotions, but she had had to admit that she felt the same way. She'd promised not to abandon him.

"Are you crazy? If she wanted you t' have the number, she would have left it for you. Every time you come sniffing around my baby she gets hurt. Leave her alone before you do more damage."

Mr. Hill dismissed him by turning away. Greyson's anger spoke before he had a chance to persuade himself that diplomacy would be the best approach. "What's your problem with me, Mr. Hill? Every since Sutton was twelve and I asked permission to date her, you've had it in for me."

Mr. Hill whirled around, his face showing that he had been waiting a long time for this chance to clear his mind. "You were seventeen—a man in those times, in these mountains—asking to date my little girl."

"Maybe you didn't know Sutton as well as you think you did. At twelve, she was developing into a young woman. I didn't mean her any harm. That's why I came to talk to you about it. I knew I loved Sutton then and I love her even more now."

"You didn't know nothing 'bout love. I know what was on your mind. You don't know nothing 'bout love now. I know what's on your mind even today. Always sniffing around my little girl."

Greyson ignored the sting of his words. "I plan on having a future with her. I'm going to make up all the time we've lost. I plan on being her husband."

"Her husband?" Mr. Hill squawked. "You'll never be good enough for Sutton."

"Not as good as Alex was?" He didn't try to tame the contempt aimed at his elder. "I may not have had the money the Galloways had, but I wanted only the best for Sutton. I tried to show you that over the years. I looked out for her. I never took advantage of her. I respected her. You kept Sutton away from me, but threw her into the pit with Alex."

Mr. Hill's face shriveled. Greyson had hit a sore spot.

"I will be Sutton's husband and no one is going to interfere with that. Now you can give me the number so that I can get to the bottom of this and bring her home—where she belongs—or you can stand in the way. But know this: If you stand in my way I'll think of you as the enemy and I'll treat you that way."

The men stood stoic, both fighting to save Sutton the best way they knew how. Out of respect, Greyson softened his tone and tried to resolve the standoff. "Mr. Hill, I love Sutton. I would never let anyone hurt her or her daughter. If they're in trouble, you have to let me help. Please give me the number so that I can get to the bottom of this."

"Hello?" Sutton's soft voice penetrated Greyson's ear.

"Sutton, it's Greyson. What's going on? Why are you still in Ohio? Your father said you're not coming back."

"He's right, Greyson. I had a chance to think things over and this is the best place for Sierra and me. I'm sorry."

"Don't 'I'm sorry' me, Sutton. What's really going on?"

Sutton sighed. After a pause she continued with a shaky voice. "I know you don't understand and I can't explain further. Believe me, everything I said, I meant. Things are out of my control. I can't be with you. I'm sorry."

"Stop saying that. Why can't you be with me? I won't accept this without you explaining what happened in the three days I was gone to change your mind."

"This is how it has to be. Good-bye."

The dial tone stunned him.

Seventeen

Twenty-five days had passed since Sutton's last conversation with Greyson. It had taken many phone calls to convince him, but finally he'd stopped calling to declare his love for her. Twenty-five days filled with meaningless conversation and dinner parties with people who could care less about her well-being. Twenty-five days of Mother Galloway directing her every move.

"Mom," Sierra scampered across the room in her footed pajamas. She rubbed the sleep burning her eyes. "I can't sleep," she whimpered.

"Come here, baby." Sutton threw back her blankets and let Sierra climb into bed beside her. Sierra snuggled against her mother's chest and soon was asleep.

Sutton stroked Sierra's red braids. Mother Galloway had begun to take an active interest in her granddaughter. Sutton liked it better when she had ignored them. Mother Galloway dressed Sierra in elaborate dresses and shiny shoes. She paraded Sierra in front of her snobby friends. The whole scene was becoming a circus. Whenever Sutton tried to intervene, Mother Galloway found a charity gathering where Sutton's appearance was urgently needed.

Sierra hadn't seemed to notice Sutton's distress with their new living situation. She had all the attention, candy, and toys she could ever want. As long as Mother Galloway continued to spoil her, she'd be content. In the end all that mattered was that Sierra was happy and that they were together.

Sutton had overheard Mother Galloway filling Sierra's head with tales of how wonderful a man her father had been. Sutton would never put down Alex to Sierra, but she also didn't want new wounds to open that Sierra would have to struggle to heal. Alex was a void in her life. Introducing him at this point served no purpose other than to make Sierra start missing a man she never even knew.

Sutton pressed her nose against Sierra's freshly washed and braided hair. They were living in a spacious, well-kept home, but she was miserable. She missed Greyson. She missed the independence she was on the verge of discovering. She missed her parents. Everyone she loved seemed so far away. She held Sierra tighter. She'd never let her little girl go. She'd endure Mother Galloway's rules as long as necessary to keep her daughter by her side.

"Mother Galloway?"

Mother Galloway looked up from her reading to see Eddie standing in the doorway to her bedroom. "Come in. Close the door."

Eddie did as he was told before greeting her with a kiss on her cheek.

"How's my baby?"

"Fine, Mother Galloway."

She raised her lips in a rare smile. "We're alone. Call me Mother."

Eddie returned her smile. He enjoyed the time he had with his mother when he didn't have to pretend to be her nephew. "I need to speak to you."

"What about?" She closed her book and dropped it on the floor next to her chair.

Eddie sat on the corner of the bed, his hands gripping his knees. Sitting there focused and serious-looking, Eddie was the spitting image of his older half-brother Alex. Watching him made Mother Galloway's heart break. No matter what Eddie had done, he would be forgiven. She could not deny her only living son anything. He knew this, which made her suspicious of his nervousness.

"It's about Sutton," Eddie hedged.

The smile was lost. "What about her?"

"I want to ask your permission to start dating her."

Her eyes narrowed.

Eddie rushed on. "Surely, you see she's restless here. And you can't miss the fact that every eligible—and sometimes married—man at your get-togethers is all over her. I was thinking if I could get to know her it might lead to marriage. If we married she'd be more apt to settle into her routine here. She'd still be a part of the family, and I could start working on the grandson you want."

Sierra's sunny disposition made Mother Galloway smile, but she needed a grandson to keep the Galloway name alive.

"What makes you think Sutton would go out with you, Eddie?"

"We get along. I'm the only man you'll let get near her. I think my chances are good."

And if Sutton disagreed, Mother Galloway had pictures that might persuade her to change her mind. "Go ahead, give it a shot."

She stared at the replica of her pride, Alex. Eddie eagerly carried out her every demand. He didn't make a move without her approval. Alex had been stubborn that way—wanting to make his own money, secure his future independent of what his father had passed on to him.

Remembering some of their disagreements made her sad. The only reason she'd endured her husband's cheating was to secure the future of her children. That's where Sutton had made her mistake. She tried to hold her marriage together with love. Mother Galloway subtly warned her the first time she came knocking on her door crying about Alex's infidelities. Being a cheat was in the Galloway blood and no amount of love and understanding would change that. If Sutton had listened years ago, she wouldn't be penniless while Alex's mistresses lived in fancy houses and drove expensive cars.

Mother Galloway had married at thirteen to get out of her father's house. Growing up a child of a miner, she'd seen her fair share of days without meals. Mayonnaise sandwiches were considered a delicacy in her shack of a home. The children in her class shunned her because she wore the hand-me-downs of her six older brothers and sisters. Her father was an ornery cuss who beat her mother regularly. Her brothers mimicked his pattern and practiced their abuse on her until they were married with wives of their own to batter.

Alex's refusal to inherit his father's money was a slap in the face. It was the source of their only arguments. Eventually, Mother Galloway learned to respect his desire to be independent and make his own way. Eddie had not been as lucky. The circumstances of his conception didn't allow it. He had never received the benefit of going to college or living as one of Hannaford's most influential family members. As Mother Galloway watched him leave her room with a hopeful smile, she promised to make up what he had missed.

"Good morning, Sutton."

Sutton turned in her chair and was instantly transported to her kitchen in her condo. Physically, Alex's cousin Eddie resembled him so closely it was uncanny. However, Eddie did not possess Alex's cocky stride and deceitful ways. When Eddie moved into the house Sutton felt that some of the burden of pleasing Mother Galloway had been lifted. Mother Galloway fawned over Eddie as much as she had Alex. But there were times when Sutton overheard Mother Galloway's harsh criticism of his business decisions. It seemed that Mother Galloway had turned over a portion of the money Alex had left her to Eddie to invest and she wasn't happy with the results so far.

Eddie pulled out the chair next to Sutton and began filling a plate with breakfast.

"I overheard Mother Galloway giving you a hard time. Is everything okay now?"

Eddie dropped his eyes in embarrassment. "Mother Galloway has very rigid expectations when it comes to her money. She refuses to return to Hannaford Valley to live. She'll do anything to avoid that."

Sutton nodded as she finished her juice.

"That reminds me. Mother Galloway says that you'll be attending a dinner tonight in support of black firefighters. I'm planning to attend that dinner and I thought it might be fun if we went together."

Sutton smiled wearily. She'd forgotten about the dinner. Mother Galloway managed her social calendar. "Actually, I thought I'd try to get out of that. I really want to spend time with Sierra."

"Mother Galloway will keep Sierra busy. I understand that she's gotten tickets to a kid's stage show. Besides, Mother Galloway won't let you off the hook that easily. Together we can make a good time out of it."

"Maybe," Sutton hedged.

"If you turn me down, I'll have to think it's personal." Eddie grinned at her. He had the same honey-colored skin Alex had.

"What is it?" Eddie asked.

"You look so much like Alex. It's unnerving sometimes."

"I'm afraid there's nothing I can do about that."

"I didn't mean it that way." She covered his hand with hers in a gesture of apology. Eddie's eyes locked on her hand. He lifted his head to meet her eyes. The intense look of longing made her pull away.

Sensing her uneasiness, Eddie laughed. "So, are we on for dinner tonight?"

Sutton gathered her empty plate. "Sure. It'll be nice to have a friend to sit with." She hoped her subtle words were enough of a hint to Eddie to clarify her intentions.

Chevy stood at a wall chart that illustrated the layout of the forest from which the paper mill acquired its trees. Greyson sat at the head of the long conference table, his squared chin resting on the steeple of his fingertips. Kirkland sat to his right, across from Chevy's vacant chair, scribbling notes.

Most of the seats at the conference table were taken. Locals with the required education and experience had been chosen to fill supervisory roles at the mill. Chevy and Kirkland were in the process of conducting quick hiring to fill vacant positions before the rapidly approaching launch date of the mill. Admittedly, Greyson had neglected his duties because he was wrapped up in winning Sutton Hill. Twenty-five days after their abrupt, unexplainable breakup, he sat immersed in thoughts of her.

"We've made a commitment to environmentalists and the government that for every tree we cut down, we'll plant another," Chevy stated. "Because of the slow rate trees grow to maturity, my men have already begun planting here and here." He pointed to the respective places on the chart. "We're also making a sizable donation from our yearly profits to a fund for preserving the Costa Rica rain forests."

Greyson's intense scrutiny of the chart blurred. His attempt to focus on Chevy's words failed. His mind left the meeting and floated back a month ago to his rented suite in Ohio. He relived the scene where he confessed his feelings for Sutton. As he pictured her eyes and heard her words, he became more confused about their breakup. She had warned him that he was coming on too strongly, pushing her, she had said. But he never expected her to run away. She had promised. She had promised to stand by him for always.

Chevy pulled out his chair next to Greyson. Grey nodded in Chevy's direction, hoping Chevy had not noticed that he had zoned out for the balance of his speech.

Greyson poured himself a glass of water as Kirkland took the floor. As he listened to his youngest brother speak of production deadlines and profitability, he wondered how Kirkland's soft-spoken manner could still keep his people in line. Although only twenty-eight, Kirkland was accomplished and respected in construction. He had performed all roles of the trade: serving as a foreman, reading blue prints, designing structures, and laying bricks. He had been instrumental in designing his parents' home, as well as putting the finishing touches on Greyson's home.

The meeting adjourned after lunch. Kirkland hurried off to run errands for their mother. Chevy lingered behind to speak to his brother.

"I finished decorating my office," Chevy said. "Why don't you take a walk down the hall to see it?"

Greyson peered at his brother from behind his desk. Seeing the enthusiasm in his brother's eyes, he accompanied Chevy to tour the office. Along the way, Chevy introduced him to workers who were busy preparing their worksites. In only two weeks the mill would make its first trial run. The first product to run the line would be a cotton-based, eight-by-eleven, pink-blush paper watermarked with red roses, Greyson's design, in remembrance of a special time he shared with Sutton.

"This is nice," Greyson stepped around the room. A table near the window with four chestnut-colored leather chairs matched the sofa. Forestry books and government manuals covered a bookshelf built into the far wall. A miniature replica of the paper mill sat on a pedestal under Plexiglas. Huge area rugs with swirls of shades of tan covered the floor. The private bathroom shared the brown-and-tan color scheme.

"You should let the designer take a stab at your office," Chevy offered.

"Whatever you want," Greyson headed for the door.

"Whatever I want?" Chevy murmured. "I'll have her come in this afternoon."

"Yeah," Greyson answered half-heartedly.

"You should stick around and meet her," Chevy called. "Maybe you'll hit it off. She's your type."

Greyson spun around on the tips of his shoes, his face a reflection of blazing hot anger. "How do you know what's my type?"

Chevy threw his hands up. "I'm just saying—anything is worth trying to get you out of this funk before the mill opens. Everyone has worked hard to complete this project—and it was a massive project. It's hard to see you walking around unhappy, like we've all let you down."

Greyson's misery wasn't as well-hidden as he believed. "I'm not disappointed in the paper mill. Everyone has done an exceptional job."

"Then why don't you show it?" Chevy challenged.

Greyson stalked to the sofa and slumped down in defeat. He loosened his tie and fidgeted with the buttons of his jacket.

"What's up?" Chevy perched on the corner of his desk with his arms folded across his chest.

"Sutton and I were finally there, Chevy. We spent time together. I told her how I felt. I told her my plans for us."

"That's great," Chevy chimed in.

Greyson shook his head. "And then it all fell apart. She up and moved back to Ohio without a word to me. I tried to call her a hundred times and she kept giving me these encrypted excuses why we couldn't be together."

"I don't get it, Grey."

"I don't either. All I know is that Sutton is in Ohio and I'm here."

"What are you going to do about it? You've been after Sutton all your life. Are you going to just walk away now? How many times have you walked away from her? How many times have you failed the challenge when it came to Sutton?"

Greyson thought about his brother's words.

"Mama has a scrapbook at home with clippings of all of your trials that made the newspapers. Do you hear me? Enough to fill a book. You can go into court and fight huge corporations but you can't fight for the woman you love?" Chevy rounded the desk, placing a safe distance between them before he made his final comment. "You don't deserve to have Sutton."

Greyson dropped his face in the palms of his hands and rubbed his eyes.

"I know there were times when I told you to back off. I said interfering was wrong, but Sutton isn't engaged or married now. *Now* is the time to chase after her."

Greyson jumped up from the sofa and headed out the door.

"Where are you going?" Chevy called after him.

"I'm going to see Sutton."

Eighteen

Greyson dialed the private detective that freelanced for Hunter, Roe & Volney the second he stepped off the plane in Ohio. Within minutes, he had an address and directions to go along with Mrs. Galloway's phone number. Hertz had a Lincoln waiting at the curb. He signed the paperwork and raced off.

Mrs. Galloway's home was located in an upper-middle-class neighborhood. Greyson boldly pulled the rented Lincoln up the stone path leading to her door and parked. While trying to steady his thoughts, he tugged at the zipper of his jacket. He reflected on the many times he had let Sutton slip through his fingers. He relived the intensity of their lovemaking in his suite. Anita's encouraging words still rang in his ears. He couldn't walk away this time. If Sutton didn't want him anymore, she'd have to explain why. He pocketed the keys and stepped from the car.

He questioned his attire as he rang the doorbell. Mother Galloway would not be impressed by his matching green khakis, black boots, and green Army jacket. Selecting his wardrobe had not been a priority when he hurried from home to the airport. He caressed the stubble on his chin. Sutton probably wouldn't want to go anywhere with him looking like a junior thug.

He stood impatiently on the stoop waiting for someone to answer the door. Jarred by the swishing of the drapes, he rang the doorbell again and again in rapid succession.

A shadow appeared on the other side of stained glass. The heavy wooden door swung open.

Shocked, Greyson took a step backward. "Alex?" he asked in disbelief. Could Alex's death be an elaborate hoax?

The man's hand tightened on the frame of the door. "I'm Eddie. Can I help you?"

Greyson had offended him, which would make his mission harder. He didn't have time to figure out who this man was or what he was doing in the same house with Sutton. He composed himself before saying, "I'm looking for Sutton Hill."

"Is Mrs. Galloway expecting you, Mr.—" Eddie's respectful tone contrasted with Alex's haughtiness.

Greyson cringed. He wanted to detach that name from Sutton as easily as he had slipped the wedding band off her finger. He let his jealousy go and stayed focused on his mission. "Ballantyne. Greyson Ballantyne. No, she's not expecting me."

"One minute." The door swung closed, sealing Sutton in and Greyson out.

Greyson shoved his hands in his pockets and waited. He turned his back to the door and waited. He surveyed the quiet upscale neighborhood and waited. The style of the home was in keeping with the Galloway property in Hannaford Valley. Greyson turned to the door, placed his hand over his brow, and tried to see through the stained glass. He waited. He checked his watch and tried to estimate how long he'd been waiting. He pushed the bell again.

Eddie appeared. "Mrs. Galloway can't see you."

Greyson's cool slipped away. He saw himself sitting at the back of the church again. "Did you tell her it was me? Did she say that?"

Eddie's face bent into a frown. "I told you, Mrs. Galloway couldn't see you."

"I want her to tell me that." Greyson's anger began to bubble in the pit of his stomach. Sutton wouldn't dismiss him after he'd come this far. "Did you even tell her I was here?"

"I won't stand here and argue with you. This is my home. I said Mrs. Galloway couldn't see you. Go away."

Eddie had chosen to place himself between Greyson and Sutton, and like any barrier, he had to be knocked down. Greyson wedged his foot in the door and pushed it open with both hands, sending the gatekeeper scurrying toward the back wall. Boldly, Greyson stepped inside the house and went in the direction opposite the scrambling man.

"Sutton! Sutton, it's me," Greyson called as he moved through the house. Eddie followed, shouting obscenities and demanding that he leave the premises.

This bravado did not belong to the polite man that answered the door. Greyson figured Mrs. Galloway had threatened Eddie in some way and he was afraid of her wrath. Or he had more to lose. He might have something invested in Sutton that depended on keeping them apart. Greyson's male instincts zeroed in on the sour expression of possessiveness Eddie gave him when he introduced himself earlier on the stoop.

Greyson shrugged Eddie off his sleeve as he continued to search the house while calling Sutton's name. Mother Galloway responded to the commotion, blocking Greyson's path as he climbed a wide flight of stairs.

"What are you doing in my house?" Mother Galloway demanded with straight lips.

"Mrs. Galloway, I need to see Sutton."

"Sutton doesn't want to see you, Greyson Ballantyne. Didn't my nephew make that clear to you?"

Greyson tried to keep a respectful tone. "He did tell me that, Mrs. Galloway, but I need to hear it from Sutton. It's very important that I see her."

"I'm sure you believe it is, but I have to insist that you leave now. I'll tell Sutton you came."

"I'm not leaving until I see her. I want to make sure she's all right."

Mrs. Galloway turned up her nose. "Do you think I've done something to harm her?" Her eyes moved pass

Greyson to Eddie who was standing quietly on the stairs. "Call the police."

Greyson turned to see Eddie's thin body scurry down the stairs and to the right.

"Mrs. Galloway, I don't want any trouble. If you could just let me see Sutton for five minutes."

"I will not have this foolishness! Sutton doesn't want to see you now or ever. She's in mourning. Losing my son has been hard on her. Why do you insist on making it worse? Go back to Hannaford Valley where you belong. Sutton and Sierra belong here with us—Alex's family. Her family."

"I won't go until she tells me that for herself."

Mrs. Galloway snorted. "Thick-headed—" She regained her composure but held on to her anger. She smoothed her eyebrows. "What do you want with Sutton?"

Greyson's eyes flickered to the ground. He didn't feel comfortable sharing his feelings with Alex's mother. "I just need to see her. She moved away without saying good-bye and—"

"And what? Why would you think she's obligated to gain your permission to leave?"

"Sutton and I—we've been friends—"

"And I'm her family. What do I have to say to get it through your head? Sutton will never see you again."

Mrs. Galloway's angry expression was transformed into something purely evil. Greyson read hatred and resentment behind her eyes. She had never been overly fond of him as a child, but he never believed she hated him.

"I'm not going until I see Sutton," Greyson stipulated.

"Well, that's not going to happen."

Greyson heard Eddie climbing the stairs behind him. He had no idea what exactly was going on, but he knew he was not leaving without seeing Sutton. He had walked away without a fight too many times. He sized up Mrs. Galloway's determination to keep him away from Sutton. He estimated the number of stairs Eddie had to climb to reach him. In a flash, he rushed toward Mrs. Galloway and deposited her in the arms of Eddie, who was in the process of taking a swing at him. They struggled to maintain their balance on the staircase while Greyson bolted to the top, never looking back.

"Sutton! Sutton, it's Greyson. Come out." He rushed down the hallway, opening doors in search of her. "Sutton, where are you?"

At the end of the hallway, Sutton backed out of a door. She knelt and said a few words before closing the door behind her. Greyson caught a glimpse of fire-red braids before the door closed, hiding the little girl's profile. He scooped Sutton up in his arms.

"Are you all right?" He plastered her face with wet kisses, wrapping her against his chest.

"Greyson," she breathed his name and his heart melted. "Why did you come here?"

"I came to take you home. I don't know what's going on and I don't care. Together we'll work it out."

"Oh, Greyson. You're always trying to save me." She pressed her face into his chest.

"Get your things. Where's Sierra?"

Sutton's tear-filled eyes stilled him.

"What is it?"

"Didn't Mrs. Galloway tell you everything?"

"She said you didn't want to see me anymore."

Sutton cupped his stubbly chin inside her hands. "Don't believe that. No matter what happens, everything I said to you in the hotel I meant."

"You promised to never leave me. Did you mean that?"

"I did, but—"

"Then tell me what's going on." His voice boomed in the hallway. "Tell me why you ran away. This wasn't your decision, was it?"

A disturbance rose from downstairs. Greyson heard Mrs. Galloway shouting. Sutton looked past his shoulder. His eyes remained focused on the distress jacketing her face.

"Greyson, listen to me. I love you."

"I love you, too. Get your things and let's go home."

"Wait. Listen to me."

Greyson glanced over his shoulder. Their time was limited. Why couldn't this wait until they were alone? He knew how she felt about him before she told him with words. Whatever she needed to say, she felt had to be said now. He ignored the noise at the bottom of the staircase and gave her his attention. "What is it, Sutton?"

"I love you. When we were kids and even while I was married to Alex. I only recently admitted that to myself, but it's true. If I have to give you up, I want you to always know that."

"Give me up? You're not giving me up. We're just getting started."

"No, Greyson. I've been forced to make a choice between you and Sierra. I had to choose Sierra. You understand that, don't you?"

"No. No, I don't have a clue what you're talking about."

Mother Galloway appeared at the top of the stairs. "Up here, officers."

The police always responded quicker in the suburbs. Greyson cursed. In Chicago, a domestic dispute would be low on the priority list.

Greyson rushed his words. "What do you mean you had to choose between me and your daughter? I told you I'd raise her as if she were my own."

Greyson's eyes followed Sutton's. The police were quickly approaching. Mother Galloway was at their heels, shouting demands. Eddie brought up the rear.

Sutton hurried to explain. "Mother Galloway forced me to make a choice. No matter how much I love you, I had to choose my daughter. Even if that meant never seeing you again."

"Sir," a lanky officer dressed in black touched his arm. "What seems to be the problem?"

The other heavy-built officer stood behind him with his hand resting on the handle of his gun. "Let's talk outside."

"No talking." Mrs. Galloway and the Alex look-alike stepped forward. "I own this house and I want him arrested. I'll file charges. And I want a restraining order. You won't be bursting into my house again, Greyson Ballantyne."

The lanky officer touched Greyson's shoulder and indicated with a nod that he should follow them out.

"Wait," Sutton pleaded. "Mother Galloway, please. You don't have to have him arrested. He won't come around again. He only wanted to make sure that I was all right."

Greyson looked over his shoulder and watched Sutton plead his case to a stoic Mrs. Galloway. Her voice choked with tears. Eddie stood next to Mrs. Galloway, watching the scene with unbridled pity. He tried to pull Sutton into his arms and, when Sutton stayed where she was, began to stroke her back in an effort to comfort her.

Greyson stopped at the top of the stairs. "Sutton, don't beg her for anything. It'll be all right."

The police guided him down the stairs.

"I'll be back, Sutton." Greyson glared at Eddie. "I'll be back."

The judge refused to hear Greyson's case until a twelve-hour cooling-off period had passed. How he was supposed to cool off locked in a cell with mentally insane criminals was beyond him. He had no fear of his cellmates; he'd been tossed in the can before. At the top of his game, he had ruffled more than his share of judges and had been found in contempt of court. The problem was feeling helpless and unable to get to Sutton. How was he supposed to cool off when the only thing he could see was Eddie holding Sutton like he knew how to calm her? Like he was the good guy, and Greyson the maniac.

The longer Greyson sat in the cell, the more desperate he felt. Who knew what was going on with Sutton? What did Sutton mean she had been forced to choose between himself and her daughter?

Greyson rested his head against the cold, white cement blocks of the cell wall. He closed his eyes and tried to make sense of what had landed him in jail. There were hundreds of questions, but no answers. It seemed that all of his efforts to be with Sutton were always thwarted by an outside force. Maybe, despite his wishes, he and Sutton were not meant to be together.

Greyson relived his past. Every decision he ever made was with the ultimate goal of marrying Sutton Hill. He decided that the trials they were experiencing were a test. A divine intervention to make him appreciate Sutton's love and to cherish it for a lifetime.

"Ballantyne, your attorney's here."

Greyson grabbed his Army jacket, which had been covering the wooden bench. He dusted off his clothes and waited for the cell door to open. He was taken to a room with a wobbly table and two chairs.

"As an attorney, I thought you had more sense than to break and enter." Brice Vance marched into the room dressed in an expensive brown suit and tan shirt. The jewelry around his wrist sparkled. He placed his briefcase on the table and met his friend with an embrace.

"Thanks for coming," Greyson mumbled in embarrassment.

"Yeah, you'll get the bill." He fished through his briefcase, finding a legal pad to take notes. "Home invasion? What happened?"

Brice stared in amazement as Greyson tried to justify his actions at Mother Galloway's house. "I don't know what I was thinking. I had to see Sutton."

Brice became animated as he rehearsed his argument for the judge. "Your Honor, he's watched too much television. He believed that he could scale the castle wall and rescue the damsel from the evil queen. C'mon, Greyson, give me something I can work with."

"That's it."

"If that's it, you'd better go in and apologize to the judge,

Sutton, and Mrs. Galloway. I'll sell the country-boy-in-love angle. Throw in your achievements as an attorney and hope for the best."

"The best being?"

"Time served. I checked the judge out. He's not concerned much with black-on-black crime, if you know what I mean."

"The worst?"

"The worst being that today's 'example day' and the judge chooses you to set an example for dangerous black men everywhere. He could hold you and send this to trial." Seeing his friend's startled reaction, he quickly added, "I don't think that's going to happen."

Greyson nodded. "Is Chevy here?"

Brice gathered his things. "He's in the courtroom waiting." Brice went to the bars and called out for the guard. "I'll see you in there. Try to straighten up. And be eloquent when you apologize."

After scolding Greyson for his stupidity, the judge persuaded Mrs. Galloway to drop the charges against him. The judge gave him a stern warning and suggested the he leave Ohio immediately. Greyson didn't want to apologize for loving Sutton too much to let her go, but he had a greater goal to achieve that his pride could not vie with.

Greyson looked around the courtroom hoping to see Sutton. Instead, his eyes fell on Mrs. Galloway and Eddie. Chevy and Kirkland sat in the second row. They looked worried. Greyson hated the turmoil he had caused.

His release was processed and Brice escorted him out of lockup. Just as with his time as a corporate trial attorney, jail time increased his fervor to win. And winning meant bringing Sutton home.

Greyson and his brothers drove Brice to the airport.

"Thanks again," Greyson said, shaking Brice's hand before he boarded his flight.

"Between the hours you and Ryan have logged this year, I'll be able to retire soon."

Greyson laughed. "You're not billing me for this, are you? This was a cakewalk."

"Yeah, whatever. You better pay my bill or else I'll put it on your credit report." Brice hid his smile as he handed the gate attendant his ticket.

"Stay away from the Galloway house," Brice said before disappearing down the walkway.

Chevy and Kirkland joined Greyson.

"Did you tell Mama and Pop?"

Chevy shook his head. "I wouldn't have told Kirkland if he hadn't been sitting there when you called."

"What are you going to do now?" Kirkland asked.

"I'm going to get Sutton and Sierra and bring them home."

Chevy and Kirkland stared at him in disbelief.

"You just got out of jail," Kirkland reminded him.

"And you two are going to help me." Greyson walked off before they could object.

Nineteen

Sutton took in a deep breath before she knocked on the door of Mother Galloway's study. She would put her anger aside and act with diplomacy. She planned to hold her head high and tell Mother Galloway that the charade had to end. She would demand that the restraining order against Greyson be dropped. She would clearly state that she had no interest in Eddie and inform Mother Galloway that her matchmaking attempts were useless. Finally, she'd say—without emotion binding her throat—she was taking Sierra and going home to Hannaford Valley.

"Enter," Mother Galloway said from the other side of the door.

Sutton closed the door behind her; Eddie wandered the house and she wanted their conversation to remain private. She felt Mother Galloway would be more receptive of an agreement where the details were kept between the two of them.

Mother Galloway sat behind her desk. Her arched back mimicked a hunched cat.

"Mother Galloway, I need to talk with you."

She swept her hand from left to right, inviting Sutton to sit down.

Sutton maintained direct eye contact. "I'm not happy here. I want you to drop the charges against Greyson. When he's released, Sierra and I are going back to Hannaford Valley with him."

She expected Mother Galloway to loudly object. When she didn't, Sutton's courage soared and she went on. "I don't mean to keep Sierra away from you. Any time you want to visit, you're welcome. We'll come here whenever I have vacation time at work." She hoped she could talk Maddie into allowing her to come back to the library.

Sutton leaned forward, resting her hands on the edge of the desk. "I want to make this work for all of us."

Mother Galloway fell back in her chair. She studied Sutton critically as she smoothed her dress. Her face turned to ice when she finally spoke. "Did you just walk in here and give me an ultimatum?"

"I didn't mean it like that. I'm not happy here. This isn't my home. I want to pick up the pieces of my life and move on. It's time that we both do that."

Mother Galloway leaned forward and spoke in a harsh whisper. "I will not forget my son."

Things were not going as Sutton planned. She remained diplomatic. "I'm not suggesting that you do."

"No, you're telling me that you already have."

Sutton was tired of playing the grieving widow. She did it out of respect to Alex and Mother Galloway when she was showcased at social events, but it had all gone too far. Greyson had been arrested. Her life was in shambles. It had to end.

"It's not like Alex was good to me during our marriage. He had so many affairs I can't count them all. I stopped trying. He was insensitive to me. He ignored Sierra. He left me penniless, while all of his girlfriends are set for life." Sutton hadn't realized how much resentment she harbored toward Alex until she listed all his transgressions to Mother Galloway. "I've mourned him long enough."

"Have you really mourned him at all? You took up with Greyson the minute Alex's body hit the soil."

"That's not true."

Mother Galloway jumped up from her seat. "How could you be so low? You know how Alex felt about Greyson. Did

An important message from the ARABESQUE Editor

Dear Arabesque Reader,

Because you've chosen to read one of our Arabesque romance novels, we'd like to say "thank you"! And, as a special way to thank you, we've selected four more of the books you love so well to send you for FREE!

Please enjoy them with our compliments, and thank you for continuing to enjoy Arabesque...the soul of romance.

Karen Thomas
Senior Editor,
Arabesque Romance Novels

Check out our website at
www.arabesquebooks.com

SPECIAL OFFER!
4 FREE BOOKS

ARABESQUE ®

A PRODUCT OF

BET BOOKS™

3 QUICK STEPS
TO RECEIVE YOUR "THANK YOU" GIFT
FROM THE EDITOR

Send this card back and you'll receive 4 FREE Arabesque
novels! The introductory shipment of 4 Arabesque novels – a
$23.96 value – is yours absolutely FREE!

There's no catch. You're under no obligation to buy anything.
You'll receive your introductory shipment of 4 Arabesque
novels absolutely FREE (plus $1.99 to offset the costs of
shipping & handling). And you don't have to make any
minimum number of purchases—not even one!

We hope that after receiving your books you'll want to
remain an Arabesque subscriber. But the choice is yours to
continue or cancel, anytime at all! So why not take us up on
our invitation to receive 4 Arabesque Romance Novels, with
no risk of any kind. You'll be glad you did!

Call us
TOLL-FREE
at 1-800-770-1963

THE EDITOR'S "THANK YOU" GIFT INCLUDES:

- 4 books absolutely FREE (plus $1.99 for shipping and handling)
- A FREE newsletter, *Arabesque Romance News*, filled with author interviews, book previews, special offers, and more!
- No risks or obligations. You're free to cancel whenever you wish... with no questions asked.

BOOK CERTIFICATE

Yes! Please send me 4 FREE Arabesque novels (plus $1.99 for shipping & handling). I understand I am under no obligation to purchase any books, as explained on the back of this card.

Name _____

Address _____ Apt. _____

City _____ State _____ Zip _____

Telephone ( ) _____

Signature _____

Offer limited to one per household and not valid to current subscribers. All orders subject to approval. Terms, offer, & price subject to change. Offer valid only in the U.S.

Thank you!

AN053A

Accepting the four introductory books for FREE (plus $1.99 to offset the cost of shipping & handling) places you under no obligation to buy anything. You may keep the books and return the shipping statement marked "cancelled". If you do not cancel, about a month later we will send 4 additional Arabesque novels, and you will be billed the preferred subscriber's price of just $4.00 per title. That's $16.00 for all 4 books for a savings of 33% off the cover price (Plus $1.99 for shipping and handling). You may cancel at any time, but if you choose to continue, every month we'll send you 4 more books, which you may either purchase at the preferred discount price. . . or return to us and cancel your subscription.

ARABESQUE ROMANCE BOOK CLUB
P.O. Box 5214
Clifton NJ 07015-5214

THE ARABESQUE ROMANCE CLUB: HERE'S HOW IT WORKS

PLACE
STAMP
HERE

you ever think you might have pushed Alex to see other women?"

"Me?" Sutton stabbed her chest with the tip of her finger. "I pushed him to see other women?"

"Yes!" Mother Galloway slapped the desktop. "Alex worried every minute that Greyson would take you away from him."

"What?"

"He saw you at the wedding."

"What are you talking about?"

"At the altar. Alex saw you. I saw you, too." Mother Galloway smiled triumphantly at Sutton's reaction. "I hoped he didn't see it, but he told me later that he did. I don't know what happened between the boys that made Greyson drop out of the wedding. I didn't care and neither did Alex. But right after the preacher asked you if you would take Alex for your husband, you looked back."

Mystified, Sutton didn't respond.

"You looked back. I thought it odd, so I turned to see what had caught your attention. You were looking at Greyson Ballantyne."

Sutton blinked several times. The gesture occurred on a subconscious level. She hadn't meant to look for Greyson. He was missing from the groomsman line. After what had happened in the church office, she had to be certain he was okay. Or could it be that on some plane, she knew her marriage to Alex was a mistake? She forced honesty with herself—she had hoped Greyson would jump out of his seat and stop the wedding.

"If you think I'm going to stand by and let Greyson Ballantyne raise Alex's daughter, you're wrong." Mother Galloway left her chair and went to the wall safe.

Sutton watched in silence while Mother Galloway removed the photos and videotape. She searched her mind for incidents that might have led Alex to believe she was cheating on him with Greyson. It did explain his possessiveness and his not wanting her to work outside the home. But it did not justify the affairs.

"Don't make me use these," Mother Galloway said as she waved the envelope and video.

"Jail!" Mrs. Ballantyne gripped her chest. "Jack, Greyson is in jail!"

Pop Ballantyne stumbled over an area rug as he ran for the phone. "What are you boys doing?" he demanded.

"It's Kirkland, Pop. Greyson came to Ohio to get Sutton and Mrs. Galloway had him arrested." He gave his father all the details.

"Where's Greyson? Put him on this phone."

There was a pause on the line. Pop listened to Greyson and Chevy in the background yelling at Kirkland. Kirkland never could keep his mouth shut, Pop thought. Whenever the boys got into mischief he only needed to look in Kirkland's direction for him to spill all he knew. A brief silence filled the connection before Greyson came to the phone.

"Sir, it's Greyson."

"What's going on there? Kirkland said you were in jail."

"Yes, sir. It wasn't as big a deal as Kirkland's making it sound."

"What do you mean? Jail is jail. Get back here—today." He glanced at his wife.

"Is he okay? Did they hurt him?"

Pop shielded the receiver. "He's fine, Mar-beth. Crazy is all." To Greyson he said, "Bring your brothers home, Greyson. And I want to see you immediately. Don't go home first. What do you mean getting your brothers mixed up in this? You're a lawyer, you know better. And I want you to apologize to your mother."

"Pop, I'm sorry, but I had to do this. Let me speak to Mama."

Mama Ballantyne took the phone. "Honey, are you all right? They didn't mess with you in jail, did they?"

"No, Mama. We'll be home soon. I'm sorry for worrying you. I love you."

Marybeth replaced the receiver.

Jack took his wife in his arms. "It'll be fine, Mar-beth. You can't let those boys worry you none. They all grown now."

"A mother doesn't stop worrying about her kids just because they grow up, Jack."

"I know." He patted her back.

"Do you have any idea what this is all about?" She looked up at her husband with pleading eyes.

"I've got an idea."

"Jack, I've always let you handle these boys, but I won't stand by and watch my son rot in jail." She pulled away from him.

"Mar-beth, what am I s'posed to do? He's out and he's okay. If I had known—"

"The boys are out of control. How come Greyson didn't come to you first? I want my boys back here—tonight. Or else you're driving me to Ohio!"

Sutton climbed the stairs after leaving Mother Galloway in the study waving the pictures around. Her mind was numb. She'd made her stand and been blindsided by her own infidelity. Alex did not deserve to marry someone whose love he questioned. She wondered why he never mentioned his doubts in the five years they were married. It made sense to her now why he refused to divorce her—he feared she would go to Greyson.

Sutton opened her bedroom door to find Sierra face down on her bed, crying.

"Sierra, honey, what's wrong?" Sutton sat next to her and stroked her back. Her daughter appeared small and helpless.

"I want my dad."

The words stunned Sutton. Never had Sierra cried for him. She hardly acknowledged that Alex suddenly disappeared from their lives.

"Why do you want Dad? I'm here."

"Dad can make that man who made you cry go away."

"Greyson?" She pulled Sierra onto her lap. "Greyson didn't make me cry. I was crying because I felt sad."

Sierra's sobs turned to hiccups. "He made you sad."

"No. It's a grown-up thing; don't you worry. Everything is going to work out." She held Sierra to her chest. "I love you."

"I love you, Mommy."

Sutton rocked her daughter until the crying subsided. "What's that in you hand?"

Sierra turned her hand palm-up, displaying a gold locket on a gold chain.

"Where did you get this?" Sutton took the locket and examined it for identifying marks.

"Dad."

"Dad gave you this necklace? When?"

"When I turned four." She held up three fingers.

Sutton smiled and helped her to lift another finger.

"I keep it in herĕ." Sierra crawled across the bed and retrieved her toy doctor's bag.

Sutton opened the locket. She gasped. Inside was a picture of Alex cuddling Sierra soon after she was born. Sutton had forgotten that time. When Sierra first came home from the hospital they were a real family.

"I want it back." Sierra reached out for the locket. "Dad said—"

Sutton dropped the locket inside her daughter's waiting palm. Sierra placed the locket in her doctor's bag and ran off to her room, all the trauma of only a few minutes ago forgotten. Kids were resilient. Sutton needed some of Sierra's tenacity now. She rubbed her eyes before dropping back on her pillow.

Alex had matured into a honey-colored prince. After losing his southern accent, he sounded like an Ivy League professor. His mannerisms reminded her of a cougar—sleek and mysterious, you never knew his next move. He could explain a situation with so many twists and turns that he would have Sutton believing that she was in the wrong. It made playing the fool easy.

"You're my number one." Alex had reminded Sutton after returning from a Christmas party at his boss's home. "You know that don't you?"

Sutton nodded. She faced the mirror while disrobing.

Alex's hands rested on her shoulders. "Why don't I make you a hot bath?"

Sutton watched his reflection for signs of guilt.

"Sierra's something else. I can't believe I helped make her."

She had fully expected him to confess to having fathered another child. He was not in the habit of becoming sentimental about their daughter.

His hands began to massage her neck. "You're doing a good job raising her. I was thinking we should go to Disneyland. You've always wanted to see California."

Sutton turned to him. Hope seeped into her chest. "Can you get time off from work?"

"I will. Do you think she's old enough?"

"Three may be a little young." Sutton turned back to the mirror. The excuses would begin to flow.

"Do you think your parents could keep her while we stroll on the beach and stargaze in LA?"

Sutton spun around. "Do you mean it?"

Alex flashed his smile.

She jumped into his arms. His step faltered.

"Don't act like I never take you anywhere," Alex said, laughing. Gawd, he was handsome.

She draped her arms around his neck. "What did I do to deserve to a vacation?"

"Nothing—yet." His lips went to her collarbone.

Alex removed the last piece of clothing separating them before the phone rang.

"Don't answer." She grabbed his hand.

"I have to. This late it might be an emergency."

He kissed his way to the receiver. He picked it up and immediately slammed it back down. It rang back immediately.

"Who is it?" Sutton asked, knowing the answer he would give her.

"Crank caller." His lips were on her again. This time the eroticism was replaced by shame.

The phone rang again. Sutton grabbed it before Alex could stop her. She watched as he sat up in the bed and scratched his bare chest.

An angry woman proceeded to tell Sutton things about her husband that she should not have known. Explicit details, in case Sutton doubted her knowledge. The sounds, positions, and sexual desires. How often, where, and when. Sutton kept the phone pasted to her ear, unable to end the call.

Stupidly she said, "Leave my husband alone."

The woman disputed her claim that Alex was "hers" with the use of violent curse words. Alex snatched the phone from Sutton's ear. "Don't talk to my wife like that—ever."

How chivalrous. Sutton bolted from the bed. Alex slammed the phone in its cradle and followed her.

"She doesn't mean anything to me." He grabbed her arm and whipped her around to face him. "It happened once. Once."

"Does once make it acceptable, Alex?"

"No. That's not what I meant. I'm weak. I need you to be strong for the both of us."

Sutton pulled out of his grasp. "Please sleep in the guestroom."

"I love you, Sutton."

He gathered his pillow and a blanket and walked to the door. "I'm loving you the best I can."

Twenty

"You stay here, big mouth." Chevy poked Kirkland in the arm.

"Believe me, I wasn't leaving this van."

"Shhh." Greyson quieted his bickering brothers. He had thought of everything. He had exchanged the Lincoln for a van large enough to carry five. He had drawn a layout of Mrs. Galloway's home as best as he could remember it. He had laid out his plan until Chevy and Kirkland knew it as well as he did.

"Are you sure about this?" Chevy asked outside the van. They were dressed in matching black jogging suits.

Greyson tried to assure him that nothing detrimental would occur. "I'm going to talk to her. If she wants to go, then I'm taking her with me."

Chevy nodded. "Then why am I dressed like a cat burglar?"

"Because I need time to talk to Sutton without Mrs. Galloway around. I don't know much about Eddie, but all you have to do is look threatening and he'll run away. Although he did take a swing at me. Ready?"

"You didn't tell me he tried to hit you."

"You can take him, Chevy. Now c'mon. Are you ready?"

Chevy studied the determination on his big brother's face. Greyson would never let him back out. Besides, he'd do anything to help Sutton. "Ready."

Greyson pulled the black baseball cap down securely on

his head. He crouched low and ran to the back of the house. Chevy followed closely behind.

Greyson's adrenaline pumped. He hadn't done anything this daring since stealing penny candy from the Five and Dime store when they were kids. They quietly approached the back porch. Chevy stooped down and locked his fingers. Greyson placed his foot in Chevy's hand, and with a boost, pulled himself up on the flat overhang of the back door. Once on top, he could see four widows. Lights shone behind two. They were the only two he could reach from this position. He held out a hand and helped Chevy climb up.

"We can still back out," Chevy whispered.

Greyson shook his head. He pulled a fallen branch from the gutter and tapped the window. He tapped again and the curtain moved. He tapped again. His heart raced. If Mrs. Galloway lifted the window, he was on his way back to jail. Knowing her yearning for only the best, he supposed her bedroom would be in the front of the house. He prayed he gambled correctly. He shuddered at the tongue-lashing Pop would give him for dragging Chevy to jail with him.

The window caught several times before it opened fully. Sutton stuck her head out. "Greyson? Is that you?"

Greyson released his breath. "It's me." He sidestepped across the roof and swung his leg inside the window. Sutton's hands held his waist until he was safely inside.

"What are you doing here? Mother Galloway will have you arrested—"

"Shhh." Greyson leaned out the window and helped Chevy inside.

"Chevy? You're here, too?"

"Greyson said you needed rescuing." He turned away while they embraced. "Where's Sierra?"

"Next door. To the left, but—"

Chevy took off.

Greyson pulled Sutton into his arms. "I came for my family and I'm not leaving without you."

"Greyson, I tried to explain—"

He captured her lips. He'd longed for this time since boarding the plane to California to attend Ryan's wedding. He kissed her until she melted in his arms. Her tongue followed his. He relished her embrace around his waist.

"Do you want to go home with me? I don't care what Mrs. Galloway has told you. We can fight her—together. You don't have to choose between Sierra and me. You can have us both."

Sutton pulled away and crossed the room. He watched the bounce of her round backside in her jeans. "Mother Galloway has pictures of us together in your hotel suite. She has a video. She says she'll use them to win custody of Sierra unless I stay away from you."

"That's crazy."

"Alex told her he believed we were having an affair and she's determined to keep us apart in honor of his memory. She doesn't want you to raise Alex's child. She's obsessed."

"Not as obsessed as I am to have you. I can't go into detail now, but I can help you fight her."

"Not with those pictures. What will our parents think when they see them?"

Their parents would be the target of rumors for months— years—if the pictures were ever made public. Greyson's mind raced for a solution. "Do you know where the pictures are?"

"She keeps them in a safe in her den."

"Show me."

"If she catches us—"

Chevy entered the room with a sleeping Sierra cuddled in his arms. He had taken the time to wrap her in a blanket and carried her bag of toys in one hand. A gym bag stuffed with clothing hung over his other arm. "What are we doing?"

Greyson held Sutton by her arms. "Try not to worry about the pictures or losing Sierra. I'm not going to let that happen. Do you want to leave with me? Do you want to be with me?"

"I promised, didn't I?"

Greyson turned to Chevy. "Follow us down the stairs and get Sierra to the van. And make sure she's warm. We'll be right out." He turned to Sutton. "Get your shoes."

He grabbed a bag off the shelf of her closet and plucked clothing off the hangers. Sutton joined him with an armload of clothing from the dresser drawers.

"Ready?" Greyson asked Chevy; he nodded. He turned to Sutton. "Ready?"

Sutton nodded, "Ready."

"Don't let go of my hand. No matter what."

Sutton placed her hand inside of his.

"Show me where she keeps the pictures."

Keeping near the wall, Sutton led Greyson by the hand down the stairs. The house was dark except for the light in the foyer. Mother Galloway used that light during the night. She worried about tumbling down the stairs during her nightly trip for a drink of water. Chevy broke their human chain and quietly slipped out the front door. Sutton tugged Greyson's hand, leading him to the study. They crossed the room in the dark and stood in front of the picture. To Sutton, the picture represented an oak tree too tall to be chopped down. Greyson dropped her bag to the floor and removed the painting with ease. He never released her hand.

"Now what?" Sutton asked him once the in-wall safe was revealed.

"Now I call the police." Mrs. Galloway clicked on the overhead light.

Sutton and Greyson swirled around simultaneously. She gripped his hand at seeing Mrs. Galloway's ghastly appearance. Evil intentions distorted her usually over-made-up face. Pink hair rollers were tied inside of a pink sheer scarf. Her misshapen bare feet gripped the hardwood floor. Sutton moved to stand partially obstructed by Greyson. He stepped over, showing he would protect her.

"I knew you'd come back. Do you think I'm too feeble to hear people moving around in my own house?" Mrs. Galloway produced a cordless phone from the pocket of her robe.

Greyson tried to reason. "Give me the pictures. I'll take Sutton and Sierra and be gone."

"Ha! You must be joking. The restraining order will do the trick. This time your connections with the court won't persuade me to drop the charges."

"Why are you trying to ruin Sutton? Your granddaughter?"

Her head whipped up. "I'm preserving the memory of my son. Sutton and I have an agreement. If she reneges, I expose the vulgar activities she engaged in with you—four months after her husband's death. I'd like to see a judge award her custody after watching that video."

"You have a serious problem," Greyson said through clenched teeth. If she watched the video, how could she categorize their lovemaking as vulgar?

Sutton squeezed his hand. Her chest heaved against his back.

Knowing she was frightened spurred his anger. "No judge will award custody based solely on your interpretation of a video. That's a lame attempt at keeping Sutton under your thumb."

"Sutton and Sierra belong here. This is the way Alex would have wanted it."

"Alex is dead and Sutton needs to start living. She's played her role wonderfully, but now Alex is dead. Realize that and get over it. With or without the pictures and video, Sutton leaves tonight. If you have a shred of decency in your heart, you'll let her destroy what you have in that safe." He moved to tower over Mrs. Galloway, dragging Sutton along by the grip on her hand. "If not, you'll regret the moment you decided to tangle with me."

"Are you threatening me?" Galloway frantically punched the phone keypad.

Greyson took the phone out of her hands and threw it

across the room, smashing it on the wall. "I'm warning you. Don't do anything to hurt Sutton or Sierra, or you'll have to deal with me. That's a promise."

Sutton tugged at his arm. "Greyson, let's go."

Greyson intimidated Mrs. Galloway with his searing glare before pulling Sutton around in front of him. "Let's go."

Twenty-one

Sutton tucked Sierra in before climbing into the double bed next to her. Greyson slept in the hotel room to her right; the warmth of his presence permeated the walls. She smiled in the darkness. He had actually climbed up on the roof, through the window, and rescued her. Every woman should have the opportunity to experience being saved by her prince.

Sutton worried that Mother Galloway would call the police and have Greyson arrested before they drove back to West Virginia in the morning. She held her breath during her shower, waiting for the ominous knock at the door. It never came. What could Mother Galloway have him arrested for? Sutton would deny that Greyson and Chevy crawled through her bedroom window; she'd say she let them into the house. No case could made for a kidnapping. As she listened to Greyson protecting her honor to Mother Galloway, she recognized she had been waiting a lifetime for him to stand up and claim her as his.

A soft tapping at the door pulled Sutton out of bed. Greyson's large frame blocked the peephole. He stepped inside, hauling a sleepy Chevy behind him.

Greyson whispered so not to wake Sierra. "Want to come out and play?"

Sutton giggled. "Now?" She looked over her shoulder at Sierra's sleeping body.

"Yes. Now. Chevy will watch Sierra. Right, Uncle Chevy?"

Greyson grabbed the shoulder of Chevy's pajamas and shook him.

"Right, whatever." Chevy grumbled, half-awake. He broke away from Greyson's grasp and headed for Sutton's bed. He climbed in and turned his back to them.

Greyson handed Sutton a bag from behind his back. "Get dressed. I'll meet you in the hall."

Sutton dressed and checked on Sierra and then Chevy, covering them both with an extra blanket from the closet before she backed out into the hallway. She turned to a smiling Greyson holding a single rose between his teeth. He had shaved away the stubble beginning to form on his chin, revealing every inch of his angled jaw and sharp, proud cheekbones. Tall, dark, with squared shoulders, he resembled the model in the old Marlboro Man cigarette ads. His high-fashion New York runway appearance severely contrasted with the sweet, southern twang that flowed from his full lips and pearly white teeth.

The black tux Greyson wore went perfectly with the sheer black dress he had chosen for her. Sutton thought her breasts too full to ever chance a gown with only the support of spaghetti straps, but she knew men had their own rationale for choosing clothing for the woman in their lives. The shoes he selected were also stereotypical: tall, skinny, impractical heels with straps that inched up her ankle. Greyson stepped to her, triggering her nervous gesture of sweeping her hand across her cherry-colored hair. Without hair accessories, she'd been forced to brush her hair straight back and flip the ends with a hairbrush. She surely couldn't borrow any makeup from Chevy, so she appeared before Greyson completely natural.

Greyson placed his hand above her head on the wall and leaned in to her for the presentation of the rose.

"Where did you get a rose at this time of night?" Sutton inquired. For that matter, where did he find a store open that could supply him with formal wear?

"I never cease to amaze you, do I?" The stress plaguing him earlier had disappeared.

"No, you don't."

"Wait until later." He shuffled his eyebrows upward seductively.

"You're mighty frisky tonight, Mr. Ballantyne." Sutton twirled the rose between her fingers.

"Uh-huh. You're looking very radiant this evening, Ms. Hill."

"That was a stupid thing you did tonight." Sutton swiped his chest with the rose. "Mother Galloway could have had you arrested again."

"Wasn't worried 'bout no Mrs. Galloway." He thickened his down-home accent. "I was worried 'bout getting my baby back."

Sutton felt a rush of blood color her face. She dipped her head only to be halted by Greyson's lips. After the kiss, he took the rose from her hands, broke the stem, and placed the flower behind her left ear. Greyson asked, "Are you ready to begin our second official date?"

Left dizzy by the fire of his kiss, Sutton nodded in reply. Greyson took her hand and led her to the elevator.

"Good job you did back there," he complimented as they stepped on the elevator together. "You never let go of my hand once. Even in the van on the drive over to the hotel."

"I don't know how I'll repay you for everything, but I will."

"Yes, you will. But not with money."

Sutton watched his profile. His eyes watched the numbers above them. The doors opened and he stepped aside, clearing her path to exit. He quickly fell into step beside her. He showed her across the lobby to a club that bristled with people and boomed with music. The twenty-something crowd curiously eyed them as Greyson went forward to pay the admission price. Rap music pumped as Greyson led her inside. He leaned down next to her ear, "Can you handle this crowd?"

Mischievously, she said, "I can handle it."

Sutton watched the young people around her giving them

the eye. Most appeared baffled by their formal dress. The crowd wore oversized jeans with jerseys and name-brand sneakers. The women displayed their bodies with cut-off shirts and short skirts. She noticed more than one woman give Greyson her full attention when they passed by. The men nodded their approval to him.

A new version of the hustle brought the profiling crowd to its feet. "Wanna try?" Sutton asked. Greyson shrugged and led her to a safe place in the back of the dance floor. By the middle of the song, they could keep up with the crowd. Toward the end of the song, sweat saturated Greyson's forehead as Sutton copied the women's seductive strutting and dipping. The record segued into a faster tempo. Greyson secured Sutton at the waist and led her to a seat at the bar.

He leaned across the bar, commanding the bartender's attention, and ordered their drinks. Sutton used the napkin underneath her glass to wipe Greyson's forehead. "Couldn't handle the flow, old man?"

"I can handle the flow fine. What I couldn't handle was you shaking your rump all in front of me when you know I haven't had any since—"

"Stop," Sutton demanded when the young man next to him started bouncing with laughter.

"You know what I mean." Greyson slapped palms with the man.

Embarrassment made Sutton hide behind her glass of white wine.

"What is that you're drinking?" Sutton watched Greyson take a gulp of his orange drink.

"Fuzzy navel." He held up the glass in question. Sutton parted her lips and he gave her a sample.

"It's good."

Greyson signaled the bartender and ordered another for Sutton. He stood possessively over her while they sipped their drinks. A young man asked her to dance and Greyson briskly turned him away.

"Can you believe he approached you while I'm standing right here?"

She smiled at his jealousy. "How are you able to afford the rental van, airplane tickets, three hotel rooms, and bail when you haven't worked in months?"

Greyson considered his deceit. He'd tell her everything. First he had to prove with his loving actions that he did not have the heart of a rich playboy. Thanks to Alex, Sutton equated successful black men with sleazy women haters.

"The hotel rooms were free. Remember, I told you about my client. I've been picking up consulting work here and there. I saved while at the law firm. Don't worry about me."

"Like I said before, I'll reimburse you for this as soon as I can." Embarrassment flashed across her face. "My finances are shaky right now . . ."

"I told you not to worry about it. I would never accept money from you."

They watched a couple clear the floor with their flourishing ballroom dance moves.

"What do you think will happen when we get back home?" Sutton asked.

"I don't know. I hope Mrs. Galloway gets over Alex's death and leaves you and Sierra alone."

"This is all my fault. Five years ago if I had stopped the wedding, none of this would be happening."

"I wish I would have done things differently, too. I could have stopped the wedding. Alex could have. We all could have done things differently, but that's what life is about. Making mistakes and being mature enough to correct them."

Greyson placed his glass on the bar, giving her his undivided attention before continuing. "I'm ashamed to tell you how many times I played out different scenarios to your wedding. The only way I've been able to live with myself is to say that all the experiences after that day brought me here today. We've both changed so much since we were kids, but one thing has remained constant—we've been good friends.

That has to mean something. The boundaries of our relationship keep changing, but our friendship is constant."

Sutton held her glass up for a toast. "To friendship."

"And more."

Greyson had to cut Sutton off after she completed her fuzzy navel because her words began to slur.

"I like this song." Sutton slid off the barstool. Let's dance."

"Dance?" Greyson steadied her. "Can you walk?"

"C'mon." Sutton parted the crowd and stopped at its core, her arms wide open to receive him. Greyson found his place, letting her hug him around his waist while he held her head next to his heart. He moved in small, rocking circles to the ballad. He liked the old Prince tune, "Diamonds and Pearls." It spoke to his heart with pleading words from a man to a woman. The man in the song would give his woman anything to make her happy and start a family. Greyson dipped to place his lips next to her ear, "How many dates should we have before I officially propose to you?"

The alcohol made Sutton giggle. "You did that on our first date, remember?" She giggled again.

Greyson downplayed the seriousness of his question by laughing along. "I guess I did."

"Do you know what I'd like?"

"What?" The hair on his neck peaked.

"I'd like another one of those fuzzy things."

"No more for you."

She snuggled up to him. "One more?"

"No. Believe me, one was enough for you."

"Please?" Her bottom lip dropped in a sexy pout. "C'mon. You know you want to give it to me."

"Now I know you've had enough."

Sutton relented and tightened her hold on his waist. He rested his chin atop her head inhaling the fragrance of the rose. A simple flower signified grand pleasure for them. The DJ spun two more slow tunes. Greyson pulled her closer, rubbing small circles into the small of her back. He couldn't count how many times over the years he'd imagined having this opportunity with Sutton. There were moments when he sat with his brothers plotting the development of the paper mill that he missed Hunter, Roe & Volney, but the moments were no more than fleeting. Sutton and Hannaford Valley were his past and his future. To cure his withdrawal from practicing law, he had let one of the partners talk him into reviewing files via computer and acting as consultant on difficult cases. With Sutton by his side he could have it all: family, his law practice, the paper mill, and the satisfaction of reviving the town.

Greyson measured Sutton's fragile frame beneath his fingertips. She felt small and delicate next to his hard body. To unleash all of his love on her at once would break her. He buried his nose in her hair and she giggled in response. He liked her carefree, teasing him with the sway of her hips. Her step stilled when he responded to the motion. She looked up at him, the giggles gone. He closed his eyes and let the heat of her eyes burn into him.

Sutton's hands slipped down his back and held his haunches.

"Let's go back to my room."

Twenty-two

Greyson watched as Sutton innocently released the straps of her shoes and looped them around her finger. She looked up from her corner of the elevator and smiled at the concentrated lust reflected in his eyes. She relaxed against the wall, watching the numbers overhead. The other couple in the elevator remained oblivious to the sexual tension bouncing between them.

All of his days, Greyson wanted this. When the doors closed behind the couple, leaving them alone on the elevator, he rushed to her corner. He wrapped his hands around the sheer black fabric of the dress and lifted her at the waist. Her legs clasped his waist. He pressed her into the wall. Their lips met as Sutton locked her arms around his neck. He pinned her to the wall, gyrating his hips, promising what was to come.

The doors parted and Greyson carried her to his room. Releasing her behind with one hand, he searched his pockets for the room key.

"Hi," Sutton giggled. Greyson glanced over his shoulder and was met with the disapproving glare of an elderly puritanical-looking couple. They hurried in the opposite direction, shaking their heads in disgust. "Good night," Sutton called after them.

Greyson used his foot to close the door behind them. Sutton tore wildly at his tux. His lips decorated her face and neck while she helped him out of his jacket.

"Don't drop me," Sutton whispered in his ear as he

moved to the bed. Her fingers deftly opened the buttons of his starched white shirt. He released his hold on her one hand at a time while she worked his arms out of his shirt. She dropped her head and ravished his chest. Never having any sensitivity in his nipples in the past, the shockwaves evoked by her nibbling made him drop to the bed.

In a flurry of motion, Greyson worked Sutton's dress over her head. She pushed his upper body down against the bed while straddling him. He reached between them to open his pants. Her breasts stroked his chest while she licked the corners of his mouth. He opened to receive her flickering tongue. His hands moved from the indentation of her waist to the waistband of her panties.

Greyson placed his hands inside to measure her stage of readiness. "Hot and moist."

He helped her shimmy out of her last article of clothing. She used her body to cover him in long, torturous strokes of burning flesh. "This is what I've wanted," he said while flipping her over onto her back and kicking off his pants. He slipped his underwear over his erection and pressed his naked body to hers. "All my life."

Greyson wrapped his arms around her middle and dragged her to the top of the bed.

"Do you have any condoms?" Sutton had the presence of mind to ask.

Greyson questioned the reason behind the need, but did not consider it the best time for discussion. He throbbed with anticipation when his manhood grazed her wet opening. He found his pants and searched the pockets for his wallet. He removed a light blue square and rushed back to Sutton.

"Give it to me."

He handed her the package as he climbed underneath the sheets with her. She examined it carefully. He scooped her up in his arms and situated her beneath him.

"I always wanted to put one of these on with my mouth like they do in the dirty movies."

Greyson's exploring lips came to an abrupt halt. "I think you've had too much to drink." He took the condom from her.

"Why do you say that?"

"You're awful feisty tonight." He settled between her legs, his erection pressing against her curly mound of hair.

Sutton took the condom back. "You encouraged my participation the last time."

"Stop talking and start participating now." He ran his tongue over her collarbone, sending a shiver across the planes of her body. He lifted her breast to his lips and began to suckle. He heard the wrapper rip near his ear. She pushed his chest as a signal for him to shift onto his back. He eagerly obliged.

Sutton kissed her way from his forehead to his navel. She sat between his legs examining him.

Greyson placed his hands behind his head and closed his eyes. He reveled in her touch. She lifted his twin pouches in her hand with the gentleness of holding breakable jewels. He moaned his encouragement for her to explore further. Her fingers formed a ring around his erection and moved slowly down the shaft. Then she moved upward, stopping at the tip. Her head came to rest on his thigh.

The sensation of quick, hot spurts of air made Greyson's body tremble. Sutton raked her fingers down the opposite thigh and his manhood convulsed. He squirmed, tightening his fingers behind his head. He wanted to allow her this time to acquaint herself with his body, but he felt a hot drop of liquid warming the tip of his erection.

Sutton's fingers moved through a tangle of hair near the base of his manhood. His thigh cooled instantly when her head bobbed up. With concentrated care, Sutton unrolled the condom onto him. She straddled his middle. She rested one hand near his head to maintain her balance. The other she used to glide his full length inside of her slippery entrance. Greyson guided her hips, allowing her to control the pace of his penetration.

Sutton exhaled when he passed the ring, confirming his

total saturation. He held her head and guided her face to his. He watched her in the shadow of the darkened room. Unbridled passion made her squeeze her eyes together. She panted and paused to wet her lips with her tongue. Her hips found a steady rhythm. Her lips formed inaudible words. Her eyebrows furrowed together as the speed of her hips increased. She tried to jerk her head backwards, but he held her firmly, wanting to see every emotion that crossed her face as she came.

A moan from deep inside Sutton filled the room. Her pelvis ground into him. The sound of her calling for him to give her pleasure triggered a wild need to fulfill the request.

Greyson rolled her over onto her back without disrupting their union. He encouraged her to wrap her legs around his hips while he mixed deep penetration with a rocking motion against her mound that sent her into jerky convulsions.

"I love you," Greyson whispered in Sutton's ear as she pressed upward, engulfing his erection in her depths. "I love you, Sutton."

Greyson held his stance while Sutton claimed every second, every drop of pleasure he'd given her. He nuzzled her neck. His tongue traced her earlobe. He cupped her breasts, grazing a thumb against the nub that reawakened the convulsions of her body.

Sutton's legs loosened on his back. He drew her knees up and began with a gentle pumping. He flexed his behind, allowing his maximum depth into her contracting walls of pleasure. The delicate quivers pulled him. Sutton's fingernails traced circles across his back.

"I love you, Greyson," Sutton whispered near his ear.

The experience of being inside of her while she spoke those words pulled him into the world of the surreal. His mind reeled. His body demanded more. Sutton put her hands against the headboard to protect her head. Greyson lifted his body and with one last lunge, he exploded. He rolled onto his back, pulling Sutton to cover his chest. She wiped the sweat from his brow as he struggled to breathe normally.

* * *

The aroma of flowers stirred Greyson from his sleep. Sutton slept with her back pushed against him. Sometime after their lovemaking, she had slipped into his undershirt. Her hair was neatly brushed to the back. On the pillow between them lay the rose he had presented to her earlier. He placed it on the bedside table on his way to the bathroom.

He flushed the condom, the question of why Sutton felt its use necessary still lingering with him. He understood the necessity the first time they'd made love; he hadn't made his intentions clear. He wondered if she understood that he wanted a permanent, monogamous relationship with her.

It could be an issue of pregnancy. Greyson wet a washcloth under hot water. As he cleaned his body, he smiled, picturing a sleeping Sierra in Chevy's arms earlier that night. Getting Sutton pregnant would be a priority soon after they were married. He was anxious to expand their family.

Greyson moved through the darkness, sorting his clothes until he found his underwear. He slipped them on over his growing erection and joined Sutton in bed. He covered them both with the sheet and then the blankets. He leaned over to kiss her cheek. His fingers combed her thick reddish-brown hair. "I love you."

Sutton smiled. "I know."

"Do you know that my life won't begin until we're married?"

"Really?" She turned to him. "My life began when you came back for me tonight."

Greyson rested his head next to hers on the pillow, too overcome with emotion to speak.

"That was a crazy thing you did—breaking into Mother Galloway's house. You could have been arrested again. You could have fallen off the roof."

"It didn't matter."

"You're an attorney. You should know better."

"I'm a man first and I know that if you aren't with me, nothing matters."

"I feel safe when I'm with you."

"You should. That's my responsibility."

"Greyson, why do you love me so deeply?"

He marveled at the question. He shrugged. "I always have."

"Why?"

"Do you need to hear it put into words?"

"Yes, I do."

"It would sound trivial to put a lifetime of emotion into a sentence."

"I need to hear it."

Greyson looked into her pleading eyes. "You are beautiful, caring, and strong. You are as refined as a politician's wife but as compassionate as a country girl. You're passionate but demure. I see the love you have for Sierra and want some of it for myself. You have all the qualities that make a perfect woman in one package. How could I not love you?"

Twenty-three

"Do you have an extra toothbrush?" Sutton called over the sound of water beating the tiles of the shower.

Greyson dipped his head under the water. "In my bag." After a minute, the temperature cooled as Sutton pulled from the water source. Another minute passed before Greyson said, "Sutton, come here."

The curtain parted and she greeted him with a sunny smile. "What do you want?"

"I want you to join me."

Her eyes warmed him from head to toe. "Do you think there's enough room for me?" Her gaze landed on his rising manhood.

"Why don't they make these showers bigger? It might be a tight fit, but the three of us will be just fine." He kissed her while pulling his undershirt over her head. His arms went to her waist and he lifted her over the rim of the tub.

Sutton eased into the heat of the water. She rolled her head, working out the early-morning kinks. Greyson poured liquid soap on a washcloth and lathered Sutton's back. Peach fragrance permeated the steamy bathroom.

"That feels good." She arched her back, causing her behind to tease him. "What happens now?"

"Now we drive back to West Virginia and wait. Hopefully, Mrs. Galloway will realize how childish she's being and come to her senses."

Sutton turned to him, her face displaying all of her distress. "What if she makes good on her threat?"

"Sutton, don't worry about that." He turned her to face the water. His hands crossed her shoulders and lathered her front. She tried to remove the cloth from his hands when he reached her intimate core but he did not allow it.

Greyson stepped from the shower to retrieve her towel as she rinsed the soap away. He secured a towel around his middle and held one open for her to step into.

"I trust you, Greyson, but I need to know why you're so certain you can handle Mother Galloway if she tries to take my little girl away."

"Listen," he closed her in the cocoon of the towel, "I'll take care of it. I know some of the best custody attorneys practicing law. Believe me, I have resources that will keep Mrs. Galloway in her place."

"The pictures were pretty bad."

"How bad?"

"Beautiful to me because I know what I was feeling at the time. Pornography to anyone else."

"I'll take care of it. No one will see those pictures."

"All right." Sutton's voice reflected skepticism.

"Hey"—he lifted her chin—"I won't let you down. I'll fight for Sierra as if she were mine. I promise. Okay?"

She collapsed against his chest. "Thank you."

"I promise," Greyson whispered against the crimson curls of her hair.

Chevy and Kirkland secured the last of their things in the back of the van as Sutton and Sierra exited the hotel. Greyson spotted them approaching from inside the van. Sutton watched his face light up as he hurried across the parking lot to meet them.

Sutton squinted up into the sun. "Greyson, this is my little girl, Sierra." She crouched next to Sierra. "Say hello to Greyson."

Greyson knelt in front of her. "Hi, Sierra. I'm very happy to finally meet you." He extended an open hand to her. Sierra ducked behind her mother.

Sutton read the disappointment marring his face. "She's shy with strangers."

"Uncle Chevy!" Sierra darted around Sutton's legs and raced over to the van. They watched as Chevy scooped her up in his arms and carried her around to the sliding door of the van.

Sutton placed a comforting hand on Greyson's arm. "She'll come around."

"Why is she so attached to Chevy?" He took Sutton's hand and they walked to the van.

"Kids are funny. Don't let it upset you. Remember, it took awhile before her mother understood how wonderful you are, too."

Greyson's head dipped. If Sierra didn't like him, there would be no relationship with Sutton. He found the little girl adorable, a snapshot of her mother when she was younger, and wanted to be close to her. Never did he want her to consider him her stepfather. In Sierra's eyes, she should be his daughter, his eldest child. He opened the door and helped Sutton inside the van. He would trust Sutton; she knew her daughter better than anyone. Sierra would care for him as much as she cared for Chevy. He climbed into the driver's seat and started the first leg of the trip.

Three hours into the drive, Greyson had to separate his bickering brothers by assigning Kirkland driving duty. Sierra giggled as the two acted no older than first graders. "Mommy, they're funny." She laughed, enjoying their antics. Sutton replied, "Yeah, they are." Greyson threw his brothers an angry look off the reflection of the rearview mirror.

Sierra sat between Sutton and Greyson, leaning on her mother while making broad strokes in a coloring book. "Mommy, I'm hungry."

"Me, too." Chevy tossed in from the front seat.

"You're always hungry," Kirkland grumbled.

Sierra giggled.

Greyson shook his head. "They don't understand that it's pitiful they're on the same level as a four-year-old."

Sutton smiled, staying out of the brothers' quarrel.

"How about some McDonald's?" Greyson asked Sierra.

"McDonald's?" Sierra beamed. He'd found her hidden instant friendship button. Until that point she'd spent the drive ignoring him. "Can we, Mommy?"

Sutton deferred to Greyson. He leaned forward. "Kirkland, find a McDonald's."

Sierra sat up straight in her seat now that Greyson no longer formed a threat.

Sutton shrugged. "Anyone who eats McDonald's can't be all bad."

"Can I help with that?" Greyson pointed to the picture Sierra had been coloring most of the trip.

Sierra fished for a crayon and held it up to him. "It's red."

Greyson smiled at her acceptance of his offer. "It sure is. Just like your hair."

"Color her hair red." Sierra pointed out a little girl riding a bike in the picture before handing Greyson her book.

A McDonald's Happy Meal with super-sized fries made Greyson a hero in Sierra's eyes. She abandoned her mother's side of the booth to sit between Chevy and Greyson. Sutton watched the patience Greyson had with Sierra as he helped her ready her food, showed her the use of placing a napkin in her lap, and slathered her fries in ketchup. He accepted her invitation to share her fries instead of eating his own. The entire meal, he conducted himself as if he were alone with Sierra, her sole caregiver. He engrossed her in conversation, finding out her likes and dislikes and agreeing with most of them.

Chevy and Kirkland headed to the van, leaving them in the booth. Greyson smiled up at Sutton as Sierra placed the remains of her lunch on a tray.

"Greyson"—Sierra's doll eyes beamed, bringing him into her fold—"can I have a french fry for the road?"

"For the road?" he laughed. "I think Uncle Chevy is teaching her bad habits already." He rested his hand on her red braids. "Sure, baby, you can have one for the road."

Twenty-four

The swelling in his pants reminded Eddie how long it had been since he'd satisfied his sexual urges. He ran a finger across the glossy image. The painful expression on Sutton's face matched that of the man kneeling behind her.

He focused on the image of his brother's lifelong rival. Somehow he could not muster as much contempt for Greyson as his late brother or mother harbored. Other than Greyson being in love with Sutton, he really had not done anything wrong to the Galloway family. Stealing Sutton and Sierra during the night seemed a bit cowardly to Eddie, but nothing to ruin Greyson over.

Eddie held more contempt for Alex, the precious child who reaped all the rewards of being the only Galloway son. Eddie, on the other hand, had been forced to claim that he had been abandoned. He did not have the luxury of a heritage.

Mother Galloway—Mother—began spending more time with her "nephew" after Alex's death, but it wasn't enough. She still had not acknowledged his existence to her high-society friends in Ohio or the husband she kept on the Galloway place in Hannaford Valley. Only recently had she allowed Eddie to visit her in Ohio. Eddie felt sure that if it hadn't been for her needing help keeping an eye on Sutton and Sierra, she would not have agreed to his visit.

Eddie fingered the videotape. He wondered if he had enough time to run it before Mother stumbled down the stairs complaining of a sherry hangover. Stirrings at the top of the stairs made him abandon the idea. He hurried to replace the photos in their envelope before locking them away in the safe.

"Good morning, Mother," Eddie greeted her at the bottom of the stairs and helped her into the kitchen. "I made coffee."

"I'd prefer tea." She groaned from old-age stiffness as she slid into a chair at the kitchen table.

She would, Eddie grumbled silently as he searched the cabinet for the tea bags.

"This hangover is murder." She rubbed her temples. Several pink rollers moved, threatening to fall onto the table.

Eddie put the teakettle on to boil. "Mother," he broached as he took a seat next to her, "I'd like to talk to you."

"Is it about the investments, because I don't want to go into that right now." She massaged her eyebrows. "The only thing we have to live off of is the money your brother left us. Besides the property in Hannaford Valley, your stepfather has very little left. We have to be prudent with every cent we invest."

Eddied cringed. Her husband was not his stepfather. And he was doing the best he could with the meager amount of money she entrusted him to invest. He exhaled his frustration before continuing. "Actually, it's about Sutton. Have you heard from her? Will she be coming back?"

Mother Galloway peered at him. After a long pause where Eddie was certain she was trying to read the emotion behind his inquiry, she spoke in a gentle tone. "I doubt that she will return."

He dropped his head. He recovered and went to the stove to check the kettle.

"I have half a mind to leave her to rot in Hannaford Valley. What charm that place holds for those able to get out of it is beyond me."

Eddie stirred the tea vigorously, the spoon clanking against the sides of the cup.

"But you were fond of her, weren't you?"

He returned to the table with her cup. "I enjoyed spending time with her. I think I had a good shot at winning her over if Greyson hadn't interfered."

"You may be right." Mother patted his hand before sipping from her cup.

He remembered Sutton's face in the photos. "If there were a way to get her back . . ."

His mother continually tried to pay back a debt that was twenty-eight years in the making. He played on this emotion to steer her in the direction he wanted her to go.

Mother stared at him lovingly across the table. "There may be a way. If Sierra were here, Sutton would surely follow."

"But how will you get Sierra back here?"

"I mean to make good on my threat. If Sutton doesn't bring my grandchild back, I'll take her to court and expose her true nature. Sutton will return with Sierra, and you can have your shot at her."

"I knew I could count on you." Eddie threw his arms around her and rested his head on her shoulder.

Mother Galloway patted his back. "Anything to keep my Alex happy."

He broke the embrace and stormed out of the kitchen.

Twenty-five

Greyson dropped Kirkland off at his upscale apartment in the capital before heading to Hannaford Valley and dropping off Chevy at his cabin.

Greyson peeked in the rearview mirror at Sierra's sleeping form. Sutton had covered her with his jacket and had rested her hand on her daughter's hip. Her attention was focused on the pitch-black darkness engulfing a farmer's field.

"It's late. Should I take you to my place for the night?" Greyson asked.

"No." Sutton watched him in the rearview mirror. "My parents will be worried."

Greyson nodded. "I guess you're right." He wanted to take them to his house and tuck them in for the night. They could deal with both sets of parents in the morning. He felt that once he took her to her parents' home, things would change between them.

"I should warn you that I had words with your father."

"Great." Dread filled her voice.

"We argued about him keeping you away from me. I'm sorry."

Sutton leaned forward and touched his shoulder. "I'm not upset with you."

They traveled several more miles, past wheat and cornfields before Sutton spoke. "Do you think Maddie will give me my job back?"

"I'm sure Maddie will hire you again when you explain things."

Sutton climbed into the front passenger's seat.

He glanced over at her. "Is there anything I can say to make you stay with me tonight?"

"Believe me, I want to, but I know my father. He'll never go for me spending the night with you—all things considered."

Greyson knew what she meant. His parents held the same values. They would never approve of Sutton and her daughter—a recently widowed woman and her child—spending the night with a bachelor. The town would erupt in gossip. Both sets of parents would be chastised for their failure to instill morals in their children. As badly as he wanted to hold Sutton through the night, he would have to wait until a more appropriate time.

The light in the front of the house came on when Greyson pulled into the Hill driveway. By the time he gathered Sierra in his arms, Mr. Hill was standing in his pajamas on the front porch. Sutton placed a hand on Greyson's arm as they climbed the stairs of the porch. Mrs. Hill directed him inside and showed him where to lay Sierra down for the night. Sutton stayed behind to speak with her father. When Greyson returned, he expected Mr. Hill to lecture him and forbid him to see Sutton again. Instead, he helped Greyson carry in their belongings.

Greyson met Sutton in the parlor once he had carried her bags to the bedroom she shared with Sierra.

"Greyson, I can't thank you enough for everything you did for Sierra and me."

Greyson's eyes shifted to Mr. Hill, who was standing near the front door, waiting for them to conclude their business. "Remember your promise."

Sutton's eyes sparkled. "I will."

"Call me in the morning?"

She nodded, her own eyes shifting in her father's direction. Greyson left her with a kiss on the cheek.

"Wait just a minute, Greyson." Mr. Hill stepped out on the porch, closing the door behind him.

"Yes, sir?" Greyson stopped on the top stair and turned to face him. He could see Sutton watching them through a crack in the curtain.

Mr. Hill tugged the edges of his robe together. "I know I've been hard on you through the years, but I was doing what was best for my daughter."

"I'm sure—"

Mr. Hill held up his hand. "I want to say that I'm grateful for what you did—bringing my daughter and granddaughter home." He paused. "Thank you."

"Yes, sir."

"Sutton's mother and I would like to have you over for dinner after church on Sunday."

"Mama? Pop?" Greyson used his key to enter his parents' home. He dropped his bag in the foyer and followed television noises into the den. His parents turned together from their place on the sofa.

His mother jumped up and ran to him. "Greyson." She patted his body for injuries. "Are you all right? What did they do to my baby?"

"There's nothing wrong with me, Mama." He hugged her aging body, relishing in the softness of her plump middle. "I'm sorry I worried you."

Pop turned off the television and joined them. "Where are Chevy and Kirkland?"

"I took them home, Pop."

"You want something to eat?" his mother asked. "You look skinny."

"Mar-beth, the boy's only been gone a coupla days."

"I know Jack, but he still looks skinny."

"Mama, I ate on the road. I'm really tired from the drive. Do you mind if I stay here tonight?"

"Of course not. I'll go make your bed."

"Thanks, Mama."

"Shut the door, Mar-beth."

Greyson braced himself for his father's harsh words. He took a seat in the chair near the door.

"What were you thinking, boy?" Pop asked through gritted teeth. "You had us worried to death. Your mother hasn't slept since Kirkland called with the news. And you're the oldest, you know better. Being a lawyer and all, I never expected you to get arrested. What were you thinking?"

"Pop, I know I should have thought it through, but I love Sutton and I couldn't sit by and lose her again, no matter what the consequences. I had to believe that she loved me enough to come home with me."

Pop's face contorted while he searched for a rebuttal.

"I couldn't be sorrier for making you and Mama worry, but I had to do it. You'd have done the same thing if Mama walked away and you didn't know why."

Remembering his own struggle to be with Marybeth, Pop softened. "What happened up there in Ohio?"

Satisfied that he had his father's forgiveness, Greyson settled back in the chair to tell the story.

Sutton watched from the stove as Greyson buttered Sierra's mashed potatoes. "Do you want pepper?"

Sierra nodded, her braids flying wildly. He peppered her potatoes.

"How about salt?"

Sierra nodded again.

"Does your mother let you eat salt?"

Simultaneously, they looked up for Sutton's approval. "A little," she answered.

Greyson complied before slicing Sierra's roast beef and placing a roll on her plate.

Sutton could feel the questioning eyes of her parents as they watched the interaction between Sierra and Greyson. Sitting down next to Greyson, Sutton placed a plate piled high with food in front of him. He continued to fuss over Sierra's food as she filled her own plate.

"What are you doing with yourself, Greyson?" Sutton's father asked while buttering a roll.

"Well, sir, I'm doing consulting work for the Chicago law firm where I worked before moving back home." He set his plate aside and pulled Sutton's in front of him. "I want to help get my parents settled before I begin working full-time again." He glanced up, but his concentration remained on cutting Sutton's roast.

Sutton felt her face warm under her mother's scrutiny. She had grown used to Greyson's obsession with preparing her food in private, but never expected him to carry on in front of her parents.

"How are your parents?" her mother asked.

"They're doing well. I want to help them settle into the new house. Moving the animals has been more work than I anticipated." He slid Sutton's plate over to her and retrieved his own. He looked up for the first time and noticed the curious stares of her parents.

Sutton hurried to keep the conversation on track. "Mom, how are things at the church? Are all the Fourth of July plans coming along?"

Faithfully devoted to her church, Sutton's mother beamed at being given the chance to share news of her charity work. She chatted on about the largest celebration in Hannaford Valley, the upcoming Fourth of July celebration. The event would begin with church service. The day would be filled with a parade, a church bazaar, entertainment, a cookout, and more. The evening's events would culminate with a children's show, awards presentation, and, finally, a grand fireworks show.

Sierra piped in, "Grandma said I can be in the show."

"I sure did, honey." Sutton's mother smiled with pride.

"This will be the first show she's ever been in." Sutton addressed her father.

"We'll have to videotape it," Greyson added to the conversation.

By dessert, everyone chatted freely. The initial misgivings of Greyson's intentions toward Sutton subsided, and Mr. Hill warmed to him. Sierra played to Greyson's soft nature for seconds on her chocolate ice cream. Sutton watched Greyson interact with her family with such ease that a stranger would have thought that long dinners together were a normal occurrence. After dinner, Sutton's parents took Sierra off to bed.

Greyson held Sutton near the front door. "I think things went well."

"I know they did. My father left us alone to say good night."

"Let's take advantage of it." Greyson pulled Sutton to him and kissed her. He pulled away when footsteps sounded at the top of the stairs. "I feel like I'm seventeen again."

"I know. I'm sorry. As soon as I can, I'll get my own place. Until then, I have to live by my father's rules and unfortunately he still sees me as his little girl."

"I didn't mean it in a bad way. I meant I feel like I'm getting a chance to catch up on all that we lost."

Sutton rested her head on his chest. She inhaled his deep woodsy scent. "I still wish it didn't have to be this way."

"Can I see you tomorrow?"

"I have to work."

"I'll pick you after work and we'll take Sierra to McDonald's." He tightened his grip on her waist. "Do you think your parents will keep Sierra afterward and let us spend adult time together?"

Twenty-six

Greyson spotted Kirkland standing in back of the construction site, wearing a yellow hard hat. Greyson greeted the construction workers still lingering at the work site as he approached Kirkland.

The home stood majestically on the back side of his parents' property, overlooking the neighborhood where he grew up and, more specifically, Sutton's parents' home. White with black shutters at every window, the house stood three stories tall. The front porch, decorated with tall white pillars, monopolized the length of the house. Upstairs were four bedrooms, all with their own bathrooms. Downstairs, a magnificent kitchen was under completion. The den, great room, living room, guest bath, and formal dining area were complete. The bottom level should have been called a basement, but it resembled an entertainment complex. The walkout patio door off the basement exited onto an elaborate play yard in back of the house. Once furnished, Greyson hoped his family would find the entertainment room a comfortable, homey place to kick back and share good times.

Kirkland saw Greyson approaching and met him halfway. "What do you think?"

"I like it—a lot. When will it be finished?"

Kirkland removed his hard hat and rustled his smashed curls.

"You need a haircut."

"You sound like Pop. Don't you know my 'fro is what's happening?"

Greyson gave him a big-brother glare. "When will my house be ready?"

"The main structure is finished. The construction company is picking up the last of their equipment today. The painters are starting upstairs in the bedrooms. The basement and first level have been completed."

"What's going on over there?" Greyson pointed to the men buzzing around with shovels and bags of dirt, stone, and hay.

"Those are the landscapers. I talked with the owner of the company and he said that the trees will go up first—the ones you wanted to line the front walk. Then they'll lay sod and construct the play yard. Those people over there are planting flowers."

"Do you think I selected a good company?"

Kirkland juggled his hard hat from one hand to the other. "I've heard only good things about them. Let me introduce you to the owner. He can show you the final plan of what it'll look like."

They started in the direction of a tanned white man wearing a matching Hawaiian shirt and pants.

Greyson turned to his brother. "I wanted to thank you for the work you put into this. You've been overseeing everything like you were building your own house. I appreciate it."

"Hey, you're my big brother."

"That's what I mean. Because of our ages, we've never been as close as we should be."

"You've always been closer to Chevy."

"We've always seemed to have more in common, but I don't love you any less. Now that I'm back in Hannaford, I'd like us to be tighter."

Shying away from the exposed emotions, Kirkland replaced his hard hat. "Since you're turning over this new leaf," Kirkland's voice lightened, "maybe you can tell me why you're building this big house. And who is the play yard for?"

Other than his recent confession to Sutton and Pop, Greyson had not shared the depth of his feelings for Sutton. As they got closer to the owner of the landscaping company, Greyson stopped and said, "I'm going to ask Sutton Hill to marry me."

"I knew we didn't go all the way to Ohio and break several laws because you were only friends."

The brothers laughed together. Their tall statures and husky voices drew the attention of the men working with the trees. Kirkland waved the owner over and introduced him to Greyson who listened closely while examining the proposed layout of flowers, trees, and bushes.

"I really like what you've done here. It's exactly as I described it to your manager on the phone."

The owner grinned at the compliment.

Greyson pulled his shades off and placed them in his pocket. "I'd like to make one change."

The owner's eyes narrowed.

"Around these bushes in the front." He pointed them out on the plan. "Right around here I'd like red rose bushes. As many bushes as you can pack in that space."

"Don't go too far out, Sierra." Sutton waved her daughter back.

Sierra stopped and watched the rabbit she'd been chasing disappear into the brush before running back to her mother. She stopped and pointed, "Mommy, there's Greyson."

Sutton turned to see Greyson's silhouette materialize on the horizon. He appeared taller than life as he approached. Even in jeans and a red pullover shirt, he looked like he stepped out of a men's fashion magazine. His strut revealed his inner confidence. The muscles flexing in his legs displayed his physical strength. She felt compelled to run to him, to live a scene she'd read in a romance novel where the hero and heroine run across a flower-covered field into each other's arms.

She took a step to go to him when Sierra patted her thigh. "Mommy, are we going to McDonald's again?"

"Honey, we just left McDonald's two hours ago. This time Mommy and Greyson are going out alone."

"Aww," Sierra pouted.

Sutton's eyes remained on the figure coming down from the hill. "Stay right here." She bent to kiss the top of Sierra's head before taking off at a run to Greyson.

Greyson removed his shades and watched as Sutton ran to him. At first his face displayed a degree of alarm until she got closer and he could see the joy propelling her to run to him. He stopped and held out his arms. Sutton ran double-time. She leapt into his arms, wrapping her legs around his middle. The impact made him falter and fall backwards.

"Are you all right?" Greyson laughed, locking his hands around her behind.

Sutton answered by brushing his lips with the tip of her tongue. She pulled him to her, kissing him through his laughter.

"I sure hope you plan on greeting me like this all the time." Greyson brushed away the loose grass blades on her shirt and pants.

"I saw you coming." How could she explain the explosion of emotions that made her run like a child into his arms? "What were you doing over the hill?"

"It's so nice out, I thought I'd walk to pick you up."

"They're about done with that house. Did you see anyone who might look like they'd live there?"

"Why so curious? Looking to trade up to someone better?"

"No. I told you that I don't like those types of men. Any man that could afford a mansion like that would not be for me. Been there, done that." Sutton peeled herself off Greyson and stood. "Aren't you curious about who's going to be living there? They had the nerve to put up a house between our properties."

Greyson stood and began brushing off his clothes. "Looks like we have an audience."

Sutton turned to see her parents watching them from the back porch. She waved and they went inside. Sierra stayed behind.

"C'mon, Sierra," Greyson called to her as they started toward Sutton's house.

Sierra took off in a lopsided run. She mimicked her mother and jumped for Greyson to catch her. He placed her on his back and jogged down the hill, leaving a trail of her tiny giggles floating through the air.

"I can't remember the last time I went to the movies on a Friday night," Sutton said as she climbed the stairs up to the back of the theatre.

"It's been a long time for me, too."

They settled in a row midway down the aisle, the same seats they had chosen as teens. Greyson handed Sutton a soda while he juggled the jumbo barrel of popcorn.

The lights went down. "I guess people still don't like to sit this far back," Greyson said, observing how the crowd sat in one area close together.

Sutton dug into the popcorn. "Too much butter." She fed him a handful of kernels.

"You always say that." He grinned at the memory. "It's just right."

"Can I have the candy bar?"

Greyson handed her a Milky Way. "You sure are not like other women. *You* eat on a date. I don't know how you keep your figure."

"High metabolism." She ripped the paper off the Milky Way. "What do you have planned after the movie?"

"Wait and see."

"I hope it includes stopping to eat because I'm hungry."

"Hungry? I fed you once today."

"That was lunch."

"That was all you get," Greyson teased. "You're going to break me with dinner dates."

"Don't be cheap." Sutton shoved his arm.

He laid his arm on the back of her seat. "Shhh."

Not being a fan of "date movies," Greyson's attention soon wandered from the big screen to Sutton. Sitting in the back of theatre came in handy when he kissed her and stroked her breasts. She tried to scold him for acting like a teenager, but his touch trailed downward, extinguishing her words.

The bucket of popcorn sat abandoned on the chair next to Greyson. The fruity taste of cherry slushy passed from Greyson's tongue to hers.

"Don't." Sutton caught his hand as it moved to the button of her jeans.

"No one is watching us." The heated moisture of his words saturated her ear.

"Not here."

"All right. Let's go." Greyson stood and pulled her up by the hand. She jogged to keep up with his long strides as they descended the stairs of the movie theatre.

"Greyson, slow down," Sutton said as he hurried across the parking lot to his Volvo.

"Get in back." Greyson opened the back door and ushered her inside.

"No. Not here, either."

Greyson entered after her, pushing her deeper into the car. "Why not here? Everyone's inside watching the movie."

"Anyone walking by can see."

"You don't want me to wait until we're back in Hannaford, do you?" He pressed his body to hers.

The poignant memory of the pictures Mother Galloway held came to Sutton. Her playful tone turned serious. "Greyson, we can't. There is already one set of pictures floating around out there."

Greyson sobered. "You're right. I'm sorry." His long finger traced her chin. "I want you so badly."

"I know. Me too." She kissed the high lines of his cheekbones. "It's getting late. We better head back to Hannaford."

Greyson relented. "What are you doing tomorrow?"

"My mother will have Sierra all day at church practicing for the Fourth of July celebration."

"Can I see you?"

The next day, Greyson wanted to ensure his chances of a romantic encounter, so he called Sutton early Saturday morning to confirm their date.

"Where are we going?" Sutton asked, the sound of the television blasting in the background.

"We're coming back to my place so that I can make love to you."

The noise on the other line disappeared before she spoke again. "What did you say?"

"I said I'm going to make love to you. Can you handle that?"

"What happened to the shy Greyson I used to know?"

"That Greyson found he wasn't getting what he wanted out of life. Are we still on?"

"Seven o'clock?"

"Six."

At 5:45 Sutton emerged from her bedroom. She carried her high heels down the stairs and put them on at the bottom. She'd spent an extra-long time styling her crimson hair in wispy curls that feathered around her face. She'd plucked every stray hair from her eyebrows, forming a perfect arch over each brown eye. She'd painted her lips with a super shiny burgundy kissing stick. Not knowing how Greyson planned to carry out his evening of romance, she selected a white knit, body-hugging dress that stopped above her knees. Sleeveless, the collar formed a choker around her neck and dipped into an open U that revealed the sparkles she'd dusted across her cleavage. The only jewelry she wore came from her mother's collection. She'd chosen a silver bracelet and stud earrings. She tugged at the band of her new shimmering toffee pantyhose and smoothed her dress.

"Daughter?" Mr. Hill called from the living room.

"Yes, Daddy?"

"Bring me a soda pop."

"Daughter," he said when he saw how beautiful Sutton looked.

She handed him the soda and did a quick spin. "How do I look?"

"Pretty as a picture. Greyson must be taking you somewhere really special."

"He is." She smiled slyly. "Mom hasn't brought Sierra home yet? They've been at the church all day."

"That women spends every minute she can down there. She said she'd call me later to drive in and pick them up. I don't like her walking home when it gets dark."

Sutton tensed when the doorbell rang. She turned to her father. "Are you sure I look okay?"

"Beautiful."

Sutton tugged at the hem of her dress. "Good night, Daddy." She kissed his cheek and raced to the door.

Her father leaned over the side of his recliner. "Can't that boy come in before you go racing off?"

"Oh, Daddy."

A gray hat, cocked to the side, partially hid Greyson's face. Sutton watched the black band as he lifted his head, exposing his sparkling eyes and brilliant smile. The gray silky shirt he wore clung to his rippled chest. Dark gray slacks covered his long legs, ending at black square-toed shoes. Nervously, he adjusted his gray-, red-, and black-patterned tie. "Gorgeous."

Like a giddy teen, Sutton batted her eyes. Whenever Greyson looked at her, she was transported back to her high-school years. "Ready?" she managed to ask.

He stepped past her into the house. "Let me speak to your father before we go."

Sutton ran upstairs to check her makeup while Greyson chatted with her father. When she returned, Greyson stood and escorted her to his Volvo.

"You're quiet." Greyson remarked when they reached his house. "Are you nervous?"

"No."

Greyson smiled, knowing she was too proud to admit to it. "Well, don't be. I know I can't do anything without feeding you first."

Stepping into the parlor of Greyson's childhood home opened a flood of warm emotions for Sutton. She'd spent so many days hanging out at this house with the Ballantyne brothers. Mama Ballantyne always treated her like the daughter she'd never had. The house had changed very little since Sutton's time there. The furnishings and drapes were more colorful. The furniture arrangement remained the same over the years. The house seemed smaller than she remembered; she noticed Greyson's frame filled the doorways and monopolized the rooms.

Greyson interrupted her reminiscing. "Mama cooked dinner for us. Would you like to eat in the dining room or in front of the TV?"

"Dining room."

"After you."

A lace covering graced the table. Two places had been set, one at the head of the table, the other to the left. Red rosebuds surrounded a bucket of red wine next to two glasses.

"Sit down." Greyson pulled out her chair. Then he moved to the stove, where he removed pots from the oven and filled their plates. "Mama wanted to fix spaghetti until I told her you were coming by. Then she put on her chef's hat and made this big meal. Pop was having a fit so she had to make enough for him."

"I hope she didn't go to too much trouble."

Greyson smirked at her over his shoulder. "You know my mama. She loves to cook for people. She's going to cook the Fourth of July celebration breakfast for all the church volunteers. She says she's looking forward to sitting down with your mother."

The aroma of home-cooked bread wafted to Sutton.

Greyson continued, "Mama met Sierra at the church and she's crazy about her. She told me to ask you to bring her around next week for lunch."

"I'll call her tomorrow and set up something."

"You know, I was hoping I could take you to the celebration." Greyson returned to the table with two plates of pork chops smothered in gravy, green peppers, and onions. Green beans with almond slivers, and fried okra completed the meal.

"I was hoping you would."

Greyson placed a basket of rolls on the table before pouring their wine. He took her hand while he blessed the food.

Sutton inhaled the aroma floating up to her nose. "Everything looks good and smells great."

Greyson pulled her plate over and began slicing her pork chop. He lifted the fork to her mouth. The pork chop was so tender it melted in her mouth. Mama Ballantyne was heavy-handed with the spices when she cooked, and Sutton loved that. Her own mother was conservative with salt and spices in her dishes because of her father's ulcer scare many years ago. Both women knew their way around the kitchen, but hot and spicy was the way Sutton preferred her food—she glanced up at Greyson—and her men.

"Why do you do that?"

"Do what?" Greyson glanced up at her.

"Prepare my food for me?"

He speared a bit of okra and held it up to her lips.

"And feed me?" Sutton asked after dabbing her mouth.

Greyson started in on his own food. "Pop controls the house, making all the big decisions. Food is my mother's way of having some say in the running of the house. She shows her love for us boys through her cooking. She wanted a girl so badly; I think cooking is the only way she knows to love big, burly boys. Now it's my way to show you my love."

Sutton's stomach fluttered. *Smart, handsome, and romantic.*

"Does it bother you? I'll stop."

"No, it doesn't bother me."

After dinner, Greyson served lemon meringue pie.

"I can't believe you remembered this was my favorite." The fact that he remembered the significance of red roses should have ceased any doubts about his devotion to making her happy.

"Of course I remembered." He lifted a slice of pie onto her plate. "The second my mama reminded me about the time she whooped our behinds for eating the lemon meringue pie she made for the church bazaar."

Sutton tossed her head back with laughter. "I remember that."

"Uh-huh. And do you remember running home and leaving us with the blame?"

"I wasn't as slick as you thought. By the time I got home, my father was on the porch waiting for me with his belt in his hands."

Sutton took the fork from his hands. She let her fingers linger on the baby-soft warmth of his hands. "Let me do that." She used the side of her fork to cut a chunk of the pie. Greyson licked his lips before accepting the fork into his mouth.

Twenty-seven

"I kinda like this plan-ahead romance." Sutton turned and lifted her head to Greyson.

"I read somewhere that married couples lose the romance as they fall into a daily routine. I thought planning a night like this would be good for us since we have to work around Sierra's schedule."

"Some men don't like dating women with kids for that very reason—among others."

Greyson dipped his face near hers and spoke softly but firmly. "I don't like it when you question me about my commitment to you and our future. Especially when you imply I see Sierra as a liability to our relationship."

Greyson had moved into his parents' bedroom. Tonight, the bed was covered with red silk sheets and a red silk comforter. The aroma of peaches lingered from his earlier bath. The bedside lamp casts their shadows on the wall opposite the bed. Soft jazz floated through the room, setting the mood for a slow, tender love session.

"Why is it that whenever I'm near you I lose all restraint and want to ravish you?" Sutton's voice was low—deep—from the bottom of her throat.

"You should never feel inhibited when we're together."

Seeing Greyson's pert nipples straining against the gray silk fabric of his shirt, she lifted her hands to caress his chest. She opened the buttons and pulled the shirt out of his pants. Her hands started at his square shoulders and cascaded down the dark skin of his chest. His oiled skin felt as soft as his silk shirt. The fine mist of hairs covering his chest felt like peach fuzz to her wandering fingers. Her eyes went to his as her hand teased his belt. Cautiously, she opened the belt and fumbled with the zipper. Instantly, he rose to her touch.

"Sutton." His husky voice made her desire him more. He grabbed her shoulders and pinned her front against the wall. She rested her forehead against the striped wallpaper as he pressed his groin against her behind. His arms came around and cupped her breasts, sending electric currents to intertwine with her nerve endings. His lips moved across her neck while his hand followed the fabric of her dress between her thighs. She sucked in her bottom lip when his hand cradled the mound at the top of her thighs.

"Grey—son." She choked out.

"This is what you came for." Down home, southern need coated his words and caused a pang of desire to stab her chest.

She tried to turn to consume his lips, but he used his body to press her into the wall. His thumbs hooked the hem of her dress. He moved his hands upward over her thighs and hips, past her waist, grazing her bosom until he pulled the dress over her head. His tongue flickered over the tender skin of her back as he unsnapped her bra. He took tiny sample bites from her shoulders as he inserted his thumbs inside the waistband of her pantyhose. Sutton's head fell back as he ground circles with his groin.

In seconds, she stood nude with her back to the wall. Greyson took a step back and removed his slacks and bikini briefs.

"What should we do now?" Greyson asked through heavy gulps of air. His eyes roamed her body. "I could run a bubble bath. We could have another glass of wine. Or maybe there's something on your mind."

Sutton watched the hand that glided down his abdomen and stroked his manhood. She opened her mouth to play his game, but desire made her speechless.

"Well?"

Sutton's eyes went from his roving hand to his inquisitive face. She backed him to the bed. Greyson helped her lie down before lowering himself on top of her.

"I want to make love to you," he whispered as he nibbled her ear. His knees separated hers and he sank into her warmth. His lips skip-hopped over her chest, across her belly. He hummed against her thigh sending a sharp, aching spasm through her body. His lips moved to the mound of flesh that desired him terribly.

"Don't." Sutton touched the top of his head.

Greyson jerked up to look at her. "Why not?" His fingers swirled around the curly reddish-brown hairs shielding her pleasure spot.

"I don't like it."

"What do you mean you 'don't like it'?" A capricious smile lifted his lips. "Weren't you the one who wanted to put a condom on me with your mouth?"

"I never said that."

"Did too."

"I had too much to drink."

"Yeah, right." He laughed. His finger traced her opening; her back arched against her control. "Talk to me." Greyson's probing made her squirm.

"I've never done it before."

"It being oral—"

"Greyson."

"You were married, how could you not have?"

"Just make love to me."

"This is a part of making love. I won't hurt you. As a matter of fact, I think you'll like this. Very much."

Greyson's head dipped out of sight. Sutton closed her eyes when she felt his hot breath between her thighs. His tongue moved into her opening. His humming vibrated through Sutton, urging her to lift her hips. Her moans encouraged him. She couldn't believe the shrill cry that filled the room belonged to her. She thrashed on the bed as Greyson taught her this new way of loving. The all-encompassing wave of sensation that moved through her body solidified her need to be loved. She pulled him to her, opening her legs to receive him.

Greyson pushed against her wetness as he reached underneath the pillow and removed the light blue package. "Okay, okay," he chuckled as Sutton hurried him in the application of the condom. He used his hand to guide himself into her cavern. When he reached the hilt, he began the deep rocking motion Sutton had come to crave.

With every thrust of his hips, Greyson whispered affectionate terms of endearment. He made promises of a future happier than she could ever dream of. He caressed her gently when his stroke became deeper than she believed she could take.

He restrained himself until she shivered before seeking his own pleasure. As he worked her body to its limit, sweat pouring from his brow, he looked as if he were riding into heaven. Erotic torture flashed across his face before pleasure lifted his eyes to the ceiling. Sutton held his behind and pulled him into her, wanting him to experience every morsel of her love.

Greyson held Sutton next to his chest. "Are you tired of hearing how much I love you?"

"Never."

He ran his fingers through the crimson wisps of her hair.

"I wish we could have told each other how we felt years ago," Sutton admitted. "My life is so upset right now. I feel like I'm taking advantage of you by bringing you into the middle of everything."

"We were brought together when it was meant to happen. I regret that we missed so much time together, but the important thing is that we're together now."

Sutton slid up in the bed and laid her head on his shoulder.

"I don't want a long engagement."

"Would you stop that?" Sutton placed her hand on his bare chest. She traced a random pattern through the short hairs.

"You think I'm joking. I'm not. I'm waiting for the sign from you that the time is right."

"I don't know when that'll be."

"You can't wait for everything to be perfect in your life. Things rarely are perfect. What we have right now is pretty close. We can work on your finances while we're together."

"The next time I get married, I want us to start on equal footing."

"I love you and you love me. That's as equal as it needs to be. I'm telling you, the time is right. We should seize the opportunity. I'd like to be married before Christmas."

"Christmas is only six months away."

"What's your favorite holiday?"

"Valentine's Day."

"Too far away."

"What's the rush?"

"The rush is that I've been waiting for you since you were twelve. I'm ready to get my life started."

"Loving you is a big responsibility."

"Yes, it is. But you're up to the challenge," Greyson encouraged.

Sutton nuzzled into the crook of his neck.

"Can we at least agree that we're dating exclusively?" Greyson asked.

"Agreed." Sutton kissed his cheek.

"Then can we do away with the condoms?" He sat up on his elbow and looked down at her.

"I have to see Doc Carter first."

"I was thinking that we could do away with them right now. You have that look in your eyes that says you want me."

"Not tonight."

"You'll make an appointment with Doc Carter in the morning?"

"I will."

"It's true that you want me, right?"

"Day and night."

Twenty-eight

"Mama." Greyson held Sierra's hand as he traveled through the house looking for his mother.

"Greyson? In the kitchen."

Greyson followed her voice and delivered an excited Sierra to his mother.

"Come give me a hug, sweetheart." Marybeth bent down and opened her arms for Sierra, who immediately ran to her. She brushed the fire-engine-red braids behind her ears. "Are you going to spend the day with me?"

Sierra nodded before looking back at Greyson.

"I should get her home right after dinner."

"Of course," his mother answered absentmindedly; all of her attention was focused on the vibrant little girl before her. "I have such a fun day planned for you! Greyson told me you like McDonald's so . . . I thought we'd drive into the capital and go to lunch. Just us girls. Would you like that?"

Sierra smiled, revealing her newly missing tooth.

Greyson stood back and watched the two interact. Sierra twisted excitedly as his mother told her about the day she had planned for them. His mother was overjoyed with the prospect of having a little girl to spoil. He checked his watch before interrupting.

"Mama, I have to get back. Chevy and Kirkland are waiting for me. We have to interview several candidates for a management position at the paper mill."

"Okay, son. We'll be fine."

"I'll be back for her after dinner," Greyson said as he opened his wallet and removed three crisp fifty-dollar bills. "While you're at the capital, would you mind buying Sierra a dress? She needs one for the Fourth of July celebration at the church."

"Sutton doesn't want to take her shopping?"

"She's tied up at work," Greyson explained. He knew Sutton was strapped for cash and that she would never take the money from him directly. She didn't have to know he purchased Sierra's dress. Sutton would never insult his parents' act of kindness; he would let her believe they were responsible. The important thing was that Sierra would have a new dress for her debut stage performance in front of the entire town of Hannaford Valley.

Greyson bent to Sierra's eye level. "Be good."

"I will." Sierra threw her arms around his neck in a tight hug. He embraced her tiny body. Months ago he didn't know that Sierra existed, but with one innocent act of kindness she stole his heart.

He stood to catch his mother's tearful gaze. He went into his wallet and handed his mother another fifty. "Maybe you could buy her a doll or something too."

Sierra jumped up and down with squeals of joy. Making her happy warmed his heart. "See ya later, Mama." He kissed her good-bye.

That evening, he scooped a sleeping Sierra into his arms from the backseat of his Volvo and carried her up the stairs of Mr. Hill's front porch. She hooked one arm around his neck and the other around her new doll.

"Hi." Greyson greeted a stone-faced Mr. Hill at the front door.

"Sutton hasn't made it home yet. Maddie wanted her to drive into the capital with her."

Greyson nodded. "She called me. I'm supposed to pick her up at Maddie's to bring her home after I drop off Sierra."

Mr. Hill's lip tightened into a straight line. Greyson was moving into his territory and he didn't like it one bit. They'd made progress at dinner, but there was still a long way to go. It was time for Mr. Hill to understand that Greyson loved his daughter and was going to be a permanent fixture in her life.

Mr. Hill reached for Sierra but Greyson handed him the shopping bags dangling from his hand instead. He wasn't ready to release the bundle of warm love from his arms. "I'll carry her up to bed."

Mr. Hill hesitated before stepping aside. "Top of the stairs to the right."

"I remember."

Greyson climbed the stairs one at a time, being careful not to falter and fall with Sierra in his arms. He gently placed her on the bed and removed her tiny red gym shoes. She pulled her doll to her chest and snuggled into the pillow. He contemplated the warm temperature and Sierra's comfort level before covering her with a single sheet. During the long, event-filled day, her braids had begun to unravel. He swiped away the stray hairs covering her round face before kissing her good night. He could picture himself doing this every night for the rest of his life.

"Mommy?"

"Yes?"

Sierra sat on the floor with her back resting on the sofa, positioned between Sutton's legs, as her mother combed her thick mane.

"I like Greyson. He's fun."

Sutton smiled. "I like him too."

Mr. Hill peeped over his newspaper. Sutton ignored his displeased expression and kept combing Sierra's hair.

"He always takes me to McDonald's."

Deftly, Sutton gathered one section of hair and began twisting the strands into braids.

"And he rides me on his back."

"I saw that."

"Daddy never did that."

Sutton concentrated on the next section of Sierra's hair. She glanced at her father, who was frowning with disapproval.

"Daddy showed you he loved you in different ways. He made sure you had a nice house and pretty clothes. He gave you that pretty locket."

"Does Greyson love me? He takes me to McDonald's."

"I think Greyson enjoys you as much as I do." Sutton tickled Sierra's underarms, hoping to distract her from asking more questions.

The night came to an end when Sutton put Sierra to bed. She took a long bath and called Greyson to wish him good night. She had started up the stairs when her father stopped her.

"Yes, Daddy?" Sutton joined him in the living room.

He shut off the television. Her mother scurried up the stairs to bed. Sutton watched, knowing her father would have a lot to talk about.

"Daughter, I've been standing by not interfering in your business—"

"I know and I appreciate that you're letting me make my own decisions."

"Yeah, well, I heard Sierra talking this evening and it disturbs me."

"Why? I thought you had made your peace about me and Greyson."

"Yeah, well," he said again.

"Daddy," Sutton scolded in an exasperated tone.

"Greyson seems to be trying to do right by you. I'll admit to that, but what about Sierra? Is it wise to let him into her life so soon after Alex's death?"

"Greyson makes Sierra happy. You heard her say so herself."

"Yeah, well," he hedged.

"Daddy, Sierra deserves someone like Greyson in her life. She's young, but she knows there's a difference between Alex and Greyson's role in her life. She's dealt with

Alex's death better than I could have hoped for. If Greyson fills that void for her, I want him to do it."

"I'm just saying—"

"I know that you're concerned and I love you for it, but this is my decision and I want Greyson to keep doing all that he's doing."

"Where are we going, Mommy?"

"We're going to see Greyson."

"Are we almost there? My legs are tired."

Sutton knelt next to her. "How can your legs be tired? They're only four years old." Sutton tickled her middle. After the giggles, Sutton pointed the way. "Do you see that hill? On the other side is Greyson's house. Do you think your legs can walk that far or should I carry you the rest of the way?"

"I don't know if I can walk, but I can run."

Sutton smiled down at her daughter's clever ploy. "Okay, be careful."

Sierra ran ahead. She stopped to pluck a fistful of dandelions from the side of the road. She tucked them in the waist of her shorts and ran to the next patch of flowers.

At the foot of the hill, Sutton could see Greyson sitting inside his Volvo. She watched as he stood and moved to the hood of the car. She immediately compared him to the busty women in tight T-shirts and cut-off shorts exploited in music videos. She watched the muscles of his thighs flex as he worked the wax into the hood. His shirt lay abandoned on the roof; the fuzz of his chest lay slicked to his chest with perspiration. He moved to the front side panel and polished the car with circular strokes. His eyebrows came together as he concentrated on his work. His body vibrated with the force of his strokes. Sutton likened the movement to his lovemaking. The water hose and a bucket sat in the dirt next to his bare feet. Perspiration glistened across the span of his shoulders. His muscles flexed. He threw the towel over his shoulder and bent to examine the rims of his wheels. Round curves defined his behind. She wanted to put her fingers in her mouth and whistle at the show he was putting on.

"Mommy, I see Greyson."

"Me, too." Sutton breathed.

"Can I go?"

"Yeah, you can go."

Sierra began her lopsided run down the hill, quickly covering the short distance to reach Greyson. He saw the flash of yellow clothing out the corner of his eye and turned to see Sierra running toward him. He knelt and she ran into his arms. He lifted her high above his head and spun her around in circles. Sutton smiled as she listened to them laughing together. He held Sierra high, looking up and saying something that made Sierra erupt in giggles. He placed her on his shoulders. The dandelions sticking up from Sierra's waistband looked as if they were sprouting from his head.

Sutton could never describe to Greyson how much he increased her love for him with the attention he showed Sierra. She understood that his relationship with Sierra would be a strong factor in determining their future. Greyson genuinely cared about Sierra. He showed it in the way he patiently listened to Sierra when she tried to tell him about her day. When she asked him to carry her on his shoulders, he lifted her without a second's thought. If she was coloring, he sat next to her and helped her complete the page. Sierra needed to form a bond with a positive male role model, and Greyson was doing that for her.

"Hi, sexy," Sutton said when Greyson reached her.

"Hi, you." He bent to greet her with a kiss. "You could have called me to pick you up."

"We didn't mind walking."

They fell into step together. Once they reached Greyson's house, he placed Sierra on the ground.

"I have something you might like." Greyson knelt down to her.

"What?"

"I went grocery shopping today and it's been so hot out, I thought I'd buy myself some Popsicles. Do you know anyone else who likes Popsicles?"

"Meeee!" Sierra sang.

"Want go in the house and get one?"

Sierra took his hand. She looked over her shoulder for Sutton's approval before skipping off with him.

Sutton sat on the porch stairs waiting for them to return. Sierra bounced down the stairs. She grabbed the rag from the bucket of water with one hand and began to mimic Greyson's moves while eating her Popsicle.

"Didn't you just finish washing and waxing your car? You shouldn't let her do that."

Greyson sat next to Sutton on the top step. "Ahh, it's okay. I'll redo it later." He laughed. "She's having fun."

"She has you wrapped around her little finger. You know that, don't you?"

"Like mother, like daughter." Greyson leaned over and kissed her lips.

"Have you been working all day?"

Greyson tore the paper away from a long, multicolored Popsicle. "I helped my father with the animals, hauled wood with Chevy, and then came back here to do some things around the house." He held the Popsicle up to her lips. She glanced at him before using her tongue to lick the length of it.

"Why did you do that?" Greyson tried to scold her, but couldn't because of the smile lifting the corners of his mouth. "You're nasty." He put the Popsicle in his mouth. "You used to do that when we were little. Spoiled. You had to have whatever Chevy had. Remember that?"

"Nope."

Greyson rolled his eyes.

Sutton watched Sierra lift the hose and try to rinse the car with the water that dribbled from the tip.

"Mama was cooking up a storm when I left there this

afternoon. I think she wants something from Pop. Want to go to dinner with me?"

"Do you think she'd mind?"

"Only if we didn't bring Sierra. They had a blast when they spent the day together. Chevy and Kirkland are going to stop by. You know she'll be in her glory with all of us there."

"Sounds good. I need to thank her for the outfit she bought Sierra for the Fourth of July celebration."

"It might embarrass her if you mention it."

Greyson wiped the sweat from his brow with his forearm. Sutton ran her hand across the sheen on his chest. His nipples responded by hardening. She glanced down at the zipper of his beige shorts. She always wanted to know she could commanded that spot with a strategic touch or brazen glance.

"Hey." Greyson turned her head away from him. "I feel like a sex object when I'm with you."

"Oh, please. This is what you asked for."

"I created a monster." He angled the Popsicle and caught the melting juices with his tongue. "You surprised me the other night. I couldn't believe you never—"

"Greyson." Sutton's eyes dipped to the ground.

"Sore spot? I'm sorry."

They watched Sierra hose down the driver's side mirror.

"How was it to be a professional model?"

Greyson shrugged. He never seemed to realize his beauty.

"Did you like it?"

"It paid my way through college. It's hard to get your professors to take you seriously when they see your half-naked body in a magazine ad for underwear. I received more propositions from my professors than I did from other students."

"Wow, that sounds just awful," Sutton said sarcastically. She rested her hands behind her on the wood boards of the porch.

"It's not all fun and glamour like most people think. You have to get up early every morning and work long hours. With my law school studies, it was murder. People fuss over you all day—'you've gained a pound; you aren't getting enough sleep; go to makeup; smile; turn right; turn left; stop smiling'. And the rejections—'too tall; too short; too fat; too skinny'. Everyone wants to be your friend because they think you can introduce them to the supermodels. It never stops. I don't see how anyone could make a profession out of it."

"How many ads were you in before you quit?"

"I can't remember. Twenty or thirty and one music video."

"You were in a music video?"

Greyson nodded. "I'll show it to you some time."

Sutton watched Sierra drag the hose to the back of the car.

"Have there been a lot of women in your life?"

Greyson stopped licking the Popsicle and looked for emotional clues behind Sutton eyes.

"Well?" she persisted.

"There have been a few."

"Tell me about them."

"No way." Greyson chuckled before eating the Popsicle. "Whatever I say will be used against me at a later date."

"That's not fair. You know my entire dating history."

"I can't help it if you only dated the man we grew up with."

"Greyson," Sutton's bottom lip protruded.

"I'm not falling for it, Sutton," Greyson laughed.

She dipped her head and batted her eyes. "C'mon, tell me."

"I will tell you that the only woman who ever mattered to me is the one I'm sitting next to right now. I did live a little before we were together, but those women were only providing me with a momentary distraction. No matter how I tried to forget you and move on, no one could take your place."

"I can't believe you've felt like this all these years." Sutton watched him with wonderment. Greyson sat next to her, perfect in every way, confessing his undying twenty-year love for her with the ease of reading the Sunday paper.

"Why not? How long have you loved me?"

Greyson's candor made Sutton blink. She had loved him for as many years. She couldn't pinpoint the day brotherly love changed into romantic love, but she'd been harboring strong emotions for Greyson for a long time. "A long time."

"I knew you loved me before you did."

"Did not."

Greyson nodded. "I know that you didn't admit it to yourself until we kissed in the church—on your wedding day. You tried to suppress it while you were dating Alex, but I read it in every gesture, every word."

"Why didn't you say something?"

"At the time I wasn't sure if it was only wishful thinking. Not until the day of your wedding."

Sutton turned her attention to Sierra. She wondered how different her life would have been if she'd become involved with Greyson instead of Alex.

"You wanted to run back down the aisle into my arms. I saw you look back."

Sutton refused to look at him. The truth of his words made her insides shiver. She remembered Mother Galloway's anger when she said the same words, "I saw you look back." Did everyone in the church know she loved Alex but was in love with Greyson?

Greyson went on. "I don't know what made you marry Alex that day. Loyalty, I guess. Maybe you did it because it was expected of you since you were fourteen. Only you know the truth. I doubt that you'll ever share it with me."

Sutton crossed her ankles. She wanted to tell Greyson to stop uncovering her emotions for everyone to see. She wanted to switch to an emotionally safe topic. Somehow, him knowing her shortcomings bothered her. Yes, she'd married Alex with doubts. Everyone told her she was lucky. She hadn't known another man, had never even gone out on a date with anyone but Alex.

Greyson sighed. "But it's all right, Sutton. I knew you loved me as much as I loved you and I knew we'd be together in the end." His hand stroked her back and she relaxed with his touch.

Greyson held the Popsicle in front of Sutton. She savored the cold sweetness. She bit off the tip.

Greyson scrutinized what was left. "You're greedy."

Sutton tossed her head back and chomped down on the ice in her mouth, fighting the brain freeze that would follow.

"And you wanted to put a condom on me with your mouth? I don't think so—ever."

Twenty-nine

Greyson sat in the barber's chair completely oblivious to the men chattering about ball games and women troubles. His eyes were fixed on the library across the street; he wondered what Sutton was doing. How had her day shaped up? Would she be off from work by the time he finished with his haircut?

"Woo-wee," Rabbit whistled. He sat by the large picture window. His haircut and shave had been completed long before Greyson climbed into the chair. Rabbit remained a daily customer in the barbershop since Greyson was a kid. The years passed and his large front teeth had long since fallen out and been replaced by ill-fitting dentures.

"Look at that car." A man known to the town as Punchy abandoned his checker game and joined Rabbit at the window.

"Forget the car. Look at that woman," Rabbit remarked.

The bell over the door tinkled. Little Man stepped inside. In his usual hyper fashion he spoke too loudly when he asked, "Y'all see that woman out there?"

The men at the window answered with a chorus of "yes." They remained at the window grunting, sighing, and reporting every detail of the woman's actions.

"Let me see what all the excitement is about." The barber abandoned Greyson and carried his clippers with him over to the window. When the cord reached its full length, he stretched his arm out to give him the extra distance he needed to stand at the window. "She is good looking. Don't belong around here. Y'all know her?"

Rabbit, Little Man, and Punchy made noises that said they didn't.

"Carver," the barber called over his shoulder, "you know this lady?"

Carver left the checkerboard and limped over to the window. He came to the barbershop every weekend to spread the latest town news. His wife—Hannaford's biggest gossip—talked his ear off every night and he shared her news at the shop every weekend.

"Don't know that gal," Carver begrudgingly admitted.

"Can a man get a haircut around here?" Greyson asked after a few minutes passed.

"What's your hurry?" the barber asked. "That girl of yours ain't off from work yet. Didn't think nobody knew about you and that Hill girl, huh?"

Rabbit and Punchy snickered. Carver looked sheepish; obviously, it was he who had told the men about their relationship.

Greyson jumped down from the chair to see what woman could command the town's attention. He took the clippers from the barber and dropped them in the chair. Once his path was cleared, he joined the men.

The woman stood next to a black Cadillac with a driver. She tugged at the multicolored vest she wore. The men in the window whistled and hooted. She ran her hands through her brunette hair then over the seams of her black riding pants. She leaned her head back and shook her thick, shiny mane. The barber pretended to faint.

Greyson tore off the cape protecting him from bits of hair. Before the entire town turned out, he needed to pull her out of view. He hurried out of the shop, drawing the men's attention when the bell over the door clamored.

"Belinda, what are you doing here?"

"Greyson!" She threw her arms around him and pressed her face into his chest. "Looking for you, of course."

* * *

"Are you sure you don't mind locking up?"

"Maddie, go. Enjoy your date."

The library didn't receive many visitors during the day, the exception being when teachers planned a class trip or the high schoolers had a report due. To justify the funds the town spent on keeping the library open, the mayor suggested housing historical records there. A special room with regulated temperature and moisture control was constructed. Birth and death certificates as well as marriage licenses were stored there. In Sutton's final phase of job orientation, Maddie had instructed Sutton on the policies for maintaining these records. Sutton checked the temperature setting of the record room before setting the electronic lock. She straightened the tables and chairs before shelving mislaid books. Once that was done, she closed all of the window blinds.

A small crowd of men had gathered on the street. Sutton stopped in the window to watch the unfolding events. At the center of the crowd's attention was Greyson standing with a beautiful white woman near a big, black car. Sutton zeroed in on the woman. She knew her. Where from?

Sutton's blood curdled when the woman ran her hands over Greyson's chest. The woman's hands had been there before; she was too familiar with the territory. Memories of Alex's betrayal assaulted her. Sutton felt her self-control withering away. The urge to run across the street and grab the woman by her long hair made the corner of Sutton's mouth twitch. When the woman tossed her head back with wicked laughter, it came back to her. Sutton had been right; she did know this woman.

Sutton closed the last blind and locked the door of the library. She hurried down the sidewalk in the opposite direction of Greyson and the woman.

"Sutton," she heard Greyson call. "Sutton, wait up."

Sutton pressed her purse to her side and hastened her step.

"Sutton"—Greyson grabbed her arm—"didn't you hear me calling you?"

She spun around.

"Hey." He held up his hands. "What's that hateful look for?"

"What were you doing with *her?* " Sutton asked between clenched teeth.

"She's a research assistant from Hunter, Roe & Volney."

"Don't pretend that she's here because of work. I saw the way her hands were roaming across your chest."

Greyson looked around at the crowd focusing their attention on them. The woman's car pulled away from the curb and disappeared down the street.

"Let's go somewhere private and talk about this." He cupped Sutton's elbow in an attempt to escort her to his Volvo.

Sutton yanked her arm away from him. "I don't want to talk to you right now. I know who she is, Greyson."

"I told you who she is. Belinda from Hunter, Roe and—"

"I know who she *really* is. I bet you've been laughing at me all this time. All that sweet talk was a joke. I should have learned from Alex."

"What are you talking about?"

"You can stop pretending. I recognize her."

A timid male voice approached from behind. "Mrs. Galloway?"

Sutton turned around to see a young black man with a slight build. "Yes?"

Greyson's voice tightened, his southern twang disappeared. "Ms. Hill," he corrected the young man.

The man clarified, "Mrs. Alex Galloway?"

"Do I know you?" Sutton asked, confused by all that was happening at once.

"I have something for you." He handed her a white legal-size envelope. "You've been served."

"Served?" Sutton asked. "What do you mean, 'served'?" she called after the man as he turned and hurried away to a waiting car.

Greyson took the envelope from her and ripped it open. He scanned the page. "Mrs. Galloway has filed for custody of Sierra."

Sutton's legs became weak. The entire valley seemed to be closing in on her. The crowd's collective face mocked her stupidity. The mountains surrounding the quaint town appeared foreboding. She took a step back. Greyson grabbed her arm.

"Let me go." Sutton raised her voice, entertaining the growing crowd. "Leave me alone." She backed away from him. "I have to get to Sierra."

"I'll drive you."

"Don't you get it? I said leave me alone."

"I don't understand what's going on, but you can forget me leaving you alone. I promised you that I would help you if Mrs. Galloway tried to take Sierra and I meant it."

"That was before I saw you with *her.*"

"Her? Belinda?"

"I don't care. Just leave me alone—forever." Sutton turned in the opposite direction and began to hurry away from him.

Greyson blocked her path. "I said I would drive you. We need to clear this up and I won't do that in front of the entire town. Now, don't be stubborn. It's not ladylike."

Sutton moved to step around him.

Greyson blocked her path again. "I won't yield on this."

Chevy went into town every Friday to collect his weekly order of supplies from the hardware store. This day he collected the sheets of wood, nails, and other supplies he needed for building a new set of shelves in the guest bedroom.

He ventured into town earlier than usual. To avoid the mocking stares and whispering, he usually visited the hardware store near closing. Knowing that Greyson would be at the barbershop, Chevy planned to meet him there and see what his plans were for the weekend. He needed help picking up supplies from a nearby town that their father needed for the animals. After their wild trip to Ohio, he knew Greyson would readily help him.

Chevy loaded his supplies into the back of his pickup truck before walking to the barbershop. He readied himself for the harsh assessments of his overalls and straw hat by the townspeople. He expected men to place themselves between him and their women—he lived in the woods and dreamt up perverted things to do to women all day, you know. He looked for the kids who would run rings around him singing their song about the crazy Ballantyne brother.

None of these things happened as he moved through the town. Instead, everyone gathered and pointed at the scene in front of the library. A new, shiny black Cadillac whizzed by him. A lost tourist searching for directions, most likely.

Chevy stopped in front of the barbershop and watched along with everyone else—until he realized the show starred his brother. He broke through the crowd and joined the confrontation. Sutton pulled away from Greyson and fell into him.

"What's going on?" Chevy looked between them.

Sutton collapsed against him.

"She's crying, Greyson." He held her with one hand and stopped Greyson's advancement by holding up the other. "Pop will have a fit if he hears you were in town causing a scene." Shame would drive their mother into seclusion for weeks.

"I need to talk to you." Greyson directed to Sutton.

Sutton's tearful eyes imprisoned Chevy's heart. "Get me out of here."

Chevy backed away from Greyson. "I'll take her home." He shared a pointed look with Greyson that he hoped conveyed his determination. If he had to directly challenge Greyson to protect the woman he considered his little sister, he would.

Greyson allowed him to usher Sutton away.

Thirty

Chevy persuaded Sutton to go back to his cabin. He told her Sierra would be upset by her mother's distraught state. Besides, Sierra was safe with her parents. Silence engulfed the truck as Chevy drove down the red dirt-and-gravel covered road. He turned off the main road and maneuvered through a thicket of trees until he reached the clearing where his cabin stood.

Sutton went directly to the bathroom to splash cool water on her face.

While she washed up, Chevy made her a turkey and ham sandwich. "Have a seat." He pointed with the tip of the knife to where she should sit. The plate was garnished with chips and a pickle. He placed a steaming cup of hot chocolate with marshmallows in front of her before he joined her with his own plate.

"Would you like me to cut that for you?" He pointed to her sandwich.

"No. Thank you." She smiled sheepishly. All the Ballantyne men had a thing about feeding her. They ate, making occasional small talk.

"Do you want to share a beer?" Chevy asked after she refused dessert.

"Yeah, that'll be good."

Chevy poured half of the bottle in a glass. He sat across from her at the kitchen table. "Do you want to talk about it?"

"I don't know." Sutton ran her fingers through her hair.

"Chevy, I really messed up my life. Now it seems I'm about to destroy Sierra's."

"What are you talking about?"

Sutton sipped from her glass before answering. "I married Alex knowing I didn't love him enough to promise him my entire life. Then I stayed when it all fell apart. He died and left me penniless. I had to run back home to live with my parents—a parent myself."

"Those were all mistakes. You were too young to see clearly."

"Well what about now? I've gone and gotten myself involved with Greyson, and because of it Mother Galloway is trying to take my child away from me."

"Hold up. What are you talking about?"

Chevy sat riveted while he listened to Sutton explain Mrs. Galloway's latest move in her power struggle over Sutton. He tossed back the bottle of beer when Sutton described the nature of the pictures and videotape Mrs. Galloway held over her.

"Does Greyson know about this? He's an attorney. He can help or he'll know someone who can."

Sutton shook her head. "He knows but I can't trust him. I saw him with *her.*"

"*Her* who?" Chevy grabbed another beer from the refrigerator.

"Did you see the woman in the black car all the men in town were gawking at?"

"I saw the car."

"I know her."

"Who is she?"

Chevy listened as Sutton disclosed their affiliation. She certainly had been through hard times since leaving Hannaford Valley. "I'm sure Greyson can explain. You have to give him the chance. Once that's all cleared up, he can help you fight for Sierra."

Sutton stacked her fists on the tabletop and rested her chin there. "I'm thinking I should be smarter this time. I'm thinking I shouldn't stay and tell myself it'll all work out. I should have learned something from the hurt I experienced with Alex." She straightened her back. "I should call it quits with Greyson and walk away before I regret it later."

"Greyson and Alex are completely different people. Greyson truly loves you and I know he'd never do anything to hurt you intentionally."

"Alex loved me too—in his own way. He used to tell me all the time that he was loving me the best he knew how. And I believe that. The problem is, why should I settle for less than everything I need?"

"That's a little harsh, isn't it? You haven't even given Greyson the chance to explain."

"Do you want to share another sandwich?"

Chevy nodded, watching Sutton as she moved around the kitchen.

"Maybe I am being too judgmental, but my child is at stake. I walked into this relationship taking the chance that Mother Galloway would do this if I did. Don't I have the right to be hard on him?"

"I suppose. But I know Greyson has been in love with you all his life. When he found out you were engaged to Alex, it ripped him apart. He wanted to talk you out of it. I convinced him that you and Alex were happy and that he should step back."

Sutton stopped working and stared at him over her shoulder.

"If I hadn't done that, you and Greyson might be married right now."

Sutton continued preparing the sandwich. Silently, they relived the New Year's she had become engaged. She brought the sandwich to the table and they began to eat.

"Not as good as yours," Sutton said.

"Talk to Greyson."

Sutton returned her sandwich to the plate. She watched Chevy's face as she reflected on her hidden fears. "You know, this is too confusing." She exhaled loudly. "Greyson loves me; I have to admit I'm certain of that. I can't begin to describe how it feels to know that your husband is sleeping around, sharing the most intimate part of your marriage with random strangers."

Sutton sipped from her beer before continuing. "This woman entered my life and refuses to leave me alone. First with my husband and now with Greyson."

"You don't know that for sure," Chevy interjected.

"I don't know what there is between her and Greyson, but I do know that she's a constant in my life. One I want to remove. The thought of having her interfere with me and Greyson . . ."

Chevy refilled her glass from his bottle of beer.

"It's like this," Sutton went on. "Greyson's love comes with an expensive price tag. The weight of knowing that he's loved me since I was twelve, that he gave up everything to come back to Hannaford Valley to try to win me. It's a heavy burden. I feel like I have to repay him in some way."

"I know that Greyson has never said that."

"No, he hasn't."

"Then don't make it harder than it has to be."

Sutton ran her hands through her cherry hair. "You're right."

"You don't sound convinced."

"It's this woman." Sutton took a bite from her sandwich.

Chevy lifted a pickle and nibbled at it, waiting for Sutton to continue.

"Greyson is handsome—a dog-gone professional model. How did I let myself fall in love with him when Alex left all these feelings of insecurity behind? Women are always going to flirt with him. Some will hit on him, not caring that we're together."

"This woman stirred up all these fears?"

"They were there—underneath the surface. She brought them to the forefront." Sutton pushed her sandwich away again. "It's like this. Imagine a faucet. The water flows freely at first until the gunk starts to build up. Then the water still flows through, but not as nicely as in the beginning. That was my relationship with Alex."

Chevy nodded.

"Imagine that same faucet when the new owners of the house take possession. They clean out the gunk, but no matter how much flushing they do, the faucet never runs as it did when it was new. That's my relationship with Greyson. I feel like the water is backing up—that's the burning sensation in my chest—and all the gunk is holding up the flow. I want to let go and love him without restraint, but I'm afraid that one day a woman will come along that will make him stray."

"Enter the beautiful woman in the Cadillac."

"Exactly. I love him too much. If he—" Sutton's voice wavered, she recovered before continuing. "If he goes to someone else, I don't know if I could handle it."

Chevy squeezed her shoulder. "Sutton," he smiled reassuringly, "you know Greyson would never do that to you."

She shook her head, scattering the negative thoughts. "You're right. Alex and Greyson are different people."

"Right."

"I have trust issues."

"Yep." Chevy took a large bite from his sandwich.

"I need to go on *Ricki Lake.*"

"Or *Montel.*"

Sutton giggled.

"What you need to do is talk to Greyson. Tell him what you've told me. He may have to go the extra mile to make you feel comfortable until you've resolved these issues."

"No. This is inside me. I need to handle this."

"Do you feel any better now that you've gotten that off your chest?"

"I do. Thank you." She rose and kissed his cheek.

Chevy diverted his eyes until the blush left his cheek. "No matter what, Greyson will not let you lose Sierra."

* * *

Sutton lay across the bed in Chevy's guestroom. After her candid discussion about her feelings for Greyson, they put their heads together and tried to find a resolution to Mother Galloway's custody petition. During their talk, she had run to the phone at least four times to call Sierra. Her father was alerted by her behavior, but Sutton never said more than that she missed her daughter.

Sutton rubbed her temples. The remnants of a migraine headache still lurked at the edge of her scalp. The two aspirins Chevy had given her were finally kicking in. The more they tried to find a solution, the more stressed she became. She wanted to run to her daughter, hug her, and tell her everything was under control. Chevy wouldn't let her go until she was calm and rational. He kept reminding her that upsetting Sierra would only make things worse.

Sutton heard Chevy, outside the door, say, "She's in the guest bedroom."

Her stomach flipped with the knock at the door. She knew that Greyson would come demanding answers. His way of being quietly assertive would prod at her will until she gave in and they talked everything out. She wasn't sure she was ready to take the chance of intensifying her migraine, but she knew she had to deal with him sooner or later. She steadied her voice. "Come in."

Greyson stepped inside and closed the door behind him. He had showered and changed out of his jeans into hunter green dress slacks. His chest rippled in a white sheer sweater; the white fabric glowed against his ebony skin. He had found his way back to the barbershop. His hair glistened, perfectly shaped close to his scalp. His sideburns were evenly squared midway down his sharp jaw line. Some of the supermodel still lingered in Greyson. He could go from coveralls and floppy hat to sleek and sexy with a snap of his fingers.

"I know you don't want to see me, but we have to talk." Greyson sat next to her on the bed. His woodsy scent entered her nostrils and calmed her nerves. "I don't understand why you're mad at me."

"I saw you with that woman on the street."

"Belinda. You said you knew her."

"It would be more accurate to say I know *of* her."

Greyson nodded, not fully understanding. Quiet, assertive, understanding. These were the weapons he chose to use against her in their fight.

Sutton hesitated before dredging up the pain of her past. "I met her in a supermarket. She hit me with a shopping basket—pushed it into me on purpose. Then she stood over me screaming that my husband loved her and not me."

Greyson's lips parted. His bushy brows rose in surprise. "You must have Belinda mixed up with someone else."

"Do you really believe I wouldn't remember the woman who did that? The basket hit me so hard that I had a bruise on my hip for a week. But I'd seen her before the supermarket incident. I racked my brain that day until I remembered. She was at my wedding.

"I confronted Alex about her. He eventually admitted that they were seeing each other. I threatened to leave and he ended it. There were more incidents after that but I could never prove she was behind them.

"I threatened to leave Alex again, but he promised to take care of it if I stayed. He told me she moved away. He had seen to it personally. And then one day, everything stopped. I figured he put her up in an apartment somewhere and she was happy enough to leave me alone. Now she shows up in Hannaford—with you. How do you know her, Greyson?"

Greyson shuffled his feet across the pattern of the carpet. "Belinda is a research assistant at Hunter, Roe—"

"You've told me that." Sutton hadn't meant to raise her voice. She took a deep breath before she went on. "I want to know how you were involved with her. I saw her hands on your chest. Do all the research assistants at that law firm have such an intimate relationships with their superiors?"

Greyson stood and crossed the room. Sutton could see it in

his face. She knew how to read the hidden look behind guilty eyes and the nervous twitching of the mouth. She knew how mortified a man needed to be for his nostrils to flare when he had to admit his secrets had been found out. She braced herself for the lie he would fabricate. If he lied to her, she would never be able to trust him again. She would never be a cohort of deceit in another relationship.

Greyson knelt before her, resting his hands on her knees.

Sutton waited. She wanted him to be truthful with her, but as she stared into his eyes, she didn't know if she could deal with what he might say.

Greyson sighed heavily. "Belinda and I were briefly involved."

"Involved?"

"We had a very short fling. I was lonely and one night—"

"I've heard enough." She tried to stand, but he grabbed her waist, fastening her in her seat.

"I want you to understand the way it was. I want to be honest with you." He took her hands in his. "I promise you that it was nothing more than me letting my hormones get out of control. I broke it off with her right after. Nothing has happened since."

Sutton studied his face for the marks of deceit. "How is she in your life and in Alex's?"

Greyson dropped his head. "I never thought anything of it."

"Of what?"

"Kirkland asked me to do a favor for a friend. He knew a woman looking for work and asked if I could find her something at Hunter."

Sutton pulled her hands away. Kirkland was the only true friend Alex had. Over the years, Kirkland had visited their home in Ohio several times. Sutton had always suspected that Kirkland knew Alex's secrets. She even suspected that he had a part in Alex's deceit.

"Sutton, if I had known—"

"They duped you just like Alex duped me."

"Wait until I see Kirkland—"

"No." Sutton pressed her hands on his shoulders. "It doesn't matter now." She studied him for a long moment. "What is she doing in Hannaford?"

Greyson stared up at her remorsefully. "Belinda didn't accept our relationship for what it was. I had to make it clear several times. She came here to deliver work to me from Hunter."

"There's no reason she couldn't have mailed it or sent it by e-mail."

Greyson looked into her eyes. "No, there isn't."

"None other than she wants you back."

Greyson's gaze did not waver.

Sutton stood and crossed the room.

"I told her again—I'm in love with you and there's never going to be anything between her and me."

"Where is she?"

Greyson hesitated to give up the information, but Sutton remained relentless until he told her at which hotel in the capital Belinda was staying. He openly answered all of her questions as she probed into the dynamics of his relationship with Belinda. He refused to discuss the intimate details of the night they shared together. Quietly and assertively, he refused, "It has no bearing on our relationship. If I tell you all those details, you'll hold them against me. Belinda is part of a mistake I made in the past. I've apologized to her and made it clear that there will be nothing between us. I never guessed this would come back to hurt you. If I had, it never would have happened."

Sutton acquiesced to Greyson's wishes. They wouldn't discuss his past with Belinda anymore. She stored the information he shared in the recesses of her mind. If Belinda remained true to her nature, she would interfere in Sutton's life again. And this time she'd be ready.

Greyson pulled the white envelope from his back pocket. "I made a couple of calls before I came here."

Sutton took the envelope threatening her daughter's future from his outstretched hand. The panic that pushed her to run to her daughter bristled through her chest.

"I'll die if I have to give up my daughter."

Greyson hurried to hold her. "That will never happen. It'll never happen because I would die if I lost the both of you. I faxed these papers to an attorney friend of mine. He's already on the case. All you need to do is keep working and taking care of Sierra. As soon as he has spoken with Mrs. Galloway's lawyer, he'll give us a call."

Sutton lifted her head. "I don't know what to say." While she pushed him away, he was fighting for her daughter.

"Say you love me." Greyson captured her lips before she could answer.

"I love you." Sutton dropped her head against his shoulder. "I can't sit here and do nothing while Mother Galloway tries to take Sierra."

"That's exactly what you have to do—nothing different. You're a good mother; keep being a good mother. Let my friend look into this. Mrs. Galloway's probably not serious about the whole thing. I believe it's a ploy to scare you back into her control."

"You're probably right. I can't picture Mother Galloway raising a four year old."

Greyson kissed her forehead. "Everything'll be fine."

"I need to get home to Sierra."

Greyson nodded. "I'll drive you."

Sutton could not sleep that night. She curled up in bed with Sierra and stroked her daughter's hair while she slept. If she were to lose Sierra—she pushed the thought away and placed her trust in Greyson. All her life, he'd been there to save her. He'd do it again this time. Not because they were lovers but because they were friends.

She didn't tell her parents about the custody battle. After meeting with Greyson's attorney, if he felt it necessary, she'd tell them. She'd have to tell them everything. And she didn't relish trying to explain the explicit pictures of her and Greyson. Meanwhile, she would do as

Greyson suggested: Keep working and taking good care of Sutton. If they did go into court, she wanted to be able to prove she was an excellent mother.

Sutton wondered if Alex would approve of what his mother was doing. He always strived to keep Mother Galloway happy, but this? Surely, he would want his daughter to be with her mother. Mother Galloway hated that Sutton was not still in mourning. Whenever Sutton thought of Alex, she grieved his absence. Not because she had lost her husband, but because of their link in time. Her long-time camaraderie with Alex was an undeniably huge part of her development into a woman. They were not good together as a couple but there would always be a place in her heart that missed his friendship.

Saturday morning, Sutton's mother took Sierra to church for more rehearsals and preparation for the Fourth of July celebration. With a vague explanation, Sutton borrowed her father's car and drove into the city. She stopped to fill the gas tank and get directions to the hotel where Belinda was staying.

Never in her life had Sutton done anything like what she was planning. She found a seat in the corner of the lobby that allowed an unobstructed view of the hotel entrance. She leafed through magazine after magazine while she waited. Several hours passed before Belinda approached the desk clerk. Sutton watched as she settled her bill.

Sutton assessed this woman who had fought to take her husband, and now Greyson, away from her. She tried to see what attracted them to her. The tight-fitting business suit clung to her straight hips and small behind. A Wonderbra enhanced the size of her breasts, hoisting them into the V of her jacket for all to see. Because she was tall, her choice of low heels showed some fashion sense. Her brown hair fell in large waves past her shoulders. She flipped it over her shoulder and tinkered with her earring. A very annoying habit Sutton hated in women. One of the bellhops tripped over his own feet in his hurry to carry her bags to the waiting black car.

"Belinda?" Sutton approached as Belinda waited for the driver to open the car door.

"Yes?" She swung around. Shock covered her face and drained it of some of its coloring. She wore foundation and blush, pink lipstick, and blue eye shadow. Sutton tried to picture her the morning after, when all the makeup had been removed by erotically induced perspiration.

"I can see that you recognize me, so I'll dispense with the formalities."

Belinda's face hardened with shaky boldness. "What can I do for you?"

"I'm going to tell you what I can do for you, Belinda." Sutton took an intimidating step forward. "I will *not* knock you down and kick your butt all the way to the airport as long as you stay away from Greyson Ballantyne."

Belinda's head cocked to the side. "Greyson?"

"Yes, Greyson."

The driver approached the women, but seeing the intensity of their conversation, stood at a distance.

With confidence, Belinda stuck out her hip and grinned. "So, you know about Greyson and I?"

"I know everything. I know about you and my late husband. I know that you seduced Greyson."

Belinda shifted to the other hip, still grinning. "You have it all wrong. Greyson seduced me—quite admirably, if you must know. But I'm sure you do know that by now." The grin disappeared, as if she was picturing Sutton being intimate with Greyson.

"When Alex dumped you, I bet you threatened his career. Did you force him to find you a new job at a new company?"

Belinda's face drooped slightly.

Knowing she was on the right track, Sutton continued. "Knowing that Alex's career meant everything to him, you held it over his head. Alex moved you away—but not too far out of his reach—to Chicago, where he found you a job at Greyson's law firm." Sutton smacked her lips. "That's something arrogant Alex would do. He was always flying back and forth to Chicago on business. You'd always be available when he needed to use your body."

Belinda opened her mouth to answer the insult but Sutton cut her off.

"You finally figured out he would never leave me. Now revenge is on your mind. You remember Alex telling you about Greyson and the way they competed over every little thing. So what do you do? You make a play for Greyson, knowing that it would tick Alex off. What happened then, Belinda? Did Alex not respond to your game? Or did you really fall for Greyson?"

"You think you have it all figured out." Belinda's calm exterior began to melt. "There are things about me and Alex you'll never know."

"Do you think I don't remember you sitting in the front of the church at my wedding?"

Belinda's posture straightened as if someone had hit her in the head with a book.

"I know about that. I know about a lot of things." Sutton guessed that Belinda had been the recipient of a house, car, or boat. She didn't need to know the specifics. She knew that a research assistant couldn't afford a chauffeured car and expensive clothes without there being more to the story. "But that's the past. You want Alex, you can have him."

Belinda's arms dropped limply to her waist.

"You see," Sutton continued, "Greyson and I are in love. That means there is no place in his life for you."

Belinda retorted, "I doubt that Greyson—"

"I really don't care what you doubt. I'm telling you like it is. I also want you to know that I'll do anything to keep him in my life. If that means clawing your eyes out because you can't listen when he tells you he's not interested, then so be it."

Sutton took a long step forward. She wagged her finger inches from Belinda's face. "Greyson is not Alex. Greyson is a good man and he loves me. You need to respect that. I'm telling you this woman to woman. I won't step aside like I did with Alex. I love Greyson too much. He's my future."

Sutton stood eye-to-eye with Belinda. Neither woman spoke. All these years, Belinda had placed herself in the shadows of Sutton's life and wreaked havoc. Standing up to her made Sutton feel liberated. Knowing that her message had been sent and understood, she turned and walked away. The bellhop and driver grinned at her as she passed.

"Sutton?" Kirkland's eyes narrowed. "What are you doing here?"

"Can I talk to you?" She glanced over his shoulder.

"Sure. I'm sorry." He stood aside so that she could enter his apartment. "I'm surprised to see you here. Greyson didn't mention that you were stopping by."

Kirkland hurried ahead of her to remove the scattered newspaper from the sofa. "Have a seat. I was in the middle of cleaning."

"I won't keep you long." Sutton sat down and waited for Kirkland to join her.

"Did you need something? Alex was my best friend; if there's ever anything I can do—"

"Did you know Alex was in financial trouble?"

Kirkland looked uncomfortable.

"He's gone now. Are you still going to keep his secrets?"

"Like I said, Alex was my best friend."

"Then you did know about his money problems. And the women."

Kirkland glanced away. "Alex is gone, there's no sense in upsetting yourself about the past."

Sutton snorted. "You sound just like Alex."

"Why are you bringing all this up now?"

"You sent Belinda to Greyson for a job. Alex asked you to help him with his dirty laundry and you did it. Without any regard to me or Sierra, you helped his mistress find work with your brother."

"It's complicated."

"How complicated can it be, Kirkland? We were friends, too. Why didn't you tell him no?"

Kirkland's voice rose to a defensive level. "Do you think I enjoyed watching Alex mess around on you? I tried to talk to him. It was like a sickness with him. He tried hard to be faithful to you, but he couldn't do it."

Kirkland regained his composure. "Alex came to me, distraught that you might leave him. You had threatened to before, but he always knew he could change your mind. When he went to the bank, he noticed you had taken a large sum of money out. He was sure you were going to run away. That's when he started moving the money out of your accounts. He didn't want you to be able to leave him."

Fascinated, Sutton watched Kirkland as he filled in the missing puzzle pieces of her life.

"Alex came to me in tears. A grown man crying like a baby. He flew into Charleston and called me at work to pick him up from the airport. You thought he was in Houston on business. He begged me to help him get rid of Belinda. He had told her it was over, but she wouldn't accept it."

"And you helped him."

"Yes, I helped my best friend save his marriage."

Speechless, Sutton stared at him.

"I did what I thought was best."

"Did Alex believe I was having an affair with Greyson?"

Kirkland made a noise of exasperation. "He was obsessed by it. I don't know why he envied Greyson so much. He was always challenging him over everything. I tried to tell him I would know if Greyson was seeing you, but he wasn't convinced."

Sutton sat back against the sofa.

"I never meant to hurt you. I know how much Alex loved you. I just wanted everything to work out."

Sutton stood and left the apartment in an angry haze. She couldn't listen to Kirkland justify his part in Alex's lies. Couldn't he see how much hurt his involvement caused?

She had more questions she wanted to ask Kirkland, but feared the answers. She'd intended on blasting Kirkland with the same wrath she used on Belinda. Seeing the regret on his face made her walk away. His being Greyson's brother complicated things further. She asked herself if she would ever be able to forgive Kirkland for his part in destroying her marriage. It would take a long time. With Alex gone, Kirkland bore the entire burden of that time in her life. For now she would leave Kirkland to his own torture. She had a feeling guilt would eat away at him for some time to come.

Sutton strutted across the lobby to the bank of pay phones.

"Hello?" Greyson's southern drawl colored the word and filled her ear with manic passion.

"Greyson, it's me."

"Hi, me."

"Can I come over and make love to you?"

"Should I pick you up?"

"No. Get undressed. I'm on my way."

Thirty-one

Sutton's laughter bounced off the windows of the car. For once, she had gotten the best of a mistress. She carefully maneuvered the car around the curves of the one-lane mountain road. If she looked out her side window, she would be peering down the side of the high mountain; she kept her eyes glued to the road.

In all the years of Alex's infidelities, she had never even considered staking out any of the women and confronting them. She had yelled and screamed and coerced Alex, all of which he viewed as empty threats after her failure to leave him. What was different about Greyson that made her want to start a catfight outside of a prestigious hotel?

As Sutton came to the end of her trip from the capital, she contemplated Greyson and his offer of a permanent future. She hadn't been widowed that long; a second marriage was tucked far away in her mind. She did love Greyson. When she thought about it, she always had—as a friend and now as her lover. Besides being a six-foot-two dark hunk of man, he was a southern gentleman. The gentle, protective, educated man beneath the good looks stole her heart. His patience calmed her. His kindness encouraged her.

She tried to visualize the photos Mother Galloway lorded over her as a symbol of when she was set free. Imagining making love with Greyson awoke all her nerve endings. As he trailed his fingers over her body, every inch of her being responded. When he made love to her, he did it with such fervor that the look in his eyes made her tremble. When he flipped into the mode that was meant to open her up to new experiences and release her inhibitions, no experimentation seemed undoable.

Sutton had just finished replaying their last session in her mind when she pulled up in front of his childhood home. She locked her father's car and ran up the steps to his front door.

Greyson swung the door open within seconds of her ringing the doorbell. "Get in here and tell me you didn't do what I heard you did."

Her broad smile laced with erotic wickedness faded. She let her gaze fall from Greyson's stony face over his bare chest, across his solid abdomen, to the bulge in his boxers. Her incorrigible grin returned. He couldn't be as mad as he sounded.

Sutton boldly stepped into his house. "What did you hear?" She dropped her purse on the sofa and turned to face him.

"This phone has been ringing off the hook. Kirkland called my mother about your little visit. Belinda called me saying you confronted her at the hotel." His tone remained angry, his face curious about her smile.

Sutton answered with a dramatic nod.

Greyson's thick eyebrow shot upward. "You did?"

The dramatic nod again. She placed her hands on her hips.

"Why would you do something like that?"

"I wanted Belinda to leave you alone."

Greyson blew out a long breath between his teeth. Studying her, he ran his hand across his chest. "You don't know Belinda. You told me yourself she attacked you in a supermarket. She could be a maniac. You could have been seriously hurt."

Remembering the shopping cart incident made Sutton's hip throb. She refused to let the memory haunt her. She pushed it away and concentrated on her mission at the present: to seduce Greyson. "Not your ordinary fatal attraction."

"I'm not joking. Let me deal with Belinda. You should have never—"

Sutton bounced around making jabbing motions with her fists. "I was ready for her."

"Stop," Greyson scolded.

Sutton froze, dropping her open fists to her side. She pushed out her bottom lip, giving him her best pout.

"You're out of control. You know that, don't you?"

"Don't be mad at me. I was fighting over you."

"I don't want you to fight over me. It isn't necessary. I told you I handled Belinda. She understands that I don't want her."

"She does now," Sutton whispered.

"What did you say?" He folded his arms across his chest.

"I did what I needed to do."

"Don't be stubborn. It isn't ladylike."

Nothing she had done that morning was ladylike, she wanted to say, but he was still scowling at her.

"Okay," Sutton complied. "I probably shouldn't have sunk down to her level."

"That's right."

Sassily, she added, "But it had to be done."

Greyson rolled his eyes. "What did you say to my brother? He called my mother and got her all upset, which brought Pop down on me. Meanwhile, I'm sitting here without any idea about what's going on."

"I didn't mean to involve your parents," Sutton said humbly.

"Kirkland runs to Mama with every little thing. You know that."

"I do. I'll apologize to your parents for getting them involved."

"You need to do a lot of apologizing."

"What?"

"I'm the man in this relationship, let me be the man."

Sutton parked her hands on her hips. "I never thought I'd hear that come out of your mouth."

"Sutton, I have been docile and given in to all your wishes. You didn't even discuss what you were planning with me. You ran off half-cocked and stirred up all this trouble."

"Me?" She pointed at her chest. "I didn't start any of this. Alex started the drama and Kirkland helped him keep it going. Even you did your part. Don't drop this all on my shoulders because I hurt your ego by taking care of the problem. If you were going to handle it, why haven't you?"

"You didn't give me the chance. Situations like this have to be handled tactfully. What do you think Mrs. Galloway will do if she finds out you drove to the capital and attacked an innocent woman? That's how she'll tell the story as she describes you as an uncontrollable, neglectful mother in court."

"I didn't think—" tears threatened. "I needed to stand up to Belinda. She's been interfering in my life for years. She would continue to do it if I didn't let her know I wouldn't take it anymore." She rushed on before Greyson could interrupt. "I needed to talk to Kirkland about Alex."

Greyson's southern accent warmed the air. "Sutton." He took several deep breaths, which removed the anger from his face. "It'll be all right. You have to remember to lay low until we get Mrs. Galloway to drop her custody suit."

Greyson walked up to her. The scowl unraveled at his eyebrows. "I still can't believe you tracked Belinda down." He pulled her into his arms. "I didn't mean to yell at you." He kissed the top of her head. "Sutton, I'm not Alex. I'll never look at another woman the way I look at you. I'll never touch another woman the way I touch you. I'll never love another woman the way I love you. Don't doubt that." He rocked her in his arms. "I'll clear this up with my parents. Kirkland and I will talk. I'll make sure this doesn't get back to Mrs. Galloway. We'll get through this together."

"Looks like you have to rescue me again."

"From what I heard, you can take care of yourself pretty damn well."

Sutton felt the rumble move through his chest. "What did you say to Belinda when she told you what I had done?"

"I told her to stay away from my baby."

Excited, Sutton jumped into his arms, wrapping her legs around his middle. She held her face inches from his. "Greyson, tell me that your body belongs to me."

"My body belongs to you, Sutton."

"Tell me that no one else can put her hands on you."

"I'd never allow it."

"Tell me that making love to me is too special to share with anyone else."

He nuzzled next to her ear and crooned the lines from a song, southern style. "I only have eyes for you."

"I love you," Sutton whispered in his ear.

"You've had a busy day. You deserve to be made love to the proper way."

Greyson tapped on the frosted glass pane of the door with *Stacy Taro* etched across the panel in large script letters. When invited, he stepped inside the one-room office.

Stacy waved him over to sit down while she completed her phone call. The moderate-sized room was filled with surveillance equipment. Various objects, with hidden cameras inside them, littered the room. Tiny hearing devices cluttered the desk. Current files were stacked high on the credenza.

Stacy chattered away in Japanese. Her father was Japanese, her mother African. Not beautiful, but wildly exotic, she encompassed both culture's features with her milk-chocolate skin and eyes that slanted upward.

"Greyson Ballantyne." She stood her full five feet and rounded the desk. "I heard you became a mountain man."

He soaked her body up in a hug. "All the rumors are true."

"Can't be. I heard you quit practicing law." She returned to her chair while Greyson took a seat in front of her desk.

"My brothers and I are running a paper mill."

"A paper mill?" She squinted in disbelief. "I don't want

to know." She pulled her chair up close to the desk. "If you're not doing the law thing anymore, what's this case you have me working on?"

"The mother in this custody case is my girlfriend."

"Now I understand." She shuffled through a stack of army-green file folders before she retrieved the one with his name marked in bold letters.

"Do you have anything? I want this taken care of as quickly as possible. I don't want Sutton to have to step into court for one hearing."

Stacy nodded as she flipped through her notes. "I got that by the bonus check you sent." She glanced up with a smile.

Greyson had called Stacy immediately upon reviewing the legal documents Sutton had received. Stacy was the best PI he knew. She had helped him with many cases when he worked at Hunter, Roe & Volney. She worked discreetly and returned results expediently.

"You sounded pretty distraught when we talked so I decided to handle this one myself."

Greyson nodded.

"I flew out to Ohio. It wasn't hard to penetrate Mrs. Galloway's social circles. They're a shallow bunch. As long as you have money you're welcomed. But her friends think pretty highly of her. Couldn't get much there."

"What's our next move?"

"Hold on." Stacy pushed back in her chair. "I couldn't get anything from her friends so I tried her nephew—Eddie."

Greyson remembered the sheepish man who'd tried to restrict his entrance into the Galloway house. He also remembered the way Eddie seduced Sutton's body with his sunken eyes.

"Well, it seems Eddie is a lonely boy. I 'bumped' into him at a social function and the rest fell nicely into place."

"What did you find out?" Greyson sat forward in anticipation.

"There are definitely pictures. Eddie has seen them. He also viewed a particularly seductive video of you, counselor."

Greyson's eyes fell to the floor.

"Mrs. Galloway is serious about using them to try to win custody of the little girl. Eddie says that it has nothing to do with doubting the mother's ability to care for the child. Evidently, Mrs. Galloway loved her son to the point of it being a fixation. She's upset that Sutton has moved on with her life and wants her to pay."

Greyson couldn't understand Mrs. Galloway's obsession with Sutton preserving Alex's memory.

"She's so obsessed with it all that it's starting to bother Eddie." Stacy placed her elbows on the desk and leaned forward. "Eddie has a secret," she whispered.

"What?"

"Mrs. Galloway is his mother."

Greyson sat back and digested the information. "That can't be right. Mrs. Galloway and her husband have both only been married once—to each other. They had one child, Alex. Eddie is lying."

Stacy put up her hands. "One thing I've learned in this PI business is that you never discredit any piece of information without checking out the possible validity of it." She leafed through the folder and handed Greyson a beige certificate of birth.

Greyson scanned the paper quickly and then read it thoroughly. "Eddie is her son."

"I did a little digging. Mr. Alex Galloway, Junior, learned his behaviors from Mr. Alex Galloway, Senior. I have a list as long as my arm of women he consorted with after his marriage. From what I pieced together, Mrs. Galloway became very sick of it. She started taking trips out of Hannaford Valley and going over to the capital, where she found that two can play the infidelity game."

"Who knows about this?"

"Eddie, his father, and Mrs. Galloway."

"How could she keep something like this secret all these years?"

Stacy licked her finger and flipped through more pages in

the file. "I gathered everything I could on the Galloways and put my own theory together. There was a time, right before Eddie was born, that Mrs. Galloway left her husband. They separated for nearly a year. I found a woman who claims she was having an affair with Alex Senior. This woman says old man Galloway loved her and wanted to start a life with her." Stacy placed her feet on top of the desk and crossed them at the ankles. "Mrs. Galloway made her husband beg for a year, but did go back to him. No one is able to tell me where she was for that year. If you look at the address on the birth certificate, we get an idea what town she was in, but that's it. No one in the town remembers her. I think she was hiding out until she delivered Eddie. Afterward, she left him with his father and 'forgave' her husband."

It was plausible.

Stacy continued, "Eventually, guilt must have gotten to her and she introduced Eddie as her nephew. That way she could be in his life but not disclose her own infidelity."

Mrs. Galloway would die from the shame. Her socialite friends would throw her out of their circle.

"What I don't get, " Stacy interrupted Greyson's thoughts, "is why Mr. Galloway hasn't caught on."

"Mr. Galloway had a massive heart attack years ago. He's partially paralyzed and unable to speak. Nurses care for him around the clock. He lives at the new Galloway place in Hannaford Valley—"

"While Mrs. Galloway and her son live in Ohio. Far away from anyone who might figure this all out." Stacy shook her head. "I always heard small towns were full of dirty doings."

Thirty-two

The library closed Friday, the first of July, as did the entire town of Hannaford Valley. Workers began the installation of the grand bandstand outside of City Hall. A concert stage where the country-western band would play was hammered together from boards and nails. The small children's entertainment stage, where Sierra would make her debut acting and singing performance, was raised next to the church. Amusement rides were assembled near the edge of town. Delivery trucks came and went the entire day. Engineers worked on the fireworks display that would be the highlight of the festivities.

Maddie closed and locked the door behind her. "Lunch is here."

Sutton exited the records room, locking the door behind her. She joined Maddie in her office for a lunch of soup and sandwiches.

"Thanks for working today."

"It's the least I could do, seeing that you hired me and then rehired me." Sutton added mustard to her sandwich.

"It's nice having you back in Hannaford." Maddie added tomato and lettuce to her sandwich. "It's terrible the way things turned out for you with Alex. Everyone believed you'd be happily together forever."

"Alex and I should have realized long ago that we couldn't stay together because it was what people wanted. We should have done what we needed to do to be happy."

The sunlight from the window behind Maddie made the black hair of her tight bun shine. "You weren't happy with Alex? He was considered the catch of the town. Heck, I know I was jealous of you all through high school."

Sutton gave her the abbreviated version of her time with Alex, while being careful not to paint a picture of a monster. Alex had his faults, but as she had recently learned, some of their problems may have stemmed from his doubts about her faithfulness. After all, he had given her the best gift of her life: Sierra.

"Are we having a girlfriend moment here?" Maddie asked. "I need a girlfriend in this town."

"I think we are. My father always complained about me spending all my time with the boys and not having female friends."

They tackled their sandwiches in silence.

"What did you decide about leaving Hannaford?" Sutton asked as she sipped from her soda.

"I'm saving. When I leave, I don't want to have to come back. No offense."

"None taken. I tried the city and it wasn't for me. I like it here." Her face beamed with a broad smile. "Especially since Greyson is here."

"Greyson? You and Greyson Ballantyne?"

Sutton nodded. "He's the best thing that's happened to me in a very long time." Sutton told Maddie about the whirl-wind romance he'd swept her into.

Maddie watched her with a faraway look. "See, that's what I'm looking for. I've taken care of my parents. I've completed my education. I want to get married and have kids before I get much older."

"You'll find the right person, I'm sure. You've done everything the right way: taking care of you and honoring your values first. Now that you've done all those things, Mr. Right will come along and you'll be ready."

The silver bell hanging above the front door rattled.

"I'll get it," Sutton said, dropping her napkin on the desk. She greeted Chevy. "Looking for me?"

"Yep. Greyson sent me looking for you." He held a bouquet of red roses.

"Sutton," Maddie called from the office, "is everything okay?"

"Come on in the office." Sutton motioned for Chevy to follow her. "We're taking a lunch break."

Sutton didn't recognize the expression on Chevy's face when he entered Maddie's office. Maddie rose from behind her desk while smoothing her hair.

"Chevy, you remember Maddie, don't you?"

Chevy removed the black Stetson and studied Maddie. "This can't be Mandisa Ingram from the booster club."

Maddie smiled and her eyes swept Chevy's body before going to the floor.

Sutton watched the silent exchange. She felt as if she were intruding. She cleared her throat. "You said Greyson sent you looking for me?"

"Ah, yeah, he did." Chevy broke his trance. "He told me to bring you these." His eyes swept back to Maddie.

"Did he say when he'd be coming back?"

Greyson had made her promise not to do anything about the custody case until he returned from meeting with his attorney. He had called periodically but had nothing to report. She hadn't heard from him in the past two days.

"Chevy?" Sutton interrupted the silent flirting between Maddie and Chevy.

"Oh. No, he didn't say when he'd be home. He left a message at my house about the flowers." He turned to Maddie. "I guess I haven't been to the library since you started working here. What do you do?"

Maddie stumbled over her words as she tried to explain to Chevy that she was the librarian and town record keeper.

Sutton tuned them out and pulled the card from the bouquet of roses. *Dear Sutton, I miss you terribly. I'll be home*

this evening. I'll pick you up by seven. Big news. I love you,
Greyson

Sutton's chest tightened. His confession of loving her always had that effect. She wondered what the big news could be. It had to have something to do with Sierra.

"Chevy," Sutton interrupted their conversation, "did Greyson say anything else in his message?"

"No." Seeing her worried expression, he turned and focused his attention on her. "He sent Sierra a doll that I delivered before coming here. That's all."

"Is something wrong?" Maddie asked, rounding the desk to stand between them.

"No, everything is fine. His note is kinda cryptic is all."

Chevy shuffled his black Stetson from one hand to the other. "I better get back to work. Are you sure everything is okay? Do you need me to do something?"

"No." Sutton smiled and touched his arm. "Thanks for bringing the message."

Chevy nodded. "Sutton, I'll see you at the Fourth of July celebration. Maddie, I'll be stopping by for some information on forestry."

Maddie smiled.

Chevy tugged his hat onto his head before leaving the office. Sutton followed to lock the door. When she returned to the office, Maddie stood with her eyes glued to the doorway.

"Did I see something going on here?" Sutton teased.

"What? No." Maddie lost her dreamy expression and returned to her seat behind the desk. "He's much different than I remember. With all the rumors about him I expected a gruff man with a beard to his knees who could barely speak English."

Sutton returned to her lunch. "I don't know how those rumors got started. Chevy is the sweetest man in town. He's quiet and humble, but strong. He's saved my butt many times." She thought of him climbing through the window of Mrs. Galloway's Ohio home. "Believe me, I know."

"He lived in Alex and Greyson's shadows in high school."

"He did. Maybe that's how the rumors started. I don't know." Sutton put her sandwich down and cleared her throat with a swig of soda. "People look at Chevy and see a man who wears overalls and lives in the woods. What they don't take time to see is that his overalls are Roc-A-Wear, a designer name label. That was a Stetson on his head. He lives in the woods—in a cabin that could be easily featured in any home magazine—and he built it with his own hands. He's quiet, but no one in West Virginia knows more about forestry than he does. I'm telling you, he's a jewel waiting to be discovered."

Maddie got that faraway look in her eyes again.

"Do you want me to set something up with you two?"

Maddie snapped out of her musings, "No. If he had wanted to go out with me, he would have asked me out."

"Maddie—"

"Sutton, really. Chevy Ballantyne and I are no match made in heaven."

Greyson rolled a barrel from the barn to the back of his house. He hauled wood from the log pile and filled the barrel. Once a fire was blazing, he jumped in his Volvo and drove to pick up Sutton.

"Daughter," Greyson heard Mr. Hill shouting when he pulled up the dirt drive to Sutton's house, "don't go running out that door."

"Daddy." Sutton's form appeared in the doorway along with Mr. Hill's.

Greyson smiled. If nothing else, dating Sutton would keep him young. He guessed it was true; no matter how old you get, you're always your parents' child. He turned off the ignition and went to pick up Sutton in the proper manner.

Once inside his car, Sutton leaned across the seat for a kiss.

"Don't do that. Your father is watching." Greyson fought her off with less than half his strength.

"He better get used to this." Sutton kissed his brow before settling in her seat. "Thank you for the flowers and Sierra's doll. What's the big news?"

"Be patient."

"Does it have anything to do with the custody case? I have to tell you, I haven't been able to sleep since those legal papers arrived. I don't know what I'd do if I lost Sierra. I don't know what my parents would do if Sierra were carted off to Ohio. I still haven't told them what's going on."

Greyson glanced over and saw the shadows beneath her eyes for the first time. He had been so happy to see her he hadn't noticed before. He placed a comforting hand on her thigh.

"Does it have something to do with the custody case?" Sutton asked again. Her voice had lost some of its earlier animation.

"It does and that's all I'm going to tell you. Be patient."

A few minutes later, Greyson pulled into his drive. He opened the door for Sutton, took her hand, and led her to the back of the house.

"Are you burning trash?" Sutton inquired, her face showing apprehension.

"Something like that."

"Greyson"—Sutton stomped the ground and crossed her arms over her middle—"tell me what's going on right now."

"All right." *Stubborn and impatient,* he thought. "I met with the private detective I hired and learned some interesting information about the Galloway family."

"You hired a private detective?"

"Did I forget to mention that?" He grinned mischievously.

"Yes, Greyson, you did."

They stood out in the yard behind Greyson's house, and as the sun began to set, he told her the entire sordid story. He explained Stacy's conjecture, adding his own spin to the theory.

Sutton shook her head. "This is too incredible to believe."

"Is it really? People have affairs all the time. What they usually don't do is hide their kids, but even that has happened before. You wouldn't believe the things I've seen men do to save their corporations. Greed and humiliation cause drastic reactions in people."

"What do I do now that I have this information?"

"You don't have to do anything. I took care of it."

"What did you do?"

"I went to see Mrs. Galloway without the attorneys present. I told her what I knew, showed her proof, and threatened to tell everyone in her social group in Ohio as well as the husband she left behind here in Hannaford Valley."

Sutton placed a hand over her gasping mouth. "You didn't."

"I did."

"Well, what did she say?"

"Edit out the cursing and she said she'd drop the custody case."

Sutton's pouty lips curled upward in an easy grin. She reared her red head back and howled with relief. After jumping into Greyson's arms and plastering him with kisses, she questioned him further.

"What about the pictures? She could still put them out there for people to see."

Greyson set her down and pulled out the envelope that was pressed against his back under his shirt. "Do the honors."

Sutton took the envelope and ripped it open. "I can't believe this is all over." She fed the photos into the blazing fire.

"It's over."

"Mother Galloway let you walk away with these pictures? She agreed to drop the custody case?"

"Not readily, but with persuasion, yes. Mrs. Galloway doesn't want her secret exposed to her uppity friends. I believe she wanted to protect Eddie, too. She became very animated when I tossed him into the mix."

Sutton dropped another photo in the flames. Charred scraps of paper floated into the air around them. "Did she ask about Sierra?"

Gently Greyson said, "No."

"Then her wanting Sierra was about her being vindictive."

"I'm afraid so."

Sutton dumped the last of the contents of the envelope into the fire. She peered inside before dropping the manila envelope in.

"Are you all right?"

"Yeah." She stared into the barrel. "It's over. It's really over. I'm happy, really. It's just that—well, it's sad that Mother Galloway has no genuine feelings for her granddaughter. I thought she enjoyed having Sierra around when we were living there."

"I'm sure she did, Sutton. She wouldn't let on to that with me. We were in the middle of fierce negotiations that affected both of your futures. She wasn't about to get teary-eyed."

"You're right." Her head popped up. "What about the videotape? There was a tape, too."

Greyson's brow came together in a display of mischief. The corner of his mouth lifted. "The video is inside—in the VCR. It's really rather interesting."

"You watched it?" Sutton's erotic mischief played behind her eyes.

Greyson nodded. "I bought popcorn. I thought you might enjoy seeing it. Maybe, re-creating the good parts. Like in those dirty romances you read." He wiggled his bushy eyebrows.

Sutton turned to him. She studied his playful grin and watched as his body readied itself for action.

"I deserve a reward. You deserve to celebrate."

"I'll race you for the remote," Sutton yelled before taking off in a full run to the house.

Thirty-three

Sierra stood in the center of the small stage near the church, wearing a burgundy velvet dress trimmed with white lace. Her tiny braids, clipped with pink and white barrettes, flowed down her back. White tights and black patent leather shoes completed the outfit she had selected on her shopping trip with Mama Ballantyne.

Mr. Hill sat forward and mouthed silent words of encouragement. Mrs. Hill stood offstage with her hands in a ball pressed to her chest. Sutton grabbed Greyson's hand, keeping her eyes locked on the stage. He leaned over to Kirkland, "Are you getting this?"

Kirkland took his eye away from the video camera. "I'm getting it. Stop asking me that." He went back to filming.

Sitting next to Kirkland, Chevy shushed them and smiled as Sierra began to recite her lines.

"Oh," Sutton exhaled, tears glistening near the corners of her eyes.

Greyson put his arm around her as he fought the lump filling his throat. After Sierra's flawless completion of her lines, the music started.

Sutton turned to her father. "Is she going to sing?"

Mr. Hill shrugged. "This must be the surprise your mother was going on about."

Sutton glanced nervously at Greyson. They both sat at attention as Sierra began to sing. The timbre of her voice did not belong to a four year old. She sang a spiritual with the emotion of a broken field slave. Greyson equated it to Countess Vaughn's debut on *Star Search* many years ago. The little girl bringing tears to her mother's eyes had no idea of the profound effect she had on the audience. No one stirred until she belted out the final note. Then the crowd jumped to their feet with cheers and a long chorus of applause.

"Did you know she could sing like that?" Greyson asked Sutton.

She wiped away the last of her prideful tears. "I had no idea."

Sierra was the last to be introduced at the conclusion of the play. The crowd erupted again. Sierra smiled, displaying her missing tooth, in the direction of her mother.

"Go to her," Greyson encouraged Sutton. He stood near as Sierra bent down and hugged her mother. He listened as Sutton told her how proud she was of her performance. His chest heated with joy and his heart melted watching them interact. It would give him overwhelming pride to be the head of this family.

Sierra turned to him and held her arms wide. "Did I do a good job?"

Greyson lifted her into his arms and settled her on his hip. "You did the best job ever."

They stood together as a model family, accepting the congratulations of the people of Hannaford Valley. Once the excitement died down, Mrs. Hill came to take Sierra backstage to change. After Mrs. Hill completed her work, they would head to the rides.

"You two go on and have a good time," Mr. Hill said, taking Sierra off Greyson's hip. "We'll see you back at the house."

Greyson and Sutton glanced at each other with questioning eyes. What had happened, Greyson wondered, that made Mr. Hill more tolerant of their relationship? Sierra waved good-bye over her grandfather's shoulder.

"What do you want to do first?" Greyson asked as they walked together away from the stage.

"I'm hungry."

"How did I not know that?" Greyson looped his arms around Sutton's waist from behind and they walked over to the tents where food was being prepared. He nuzzled against the soft cotton fabric of her pink shirt. Her thick legs flowed from underneath her miniskirt. During the entire stage play, he had been contemplating running his palm up from her knee to the burning area between her thighs. Sutton probably had had the same thoughts because she'd caressed his bare knee on several occasions—when she thought Mr. Hill wasn't watching.

"The sun will be going down soon," Sutton remarked after eating a Polish sausage and fries. "Do you want to head over to the grand bandstand for Mayor Meriwether's speech? We should get a good seat for the fireworks."

Greyson had his own fireworks planned for the evening. He checked his watch. "We have a little time. How about a ride on the Ferris wheel?"

They walked hand in hand to the Ferris wheel. Once they got on, the ride stopped when they reached the top. The mountains obstructed the view of the capital and any nearby towns, but not the stars. Millions of stars sprinkled the black sky.

"Do you think that there are other worlds out there?" Sutton asked. "Maybe another world where we each have a twin." She giggled. "I bet our twins got it right the first time."

"Maybe." Greyson pulled his gaze from the twinkling lights in the distance to Sutton's sparkling smile. "Remember how we would ride the Ferris wheel over and over at the state fair? We used to sit at the top, looking out into the world, making plans for our future."

Sutton snuggled up to his broad chest. "Most men aren't good at remembering romantic things like that."

"We weren't being romantic then. We were just kids. Dreaming about the future."

Sutton locked her eyes with his. "Did all your dreams come true?"

"Almost." He kissed the top of her red-brown hair. "Almost."

"I think if I had known how you felt, I wouldn't have married Alex. Your kissing me at my wedding clouded my head, but I never fully understood the depth of what you were feeling. I wonder how things would have been different if you and I had married five years ago."

"Don't think about that now. It's in the past."

"I want to say this. I want you to hear this. One problem after another has come up since we returned to Hannaford Valley. I really appreciate you standing by me. You didn't have to incur the expense of bringing Sierra and me back from Ohio. You certainly didn't have to hire a PI and a lawyer to help me keep custody of her." Sutton paused to settle the emotion quivering in her throat. "I want you to know that I love you is all."

Greyson placed his hands on each side of her face and softly kissed her lips. He took her pouty bottom lip between his teeth. She giggled. His tongue found the corner of her mouth. She opened to receive him and he slipped inside her mouth. Her hand rested on his knee, absorbing his heat. As he wrestled with her tongue, her hand moved upward. He twisted his tongue around hers with a tenderness that contradicted Sutton's ardent stroking of his thigh. Their synchronized breathing became heavy. Her fingers inched under the leg of his shorts. He suckled the tip of her tongue as her hand found its way to his crotch. She cupped him, caressing lovingly. He liked the drastic change since the movie theatre. Suspended in air, underneath the stars with Sutton learning his body, Greyson never wanted the Ferris wheel to move. He held her in his embrace, kissing her until the Ferris wheel returned them to the world below.

Mayor Greg Meriwether was voted "most likely to succeed" in high school. He stood over six feet tall with a full blond beard and mustache. His booming voice never carried negative words. His genuine love of all the people of Hannaford Valley made his second run for mayor go unchallenged. He stood with a broad smile on the grand bandstand underneath the banner that read "One Community, One People, One Family." He had proved on several occasions that the banner was more than a campaign slogan. He governed the town by this principle. His ancestors had governed Hannaford Valley for five generations. During an era when black Americans were forbidden to own property, were killed for looking a white man in the eye, and were considered by society to be worthless individuals, the Meriwether family treated all of the town's citizens equally. The town had its problems, but everyone was a member of the extended Hannaford Valley family.

The crowd laughed sporadically throughout Mayor Meriwether's lighthearted speech.

"I'm getting the signal from my wife that says my time is running out. Y'all know how much I like a captive audience." Meriwether pulled at his suspenders as he laughed. "Before we get to the fireworks, I need to announce the Citizen of the Year."

The mayor's tone turned serious. "This year started off as a challenge for Hannaford Valley. Our economy, such as it is, was failing. The valley's budget didn't balance. Many of you sat in my office with stories of economic despair. Many of you were considering leaving our quaint town to venture to the capital, where jobs are more plentiful."

Mayor Meriwether paused. "With that said, we pretty much needed a miracle to turn things around. And that miracle came to us in the form of this year's Citizen of the Year."

The mayor's mood lightened. He pulled a piece of paper from his suit pocket. "The Citizen of the Year has acted single-handedly to turn this town around. Until tonight, he has acted anonymously. He is responsible for building a day-care center in the church. A generous donation has been offered for the renovation of City Hall. The school board has received enough computers to open a lab in each school. He's also responsible for the restoration of the paper mill, which will employ five hundred workers. It's the spark that will ignite Hannaford Valley."

The mayor picked up steam. "He's a good man with down-home family values. That's what brought him back home. Instead of this being a Fourth of July celebration, we should rename it Ballantyne's Day."

The crowd erupted in applause.

The mayor lifted his voice over the crowd. "Ladies and gentlemen, this year's Citizen of the Year is Greyson Ballantyne."

Sutton sat stunned as she watched Greyson climb the stairs of the bandstand to accept his plaque and make a quick thank-you speech. She had no idea. She searched her memory for the explanations he had given her about his state of employment. He was doing consulting work for Hunter, Roe & Volney, he said. Helping to get his parents settled into their new home, he told her. Sutton listened to the people around her whisper that Greyson had purchased his parents' new house. Her eyes darted around to the single women in the crowd who began making plans to seduce the handsome, wealthy bachelor.

The heartbreak of Alex's infidelities rushed at her. She remembered Belinda. They had talked on several occasions about her fears of dating a "corporate roller." Why didn't Greyson tell her about his status in the community? Why had Greyson kept all of this a secret from her? She didn't know Greyson as well as she believed she did. She stood and excused herself, running from the bandstand area. She felt humiliated and betrayed as she hurried through town toward home.

Sutton rushed up the stairs and fell across her bed, her eyes glued to the ceiling. *This is all wrong,* she told herself. The entire scenario made no sense. Why would Greyson lie about the man he is? *Who is he?*

She let her eyes close on the night, losing herself in thought.

How could Greyson remember the smallest details of her life that were enormously important to her, yet not be forth-coming? How could he stand by her in all of her recent trials and not share all of himself with her? *I can't do this again. I can't stay in a relationship thinking everything is one way when it's really something totally different.* She had discussed her fears about starting a new relationship with Greyson many times. While lying tangled in his bed sheets, she'd revealed her insecurities about dishonest, disloyal men. How could he keep secrets from her?

The roses.

Two months before Sutton turned thirteen, she'd knelt in Mama Ballantyne's garden, learning the finer details of nur-turing a rose garden. She had grown fond of spending time with Mrs. Ballantyne, learning the craft of gardening. Mrs. Ballantyne crossbred flowers, sometimes with amazing re-sults. Still, the simple red rose became Sutton's favorite flower. It stood majestic and symbolized romance.

As her birthday approached she confessed to Greyson on his front porch that she had never been kissed. She told him that the girls in gym teased her about her father's strictness when it came to boys.

"Sure, I'll teach you to kiss," Greyson answered her request.

Sutton leaned toward him, her eyes closed and lips puckered.

"Not like this. Tomorrow. Tomorrow, I'll pick you up after school."

Several teachers scolded Sutton during the following school day. The only thing on her mind was that Greyson would be standing outside the school at the end of the day waiting for her. It wouldn't be the first time; he often picked her up and walked her into town to hang out at the new arcade. But this would be different; they had planned a "tryst." After this afternoon, she would be well on her way to becoming a woman. The girls in gym wouldn't be able to tease her because she would have a story to share. Of course she wouldn't tell them the boy she kissed was her friend Greyson. She'd make up a friend of a friend from the capital.

"Hi," Greyson greeted Sutton at the foot of the stairs of the junior high school.

She fell into step beside him without a word. Now that the time was drawing near, butterflies fluttered inside her stomach.

"For you." Greyson pulled a perfect red-black rose from inside his shirt.

Sutton hoisted her backpack on her shoulder and accepted the flower. She held it to her nose. Being selected especially for her, it smelled sweeter than all the times when she had sniffed the roses in Mrs. Ballantyne's garden.

Greyson escorted her to the playhouse that had started to shift to the right. They hadn't been inside together since the boys entered eighth grade, leaving Sutton behind in elementary school. Inside, Greyson had prepared for their lesson by placing a spread over the dirt floor and scattering the petals of red roses over the blanket. Sutton glanced back at him as she climbed inside.

The butterflies in her stomach turned into a line of geese flying in circles. Greyson had put much tender care and thought into what Sutton believed would be a quick peck on the lips before she ran home, embarrassed she'd gone through with it.

Sutton shed her backpack in a corner and sat with her knees drawn up to her newly developing chest. Greyson sat in the same stance next to her.

"Did you get the roses from your mother's garden?"

Greyson nodded.

"Have you kissed a lot of girls?" Since he was sixteen, almost seventeen, she was sure he had. Alex bragged about it all the time.

"Only a few." Greyson's eyes flickered in her direction.

Silence permeated the room, vying for dominance with the sweet aroma of rose petals. Sutton ran her hands through the petals, spraying them about her feet.

"Ready?" Greyson asked pointedly. She'd never seen him look more serious.

Sutton nodded. She closed her eyes as Greyson's face came near. She puckered her lips. Her heart beat wildly and the geese in her stomach dipped when she felt Greyson's face heat her space. Very gently, he placed his lips next to hers. He lingered. Sutton opened her eyes. His were closed. She closed hers. Greyson pulled away.

"You have to open your mouth," Greyson instructed with medicinal words, but his maturing voice became husky with desire.

"Open my mouth?" Sutton questioned.

Greyson nodded.

"Are you sure?"

Greyson nodded again.

She inhaled. Exhaled. Nodded.

Greyson closed his eyes and entered her space again. Sutton closed her eyes and opened her mouth when his lips met hers. When the tip of his tongue crossed her lips, a path of warm electrical current flowed from her chest out to her limbs. Greyson's hand came up behind her back and encouraged her to accept him. She let him taste the corners of her mouth even as her head became light enough to float away. The stiffness of her back relaxed under his caress.

Greyson pulled away. "Okay?"

Sutton nodded, unable to speak.

"This time, follow me. Use your tongue to do what I do."

Sutton nodded. Closed her eyes.

Greyson entered her space. His lips met hers; his tongue entered her mouth. Sutton followed his movements. As her body began to heat again, the confidence of her tongue increased. She chased Greyson's tongue, following it inside his mouth. She leaned into him as the hold on her back became firmer.

Greyson pulled away, only inches, and stared into her eyes. "Sutton," he whispered before taking her lips again.

Sutton's arms wound behind his neck. Greyson's kiss probed deeper. He pulled away to treat her with quick pecks while rubbing circles in the small of her back. He watched her as he flicked his tongue along the corners of her mouth, daring her to catch him. Sutton closed her eyes and studied his lesson.

Greyson wrapped his arm around her waist so tightly she felt sure he would crush her. He awkwardly lifted his body over hers while laying her back on the blanket. Sutton inhaled the scent of roses. A new ache stirred between her legs. The ache throbbed. Greyson's hand accidentally grazed her breast as he reached to cup her chin.

"Grey!"

They jumped apart at Chevy's voice.

"Grey! Mama wants you."

They scurried out of the makeshift playhouse. They studied each other for signs of guilt as Chevy approached. Kirkland trailed him, dragging a yellow kite on a long string.

"What?" Greyson asked with an edge when Chevy and Kirkland came near.

"Mama said come home. She wants to know if it was you that picked the red roses out of her garden." Chevy looked between them suspiciously.

"Yeah," Kirkland added, "Pop says if it was, you gonna get it bad."

"What y'all doing?" Chevy glanced over their shoulders at the playhouse.

"Nothing," Sutton and Greyson answered together.

Chevy took a step toward the playhouse. Greyson blocked his path.

Chevy cocked his head to the side. "What y'all doing in that old playhouse?"

"Nothing," Greyson answered with more conviction.

"Ooooh, I'm telling Mama," Kirkland said and took off

in the direction of the house. The bright yellow kite skirted the ground behind him.

Chevy looked between them. Sutton looked to the ground. Chevy leaned over and picked a rose petal from her hair.

Thirty-four

Greyson stepped down from the bandstand to find Sutton missing. It wasn't hard to imagine that she had been shocked to learn of his wealth. To learn he was one of the guys she vowed never to trust again. He thought, *I should have told her long ago. I was going to tell her everything tonight.* He had pictured disclosing his secrets in a restaurant at a table covered with rose petals. She would tell him that she loved him so much that it didn't matter. They would fantasize about the lavish future his wealth could bring them. Sutton running off before he completed his acceptance speech was not what he had expected. If only he had known he would be receiving the award, he could have prepared her. He tucked the plaque into the crevice of the seat as he drove to her house.

Greyson rang the bell. Sutton didn't respond. He knocked on the door. "Sutton, open up." He thanked his lucky Ferris-wheel stars that her parents were still at the celebration.

The door swung open. "You lied to me."

"I didn't lie to you. I didn't tell you everything, but I never lied."

"Lying by omission. It's the same thing, Greyson. Don't play lawyer with me. I made it clear how I felt about getting involved with men like you. You should have been honest with me then."

"Men like what? What are men like me like? Do you think I'm a different person than the man you confessed your love to on the Ferris wheel because I'm successful? I can't apologize for having enough money to spoil the people I love. I worked hard and paid my dues. It's not like I robbed a bank or sold drugs."

"So what do you want me to do?"

"What do you want me to do, Sutton?" Desperation and anger fueled his words.

"I think we should give each other space."

"No. We've spent our entire lives apart. How much space do you need?"

"I don't know you. I thought I did, but watching the mayor talk about you tonight showed me a side of you I never knew. I can't go through that again—finding out the man I'm with is someone completely different."

Greyson lowered his voice to a gentle, persuasive tone. "Get to know me now. Let's go back to my place and talk."

Sutton shook her head no.

"What? Are you going to push me away? You're not going to give me a chance to explain?"

"I can't. I can't listen to you justify your wrongs. I can't be the fool again."

"I have waited my entire life for you. I have sacrificed everything to be with you."

"I never asked you to do those things."

"You don't have to ask when someone loves you."

"What do you want me to do about what you sacrificed?"

"I want you to stop being a self-centered—"

"Self-centered!"

"—spoiled little girl and give me the respect of granting me a conversation with you. I've always stood back and watched while you made decisions that I knew were not right for you. I won't do that anymore."

Sutton studied Greyson from beyond the screen door.

"You love me? You owe me this much."

Sutton's bottom lip fell into its pouty form.

"Don't be stubborn; it's not ladylike. One conversation and if I can't make you see how wrong you are, I'll never bother you again."

Thirty-five

"Where are we going?" Sutton asked as Greyson drove past his parents' property.

"I want to show you something." He drove through the darkness along the perimeter of his land. He took a winding road outlined with tiny torchlights up the path leading to the big house that looked down on her backyard.

Sutton remained silent as Greyson pulled in front of the house and cut the engine. He rounded the car and opened her door. "Come inside."

Possible theories ran through her head as she watched Greyson retrieve a key and open the front door. She followed him inside to a foyer that had skylights in the ceiling. Directly in front of the front door was a grand staircase with a winding white rail.

"What are we doing here?" Sutton asked, following him into a huge room with a fireplace. The furniture was covered with white painter's cloths.

Silently, Greyson pulled away the cloth from the leather sofa and instructed Sutton to sit with him.

"Everything you heard the mayor say is true. I have a lot of money."

Sutton figured as much.

Greyson continued. "Sutton, the last few years of my life were completely dissatisfying. I couldn't figure out why. I was named the first black partner at Hunter, Roe & Volney. I had a solid reputation in the Chicago community. I had enough money to buy anything I needed to be happy. Companions came in and out of my life. But I wasn't happy."

Greyson sat forward on the sofa. "Why wasn't I happy when everything I worked for had come to fruition? I missed my family and Hannaford Valley, but I could come visit whenever I wanted. That wasn't it. One day it became crystal clear. I was still in love with you. From that day on, everything I did was with you in mind."

His voice lifted. "I cut my expenses and started saving money. I invested heavily. I talked with my mentor at Hunter and promised him only two more years of practice. When the two years were up, I resigned from full-time practice at the law firm and came back to Hannaford Valley."

He turned to her and looked deeply in her eyes. "My plan was to help rebuild the town and have you in my life."

"But you didn't know I would be here."

"No, I didn't. That's why I started construction on this house. I figured I'd build us the grandest house you could imagine, start up the mill again for job stability, and come to Ohio and take you away from Alex. I loved you that much."

Sutton's mouth dropped. This house belonged to Greyson? He loved her and intended to take her away from her husband and marry her? How could a man love a woman so devoutly, so unconditionally? Life with Alex proved the opposite—a man could say he loved a woman and treat her with contempt and disrespect. Her head swam. What was she to do with all the love Greyson offered?

"Oh, yeah," Greyson continued to explain. "I was jumping on a plane and coming to Ohio and not leaving without you. Things didn't turn out the way I planned. Alex was killed. You had a child. And then all the other problems rained down on you, which kept you preoccupied. But I hung in there because I knew that everything I wanted was still within reach."

"How could you risk everything not knowing how I felt about you?"

"How could I not? Knowing how I felt about you? Being home, starting the mill, helping the town—it all made me feel good, but there was still something missing. I knew that I would never be happy, my life couldn't begin, until you were in it. There was no room to negotiate. There still isn't."

"I don't know what to say."

"Say that you see me for the man I am and not what Alex represented. Everything that I've acquired has been with the hope of making you happy."

"I don't know if I'm ready, Greyson. I'm not in the same place as you are." She crossed the room, away from the thickness of his emotions.

"What is it?"

"I'm broke, I have a child and recently lost my husband. What can I offer you? I want to know that I bring something positive into the relationship. If I don't, you'll begin to wander after the newness wears off."

Greyson laughed. "Sutton, are you listening to me? I can't believe you don't see what you've given me already. You love me openly, honestly. You make the sweetest love to me my body has ever known. And Sierra," he smiled, "is the most precious child I've ever met." Greyson crossed the room and took her into his arms. "Everything about you makes me happy. Don't I make you happy?"

Sutton felt free since being with Greyson. He opened a new world of love to her. "You make me very happy."

"Then why the hesitation? We love each other. I adore Sierra. It's time to become a family."

"Greyson, I need to think about it a little longer."

"I told you I'm not going to stand around and watch you make the wrong decisions in your life. I'm the right choice for you and I say we get married."

Before she could protest, he captured her lips in an aggressive kiss that closed the door on her doubts. He separated from her and briefly left the room.

When he returned, he said, "Sit down." Greyson helped

her to the sofa before dropping to his knees. He pulled out
a small ring box and flipped the top open. Inside was the
most gorgeous ring she'd ever seen. Tanzanite surrounded
by diamonds, the ring resembled a rosebud.

"Sutton Hill, I've wanted you all my life. Will you marry
me?"

While Sutton tried to fight off the emotion jamming her
throat, Greyson placed the ring on her finger.

"Will you marry me?"

Sutton nodded, tears threatening to fall.

"The lawyer in me feels the need to tell you that once you
seal this deal, it's for life. I would never, ever entertain the
idea of divorce. If we have problems, we work them out. We
love each other for the rest of our lives. Understand?"

Sutton nodded again.

"And it must be understood that I want more kids—lots
of them. Enough to fill this house."

Sutton nodded with a smile.

"There's a bunch of rooms in this house."

She laughed.

"Oh yeah, one last point of the contract. You must allow
me to love you with all my heart and you must love me just
the same for the rest of our lives. Agreed?"

"Agreed."

Greyson sat forward on his knees so that his face was
only inches from hers. "I can promise you that I will continue to love you even after I'm dead and buried."

"I know." She could feel the truth of that statement.

"Now answer me with words, will you marry me?"

"Yes, I'll marry you."

The following Saturday, Greyson and Sutton were married in the great room of the new house he had built for his
wife.

"If you build it, they will come." Chevy jokingly repeated
the line from a popular baseball movie. Greyson knew the

laughter only covered up Chevy's sadness. He'd seen the elaborate cabin built for two.

"Family." Greyson stood and clicked his spoon against his champagne glass.

The small crowd of immediate family and friends quieted down. The short notice did not hinder Greyson's friends, Brice and Ryan, from making the trip. The mayor postponed a business trip to escort his wife. Both families of in-laws came elaborately dressed. Keeping the ceremony small when they were both lifelong residents of Hannaford Valley proved a difficult challenge. Eventually, Greyson agreed to allow the valley's newspaper reporter and photographer to attend the ceremony.

Sutton looked up at him from her seat next to her father. Her new husband stood regal, majestic at the front of the room, reminding her of his appearance over the hill in back of her parents' house.

Greyson beamed with pride as Sierra came over for him to lift her up into his arms. He secured her on his hip with a kiss before continuing. "We want to thank you all for coming. Especially on such short notice. I really love Sutton and didn't want to wait another day to have her as my wife."

Sutton's heart shifted as everyone oohed and ahhed.

Greyson continued. "Because of the quick wedding date, we've postponed our honeymoon for awhile."

Sutton smiled. Every day with him would be a honeymoon.

"Anyway, I wanted to give my wife something special for marrying me." He handed Sierra to Chevy.

"Sutton, your new brothers-in-law called in a few favors and negotiated the deal that makes this gift possible."

Sutton looked between Chevy, who was grinning ear-to-ear, and Kirkland who couldn't bring himself to meet her gaze. Time would heal their rift, but today was her day and she wouldn't allow past history to ruin it.

Greyson smiled. "The University of West Virginia has agreed to place a college annex here in Hannaford Valley."

Sutton slowly rose from her seat.

Greyson and Sutton watched each other as if they were alone in the room. Greyson's voice dipped to a seductive tone privately directed to his wife. "I've already paid your enrollment fees. All you have to do is decide on a major and select your classes."

Sutton made her way across the room.

"I know how much your education means to you." Greyson looked down into her emotion-filled face as she stood in front of him.

"My gift to you, wife," Greyson whispered.

"I can go to school and study anything I want? You don't worry about it taking time from our marriage?"

"You being happy is my primary concern. Sierra and I can take care of ourselves while you get your education."

Sutton gazed up into his eyes. "I love you so much."

Greyson wrapped her into his arms and took her lips in a kiss that made the crowd moan.

Thirty-six

After delivering the bouquet of mixed flowers to her father's grave, Sierra ran back to the Volvo and sat in the front seat with Greyson. He pulled out the contents of her McDonald's Happy Meal and helped her slather her fries with ketchup. He glanced out the window and watched Sutton standing over the cross on the Galloway place that marked Alex's resting place. He glanced toward the menacing house and wondered if Mr. Galloway was alert enough to see them.

"Greyson?"

"Yeah, honey?" His attention went to a smiling Sierra.

"Can I have more ketchup?"

"More?"

"On my hamburger."

Greyson opened a packet and spread it across the hamburger. His gaze kept wandering to Sutton.

"Greyson," Sierra called, exasperated.

"Yes?" She had his attention again.

"You didn't give me the first bite."

"I'm sorry. I forgot." He took the hamburger from her lap. "But don't pout; it's not ladylike." He lifted the hamburger to her lips while she took the first bite.

"I get the first bite because—"

"Because I love you." Greyson kissed the top of her fiery-red hair.

His eyes went back to Sutton as he stuffed a handful of

fries into his mouth. If she had been in the car, she would have scolded him for spoiling Sierra. He told her that as Sierra's stepfather his job was to spoil her rotten. Sierra had begun to be stubborn with Sutton, but minded him without question. He sat Sierra down and they had a long talk over a Happy Meal and things went back to normal.

Sierra swung her feet back and forth against the seat as she chewed her hamburger.

Greyson glanced at the clock on the dashboard. "Maybe I should go get Mommy."

"She'll come back soon," Sierra said never taking her eyes off her hamburger. "Can I have more ketchup?"

Sutton stood over Alex's gravesite knowing that Greyson's eyes were riveted to her back. He was probably watching the clock, tempted to join her. He wouldn't. She wanted to come to the gravesite alone, but he'd insisted on driving her. Alex died six months ago to the day, and they were married now, but Greyson still harbored moments of jealous doubt about her lingering affections for Alex.

"Well." Sutton shifted her weight from foot to foot. She reflected on the good times of their relationship. Kneeling down on the thick green grass, she placed her flowers next to Sierra's.

"This feels weird. How would I speak to you if you were here today?" She contemplated the question. "I guess I would ask you if I ever made you happy. If our marriage made your short time on earth happy, then I wouldn't change a thing that happened between us. I did a lot of growing up. Sierra was born. You achieved the wealth and status you craved all your life."

Sutton sat near the cross, her legs tucked beneath her. "I want you to know that I never cheated on you. My feelings for Greyson stayed buried until after you died. I honored my vows to you. It's important that you know that."

Sutton remembered Mother Galloway's harsh words. She

took a cleansing breath. "After today, I will have no negative memories of our time together. I'm letting that go. As Sierra grows up, she'll know what a dynamic, determined man you were. I see those qualities in her already."

She thought of the locket. "I think you built positive memories with your daughter that I'll never fully know about. Sierra loves you; she really does."

Sutton plucked several blades of grass from the ground and broke them into tiny pieces. "My favorite memory of you is my prom night." Her face lifted at the memory. "You were at the university taking your finals. I cried and cried when you called and told me you wouldn't be able to escort me. I was so distraught my father wanted to kill you, although he encouraged me to support you and the fact that you were securing our future. I did as you said, went to the prom alone." Sutton clutched her chest. "When you walked through the door, dressed to the nines, my heart almost exploded in my chest. That was the night I knew I would marry you. As focused as you were on your career, you gave up a night of studying for finals to be with me."

Sutton tried to pinpoint when things became sour between them. Recalling her earlier proclamation to forget the negative, she focused on the magic of prom night.

A car door opened. She turned to see Greyson standing at his door, arms resting on the hood of the Volvo, peering at her over his sunglasses.

"I was faithful and I tried to make it work when we were together." She paused. "I'm married to Greyson now. He's a wonderful father to Sierra." She rose to her knees. "I will honor your memory, but I will love my husband."

Sutton stood and said a silent prayer. She made the sign of the cross over her chest and walked away.

Greyson studied Sutton's face for any sign of emotion after visiting her first husband's grave. She fastened her seat belt and glanced back at Sierra playing with her dolls.

Greyson started the engine and put the car in reverse.

"I want to go to Ohio and talk with Mother Galloway," Sutton blurted out.

Greyson hit the brakes. "Absolutely not."

"I really wasn't asking your permission, Greyson."

Greyson turned the car half a circle, put the gear in drive and started home. "Good, because you'd never get it."

"Why are you being this way?"

He glanced in the rearview mirror. As he suspected, Sierra had dropped her dolls on the seat and was watching them. "We'll talk at home."

Sutton settled back in her seat. Her bottom lip dropped into pouting position. This would be a hard fight to win.

Once they reached home, Greyson went directly to the basement, while Sutton took Sierra upstairs to bed. No words had passed between them since her announcement that she wanted to make a connection with Mother Galloway.

Greyson opened the door of the mini refrigerator. He took out a banana, strawberries, and orange juice. He dumped a tray of ice in the blender and followed with the rest of the ingredients. His hand rested on top of the blender as he watched the mixture swirl.

He knew going to Alex's grave was a bad idea. That was why he insisted he go with her after church. Thank goodness when church ended her mother had roped them into coming over. After that he had to keep his promise to Sierra to drive to the capital for a McDonald's Happy Meal. But Sutton wouldn't let it go. Before he could make the turn that would take them home, she reminded him to drive to the Galloway place.

Greyson sat at the bar sipping his drink when Sutton came down the stairs. She had changed out of her dress and wore a white terry-cloth robe. As he watched her approach, the only thing he wanted to do was to carry her upstairs to their bedroom and make love.

Sutton sat on the barstool next to him. He slid a glass over to her.

"Thank you," she mumbled, never looking up at him.

Unable to hold his anger any longer, Greyson challenged her. "Why do you want to go to Ohio and dredge up the past?"

"Dredge up the past? Why is it that whenever you talk about my life with Alex you make it seem dark and vile?"

"Please." Greyson hopped down from the stool and crossed the room. That time period happened to be the darkest era of his life.

"I never had the chance to clear up things with Mother Galloway. You handled the whole custody petition."

"That's right, I did. Leave it alone."

"I can't. Greyson, this is about more than her trying to take Sierra. Mother Galloway is hurting over Alex's death. I've gone on with my life. She has no contact with Sierra. It isn't right."

"Are you forgetting that this woman was blackmailing you? She wanted to end our relationship and she tried to use Sierra to do it. Who cares if she's hurting?"

Sutton rested her cheek against her fist. She watched Greyson pace the floor, his response too exaggerated for their argument. "This isn't like you. You are the kindest, most understanding person I know. Why wouldn't you want me to clear the air with Mother Galloway?"

"I think that the past is the past and you should leave it there. Alex is gone—"

"Yes, he is. But Mother Galloway is still hurting and right now she thinks I've turned my back on her and on her son." Sutton left her stool and approached him. "Alex and I had our problems, but before we were a couple we were friends. I remembered that today at his gravesite. I have to respect that."

"Respect Alex? What about your husband? Remember me?"

"That's why I'm discussing it with you."

Greyson turned his back to her. "For me, this is much deeper than making friends with Mrs. Galloway. She's a threat to my family."

Sutton touched his arm, encouraging him to face her.

"I know that I came into your life right after Alex's death. Your father may have had a point. I didn't allow you time to grieve before I was there making plans for our future." He held his palm next to her face. "Maybe I wasn't playing fair, but I couldn't let you get away again. Now when I think things are safe you want to befriend Alex's mother."

"Safe?" Sutton took a step back and watched the stress lines of his face deepen. "Could you possibly believe that I might leave you? That I might abandon what we have together?"

Greyson answered without words.

"I can't believe you." Sutton took a deep breath, her expression hardened. "I'm getting on a plane to Ohio first thing in the morning and I'm going to salvage Sierra's relationship with her grandmother." She marched to the stairs, stopping before she took the first step. "I'm getting on a plane tomorrow night and coming home to my husband. Who—if he knows what's good for him—will have red roses next to the bed when I get home and be waiting to make love to me."

Greyson watched with confused emotions as Sutton slowly climbed the stairs. "Sutton," he called.

She stopped.

"Don't be stubborn; it's not ladylike."

She took a step and then stopped. "Will you look after Sierra while I'm gone?"

"Actually, I thought I might go with you."

"I need to do this alone."

"How did I know you would say that? I want to go with you."

"How will Mother Galloway react if you're with me?"

Defeated by common sense, he watched the movement of his wife's behind as she climbed the stairs.

"Will you look after Sierra while I'm gone?"

"Of course." Pop's talk the night before his wedding warned of the many compromises he would have to make in his marriage. "Sutton?"

"Yes, Greyson." She turned to him with a wicked smile.
"Yes?"
"Yes." She giggled.
"Make-up sex?"
"I said yes."

Thirty-seven

The look of annoyance drained from Eddie's face when he saw Sutton standing on the stoop. "Sutton? I never thought I'd see you again." He pulled her inside. "How are you? How's Sierra? Is something wrong?"

His uncanny resemblance to Alex still shook her. "Everything's fine. I hoped I could talk with Mother Galloway."

He studied her for a long moment. "Is it true you married Greyson Ballantyne?"

Sutton nodded.

"I had hoped—"

"Hoped what?"

Befuddled, he backed down. "Never mind. Come in the den and I'll get Mother Galloway."

Sutton sat nervously in the den, staring at the picture that hid the wall safe. Mother Galloway had not told Eddie that his secret had been discovered.

"She'll be right in." Eddie joined her. He sat on the edge of the massive desk making small talk until Mother Galloway entered the den. "Don't be a stranger."

"I won't." She pulled her hand away from him.

Mother Galloway wore a stylish snakeskin pantsuit. Tight curls framed her made-up face. She pulled her chair up to her desk. "You've returned," she stated flatly.

Sutton clutched her purse. "I wish things hadn't turned out this way for all of us. I've been thinking we could salvage the relationship between you and Sierra."

"Sierra? What about my son's memory?"

"I don't mean to sound harsh, but Alex is dead. We are still alive. I'm picking up the pieces and trying to make the best of my life. You should do the same."

"Who are you to step into my house and give me advice?"

"I'm your daughter-in-law, Alex's widow. I've gone on with my life, but I'll never forget the good times between us."

"I would never know it. You ran off and married that Ballantyne boy before my son's body was cold."

"I won't discuss my relationship with Greyson with you other than to say that he supports what I'm doing today."

Mother Galloway's manicured nails gripped the edge of the desk. "And what is that?"

"I want to offer you a chance to spend time with Sierra. She is the only remaining part of Alex on this earth. I thought you'd like to preserve your relationship with her."

Mother Galloway's mouth softened. Obviously, she had been so determined to seek revenge on Sutton that she had forgotten that Sierra was a part of Alex.

"Mother Galloway, I can't do anything to bring Alex back. Me holeing up in the house grieving will not do it. But I can offer to share what is left of him."

Mother Galloway silently considered the offer. She had bonded with Sierra the short time they lived in her house.

Sutton went into her purse and handed Mother Galloway a small box. "Alex gave me these when he loved me the most. I wanted you to have them."

Mother Galloway opened the small box. Her hand went to her mouth. Tears threatened.

"I'd like you to keep them in the Galloway family. Maybe pass them on to Eddie's fiancée. Or give them to Sierra when she marries."

Mother Galloway removed the elaborate wedding set and slid them onto her pinky finger.

"Alex's wedding band is there too."

Mother Galloway's eyes darted her way before examining the box for the last ring.

"Eddie is a good person. He's lonely for his mother. You could have your son and your granddaughter in your life."

Tears streaked the foundation of Mother Galloway's cheek. She cleared her throat. "It took a lot for you to come here like this. Especially when I should be the one coming to you."

"We had a good relationship before Alex died. He'd want us to be friends. He would want his daughter to know you. It doesn't matter who takes the first step."

Mother Galloway carefully placed the rings back in the tiny box. "Sutton, you have been open with me. I will be open with you. My son did not behave as a husband should with you. You stood by him no matter how bad it got. I admire you for that."

"Alex was special in his own way."

"You forgave what I tried to do in my grief and made this gigantic step to preserve my relationship with my son's daughter. I can meet you halfway."

"Thank you." Serenity eased the tension in Sutton's chest.

"Thank you for forgiving an old, foolish woman. I've made a lot of mistakes in my life. Maybe I can start to clean some of them up."

"Ladies, I'm home." Greyson closed the door behind him.

Greyson placed his briefcase on the floor at his feet and draped his wet overcoat over it. He stood and waited for Sierra to round the corner. He stooped down when he saw her running to him, red braids flying wildly behind her. The flash of her bright smile made his heart go loop-de-loop.

"Hey, you almost knocked me over."

"What did you bring me?" Sierra giggled.

"I brought you me. Isn't that enough?"

Sierra stuck her hand inside his suit jacket. Greyson wiggled, being sure not to drop her during their nightly ritual.

"Okay, okay." Greyson gave in when Sierra tickled him.

"I give up." He placed her on the floor and pulled a sucker from his overcoat.

"Thank you." Sierra locked her hands behind her back and twisted shyly at the waist.

Greyson pinched her healthy cheeks between his fingers. "That smile is thanks enough. That and a kiss." He knelt low for her to plant a kiss on his cheek. "Yeah, that's the stuff. Where's your mother?"

Sierra took his hand and led him into the kitchen.

"Hey, husband." Sutton didn't look up from the books and notepads spread across the kitchen table. At the far end sat a crayon box and coloring book along with a glass of milk.

"Hey, you." Greyson kissed Sutton when she lifted her head.

"Uggh," Sierra groaned before climbing up in the chair with her coloring materials.

"You're late. And you're wet."

"Raining hard out there."

"We ate without you—sorry. Let me fix your plate."

"No, keep studying. I can do it after I get out of this soggy suit."

Sierra followed him up the stairs to his bedroom. She laid on her stomach across their bed watching cartoons while Greyson took his shower. When she heard the water stop running, she chatted on and on about her day. He took her across the hall to her bedroom and read her a story before tucking her in for the night.

"Greyson, put my sucker over there so I can find it when I wake up."

"Yes, ma'am." He placed the candy where she instructed before closing the door and joining Sutton in the kitchen.

"What are you studying?" Greyson asked between bites of dinner.

"Logic and it's killing me." She looked up at him with devilish eyes. "You know I love you, don't you?"

Greyson's lips curled upward. "Oh, no. That won't work on me."

Sutton pushed back her chair.

Greyson diverted his eyes to his food. "Not working."

Sutton craned her neck so that her face obstructed his vision.

"Go on, now. I'm eating."

"Honey." Sutton slinked out of her chair and wrapped her arms around his shoulders.

"I had a long day."

Sutton wrangled her body into his lap. She placed a light kiss on his neck. "You're an attorney. You probably aced your logic course. I'm stuck on this one theory."

"Sutton, remove yourself from my lap and do your homework," Greyson scolded behind erotic eyes.

"I bet that if I sit in my instructor's lap like this she won't turn me down."

"You know you need a spanking, don't you?"

"You'll help me?"

"Of course I'll help you." He wrapped his dangling arms around her waist. "I love this. You, me, Sierra. You have no idea how good I feel when I come home and you're here waiting for me." His eyes glazed over. "I feel like my heart is going to explode every time she runs to me and the padded feet of her pajamas pat across the floor."

"I have the same feeling when you walk up to me and say, 'Hey, wife.' If someone had told me we'd end up this way when we were kids—"

"You wouldn't have believed it. I knew we'd be together. I just didn't know Sierra would be a part of the blessing."

"I wouldn't have believed it, but I sure did wish for it."

Thirty-eight

Sutton entered the darkened house as quietly as possible. She figured Greyson would be worried that she hadn't returned from the library immediately after her shift ended. Taking advantage of getting off early, she'd hidden herself at a back table in the library and studied for an upcoming exam. In the foyer, sitting on a new cream marble pedestal, was a huge vase of red roses. She smiled. She hooked her jacket on the brass coat tree and moved into the kitchen. She pulled leftovers of fried chicken and spaghetti from the refrigerator. Mama Ballantyne had provided dinner for her family in her absence. She heated her dinner, poured a glass of milk, and sat at the kitchen table. The only light in the room came from the hood over the stove.

Sutton kicked off her shoes as she ate. As she dug her fork into the fried chicken, she thanked her higher power for the blessing of her family—immediate and extended. Things had gone the way she'd hoped with Mother Galloway. They definitely had a place to build from. Sierra would learn about her father from Mother Galloway. They would share granddaughter-grandmother moments. Sutton remembered the numerous cultural and high-society events Mother Galloway dragged Sierra to when they lived with her. Actually, Sierra seemed to enjoy these outings. With all three sets of grandparents in her life, each with their own unique way of loving her, Sierra would become a well-rounded adult.

After many nights of debating with Greyson, he had

come to understand her need to pay off the balance of her IRS debt with her own earnings. She suspected that Greyson had hoped she would go to college part-time and care for him and Sierra full-time. It didn't seem right to her that he be saddled with Alex's debt. She contacted the IRS and made payment arrangements. She met with Maddie and made a schedule that would allow her to work in the library, attend classes, and still have plenty of time to devote to her family.

Sutton rinsed the dirty dishes in the sink and placed them in the dishwasher before heading upstairs to bed. Friday was the longest day of the week for her. She took Sierra to one of the grandparents' house—they alternated weeks looking after her—went to the university annex for a full day of classes, and then finished the day at the library. Greyson picked up Sierra after work, made dinner, and put Sierra to bed. This Friday, Maddie closed the library early to catalog the contents of the historical documents in the records room.

Sutton stopped on the second stair. She heard the television playing in the den, the light from the moving pictures flickering out into the hallway.

Inside the room, Greyson lay sprawled across the sofa, his feet dangling over the end in his robe, barefoot. Beneath him on the floor, Sierra had made a pallet, a sheet pulled up to her chin, her doll wrapped tightly in the crook of her arm.

This is so beautiful, Sutton thought, wishing she had the artistic talent to pull out charcoal pencils and capture the moment on paper. She tiptoed quietly over to Sierra and gathered her in her arms. Sierra's eyes never opened as Sutton carried her upstairs and put her to bed. Sutton kissed her daughter's cheek and went back downstairs.

Greyson's eyes flitted open when she cut off the television.

"Hi, husband." Sutton leaned over and gave him a kiss.

"Hi, you." Greyson's fist swiped at the corner of his eye.

"You fell asleep on the sofa."

"Where's Sierra?" He sat up in one jerky motion, his eyes

darting around the room, trying to become acclimated to his surroundings. "She wanted a drink of water and then couldn't get back to sleep, so we came in here and—"

"Greyson," she placed her palm inside his robe against his bare chest. "I took her upstairs to bed."

He fell back down on the sofa, relieved. He wiped his eyes again.

"You should go up to bed."

Greyson stretched his tall body. "Are you just now getting home from work? I thought you were getting off early today."

Sutton sank to her knees and rested her head next to the soft cotton of his robe. "I stayed to study."

"Hmmm." He sounded as if he were drifting toward sleep.

Greyson watched her sleepily, his eyes finally losing the battle and giving in to his exhaustion. She watched his face become slack, his breathing regulate to a slow, even pace. The arm he draped over her shoulder slipped down her back.

Greyson was the man dreams were made of. He was the man women pictured when they described the man they would marry. He loved her with all her blemishes in his own, unassuming way. Maddie asked her once if she tired of the roses he gave her. She answered by explaining that each rose was meant to show how much he loved her. Greyson never gave her roses after a fight or when he forgot to stop by the store to bring home a quart of milk. Greyson gave her flowers when his heart burst with love and happiness. He never gave her roses when she was in a bad mood or overwhelmed by home, school, or work. He gave her flowers when making love to her did not show her the depth of his love and devotion.

Sutton stood and straddled Greyson's middle. Thinking of the way he cherished her made her want to be consumed by him. She wanted his body to loom over hers, drinking her in, making her a part of him. She yearned for him to make her feel safe and protected.

"Greyson," she whispered next to his ear.

"Hmm?" he asked without opening his eyes.

"I want you to devour me."

Greyson's eyes opened at the same slow, steady pace that a smile lifted his lips. "I'm tired, honey." He looped his arms around her waist.

"I know you're messing with me." Sutton giggled before outlining the rectangular shape of his sideburn with her tongue.

"Stop, baby." Greyson's fingers pressed into the flesh of her hips.

Sutton leaned forward to cut off the lamp near his head.

"I'm getting mixed messages from you." Sutton rubbed her pelvis against the growing hardness in his boxers.

"How about I clear it all up by saying I love you."

At the serious tone of his voice, Sutton placed her face directly in front of his in an attempt to read his expression in the dim light. They remained inches apart in the darkness. The rhythmic blinking of his lashes matched the beating of her heart.

"I want you to disassemble me, wreck me, weaken me."

"That would ruin you," Greyson whispered, his lips grazing hers they were so close.

"You do that to me sometimes when we make love."

"I do?" Shock filled his words.

"Yes, you do, but you always put the pieces back together."

"I don't know if I like having that power."

"You like it, Greyson, and you use it strategically."

"No, I don't know my own strength. You'd have to love me a hell of a lot to let me have that power over you."

"I'd have to love you and trust you with my life."

Greyson cupped her face between his hands.

Sutton asked, "Why do you love me differently? Sometimes softly, like I'm breakable. Other times hard, like I might escape. Occasionally, tender and rigid, wrecking me."

"Because you need it."

"That's all?"

"And because I need to do it," Greyson confessed. "I need to know I have that power over you."

"So, what will you do to me tonight?"

"Tonight, I will wreck you and then I'll put the pieces back together. In the morning, I'll remind you that you're my wife by worshipping your body. And before I leave for work, I'll make you chant, in two different languages, that I'm your husband."

Thirty-nine

"Mama? Pop?" Greyson walked through his parents' home, noticing how his mother had completed decorating it. He found them in the den.

"Hey, son." His mother pushed his father's arm from around her shoulders.

Greyson concealed his smile. "I came for Sierra."

"You look real neat in that suit," Pop acknowledged before surfing the channels.

"Thanks, Pop." Greyson kissed his mother's cheek and sat on the chair across from them.

"Sierra's not here," his mother answered.

"Where is she?" A brief panic swept through his gut. Sutton had asked him to pick Sierra up from his parents' house after he finished working because she had a late class in town. He was sure of it. She wanted to walk into town because the weather was nice that morning but he'd insisted that she take the car; it would be getting dark when her class was over. She had gone on and on, around and around about it, saying that she felt "funny" driving the new Maxima. She worried people would think she was being pretentious. He'd ended the argument by saying, "I bought you the car because it's dependable. Depend on it."

Greyson's mother talked while his mind wandered off. His father called his name with a worried expression on his face.

"I'm sorry?"

"You workin' too hard over at that paper mill?" Pop angled his face in concern.

"No, I was thinking about something. Where did you say Sierra was at?"

Mama glanced at Pop before answering. "Her other grandparents picked her up late this afternoon. They were going to the capital and thought she'd want to ride along. Lord knows that chile loves her McDonald's."

Greyson smiled at the truth of it.

"Son," Pop started, "you doin' real good by them girls. Y'all make a nice family."

"Thanks, Pop." Every award he'd ever won paled next to his parents' pride in his lifestyle.

His mother broke into the emotional heaviness of the room. "Any chance more grandchildren might be coming soon?"

Greyson felt his skin flush. Talking about having kids was talking about having sex, once removed. "Sutton and I have talked about it, but we want to wait until she's finished school. That's extremely important to her and I don't want to make it any harder for her to do."

His parents shared a look he couldn't read.

"I talked to Sutton about it this morning," his mother said, "and she said to ask you about it."

"She did?" Greyson smiled. Of course she did—coward. "Mama, kids are a little ways away for us."

"You want to have more kids, don't you?"

"Mama, don't worry. When the time is right, we'll give you plenty of grandkids."

Mama opened her mouth to say more. Pop placed his hand on her thigh. "Leave the boy alone, Mar-beth. You want kids that bad, we can make our own."

"Jack!"

Pop winked at Greyson.

"I'd better be going." He stood and inched to the door.

"We're proud of you," Pop called as he left.

Greyson saw Sierra helping Mr. Hill with yard work from

a distance down the road. Mrs. Hill sat on the front porch in a chair rocking and fanning while watching their activity.

Sierra ran to him, jumping into his arms. Sutton began the ritual, Sierra copied it, and Greyson loved it.

Sierra began to chatter about her day immediately, giving him all the details of how his mother let her make cookies and his father took her into town and let her buy candy. Then she went on about the second part of her day.

"Grandpa took me," she said about her trip to McDonald's. "You weren't there to give me the first bite."

"I bet it was still good."

Sierra giggled.

Greyson greeted Mrs. Hill with a kiss. "Thanks for taking Sierra."

"You never have to thank me for keeping my grandchild. She's coming to stay with me next week while Sutton takes her exams." She pinched Sierra's leg, setting off another round of giggles.

"Go say good-bye to your grandfather." Greyson sat her down and followed at a distance. He waited until they hugged and kissed before he stepped forward and offered his hand.

"She's a good girl," Mr. Hill said, watching Sierra run to the car.

Greyson watched her climb into the backseat and try to put on her seatbelt. "I love her to death," he said, his voice dropping as it filled with emotion.

Mr. Hill grasped his shoulder. "I can see that. I can see you love Sutton, too, by the way you do right by her. She should have married you in the first place."

Greyson turned to him, unaccustomed to his approval. He had to recall the morning's weather report; was a full moon expected? Complimented by two of the most emotionally stoic men he knew in one day. Sutton wouldn't believe it.

"Thank you, sir," Greyson managed. "I better get Sierra home to bed."

"All right then." He returned to his lawn project.

Once Sierra found out Sutton wouldn't be home to put her bed, she became disappointed but easily conned Greyson into milk and cookies before bed. He sat with her at the kitchen table and listened as she rattled off the rest of the details of her day. He smiled as he imagined Sutton's face at the same age. He couldn't remember meeting Sutton before she was seven or eight, but at this age Sierra was the duplicate of her then.

Sierra climbed into bed when Greyson refused her any more cookies.

"What's that?" he asked, sitting next to her on the bed.

Sierra carefully pulled a gold locket from beneath her pajama top. "My daddy gave it to me." Seeing his expression she quickly added, "My other daddy."

Realizing his jealousy over not being her "real" father, he quickly cleared his expression and apologized. "It's okay. I knew your daddy."

"You did?" Sierra appeared confused by the possibility.

"I did. He loved you very much." He paused to ponder the truth of his words. He had no proof otherwise, he had no right to place doubt in Sierra's mind, and it really wasn't his business. His only concern should be loving his stepdaughter as if she were his own, and he did.

"Can I see?" he asked.

Sierra lifted the locket. Greyson flipped the face open and was hit by overwhelming emotions he couldn't describe. Seeing Alex and Sierra together in a portrait so obviously filled with mutual love made his rational thoughts scatter. He examined the picture thoroughly but quickly. He wanted to memorize every detail of the tender pose so that he would not have to ever look at it again.

Sierra yawned.

Greyson helped her tuck the locket inside her pajamas. "Good-night." He kissed her cheek before dousing the light.

"I love you," Sierra said sleepily as he pulled the door up behind him.

He froze as a wave of pure, sweet affection moved through him. He had wondered if Sierra would ever see him as a father figure or someone she loved. Tonight she had made the indirect reference to him being one of her fathers. Now she told him she loved him without any of the fanfare he expected with the first time, but it set fireworks off inside his chest.

"I love you too, baby."

If this is what it felt like to have a child love you, maybe it was time for him and Sutton to start having more.

Greyson went down the hall to the bedroom he shared with his wife. He sighed away the emotions threatening to bring tears to his eyes. He always wished, but never truly believed, Sutton would be his wife.

From his drawer, he pulled a pair of silk pajamas Sutton had bought him on her last trip into the capital. The deep blue silk resembled indigo. Sutton told him that shade looked radiant against his dark skin. She'd ended his habit of sleeping in boxers and white T-shirts. If she found pajamas sexy on her man, he was more than happy to oblige. Especially tonight when all the hard work at the paper mill, paired with the open emotions of their parents, made him want to share his love with his wife in the longest, deepest way he knew possible.

Greyson hummed along to the easy-listening radio station as he covered his face with shaving cream. The barber had shaped his sideburns earlier in the week but he still required a daily shave to keep his face free of stubble. He usually did this in the morning while dressing for work, but he had things on his mind that he hoped would keep him occupied late into the night. If everything went well, he would be too tired to leave the bed early enough the next morning to shave before work.

Greyson examined his face intensely with a hand mirror. Satisfied that all the facial hair had been cut away, he checked on Sierra and then stepped into the shower. He closed his eyes and relaxed under the steamy hot water.

The paper mill was finally up and running. The people of

Hannaford Valley were earning money. He could see it in the way the town began to sparkle again. The weary were smiling. Ailing houses were being repaired. The singing in church had extra pep.

His life was finally where he wanted it to be.

He and Kirkland had drove outside of town last week and had a drink. Because Kirkland was younger than he and Chevy, they had never done that together. They sat in the bar for hours, talking more than drinking. Greyson learned more about his little brother that evening than he had his entire life. Kirkland was a mama's boy but he was also very intelligent. His knowledge of the construction industry was more than learned behavior. Kirkland possessed a formal education that continued even today.

Kirkland remained focused on his career and his mother and had little time for a social life. Greyson asked him about his history with women and if there was anyone special in his life. Kirkland shied away from the subject. Greyson prodded, his big brother prerogative, and Kirkland admitted to never having had a serious relationship. He said he wasn't ready for that in his life yet and Greyson backed off, respecting his decision. Chevy, on the other hand, was past ready.

Greyson stepped from the shower and wrapped a towel around his waist, grabbing another from the towel rack for his head.

Chevy openly admitted that he wanted a special woman to consume his days and nights. Greyson knew about the rumors the townspeople spread about Chevy and wondered why he didn't move away in search of his perfect woman. But he knew Chevy was too shy and too rooted in Hannaford Valley to ever leave his home. Even if it meant being alone for the rest of his life, Chevy would never leave. Greyson remembered the vanity Chevy had built in the cabin and his heart became heavy.

Greyson stood in front of the mirror and spread deodorant underneath his arms. He splashed aftershave on his face, grabbed some lotion, and sat on the edge of the bed.

Sutton had mentioned that she believed there was a spark between Maddie and Chevy. Greyson fished for information with Chevy, but Chevy didn't have the confidence to approach her. Sutton suggested a little matchmaking, but Greyson discouraged her. If it backfired, the rumors would flare up again with new vigor. He couldn't be responsible for that. As he sat on the side of the bed, oiling himself for his wife's enjoyment, Greyson wanted Chevy to have what he had. Maybe inviting them both for dinner wouldn't be a bad idea.

Forty

Sutton closed Sierra's door and made her way toward the light in her bedroom. Illicit thoughts triggered a riot in her body when she inhaled the warm, woodsy fragrance of Greyson's bath ensemble. What designer brand he used changed from time to time, but he used only matching fragrances in his shave, bath, and oils. She had learned his habits well enough to know what scent accompanied what mood he was in.

His clean-shaven face brightened when she entered the room. This was the kind of love she needed. When she came into his space, no matter what the setting, his eyes shone and his smile broadened.

"Hi." She dropped her bags on the nearest table.

"Hi, you." Greyson sat against the headboard of their bed, reading the paper. He was wearing her favorite pajamas.

Sutton kicked off her shoes and pulled her shirt from the waistband of her pants. She'd had a long, invigorating day and couldn't wait to tell him every detail. As she dashed around the room, undressing and grabbing her nightgown, she told him about the discussion about reparations she'd had with her sociology instructor.

"Mrs. Ballantyne?"

Sutton turned before entering the bathroom.

"Would you stop chattering long enough to come over here and give your husband a kiss?" Greyson held his long arms wide open for her.

Sutton dropped everything and ran, jumping into his arms. She kissed him wildly over his freshly shaved face before settling at his lips, savoring his tongue.

"You better stop jumping on me like that. You might break something and then we won't be able to make any babies."

Sutton patted the affected area, getting the response she desired.

"I had dinner with Chevy out at the cabin before class tonight."

A flicker of jealous surprise crossed Greyson's face but he held back the words.

"He's very lonely. I don't know why he won't ask Maddie out. It's obvious that they like each other."

"I think we should stay at the periphery with those two. We could invite them to dinner but let them find their way to each other."

"I could—"

"No." Brotherly wisdom hardened Greyson's mouth. "Really, we should let them get together in their own time, in their own way."

Sutton knew he was referring to the difficulty that had surrounded their union and the sweetness they savored once everything fell into place. She relented. "If you believe it's best." She bounced to the bathroom. "I will try to get them over for dinner this weekend, though."

"Make it next weekend," he called after her. "I want some alone time with you this weekend."

Sutton grinned to herself. Hearing Greyson being possessive about their alone time or family time was one of his sexiest qualities. As she readied herself for bed, she recalled all the years they spent apart but together—joined together at the heart. As they were both beginning to understand, the time had not been right for them to be together. For whatever reasons, they needed to be apart to experience life before they came together to share it.

"Sutton," Greyson called from the bedroom, "how much longer?"

"I'm almost done." She slipped her gown over her head. "Tell me about your day."

She could hear the lilt smooth out the depths of his voice when he talked about the paper mill. When they first married, she worried he might regret what he given up to return to Hannaford Valley. As time passed, and the mill revitalized the town, she knew his soul was at rest. There were times when he hungered for the competitive debate of practicing corporate law—she could see the shadow cover his face when he watched a controversial trial on Court TV. When those times came, he spent an extra hour or so in his office consulting on a case with Hunter, Roe & Volney. There had even been a time when he sat second chair on a particularly trying case. But he soon began to miss Hannaford, calling home three or four times a day until he could leave the hustle and bustle of Chicago. Then things would settle back into their normal routine until the mood returned again.

During these times, Sutton respected his need and offered him his space. As he did with her schooling. When he left her to fly to Chicago or became absorbed in a case, she missed having his undivided attention. That was because she had come to cherish it so. But never once did she feel the dread of a secret life at the pit of her stomach. Worrying about him with another woman did not have a place in their marriage.

"Sutton," Greyson asked, "who's the professor that kept you late tonight?" She had known he'd get around to asking once he'd finished sharing his day.

"My soc professor; I've talked about him before, remember?" She pulled the brush through her reddish-brown hair one last time before spritzing perfume on her neck.

"I remember," he sulked.

"I like all of my classes, but his challenges me the most." She went on to tell him about the debate over reparations that ran over class time. She had stayed behind and the two of them had continued sparring. He was open to hearing all of her ideas, but she had to have a plausible theory she could use to support her beliefs. She understood why Greyson liked practicing law.

"I hope your professor understands that you're married."

Sutton studied the tanzanite and diamond ring on her finger. There was no way he could have missed it.

"We should start limiting these late-night sessions between you and the professor." Envy colored Greyson's words. "We wouldn't want him to get the wrong idea."

"We?" Sutton teased.

"I didn't want it to sound like I was telling you what to do," he mumbled.

"But you are."

"I can drive you to class next week, and pick you up, too." His voice dropped but she heard him clearly. "I'd like to check this guy out." The newspaper snapped.

Sutton came out of the bedroom and stood at the foot of the bed. His words touched her on a surprisingly emotional level. It didn't matter that her professor was bent over from age, married, and had grandchildren. Greyson loved her and worried that someone else might see her as he did. She didn't have to stay up during the night wondering whom her husband was bedding down with. She didn't have to listen to lame itineraries to explain missing hours. Her heart didn't break every time he walked out the door. In this relationship, Greyson loved her and wanted to share himself only with her and he wanted the same from her. He made a point of letting everyone know he was her husband, because in this relationship, he knew he had something worth fighting to keep.

"What did I say?" Greyson moved to the foot of the bed when he saw her face. She held up her hands, stopping him from coming any closer.

"Sutton, I didn't mean—"

She wiped away the tear that made it past the rim of her eye and down her cheek. "I want to thank you."

"Thank me?" Worry and nurturing clouded his smooth face.

"You have given me so much. I don't mean this house and the car. I mean the way you love me."

Greyson's body relaxed.

"Your jealousy turns me on."

His lips parted in a seductive smile that let Sutton know he would make good love to her tonight.

"You came into my life and took me into yours despite all the turmoil I was in. You never turned your back on me or my problems. You've supported me going back to college, even though it meant less time for us to spend alone and more responsibility for you around the house." She studied the lines of his face. "You gave up your whole life— Chicago, law—to be here with me."

Greyson interrupted. "I didn't give up my life. You are my life, Sutton. You and Sierra. Don't make it sound like I'm a saint. I fought to be where I am and I'm happy."

Another tear flowed down her cheek.

"Don't cry, baby."

"I want you to know that I not only love you, I appreciate you."

Greyson's eyes went to the carpet while he composed himself. When he looked up at her, his eyes were serious, his voice husky. "I appreciate what you've done for me too, Sutton. I never felt alive, happy until we became a family. Sierra is incredible—" he beamed— "Did I tell you she told me she loves me tonight?"

Sutton's throat tightened. She smiled.

Greyson settled back against the headboard as he spoke. "You anticipate my every need. You know what I want before I realize it and have it waiting for me when I do. You fill this house with love in everything you do. Sutton, I love you with all my heart." His eyes narrowed in heated passion, "Now come to bed, please. I have something I want to show you."

Emotion made way for play. Sutton burst out laughing. "Dang, Greyson, we were being all serious . . ."

"See, that's how you think. I really have something to show you—and it isn't that. I showed you that this morning."

Sutton climbed under the covers with him. Greyson went inside the bedside drawer and pulled out an elaborately wrapped rectangular box several inches thick.

"What do you have to show me?"

"We ran our first order today at the paper mill." He removed the red ribbon surrounding the box and discarded the top.

Only her husband would think to make a gift of a ream of paper. Another quality in Greyson that she found unique and wonderful.

He handed Sutton the top sheet. She held it up to the light. The pink bonded paper was embossed with a pattern of red roses. She ran her fingers over the smooth, thick paper. He had taught her that you could judge the quality of paper by the amount of light that shines through a single sheet when held to the light. She waved the thick paper back and forth, enjoying the melodic sound it made. Finally, she brought it to her nose in an attempt to determine the type of tree used for its conception—Chevy taught her about that—but she wasn't very good at that part of the inspection process.

"It's called The Sutton."

Her eyes went to him. He ran his fingers over the thick, rich paper in the box on his lap.

Sutton could no longer hide her emotion, "Why do you keep doing things like this for me?"

"Because I've loved you forever."

ABOUT THE AUTHOR

Kimberley White is the author of several novels. She is a critical care nurse who resides in Michigan with her family. She loves to hear from her readers.
Email: kwhite_writer@hotmail.com
Snail mail: P.O. Box 672, Novi, MI 48376.

COMING IN JULY 2003 FROM
ARABESQUE ROMANCES

__COME FALL

by Marcia King-Gamble   1-58314-399-8 $6.99US/$9.99CAN

Vivianne Baxter was the spokesperson for a prestigious not-for-profit organization until she was charged with sexual harassment, disgraced, and took refuge in Venice under a new identity. But when she realizes that the accidents dogging her trail are anything but, she has to rely on Sage Medino, a suspended FBI agent with his own secrets.

__COMFORT OF A MAN

by Adrianne Byrd   1-58314-428-5 $6.99US/$9.99CAN

Brooklyn Douglas has her hands full raising a teenaged son and running her own business. What she doesn't need is everybody trying to hook her up with "a good man." The last good man turned into a *no-good* husband who left her for another woman. Can't she just find a mind-blowing lover with no strings attached?

__LOVE ME ALL THE WAY

by Simona Taylor   1-58314-387-4 $5.99US/$7.99CAN

After an innocent deception shattered Dr. Sarita Rowley's marriage to Dr. Matthias Rowley, her only way of gaining access to their beloved reef rescue project is to use an assumed name. When Matthias falls ill, Sarita tries to save the reef and rebuild their relationship. But it will take a terrifying threat to make Matthias open up his heart to Sarita, and grasp a second chance at love . . .

__YOU REMIND ME

by Linda Walters   1-58314-356-4 $5.99US/$7.99CAN

Sloan Whitaker has sworn off relationships, and her newest assignment to cover the Barbados Jazz Festival is just the diversion she needs. But that's before an airport mishap sweeps Norwood Warren into her life . . . before this charismatic native of Barbados seduces her with a passion that scuttles all her intentions.

Call toll free **1-888-345-BOOK** to order by phone or use this coupon to order by mail. ALL BOOKS AVAILABLE JULY 01, 2003.

Name _____

Address _____

City _____State_____Zip _____

Please send me the books that I have checked above.

I am enclosing $_____
Plus postage and handling* $_____
Sales Tax (in NY, TN, and DC) $_____
Total amount enclosed $_____

*Add $2.50 for the first book and $.50 for each additional book. Send check or money order (no cash or CODs) to: **Arabesque Romances, Dept. C.O., 850 Third Avenue, 16th Floor, New York, NY 10022**

Prices and numbers subject to change without notice. Valid only in the U.S. All orders subject to availability. **NO ADVANCE ORDERS.**

Visit our website at **www.arabesquebooks.com**.

COMING IN AUGUST 2003 FROM
ARABESQUE ROMANCES

__SAVING GRACE
by Angela Winters   1-58314-335-1 $6.99US/$9.99CAN
Grace Bowers is determined to bring down the company that discriminated against her father thirty-five years ago. Hiring Keith Hart to handle the expansion of his growing restaurant is her first step. Suddenly she and Keith are working together—and fighting a potent attraction that makes becoming real-life partners incredibly tempting . . .

__MEANT TO BE
by Mildred Riley   1-58314-422-6 $6.99US/$9.99CAN
When a young boxer turns up dead, nurse Maribeth Trumbull is determined to find out what happened. But police officer Ben Daniels is dead-set against her digging up evidence on her own. While she may be drawn to the irresistibly sexy cop, Maribeth has no intention of surrendering her hard-earned independence . . .

__CAN'T DENY LOVE
by Doreen Rainey   1-58314-432-3 $5.99US/$7.99CAN
Tanya Kennedy longs for something her dependable boyfriend Martin can't seem to provide. Disillusioned, Tanya refuses his marriage proposal . . . and runs straight into her ex, Brandon Ware. Once, Brandon filled her life with passion, but he also left her feeling bitterly betrayed.

__MY ONE AND ONLY LOVE
by Melanie Schuster   1-58314-423-4 $5.99US/$7.99CAN
Determined to recover from her brother's disastrous mismanagement of her career, star Ceylon Simmons has worked herself to near collapse. She's come to find refuge on sea-swept St. Simon's Island. But when she discovers that the man she's always loved from afar is also visiting, she realizes there's no safe haven from their desire . . .

Call toll free **1-888-345-BOOK** to order by phone or use this coupon to order by mail. ALL BOOKS AVAILABLE AUGUST 01, 2003.

Name _____

Address _____

City _____State_____Zip_____

Please send me the books that I have checked above.

I am enclosing $_____
Plus postage and handling* $_____
Sales Tax (in NY, TN, and DC) $_____
Total amount enclosed $_____

*Add $2.50 for the first book and $.50 for each additional book. Send check or money order (no cash or CODs) to: **Arabesque Romances, Dept. C.O., 850 Third Avenue, 16th Floor, New York, NY 10022**
Prices and numbers subject to change without notice. Valid only in the U.S. All orders subject to availability. **NO ADVANCE ORDERS.**
Visit our website at **www.arabesquebooks.com**.

Own the Entire ANGELA WINTERS
Arabesque Collection Today

__**The Business of Love**
                1-58314-150-2 $5.99US/$7.99CAN

__**Forever Passion**
                1-58314-077-8 $5.99US/$7.99CAN

__**Island Promise**
                0-7860-0574-2 $4.99US/$6.50CAN

__**Only You**
                0-7860-0352-9 $4.99US/$6.50CAN

__**Sudden Love**
                1-58314-023-9 $4.99US/$6.50CAN

__**Sweet Surrender**
                0-7860-0497-5 $4.99US/$6.50CAN

More Sizzling Romance From
Leslie Esdaile